W9-AUA-023

THE ENLISTED MEN'S CLUB

Gary Reilly

Running Meter Press
Denver

The Enlisted Men's Club
by Gary Reilly

Copyright 2014 by Running Meter Press

All rights reserved. No part of this book may be reproduced in any
form whatsoever without the prior written permission of the publisher.

Published by

Running Meter Press
2509 Xanthia St.
Denver, CO 80238
Publisher@RunningMeterPress.com
720-328-5488

Cover art and book design by Nick Zelinger

ISBN 978-0-9847860-7-7
Library of Congress 2014933115

First edition, 2014
Printed in the United States of America.

This book is a work of fiction. Any resemblance to actual persons,
living or dead, business establishments, locales, or events is
entirely coincidental.

Also by Gary Reilly:

The Asphalt Warrior Series:
The Asphalt Warrior
Ticket to Hollywood
The Heart of Darkness Club
Home for the Holidays
Doctor Lovebeads

Introduction

When writer Gary Reilly died in 2011, he left behind a trove of manuscripts. In all, there were more than 25 novels, all unpublished. Each was carefully crafted, rewritten countless times and polished to his high professional standards. He also left one more sheet of paper—his three-sentence will. His last directions gave me and my friend Mark Stevens permission to publish his works.

Mark and I immediately established Running Meter Press for the sole purpose to carry out Gary's wishes. In 2012, in association with Big Earth Publishing in Boulder, Running Meter Press launched *The Asphalt Warrior*, the first in a series of eleven comic novels featuring Denver cab driver Brendan Murphy, a.k.a. "Murph."

To date, we have published the first five in the series, each one of them reaching the top three in *The Denver Post's* Local Bestsellers List. The second novel, *Ticket to Hollywood*, was a finalist for the 2013 Colorado Book Award.

But Reilly was not just a writer of humor. He created mysteries, science fiction and deeper literary works. It is now time to expose readers to Gary's more serious side.

Based on his own experiences in the U.S. Army, including a tour of duty in Vietnam during the war, Reilly wrote a trilogy about Private Palmer, a draftee adrift in the military bureaucracy, trying to make sense of his existence, facing an unknown future.

The Enlisted Men's Club finds Private Palmer stationed at San Francisco's army base at The Presidio, awaiting orders. He's been trained as a Military Policeman but struggles with the Army's power structure and codes of behavior. He focuses on killing time, finding cold beer and thinking up ways to survive each day. More than anything, that means avoiding the "shit details." The trick, Private Palmer decides, is not care about anything for the next eighteen months. To his surprise, that's the most difficult challenge of all.

Reilly's range is apparent in this new series. Palmer in his own way is as memorable a character as Murph—and struggles just as much with his role in organizations, among friends and with the value of his time and work. We believe, like us, readers will sign up for a full tour with this flawed but sympathetic soldier.

And to fans of *The Asphalt Warrior* Series, don't worry, Murph's taxi will arrive soon for another whacky trip.

Mike Keefe
2014

PROLOGUE

OAKLAND

As soon as the sergeant in the tower put the formation at ease, Private Palmer began rubbing the cross-stitched scar that ran from the base of his clenched fist to the cleft of his cocked elbow. A light rain had ended only a few minutes prior to the formation so it was cold out on the tarmac, and though his arm didn't hurt, the damp weather 'made him feel protective toward the damaged bone which, the doctor had assured him, was stronger now than it had been before the accident. But Palmer didn't really believe that because it sounded like the sort of horseshit a Drill Sergeant might tell a man to teach him not to be afraid. The army doctor had opened the skin on the soft white underside of the forearm, so people never noticed the damage unless Palmer deliberately turned it up to show it to them, or if he reached out with his left arm to pick up, for instance, a beer.

He listened for his name even though he didn't expect to be called. He expected to pull shit details for four days, and on the fifth day hear his name called over the PA. This was not only what his brother Phil had told him would happen, but what he had gathered from other men who had been here a day or two longer than him and were therefore veterans, short-timers, men who would be going to Vietnam ahead of him.

The NCO in the tower slowly recited the names on the manifest for the next scheduled flight. After each name went out over the loudspeaker the sergeant looked up from his list to make certain that one body out of all these thousands was edging through the ranks toward the side of the formation. It took twenty minutes before the last name was read off the list, a Z name, then the NCO told the remaining men to close up the ranks. They did this reluctantly because it was shit detail time.

A squad of E5's oversaw this cute culling of men, this draft that made everyone groan but which possessed an element of excitement because it was like a lottery. The strategy of the NCO in the tower was capricious, in that rather than ordering the troops in the front rank to fall out for the first detail, he pointed at five men in the middle of the formation and sent them off to sweep and mop the operations building. This process left a patchwork of empty spaces within the formation, like holes in a page of postage stamps, and some men began to slip surreptitiously from one rank to another in the hope that they wouldn't be a part of the next squad picked. But the NCO began telling the troops to tighten up the formation and fill in the holes. Palmer's only real worry was that he would get picked for KP, which would involve eighteen hours of hot, sloppy, shitty kitchen work, and he had better things to do with his last days in America.

The KPs were not chosen until the formation had been reduced to half its original muster. A moody silence settled over the tarmac because everybody knew what was coming. Palmer wished he had gotten picked to push brooms or mop latrines because the lesser shit details lasted only an hour, which would leave him plenty of time to drink beer.

The NCO counted off fourteen men on the right side of the formation and told them to fall out and hand over their

ID cards. This was only the first group of KPs. There were six kitchens Palmer knew of that needed a new roster of bodies every morning, so he paid close attention to the procedure, looking for an opening that might be taken advantage of by a man willing to risk dodging a detail. But he had never encountered any detail as tightly supervised as Oakland KP. The sergeants confiscated the men's military ID cards, they made them sign a roster, and they required them to spend the night in some sort of special KP barracks, with work-call at three in the morning. To escape KP would be tantamount to escaping from Alcatraz.

The sergeant chose fourteen men near the left side of the formation, then another fourteen near the left, then switched to the rear ranks, continually telling the remaining men to close it up, fill in the holes. He seemed to be enjoying his chore, which aggravated Palmer's oppressive sense of entrapment and which aroused the loathing he reserved for prima-donna officers and chump sergeants, like the E6 who had made him get his hair cut when he first signed in even though he had known it was going to happen. When Palmer had arrived at the Oakland Army Replacement Depot, he hadn't been to a barbershop in more than six weeks.

Then it was over. All the requisite KPs had been chosen and were standing off to the side of the formation in silent pissed-off ranks, signing rosters and handing over their ID cards, the kiss of death, because once they had your ID card you were fucked.

But Palmer had been lucky. No KP and no shit detail for this evening. He could now head straight for the enlisted men's club.

When he had arrived at Oakland on Monday he already knew how to find the place, having visited it with his brother a few months earlier, but this knowledge didn't give him an edge. The club was already half filled by the time he stepped through the doorway. An E6 seated on a chair by the door barked at him to uncover, then demanded to see his ID card. Palmer took off his cap revealing a head nearly as naked as a basic trainee's, the flesh stark white beneath his close crop like a rubber skull-cap revealing the faint but distinct line of a tan that he had gotten sitting on the sands of Sunset Beach celebrating his twenty-first birthday with two friends.

He went to the bar and ordered a pitcher of beer and one empty glass and carried them across the room. He was pleased to find vacant the same booth where he and his brother Phil once had sat the day Palmer came to Oakland bent on a mission that even now he did not regret having accomplished, though he had wondered if he might end up some day regretting it. Never volunteer, and that's no joke.

A few minutes after he got settled in the booth, he heard a voice say, "Are those seats taken?"

He looked up at the eager faces of three GIs dressed in the same olive-drab jungle fatigues that he was wearing, multi-pocketed rip-stop fabric baggy in cut, the shirt tails hanging untucked and thus a bit unmilitary, a uniform designed for the tropics.

"No," he replied.

"Would you mind if me and my buddies sat here with you? There's nowhere else to sit down in this place."

Palmer said yes, completing the ritual of proper barroom etiquette. The three men slid in, one of them setting a pitcher down on the table and telling Palmer to help himself. They were happy now, just like Palmer, happy and apprehensive, sitting in a booth in a bar on their way to Vietnam.

He wouldn't tell them that he was a Military Policeman until after they had shared a few beers and told each other what state they called home, and where they had taken basic training, and had exchanged a few funny stories about their brief time-in-service. Palmer had learned that people didn't seem to mind that he was an MP, a cop, a pig, as long as they had gotten to know him a little bit beforehand and realized that he was no different from them, a draftee who had gotten sent to MP school instead of Infantry or cook or clerk school. He would tell them he was an MP after the group had shared a few beers and jokes with him, and finally asked the specifics of his military occupation.

When his own pitcher was empty, Palmer accepted their offer. He reached for their pitcher with his right arm, always conscious of letting it do the heavy work and protecting what he thought of as his weaker left arm, even though the doctor had assured him that it was as strong as ever. With his left hand he reached out to hold his glass steady, exposing to his new drinking-buddies the ugly pattern of sewn flesh.

One of them asked, as someone always did in a bar whenever Palmer unconsciously or else deliberately (as he often had done in the beginning) let strangers see the needlework, "How did that happen?"

Another man said, "Did you get that in Vietnam?" which Palmer also had heard before.

"No," he replied. "It was just an accident."

This was when he told his new drinking-buddies that he was a Military Policeman, and that his arm had been broken a few months earlier when he had been stationed at the Presidio of San Francisco, just across the bay.

PART ONE

CHAPTER 1

The ground is damp where Private Palmer is standing, sandy, with some sort of small-leafed green vine which wraps itself around everything planted in the earth—the white wooden legs of the NCOIC tower, a picket line of telephone poles, even the rows of smooth white rocks as large as footballs which border the sides of the dirt drive leading into the rifle range.

The sky is overcast and the wind is blowing hard, making Palmer's fingertips ache each time he pinches a brass-jacketed round of ammunition and tries to stuff it into a spring-loaded magazine. His gloves are in the pockets of his field-jacket because this isn't the kind of work you can do wearing gloves, you have to do it bare handed. Colorado raised, he's used to the stale dry mile-high bite of lifeless Rocky winters, not these damp, heat-sapping, muggy mists blown inland from the coastal waters at dawn. San Francisco Bay is hidden by barren brown hills which border the rifle range, but he can still smell the odor of beached fish in the air.

Four other men are working the detail alongside him at a wooden table, all of them shielded by a canvas roof which lifts and pops in a wind which sends loose bullets rolling across the table. Palmer ignores the soft sound of the occasional slug hitting the sand beside his boots. The crackle of M-16 fire and the sweet stink of gun smoke is carried to him on the wind, the sounds and smells of basic training that he had liked, and even misses, and thinks about often: the pleasant stretch of a gut filled with fried eggs at dawn prior to the mile run, the long marches to the ranges, the PT with its daily-dozen, the bizarre ache of overworked calves wracked by Charley-horses throughout the night, and the strangeness of falling asleep the instant his head hit the pillow. He had liked it all, but wouldn't go back. He picks up an empty magazine and stuffs a bullet into it, and begins daydreaming about Denver, his home, which is just about all he has ever thought about and ever will think about while he is in uniform. Going home.

The magazine grows heavy in his hand as it grows full. It is designed to hold twenty rounds of ammunition, but he inserts only eighteen because everyone had been told in basic training that twenty rounds could jam an M-16 during combat, an error brought to light not by the blueprints rendered by college-educated civilian engineers but by the men who had to carry the weapons into the field at the beginning of the war and put them to practical use. Something to remember if he ever gets sent to Vietnam.

His platoon leader, Sergeant Sherman, is huddled against the wind in a rubber rain-poncho next to one of the three blue buses which had brought Company D north across the Golden Gate Bridge to make this shoot. The sergeant is holding a cup of coffee with both hands but not sipping from it, using it only to warm his fingers, just as Palmer is blowing hot hungover breath at the tips of his own fingers that he keeps inspecting to see if they might be turning blue, which they are not. Sgt. Sherman is wearing a Smokey Bear hat wrapped tightly in translucent plastic to ward off the rain which keeps threatening to fall but never does. Sherman's eyes water easily in the cold and grow red around the rims like that of a drinking man, although Palmer does not think he drinks. A veteran of the Korean War, Sgt. Sherman is a bit younger than Palmer's father, a veteran of WWII who did not hang around in the army after the shooting stopped.

Sgt. Sherman sets his cup down on one of the steps inside the open door of a bus and picks up a clipboard and starts heading toward the ammo pit. Seeing this, Palmer knows that his turn on the detail is over. He quits stuffing bullets and digs out his gloves and tugs them on while his buddies continue to work. Sgt. Sherman double-times the last few steps up to the ammo pit and hollers, "You five men go up to the firing line!" He takes out a pencil and starts checking off names. "Everyone pick up two loaded magazines and bring them along!"

Palmer grabs two out of the small stack he has been building and carries them at his side like paperback books, unaware that one of them is a sort of time bomb.

The first to leave the ammo pit, he's the first to arrive at the crowd of men milling around the base of the tower listening to a Range NCO recite the proper procedures and rules of weapons safety. The NCO is wearing a blue helmet and the tailored fatigues that every permanent-party personnel instructor whom Palmer has ever encountered seems to prefer, weirdly skin-tight pants and a field-jacket one size too small. Captain Weller, the commanding officer of Company D, is standing alongside the NCO dressed in the same sort of outfit with the exception of two vertical parallel silver bars decorating the front of his blue helmet. Palmer listens with only one ear to the instructions because they are a repetition of all the rules of all the ranges he had ever fired on during his four months of training: keep your weapon set on safety, keep your muzzle pointed downrange, all the common-sense rules that he thinks he knows and doesn't need to be told twice about. He looks out at the fan-shaped field-of-fire where concentric earthen berms have been planted with man-shaped targets, plastic and steel mechanical-devices which are said not to be working well today.

"Find a buddy and take up your position on the firing line!" the NCO shouts.

Palmer has been with Company D only one week and doesn't really know anyone well enough to buddy-up with. None of the men of his squad are in this group so he stands back and waits for the crowd to thin, to see who might be left over. But Sergeant Weigand, a third-platoon NCO, spots him and shouts, "Palmer, you go with Courtney!"

Palmer steps up to the rifle rack and picks out one of the battalion M-16s that the company is using today for record-fire. He doesn't know much about the M-16 because he had trained in basic on the M-14 even though the Vietnam War has been going on for years. His only practical experience with the M-16 had taken place during one day of training at Military Police school in Ft. Gordon, Georgia, where he was allowed to fire it only one time, but that was enough to intrigue him with its toy-like kick which could be resisted easily with one hand on the pistol-grip. On that day he had also fired the M-60 machine-gun and the M-79 grenade launcher, the weapons which, the trainees had been told, they as Military Police-men would most likely be using when they got to Vietnam, including the .45.

He carries the rifle up onto the berm fronting the range and walks toward Specialist Fourth-Class Courtney, who is already at his position peering out at the targets with one hand raised to shade his eyes, now that the sun is beginning to break through the low clouds sending streaks of light down onto the fields and roads and white wooden barracks buildings of Fort Cronkite. Palmer doesn't know Courtney beyond having seen him around the company area. Courtney is in his platoon but bunks down the hall in the second squad. He is taller than Palmer, tanned and lean, and standing there with his palm shading his eyes he looks like an artist's rendering of a Combat Infantryman, a figure you might see on a recruiting poster or a movie advertisement: serious, wary, and confident, a soldier studying a terrain inhabited and dangerous.

The range is small, with room for only ten firing positions, not at all like the massive spreads of basic training where dozens of men could fire at a time, where the far tree line had been hacked low by flying lead over decades creating barkless white pocked living trunks devoid of branches. One day during basic a deer had run across a rifle range, and the NCO in the tower had shouted, "Cease fire!" Everyone took their fingers off the triggers and watched the deer's erratic panicked sprint between the targets, and Palmer was certain that every single trainee wanted to shoot at those flashing brown broad fleet ribs because that's exactly what he wanted to do.

He approaches Courtney, and because he would like to be polite and demonstrate military courtesy to a man who has been in the company longer than him, he offers to let Courtney fire first.

Courtney lowers his hand and turns his head and looks at Palmer as if seeing him for the first time, which maybe he is because they have never spoken to each other in the company area.

"You go first," Courtney says. "I want to see how the targets are falling."

Each plastic target is designed to fall flat when struck by a bullet and spring upright for the next round to knock it back, but most of the targets are rusted, or else just pieces of shit because they either don't go down at all, or else don't come back up after they do go down. And because nothing is working properly, everyone is marking false hits on the scorecards, indicating that each man, whose bullets may or may not have hit any target, is an Expert with the M-16, officially, and for the record. It's a joke of course, an exercise in paperwork, whereas record-fire in basic training had been an absolutely monumental event, the final tally of eight weeks of training which, the trainees were reminded constantly, would determine the course of their army careers. Palmer had interpreted this to mean that a man's ability to hit a target would pretty much determine whether or not he would come home alive from Vietnam.

But today's shoot lacks any sort of dramatic underpinnings. Palmer hands Courtney one of the two magazines and goes out to the firing line and flops belly down on a square of canvas staked out on the ground. He works his elbows around and points his weapon downrange and waits for the man in the NCOIC tower to tell everyone to lock-and-load. A ground-level breeze starts blowing his way, he can see its airborne debris coming, and he lowers his head with his face to the ground and lets the steel helmet take the brunt of a spray of grit which rattles against his steel pot like hail on a Quonset roof.

"Listen up on the firing line! Insert your magazines and lock-and-load!"

Not a large amount of adrenaline but a thin flow always lights up Palmer's spine whenever he chambers a round and feels a rifle come alive in his hands.

"Ready on the left? Ready on the right?"

Palmer's heart starts beating faster, as it always does when he knows he's going to be throwing lead at things shaped like men.

"Commence firing!"

The first shot flips brass ringing past his ear to the ground, and Palmer is inside it instantly, the fine sensation of being close to a weapon's pump as he touches something out there with a spiraling reach. The target doesn't go down, but he knows he hit it because he saw the plastic shoulder shudder. He moves his sights to a target five meters to the right, and when he squeezes the trigger he sees the man-shape snap back and disappear beyond the berm. A gratifying feeling of cause-and-effect. He's doing something out there.

He wastes three more shots aiming at tiny silhouettes that are far away but which he wants nevertheless to try for, then he takes a bead on a target only thirty meters out and fires two rounds. Nothing. The men on either side of him are shooting at targets which sway but do not go down, like enemy who are wounded but can still fire back, and this leads to a lot of bitching and laughing along the line.

They are not allowed to fire their weapons on full-automatic today, so Palmer concocts a counterfeit-automatic by tapping the trigger like a telegraph key. He's emulating the M-60 machine-gun, attempting to re-experience the belt-fed pleasure of sitting cross-legged at the range in MP school firing bullets across five-hundred meters of flat earth, the rounds weaving a vicious arc like water from a fire hose. He had been allowed to fire the weapon only one time because there was an entire company to get through, but during that moment a craving blossomed inside him, the desire to spew limitless lead. He empties his M-16 in three seconds.

"Cease fire! Clear your weapons!"

His turn has ended, and now he's an Expert even though he had knocked down only three targets. He walks back behind the firing line and waits for Courtney to sign his score-card as the official witness. Courtney marks a total of eighteen hits. He presses hard when he writes. His signature is dark and thick and bold along the bottom of the card. Palmer takes Courtney's blank scorecard and signs his own name light and fast, like a guilty man in a hurry.

Courtney marches out to the firing line and drops into the prone position and aims his weapon downrange. Palmer takes a few seconds out of his military day to mark eighteen hits on Courtney's scorecard, then he starts thinking about the beer he will be drinking this evening at the bowling alley just down the block from Company D.

He had drunk in the bowling alley the previous evening, so he has a flicker of a hangover, and can taste a residue of Budweiser on the back of his tongue that hadn't been washed away by this morning's gargle with Listerine. It tastes good.

The man in the tower tells everyone to lock-and-load. The ratcheting of weapons along the line distracts Palmer momentarily, but his attention soon drifts back to beer. He decides he won't bother to go to chow in the mess hall this evening. He will head straight to the bowling alley right after formation. He will beat the crowd.

The men begin firing their weapons, and the odor of scorched brass makes Palmer think of the hamburgers they sell at the bowling alley. Wrapped in foil and warmed in an oven, they are no worse or better than mess hall burgers, and he will probably order one after he has his first beer for the evening. A beer, then a beer and a burger, then he hears a loud silence coming from Courtney's square of canvas and realizes that the man has stopped firing.

Courtney rolls onto his left side with the muzzle of his weapon raised to the sky. Cursing softly and pawing at the bolt mechanism, he's trying to get a thumb into the ejection port because his weapon has jammed. He finally gives up and raises his hand, and Palmer turns and raises his own hand signaling for a Range NCO.

Sgt. Weigand double-times over and squats next to Courtney and examines the weapon.

"Did you load Courtney's magazine?"

Sgt. Weigand is standing in front of Palmer with one arm extended, the gold length of an unexpended bullet lying in his palm.

"Yes, sergeant."

"You loaded this bullet backwards."

Palmer looks down at the bullet, probably the fifth or sixth in the magazine.

"You loaded this bullet backwards," the sergeant says again, as if he isn't entirely certain that Palmer understands the crux of the problem.

Palmer glances at Courtney lying belly-up in the morning sun.

"I'm sorry, sergeant."

"Sorry doesn't cut it, Private Palmer."

He knows this, but doesn't know what else to say.

"Courtney, you fire again with the next group!" Weigand hollers. Then he grabs the scorecard out of Palmer's hand, the card which has eighteen hits marked on it even though Courtney had fired less than seven rounds.

Palmer is mortified.

His right hand twitches and he almost snatches the card back. But Weigand just tears it in half and tells him to go get a new magazine for Courtney.

Palmer turns and begins double-timing back toward the ammo pit, certain that Sgt. Weigand had seen the false hits. But on this day of frauds, Palmer's fraud has been absorbed.

When the last group to shoot for the record is on the firing line Sgt. Sherman corrals the rest of the company and puts everyone to work policing the grounds. In a few minutes the troops will be getting on the buses and heading back across the Golden Gate Bridge to the Presidio, to the top of the very hill which anchors the southern suspension wires of the bridge. Crowning the hill is a series of three-story, white-stucco barracks surrounding a quadrant of closely-cropped grass. Palmer knew he was in California on the day he arrived at the Presidio and saw this arrangement of red-roofed Spanish architecture in lieu of the dull wooden barracks which he had grown used to during his four months of training. On that day he thought he had arrived in paradise.

Now he is lurking near the parked buses embarrassed about his bullet blunder and wishing he had been assigned to duty in Alaska. He avoids eye-contact with anyone who might have heard about it. Fuck-ups travel fast in the army. He had never before heard of anyone loading a bullet backwards into a magazine, not in basic training where you might expect that sort of error, and not in MP school. It is the kind of mistake that he never would have even conceived of, until he did it.

He debates whether or not to mooch a cigarette from someone nearby. He's pissed-off at himself and feels like smoking, but the problem is that he has been trying to give up smoking ever since he was sworn into the army. He wants to use these two years as the time in his life when he will shape up, cut out the smokes, get serious about an exercise program, and purge all his bad habits. But now he wants a cigarette, a little taste of home, but he will have to cadge it from someone who might have heard the bullet story. He finally wanders by himself across the road into a field and begins pretending to pick up litter, ignoring any scraps of paper or cigarette butts he happens to encounter. It's amazing how many smokes get tossed on a military reservation.

He can see SP4 Courtney from here, standing beside the NCO tower talking to SP4 Tichener, a black GI from Atlanta who, in the chain-of-command, is Palmer's squad leader. When the two men glance in his direction, Palmer assumes that Courtney is telling Tichener that one of the men in his squad had better be watched closely so he won't put someone else's life in jeopardy. They laugh. Very likely they are not talking about him at all, but he is paranoid. He's one of the new men in Company D, and is worried about being looked down upon as a dud by the veterans, which would include any man who has been in the company at least one day longer than him.

When he sees the last group move off the firing line and head toward the buses, he drops a wad of yellow legal-paper that he has been carrying around as a decoy and joins the crowd. He doesn't want to mingle with anyone who might have heard about his fuck-up so he climbs onto a bus right away. He takes a seat halfway down the aisle and gazes out the window and tries not to look anyone in the eye. Everyone begins filing on behind him. Then Sgt. Sherman comes running down the road screaming, "I didn't give the order to mount up!"

A clammy feeling grows in Palmer's gut. He's not yet used to the dignity of permanent-party status, so he waits for the sergeant to order everyone to dismount as if they were a pack of basic trainees. But Sgt. Sherman only stands outside the bus red-faced and fuming—he likes things done the army way, slow and complicated.

The battalion driver hops in and settles onto his seat and closes the door. But before he can start the engine there's a hammering of fists on the glass, and he cranks the door back open. Courtney and Tichener climb on.

Palmer turns his head and stares out the window, thinking that the thing you want most not to happen is the thing that always happens. Courtney and Tichener make their way toward the rear where they will have to stand because the bus is overcrowded. As they shuffle past his seat, Palmer closes his eyes and leans his head against the cool glass of the window and pretends to be asleep. When the engine starts up, he can feel the vibrations inside his skull. It feels good. The driver shifts gears and guides the bus across Ft. Cronkite toward a road which weaves up one of the encircling naked hills toward the intersection of California Highway 101, which will take them to the Golden Gate Bridge.

As the bus makes the climb, Palmer parts a single eyelid to observe the scene of his debacle growing smaller below. When the bus crests the hill and stops at the intersection to wait for an opening in traffic, somebody shouts, "Hey, Palmer!" He recognizes the deep bass voice of SP4 Tichener, but he keeps his head pressed against the glass and closes his eye.

"Listen up, Palmer! Courtney here says if you ever get to Vietnam, stay out of his foxhole!"

The ensuing laughter of the troops is like hot breath blown against the back of Palmer's neck.

"Wake up, Palmer! No sleeping on my bus!"

"He heard you," Courtney says loud enough for everyone to hear. "He's embarrassed."

Palmer can't believe it. Nailed in public, and not by a mere wisecrack, but by The Truth.

He thinks about pretending to wake up—to look around as if perplexed, as if to say, "Is someone speaking to me?" But as the bus pulls across the highway and turns left toward the bridge, he keeps his eyes closed and keeps his head pressed against the glass. He has been pretending to wake up all his life.

CHAPTER 2

The following dawn Palmer remains in his squad room until the last possible moment, taking his time snapping the green MP scarf around his neck and stuffing it into his fatigue shirt and checking to make certain the flaps of his pockets are properly buttoned. His hangover is only a little worse than yesterday's, with a slight dizziness which, after he steps to the door of his room which opens onto the long porch of the stucco barracks, is relieved a bit by the chill morning air and the cleansing taste of a fading fog. He doesn't normally drink to excess on week nights, and has intentionally tried to avoid it ever since he was sworn into the army, but the previous night he had felt justified, which is almost always the first step in any drinking he does.

It's a few minutes before six. The rest of the company is standing on the sidewalk waiting to be called into formation. In this darkness it is difficult to see the details of the faces of the men unless Palmer stands close to them, which he deliberately does not do. Still embarrassed about his fuck-up on the rifle range, he's certain it must be the subject of every throat-clearing and smoke-hacking conversation on the sidewalk.

Second Lieutenant Norbert, the company Executive Officer, is standing just inside the open double-doors of the central foyer. Behind him is the bulletin board with its daily quota of rosters and announcements, including the names of the men who have received orders to go to Vietnam. The KP roster hangs there too, with Palmer's name already on it even though he has been here only a week. During training he had always signed up for pots-and-pans whenever he was assigned KP because the cooks always left the pots-and-pans man alone in his tiled corner of the kitchen, and Palmer intends to keep right on doing it here. It's always a race to the kitchen at four A.M. to sign up for pots-and-pans, because everybody wants to be left alone.

Sgt. Sherman calls the company to attention. Lt. Norbert marches out onto the grass and stands in front of the formation to take the morning report. As the platoon leaders give the all-present-or-accounted-for, Palmer stares at the sky which is paling by degrees revealing the frosted grass of the quad which is the size of a football field and mown to a military inch like a lifer haircut. The massive stucco buildings surrounding the quad are evenly-spaced and form a pattern in the shape of a question-mark with the bowling alley serving as the period at the bottom, just across the street which borders the far end of the quad. Cattycorner from Company D and isolated from this pattern of punctuation stands the Presidio stockade. Surrounded by a high fence topped with barbed-wire, at each corner of its perimeter stands a wooden tower where an MP guard sits on a stool with a loaded shotgun either under his arm or within easy reach.

Fascinated by nothing more than its presence, Palmer stares at the stockade wondering if there has ever been a break of any sort, a mass escape perhaps, or a lone man going over the wire and an MP unloading a wad of buckshot in his direction. Palmer has heard that whenever an MP kills a prison escapee, he gets transferred to another duty station. Company A runs the stockade. Palmer could have become a stockade guard if he had gone to confinement school at the end of MP school, but that would have meant more training at Ft. Gordon, and by that time, with four months in the army, he was sick of being a trainee. A buddy named Gilchrest had volunteered for it and already has orders to pull a tour in a stockade in South Korea where, according to his most recent letter, it looks like he'll be spending his nights freezing his nuts off, which, Palmer supposes, is better than getting them shot off in Vietnam.

When the morning report is completed, Sgt. Sherman dismisses the formation for chow. The troops rush onto the long porch and form a line at the door to the mess hall. When Palmer gets inside, he finds he can eat only three strips of bacon and one forkful of egg. Coffee too, and milk for its chill. He's too hungover to eat much, but doesn't regret drinking the previous night because he knows that during the day the hangover will eventually fade away and make room for the next one.

He lingers over his tray of food though, killing time in order to avoid going back into the billets where men are sweeping and mopping floors and scrubbing urinals and putting the building into shape for the upcoming military day. He sips his coffee and toys with his cooling eggs until the mess hall is nearly empty, then turns in his tray at the kitchen window where a KP who had signed up for the job of dishwasher at the morning roster-race is collecting trays and scraping leftovers into a trash barrel. Palmer exits through the door leading into the billets and takes his time going down the hallway to his squad room.

Six men are quartered in his room, which is only large enough to hold three double bunks and a row of wall lockers, a corner room at the far end of the porch. Palmer has the top bunk in the middle where he goes to work folding neat hospital-corners on his blankets, then undoing them and redoing them in order to avoid going into the hallways where the real work is being done.

He thinks about hopping on top of his bunk for a quick nap to ease some of the weariness of his hangover, but Sgt. Sherman walks in with a look that Palmer already has become familiar with: chin drawn toward the breastbone, pale gray eyes wary, lips creased with disapproval. It's as if, after only one week, Sgt. Sherman understands that he had made a mistake when he hand-picked Private Palmer from the pack of MP school newbies who had marched around the quad from battalion headquarters for their assignment at Company D. A few inches taller than the rest of the troops, Palmer's hair had recently been cut in a Denver barbershop. Palmer had looked deceptively STRAC that morning.

Sgt. Sherman crooks a finger, "Come with me, troop," and leads Palmer down the hallway past the Coke machine and into the latrine where he tells his troop to grab a mop.

Palmer doesn't say anything. He doesn't smile or grovel or acknowledge in any way that Sherman had nabbed him fucking-off, which is exactly what he had been doing at his bunk. He chooses a mop from the storage closet and starts dragging the rag strings around the shower room floor, and picks up where he had left off at the rifle range the day before. Which is to say, he begins daydreaming about home.

At seven A.M. formation Palmer is a bit worried about being put on a shit detail with SP4 Courtney because he doesn't want to end up the butt of good-natured but intolerable wisecracks for an entire morning. But Courtney is sent off with a group of men to haul laundry bags down to the main post in a deuce-and-a-half, and Palmer is picked with five other men to march around the quad to battalion headquarters to do whatever jobs that small unit can't or won't fill with its own corps of elite, starch-pressed, clean-shaven clerk/typists.

When they get inside, a battalion sergeant sends Palmer and another man up to the supply room on the third floor where a Hawaiian lifer E7 is waiting for them. He puts them to work sorting and inspecting equipment for possible damage — rips in canteen covers, chipped blades on bayonets, pistol belts frayed or unsalvageable. The man Palmer is working with is a Specialist Fourth-Class named Thorpe, whom he has never spoken to before.

They begin digging out equipment stored in deeply-recessed shelves in the walls and piling it in the center of the floor. It will be easy work, out of the weather and within the dim confines of the long, low-ceilinged attic room, so Palmer feels he has lucked out. He could just as easily have been sent down to the motor pool to wash jeeps all morning, a mind-numbing job that he had done the day after he had arrived, so he's satisfied with this. He wouldn't mind doing this particular job for the next nineteen months. It doesn't engage his intellect, and it allows him to daydream about women or the bowling alley, or to continue thinking about Denver and his discharge.

They work for an hour stacking piles of refuse under the dull eye of the sergeant who stays busy fiddling with paper-work at his desk. Then, "Smoke if you got 'em," he says, and tells them he's going downstairs to get a cup of coffee. Before the sergeant leaves he hands them an ashtray, the kind of cheap, machine-stamped, tinfoil flower found in bars and bowling alleys. But Palmer is still caught up in the myth of giving up smoking, so he doesn't have any cigarettes on him.

SP4 Thorpe walks across the room and sits down on a footlocker and tweezers a Winston from his shirt pocket. Palmer knows he's not going to quit smoking today because he's still pissed at himself about the rifle range, so he crosses the room and asks Thorpe if he can borrow a cigarette.

Thorpe doesn't say anything, but does reach in and pull a tube from his pocket. He holds it up to Palmer, who tries to make eye contact, to either start a conversation or at least nod his gratitude, but Thorpe won't look at him. Thorpe's lips are thin and pinched, his face pale like the underbelly of a fish, the flesh stretched tightly across the cheekbones and jaw. There's a strange sort of squint about his eyes, inbred, and not from any bright light in this dim place. The problem is, Palmer also needs a match (want me to smoke it for you ha ha) so he feels a bit awkward asking a second favor from a man who won't even look at him. His own Zippo is lying on the top shelf of his wall locker, a basic training souvenir that he doesn't want to throw away. Soldiers are always cluttering up their lives with duty-station doodads and sentimental crap like engraved lighters or embroidered silk pillows that they think they'll treasure into old age in the belief that these are the most significant things they will ever possess in their lives, and Palmer is one of those soldiers.

"Got a light?" he says.

Maybe to let Palmer know he's annoyed too, Thorpe takes his time digging his Zippo out of his pocket. He holds it up without looking at Palmer, who takes it and lights up and hands it back. "How long have you been stationed here?" Palmer says.

There's a strange croak in Thorpe's voice as he answers. "Seven months."

"I took basic training at Fort Campbell. Where'd you take basic?"

"Fort Lewis."

No elaboration. Thorpe doesn't want to talk. He just wants to sit and suck smoke and blow it softly into a thin breeze created by a hidden crack in the attic near a window which had been sealed shut by layers of paint years ago. This pisses Palmer off because the communal oppression of a shit detail is a thing to be shared, is one of the ways you make buddies in the army. So he decides to go on talking, and maybe bug Thorpe a little.

"My brother Phil graduates from basic in Ft. Lewis this week," he says. Phil is three years older than Palmer, went to college until he had acquired enough credits to invalidate his student deferment. Phil knew he was going to get called up anyway, so he had volunteered for the draft.

Thorpe turns his head and looks up with that stretched squint and gives Palmer what must be a smile. But it's thin, like a cop smiling at a man who isn't amusing him. It's a reaction though, something anyway, and having gotten it, Palmer loses interest in the conversation. Thorpe's sullenness reminds Palmer a little of himself when he's suffering from a bad hang-over on a work day and wants to be left alone. So maybe a hangover is the problem, and he can commiserate because he has a small one himself. But he decides instead that Thorpe is just an asshole.

Palmer finishes his cigarette and crushes it out in the stamped tulip. Without another word he crosses the room and sits down and starts sorting canteen covers.

At eleven a.m. the sergeant tells them to put everything away and knock off for chow. They stow all the unexamined articles of war back into the shelves and head for the door. Just before they walk out, the sergeant tells them to inform their operations sergeant that he won't need them in the afternoon.

As they stroll around the quad toward Company D, Palmer thinks about the sergeant's remark. If the battalion supply room doesn't want them back, Sgt. Sherman would not necessarily know about it, which means Palmer and Thorpe might be able to avoid work details in the afternoon.

He doesn't say anything to Thorpe about this right away though. He wants to think it over because he's never liked involving other people in his schemes—it complicates things. But he realizes that he's bound to Thorpe in this situation, and is sorry now that he hadn't been a little friendlier in the supply room.

When they get back to the barracks, Palmer goes into the latrine and washes the attic dust off his hands, then goes out to the porch and joins the moving queue in front of the mess hall door, where he continues to think about this vague plan which is giving him a kind of thrill due to its perceived hermetic nature. He has successfully dodged more than one shit detail during his brief time in the army.

Before basic training, in the reception station when everyone was still unassigned and receiving their uniforms and filling out paperwork, including one mandatory letter home written in an auditorium telling their parents that they were alive and weren't being brutalized, he had dodged his first detail ever. He had walked out of a mess hall one noon and a moment later heard someone open the door behind him and yell, "Trainee!" He knew who it was and what he wanted. This was how the cooks always did it, nabbing trainees at random for impromptu KP that lasted for hours. Instead of looking around, which was the mistake he had made the day before, Palmer kept right on walking. The cook screamed again, "Trainee!" and in desperation Palmer rushed around the corner of the mess hall and encountered a crowd of new recruits standing outside a barracks. He edged into the crowd and stood stock-still trying to control his heavy breathing, believing that he would be invisible in the identical green garb and bald-headed capped mass of milling men who would serve as his camouflage. His heart was pounding from a burst of adrenaline shot through with pure elation, because he knew he was going to get away with it, and he did.

But the plan for this afternoon does not entail bovine panic and freak luck. It has to be thought out carefully. He stares at his lunch tray as he chews, wishing again he did not have to involve Thorpe because if he did this alone it would be relatively easy to pull off, and if he got caught, he could play dumb, his perpetual ace-in-the-hole.

Second and third platoons are billeted in opposite wings of the second floor, but Palmer doesn't know which platoon Thorpe belongs to, so he just roams the hallways looking into empty rooms until he spots Thorpe sitting on the edge of a bunk. He's polishing a boot. It's an odd thing to be doing at noon, but Thorpe already has struck him as an odd bird.

Palmer knocks on the open door, even though it isn't barracks protocol, and walks in.

"Hey Thorpe, I'm glad I caught you," he says, putting as much conviviality into his voice as he can muster.

Thorpe doesn't look at him, doesn't even slow down making circles with the rag on the toe of the boot held upside down with a fist shoved into the ankle.

"I don't know what your plans are," Palmer says, "but since we don't have to go back to battalion supply this afternoon, I was thinking we could maybe, you know, take the rest of the day off."

Thorpe stands up and places his boots side-by-side under his bunk, then stows his rag and Kiwi in his wall locker. Palmer assumes he's thinking it over, but after he closes the locker Thorpe walks out of the room without a word.

Nonplused, Palmer stares at the doorway as if expecting Thorpe to walk back in and whisper that the coast is clear and the idea sounds swell. Palmer looks around at the wrinkled blanket where Thorpe had been sitting. He's never experienced such peculiar rudeness, such a blatant snub, and he doesn't know what to make of it.

He walks back downstairs knowing that there is no plan now. Thorpe has trashed a rare opportunity, and this angers Palmer, and serves to confirm his belief that it's futile to include other people in his goldbricking. A lesson learned.

He heads down to his squad room and climbs onto his bunk in violation of barracks protocol, and sleeps until afternoon formation is called.

At one p.m. the troops gather on the front sidewalk at attention and wait while the members of the cadre refer to the lists on their clipboards and consult one another about the afternoon's business. After the troops have been dispersed to their various details, Palmer looks around but doesn't see Thorpe anywhere. Sgt. Sherman is standing near the porch scribbling notes on a clipboard. Palmer feels like a traitor to himself as he approaches the man.

"Sgt. Sherman, the battalion supply sergeant told me and Thorpe we don't have to go back to the supply room this afternoon." He specifically mentions Thorpe's name just in case the prick has concocted some private scheme of his own to hide out for the day.

Sgt. Sherman frowns at his clipboard. Loose cannon. He tells Palmer to hang tight while he runs into the operations office to see what goes.

Palmer steps up into the shade of the porch and stares across the quad toward the plastered facade of battalion headquarters glowing white beneath the cloudless blue noon sky. The last of the Company D troops come out the front door and go around behind the barracks, and the building grows so quiet that he can hear the soft clicking of typewriters down in the staff offices. One man who had graduated from MP school the same week he did already has become a clerk/typist. Palmer doesn't envy the kind of work the man has to do, but does envy the fact that he'd copped a dick job. He'll get promoted sooner, and will become friendly with the officers and NCOs, and will never get put on a shit detail. But he's confined to an office all day, which Palmer doesn't think he would be able to stand because he couldn't slip outside at will to have a smoke, or to just get away. In spite of the in-herent dull nature of shit details, you do get sent to different places to do different shit.

Sgt. Sherman steps onto the porch. "Take the afternoon off, Palmer. You're going on guard duty at the motor pool tonight."

Guard duty. Palmer is instantly infuriated. His plan for the evening had been to drink beer at the bowling alley and play the pinball machines until ten P.M. But he tries not to let his anger show, because back when he was sworn in he had made a vow that if he was going to take part in this army business, he would never gripe aloud about any assignment, would perform whatever job they ordered him to do, and would never refuse any mission, so that he would come out of these two years clean. If there is one thing he cannot stand it's a griper—basic training was infested with them, the whiners, the pussies, the duds who made things harder for everybody else. What made them think they were above the humiliations that were every yardbird's due?

He nods at Sgt. Sherman but keeps the blank look on his face that he always wears whenever speaking to anyone above the rank of corporal.

"Be ready in the operations office with your field-gear at seventeen hundred hours," Sgt. Sherman says.

Palmer says yes sergeant and steps off the porch and walks away from the company area fast before anything else crops up. He heads down the gentle slope of the sidewalk toward the bowling alley, but turns left at the corner and walks one block over to Lincoln Boulevard, the main two-lane asphalt road which loops all the way around the Presidio from the Lombard gate to Baker State Beach. He stands on the shoulder of the road waiting for the traffic to clear, and waiting for his fury to evaporate.

The far side of the road is shaded by pines, as well as trees with trunks wrapped in creeper vines which aren't evergreen but which are said to stay green all year, giving off an over-whelming odor of chlorophyll which permeates the Presidio all the way down the hill to main post. When the traffic thins he runs across the road toward a patch of mown lawn, a kind of park where a mock ICBM missile is set up on permanent display. He had taken a picture of it on his first day here when he hadn't yet been assigned to Company D and had nothing to do but roam around the quad looking things over. He had taken a motion-picture of it, an 8mm home-movie which was no different from the movies he had taken in basic training and MP school, movies of things not moving—barracks, signposts, tanks, sometimes soldiers. Everyone else was taking snapshots with the cheap Instamatics they had bought at the PX, but his idea was to manufacture a kind of living scrapbook depicting his stretch in the service from basic training to his discharge.

He kicks his way through a hedgerow of bushes toward a spot that PFC Gunther, another MP school acquaintance, had shown him a few days earlier. Gunther had referred to the spot as his thinking place, but since he's from The South he had pronounced it "thanking place." In basic training, the men from the North were continually mimicking and mocking the men from the South, and not just their heavy accents but their idiom too. Palmer once heard a man from Michigan say to a man from Alabama, "Approximately how far is 'yonder'?"

He emerges from the bushes and steps onto a naked patch of earth at the edge of a cliff overlooking the Pacific Ocean, and gazes at a panorama which would look pretty good on film: to his right, the Golden Gate Bridge set against the blue hills of Marin County; in front of him, the green and unbroken surface of the ocean defining the earth's curve at the horizon; to his left, further along the coastal cliffs southward, Baker State Beach, and beyond that, a pastel clutter of civilian houses bordering the perimeter of the Presidio.

He sits down on the flat shelf of earth, a small clearing surrounded by bushes. He picks up a rock and chucks it into the air but doesn't watch it fall. Instead he watches seagulls circling seals charging in bullet-bodied packs toward the shoreline rocks white with bird-shit poking from the surf like teeth. A cool wind is blowing, but the sun is hot on his legs and feels good. He looks at the Golden Gate Bridge, at its shadow floating in its entirety upon the surface of the bay. As a kid he had always assumed that the bridge was painted gold like its name. His father had sailed beneath the bridge on a troop ship headed for the Philippines in 1942 and served three years in the same latitudes as Vietnam, dropping fifty pounds from his six-foot frame. Palmer had expected to be sent to Vietnam straight out of MP school, had expected to be sitting right at this moment in a foxhole ducking bullets in the Mekong Delta. Instead, he's sitting on a breezy cliff on the northernmost tip of the San Francisco peninsula, pissed-off because he can't get drunk tonight. So Gunther from The South was right. This is, after all, a good place to sit down and think things over.

Palmer stands up and brushes the dirt off his ass and walks back to the barracks to sleep until guard duty begins. This will be the first real guard-duty he has ever pulled in the army, so he doesn't know how it will go, but does know that, like most army work, it probably will be simple and tedious, and that he should get as much sleep as possible before it begins. This he had learned long ago.

CHAPTER 3

Three men have been scheduled for guard duty, Palmer and two men from the second and third platoons. They are already in the operations office when he arrives, dressed in field-gear and wearing helmets inside the barracks which surprises Palmer because he still has the mind-set of a trainee who had been taught that wearing a hat indoors is a cardinal sin. But Sgt. Weigand doesn't say anything about it, just as he didn't say anything about Palmer's cheating on Courtney's scorecard. He's Charge of Quarters tonight, CQ, and will be acting as sergeant-of-the-guard if anything comes up, although he says nothing ever comes up at the motor pool.

He reviews their special orders and tells them not to let anyone inside the fence except the Officer of the Day, Lieutenant Norbert. The field phone is beside the motor-pool office door but don't use it unless there's a real emergency. Stay on your feet, walk the perimeter, and don't sit in the goddamn jeeps. Then he goes into a story about the last man who was caught sitting in a jeep and ended up confined to quarters for a week. It's another last-man-to-do-that story, like the man Palmer kept hearing about in basic training and MP school: the last man who dropped a live grenade (and lost a foot), the last man who let a prisoner escape (and had to serve the prisoner's sentence), the last man who set up a Claymore mine backwards (they never even found his dog tags). Always the same guy bumbling his way through training, fomenting one disaster after another, and continually losing stripes. But Palmer never got to see him

in action, because everywhere Palmer went, the poor dud had
already fucked-up and left.

Sgt. Weigand assigns Palmer the first shift, six-to-eight
and midnight-to-two, and lets the other men go back to their
bunks. There's one M-14 that the guards will be trading off
throughout the night. Palmer is given a flashlight, and two
magazines of live ammo that someone else had loaded. The
CQ runner drives him down to the motor pool at the edge of
the San Francisco Bay.

The runner is a PFC named Lomax from the second platoon.
He waits with the engine idling as Palmer unlocks the padlock
and drags the gate open and steps inside. Lomax hollers, "Back
in two hours!" and punches the accelerator and races across
the asphalt flats toward the main road.

A fenced acre, the motor pool sits on a long coastal strip
of land east of the Golden Gate Bridge which, as the sun goes
down, begins glowing with white bulb light outlining the
span of the road-bed. Palmer can see the windows of a WAC
barracks a quarter-mile in the opposite direction, a single
wooden WWII building surrounded by a barbed-wire fence,
like the stockade but without guard towers. The place was
pointed out to him and a few other new men when they were
taken on a bus tour of the Presidio two days earlier to famil-
iarize them with the layout of the reservation that they would
one day be patrolling as enforcers of Sixth Army law.

He stares at the barracks wondering if WACs in bras will
walk past the windows. Then he turns and begins patrolling
the perimeter fence, walking slowly to make it look like he's
working, in case someone happens to be watching. Beyond
the back fence of the motor pool is the dirt wall of a cliff, a

palisade like the drop below the thinking place. On top of it runs a part of Doyle Drive, a civilian freeway which cuts straight through the Presidio to the Golden Gate Bridge. Palmer takes note of the cliff because no one would be able to see him very well if he hung out back there, especially in the dark, an ideal place to fuck-off. He tightens the zipper of his field jacket at the neck as a sea breeze snaps loose canvas on the back of a deuce-and-a-half stirring up dust and a few newspapers which had been overlooked by whoever the drudge was that had policed the motor pool earlier in the evening. It would have been a private of course, an enlisted man like himself.

He comes to the long white one-story wooden building which houses the motor-pool sergeant's office and the garage bays where vehicles in daylight are repaired, though the bays are empty now. Red toolboxes line the rear wall of the garage, padlocked and secured, the only things he can see that a thief might be able to steal from this place and expect to get away with. He continues on around the perimeter until he's made the entire circuit and returned to the front gate. He looks at his watch. Twenty minutes have gone by. There are one hour and forty minutes left.

He calculates that with five slow strolls around the perimeter, his shift will be over. But he's not about to stroll around this place five times. He cuts straight through the rows of jeeps and two-and-a-half ton trucks and heads for the darkness and anonymity of the last line of vehicles parked at the base of the cliff.

He picks a jeep hidden especially well behind a big truck and sits down on the front seat and lays his rifle across his lap. He takes out a fresh pack of Camels that he had bought at the PX earlier in the evening, the oppression of guard duty being his excuse now. He lights a cigarette and breathes the smoke deeply and coughs and stares at the flat asphalt apron which fronts the motor pool, and beyond that, Mason Street which runs the entire length of the marina past the WAC barracks to the Presidio gate near the Palace of Fine Arts.

It's too dark to see the waters of the bay now, but he can hear the clanging of buoys and the dull chug of boats driving toward the lights of Sausalito. He can see the night glow of Oakland where he knows that Jack London had lived, starved, wrote, rode horses, and died. He can't see Alcatraz Island from where he sits, but does know that in 1962 some prisoners had escaped from it and were never seen again, the escape reenacted on a TV show. "Swept to their deaths by the frigid swift currents beneath the bridge," said the announcer, a mortifying statement, children so often able to identify closely with desperate adults. Was a GI on guard duty in this very place in 1962, smoking illegally like Palmer is smoking while criminal corpses drifted past in the bay? Then he sees lights coming across the flats, the headlights of a racing jeep, and he's certain he has been seen, certain that he has been caught fucking-off.

He hops out of the jeep and tosses his cigarette to the ground and stamps the sparks black. He holds his rifle at port-arms and begins walking toward the main gate, not too fast though because he's been in the army long enough to know that cheap shit like spying on a working man could happen but isn't likely, so he's only a little panicked as he makes his way toward the gate. When he gets close he slows to a stroll to make it look as though he's just completing another circuit of the grounds.

The jeep pulls up at the front gate with its headlights shining through the cyclone fence. Palmer stays off to the side so the driver can't see him because there's always the unlikely possibility that this is someone actually trying to break into the motor pool.

But he recognizes the driver. It's Lt. Norbert making his rounds. The lieutenant gets out of the jeep and walks toward the fence, and only then does Palmer realize he isn't quite sure of the procedure for acknowledging the presence of someone he recognizes on sight. He knows how to challenge a stranger, an enemy, but what do you say to someone you know but who doesn't know you? A small thing, but strange to him at this moment. He decides that since they're practically strangers anyway, he will go by the book.

"Halt! Who is there?"

The lieutenant stops. "I'm Lt. Norbert, Officer of the Day."

"Advance, lieutenant."

The man approaches the fence and peers curiously at Palmer's face.

"May I see your military identification card, sir?" Palmer says.

The lieutenant seems a bit surprised to be going through this rigmarole, but not annoyed. He takes out his billfold and digs through the pockets and pulls out his military ID. Palmer asks him to place it flat up against the fence, and he does so. Palmer shines his flashlight on the photograph, then pokes the light into the lieutenant's face which might be discourteous but is by the book. His face is the same as on the photograph, the

ID has been made, and now Palmer doesn't know what else he can do in terms of identification to protect the motor pool (a saboteur would probably possess forged documents anyway) so he lets the man inside.

"That was an outstanding challenge, Private Palmer," the lieutenant says, squinting at the name-tag on Palmer's field jacket. "Most of the guards at the posts I visit don't seem to understand proper military procedure."

"Thank you, sir," Palmer says quickly.

Palmer has never been very comfortable around officers. They are like old ladies in that you never cuss or say "fuck" around them, or spit, and never laugh without being invited to laughter by their tepid jokes.

"I'm going to take a look around, Palmer. You may accompany me." Lieutenant Norbert takes the flashlight from Palmer and steps off on the left foot and heads toward the motor-pool office. Palmer hurriedly secures the gate and catches up, and follows at a distance of one pace.

The lieutenant sweeps the flashlight beam across parked vehicles as if he's inspecting them, making sure they aren't damaged or stolen. They make a quick pass along the vehicle bay, the circle of light slithering up slats or dancing beside the lieutenant's booted feet. Palmer can't tell if Lt. Norbert is just putting on a show or what the hell he's up to. When they come to the motor-pool office, the lieutenant turns and says with an officious grin, "Why don't you wait outside here, Palmer. I've got to make a phone call." He opens the door and steps into the office where a low-watt bulb is burning, and shuts the door tightly behind him.

It's a flimsy door and doesn't shut very tightly at all. Palmer could probably hear him dialing the phone if he stood right next to the door, which he does. He edges as close as he can, prepared to move away fast if he hears the phone being hung up. The lieutenant dials seven numbers, waits a moment, then says, "Hi, honey."

It's difficult to make out distinct words, even though Palmer has his ear pressed practically against the door. He starts grinning, thinking how great it is that an officer would take time out of his duties to ring up his girlfriend, just like a goldbricking enlisted man.

The lieutenant's voice grows louder and he says he'll try to make it over to Sausalito and see her as soon as he can. Palmer looks at the lights of Sausalito sprinkled along the far dark Marin shore where the lieutenant's girlfriend is talking on the phone right at this very moment, nude on a couch Palmer hopes. There's bit of throaty laughter as the lieutenant says, "Yeah. Okay. Yeah." Then his voice gets low, and Palmer figures the lieutenant is getting ready to say something dirty and hang up, so he moves off a few feet and stands with his back to the door and stares at the bay with his rifle at port-arms.

There's a bit of a bounce in Lt. Norbert's walk as he steps outside. A smile of impending satisfaction makes his teeth gleam in the light from a bulb on a nearby telephone pole. "I'm finished here, troop. Things looks secure."

Palmer accompanies him back to the gate. As the lieutenant steps outside he turns and glances at Palmer's name-tag again. "You're doing an outstanding job, Private Palmer. I'm going to make sure Captain Weller hears about this."

Palmer is instantly elated. In the company only a week, and already he has impressed an officer. In fact, this is the first time an officer has taken note of, and personally commented upon, anything he's ever done. Palmer straightens his spine and performs a rifle-salute. "Thank you, sir." He closes the gate and locks it and watches as the lieutenant climbs into the jeep and starts the engine, fires the headlights, and wheels across the asphalt flats to inspect the next guard post.

Palmer is amazed. Such a generous remark from an officer for having done what he was supposed to do only because he didn't know what else to do. He wonders how the CO will react when he hears about this. It changes the mood of Palmer's entire night. He shoulders his rifle and begins walking the perimeter at a fast pace, and makes the circuit in five minutes.

By the time he's back at the front gate he's grinning, not laughing aloud but feeling like laughing, pausing to peer at the lit windows of the WAC barracks, then moving on, laughing once finally, a goofy yuk that echoes off the palisade. He's certain that he's got it made now at Company D, certain that when Captain Weller hears about this, Private Palmer's name will rise to the top of the next promotion list.

When his shift ends and the next man arrives to take over, Palmer doesn't tell him about his good luck, doesn't tell him that the way to impress the Officer of the Day is to give him a formal sentry challenge. He doesn't want to share his glory with anyone. He wants it to be his secret, like a cache of gold, like a bird in the hand, like the keys to the fucking kingdom.

CHAPTER 4

Palmer wakes up the next day at noon buoyed by the same sense of satisfaction that had lulled him to sleep at two-thirty in the morning, the sense that he is making some kind of progress in the army at last. He eats chow in the mess hall, then strolls around to the alley behind the barracks to smoke his first cigarette of the day and to think a bit more about his encounter with Lt. Norbert the previous evening. This thing's got a grip on him.

During basic training he had performed every difficult mission and simulated stunt in the field uncomplaining and eager to learn how to be a good soldier, and yet throughout all that he had gained nothing but a feeling of uneasiness, because the Drill Sergeants never seemed to take notice of the effort he was putting into things. But still he believed that a reward for his hard work was inevitable, and would come to him during the final week of basic in the form of that broken-backed wistful strip of yellow rank insignia referred to by everyone as "mosquito-wings," the designation of Private E2. He wanted his stripe very badly out of basic. Less than a quarter of the company would be receiving this badge of recognition for outstanding effort, and he fully expected he would be one of them. But when the day came and the Drill Sergeants gathered the trainees together in a classroom and handed out stripes to those who had made the grade, Palmer's name wasn't called. He couldn't believe it. He had worked so hard, had never complained, had never made waves, had never talked back or screwed up or caused any kind of trouble. In fact a few of the men who did get promoted had caused their Drill Sergeants some form of minor grief at one time or another during training, and the rest seemed to be men whom Palmer had frequently observed talking to the Drill Sergeants after hours, shooting the shit, cracking jokes, and generally kissing lifer ass. So Palmer didn't get his mosquito-wings until the end of MP school, the insignia which currently decorates the arms of his Class A uniform coat hanging inside his wall locker. He has no idea how long it will take to get promoted to Private First-Class, but with this Norbert thing, who knows?

He lights a second cigarette as a deuce-and-a-half loaded with cardboard crates rolls up the alley in low gear and makes a turn into the Company D parking lot. The white stenciled insignia on the bumper indicates the truck is from a quartermaster company. He hears another truck coming behind it. He moves out of the way and watches as it pulls to a stop, blocking the alley. Both trucks idle in neutral belching fumes. Working vehicles never seem to get shut off in the army—government gasoline is free.

Formation is due to begin in a few minutes, so Palmer field-strips his cigarette and walks around to the front sidewalk and falls in with the first squad of the first platoon. Captain Weller marches out onto the lawn and faces the formation and puts them at ease. "Men, I've got some good news to pass along to you. We've had new wall lockers on order for two months now, and they're being delivered this afternoon. We're not only going to get rid of your old wall lockers, we're getting rid of your wooden footlockers, too."

The captain looks extremely pleased to be delivering his newsflash, grinning in the shade of the bill of his saucer cap.

He signals the First Sergeant to take over the formation, and Top comes off the porch.

This detail sounds okay to Palmer, and now he knows what's in the crates on those trucks. Wall lockers hardly weigh anything, so this won't be a bad detail at all. He had delivered sofa-beds during one of his shit jobs as a civilian, so he knows all about leaden burden and scaling staircases and standing cumbersome crap on end to squeeze your way around landings or through tight doorways.

Top faces the troops and takes an unlit cigar out of his mouth and says in his ragged commanding lifer voice, "Men, if you had any plans to take off at five o'clock tonight and drink beer and chase pussy, you can shelve 'em right now."

Everybody laughs. Everybody loves it when an old sergeant says "pussy."

"I'm giving you one week to complete this mission. You're going to work on these lockers at oh-seven hundred hours every morning, and you're going to stay on the job until twenty-two hundred hours every night."

This part doesn't sound so good because the bowling alley closes at ten P.M. on week nights. But since one hundred and fifty men will be taking part in this mission, he doesn't see why the job shouldn't be finished by tomorrow evening.

Top turns the company over to Sgt. Sherman, who calls the troops to attention and tells them to fall out to the parking lot and start hauling crates. As the men crowd around the trucks, Palmer can feel the excitement in the air that is always present whenever GIs are working like a team toward a goal that they understand and know they can handle. Four men hop up and crawl around on the crates and start sliding them out, but it's not until Palmer steps up to the tailgate that he gets his first good look at the cardboard boxes. A real good look. They're no thicker than mattress boxes, and he suddenly realizes that these bastards are coming unassembled.

Men elbow past him to get up close and grab hold of what they believe to be wall lockers instead of stacks of sheet tin. Palmer can't believe it. The contents of these boxes will have to be put together by hand. His previous estimate undergoes a radical recalculation, and he envisions this detail dragging clear into Friday of next week, beginning every dawn and lasting until closing time at the bowling alley. It looks like Palmer is never going to get any beer.

He hangs back as the ebb of bodies lurches toward the truck, wondering why the hell the army couldn't pay a bunch of damn factory workers to put those fuckers together. When the first vehicle is empty, the troops back off and take a breather while the next truck in line maneuvers into the parking lot. Palmer hears another deuce-and-a-half coming up the alley. He looks around at all the men grinning and stretching their muscles and cracking jokes like they don't have a clue, then he walks over to the porch and looks at a growing stack of crates outside the mess hall door. Sgt. Weigand is supervising the carrying of boxes into the foyer and up the stairs, which involves a tight 180-degree turn on a landing midway up.

Thank God I don't bunk upstairs, Palmer thinks, then notices two men squatting and tearing open a lone crate at the far end of the porch near the door which leads into his squad room. Top and the CO are standing over them giving instructions. Palmer walks over to see what's going on and discovers that Top wants to assemble a locker right here on the porch as a model so that any tricky arrangements of bolting might be foreseen and thus corrected before everyone in the barracks starts making the same mistakes.

It's obviously a ridiculous plan, because nobody is going to wait around for a model locker to be built, they're just going to dive in and make their own mistakes, especially the men upstairs. But Palmer sees a possibility in this situation, so he starts helping the men lift out tin and lean it against the wall. He digs into the open cardboard crate and comes up with a small paper bag filled with nuts and bolts and braces of various sizes. He finds a small booklet containing the instructions for assembly, and he immediately hands this to Top, and in doing so he becomes one-of-the-men-on-the-porch. When the unloading of crates begins again, he stays right where he is with Top and the CO hovering over him giving advice like abrupt fathers supervising bicycle assembly at Christmas.

The rest of the company gets back to work dragging crates off the rear of the new truck and hauling them along the sidewalk under the sun which is getting hotter, but Palmer remains where he is. He doesn't have to haul crates now because he has become one-of-the-men-on-the-porch.

He discovers quickly that the job is as complicated as he expected it would be, with three long sheets of tin for the walls, and two smaller sheets for top and bottom, plus double-doors (the new lockers are extra wide), plus all the shelves and dividers and attachments which will make up the guts of the thing. Palmer can see that this easy assignment will very likely last all afternoon.

He was right. The model locker isn't even half-built before the troops are allowed to knock off for chow. At a quarter to five, word goes around to get ready for evening formation, and all the sounds of rattling tin and men arguing about how to do things right cease, and the troops come out of the building and stand on the sidewalk with the eagerness gone from their faces because the simple part, the hauling of boxes, is coming to an end, and before them lies the interminable job of inserting bolts and tightening them with pliers and having to undo them because the panels were put together in the wrong order because Palmer was right about the other thing too: nobody came out to look at the model.

He's no longer worried about beer though. He's had all afternoon to flesh out his plan. He'll go to the bowling alley at five P.M. for hamburgers and a few Buds, and be back at six o'clock to resume work. And he knows exactly how much beer he can drink in an hour. When he was a nineteen-year-old civilian he once took a bet that he could drink an ounce of beer per-minute for sixty minutes, and he won.

Formation is brief, with Top only telling the men to keep up the good work. After he dismisses the troops, everyone except Palmer queues up in front of the mess hall door. Palmer heads down the sidewalk toward the bowling alley, but gets no further than the corner of the barracks.

"Palmer!"

He stops and turns around and sees Sergeant Armand of the second platoon standing on the sidewalk with his fists on his hips. Sgt. Armand is a black E6 who possesses a Combat Infantryman's Badge. The bill of his cap is tugged low to his eyes. His faded and starch-pressed fatigues are tailored to hug his muscular physique. The black toes of his jump boots glisten like balls of glass. "Where the hell do you think you're going, Palmer?"

"To the bowling alley."

"Negative, Palmer. Nobody leaves the company area tonight."

It's obvious to Palmer that Sgt. Armand just now made up that rule. Neither Top nor the CO had said anything about what the troops could or could not do during break-time. And while Palmer has never talked back to a sergeant before, this seems a violation of a right, although perhaps a minor right—a minuscule one even. But more than that, it's simply stupid. It's the panic of sergeants.

"I'm just going to get a hamburger and come right back," Palmer lies.

Sgt. Armand comes at him fast and grabs hold of his upper arm. "Are you trying to bust my balls, private?" He leads Palmer to the porch. "You get in line and chow down and then you get back to work."

Palmer takes his place at the end of the line and stares at the pimpled neck of the man in front of him. Nobody laughs or makes a wisecrack. The porch is silent except for the occasional creak of the screen door opening and closing. Palmer is disgusted, but his anger works for him, helps to focus his thoughts for the fabrication of something like vengeance but is merely a solution, because he doesn't have time for vengeance.

He steps into the foyer of the mess hall and signs the chow sheet as "Mickey Mouse," which everyone does for a joke now and then, also scribbling such personal favorites as "Tom Terrific" or "Froggy the Gremlin" because the cooks never check the signatures anyway. He goes into the mess hall and picks up a tray and stands in line, but after he has filled it with chicken and potatoes he doesn't go into the dining room. He steps around the serving counter and enters the kitchen.

It's hot back there, humid and sweet with the stink of cherry pie and dishwater. Cooks are sweating in their fatigue whites in front of the ovens, stirring steaming pans of beans or soup. Palmer walks up to a cook turning chicken with tongs at a stove. "Excuse me, sergeant, have you seen Private Lauderman?"

A big man, heavy, six-four, the cook looks down at Palmer through thick lenses of fogged eyeglasses, and says no.

"I was told he's on KP and I need to talk to him. Is he in here?"

"I don't know, look around," the cook says, turning away before he's even finished speaking. Palmer had known he would be able to take advantage of the man's indifference. Lifer sergeant cooks don't give a shit about the problems of draftees.

Palmer walks deeper into the tiled cavernous kitchen out of view of the dining room where Sgt. Armand might be watching. He steps up to a man scrubbing a pan in an alcove and looks him over as though he might be Private Lauderman, who was in fact a jerk Palmer had known in basic who would never loan anyone cigarettes.

Without looking around to see who might be watching, Palmer sets his tray on a countertop and walks toward the back door as though he is supposed to be walking toward the back door. He pushes open the screen door and steps out into the sunshine and strolls over to the alley and disappears behind the barracks next door.

There are no other customers in the snack bar, only a single group of lifer wives out in the lanes bowling. The crowd that Palmer is always trying to beat will be coming in soon, MPs from A or B or C companies, or engineer or signal corps troops who don't have to go back to work at six P.M. The pinball machines in the foyer are silent, so Palmer can clearly hear each lifer wife squeal whenever a bowling pin falls down.

He takes a long drink from his first bottle of beer, lights a cigarette, inhales deeply, and sighs with contempt. He's contemptuous of anyone who won't risk the things he'll risk, guys like that chickenshit Thorpe. On the other hand, he's in complete awe of anyone who will do things he would never do, like put in for a transfer to Vietnam. He's heard about three Company D men who have already done this. But never volunteer, and that's no joke to him. He once volunteered in basic to help set up twelve-man tents in a sleet storm because he thought he would get better treatment from the Drill Sergeants, but all he got was a frostbit ass. And anyway, of all the places in the world he would go to on purpose, Vietnam isn't even on the list.

He orders another beer.

As he drinks, he glances constantly at his watch, though not out of irritation but like a timekeeper at a football game careful about the seconds. The snack bar begins to fill with troops off work for the day. His bad luck to get assigned to Company D instead of C or B. If he was in C Company right now he would be pulling road patrol instead of enduring the queen bitch detail of all time. He is beginning to feel the creep of alcohol in his brain, and it makes him feel reckless, makes him want to talk to all these strangers and blow off the night and stay here boozing until ten P.M.

This thought makes him smile, because he does know one thing about himself: if the consequences were not so dire, he actually would stay here drinking. But he's not out of control. He likes to think that there has never been anything he has ever done drunk that he didn't do willfully, that booze was merely his camouflage, that he always knew what he was up to whenever he got too loud, or insulted his friends, or simply said embarrassing things in public. The proof to himself that he's under control in this instance is that, after he finishes his fourth Budweiser at five minutes to six, he gets up and walks outside.

The spires of the Golden Gate Bridge towering over the large Quonset roof of the bowling alley are lit true gold now by the setting sun. A blanket of fog is sliding beneath the road-bed of the bridge, broad roiling gray and white billows which never seem to appear when you've got a fucking camera handy. It's too nice an evening to go back to work, but the booze starts making Palmer feel both competent and magnanimous, and he starts thinking about tracking down Sgt. Armand and apologizing for being insubordinate. Wouldn't that be something? A beer-breath E2 confessing sins and asking forgiveness and fabricating a jolly camaraderie with a pissed E6? This is the real danger of excessive alcohol consumption and not, for instance, liver damage: tactical errors manufactured by a brain gone to ruin and delighted with itself.

He returns to the company by the alley route, but passes behind the barracks so he will circle around and approach the porch from the opposite direction of the bowling alley, just in case Sgt. Armand is watching for him. He finds the men of Company D milling around on the front sidewalk having last smokes while waiting for work-call.

Feeling cagey, Palmer lights up and mingles with the troops. He's high and he's happy, and at six o'clock he doesn't return to the porch to work on the model locker. He leaves that to the two strangers, and goes into his squad room and gets to work helping Keillor crack open a new crate.

There's only enough space in the room to assemble two lockers at a time, so they have to maneuver sheets of tin around the three double-bunks like a giant slide-puzzle. The first hour of assembling is fun, as Palmer fumbles with bolts and accidentally strips threads and ends up hiding the results in his pockets. The men smoke and crack jokes, and Palmer is a bit loud which he's never been before, so maybe the other men know he's been drinking, can smell it on his breath maybe, but they play the game.

He goes to work on a sliding drawer which will slip into the bottom of a finished wall locker to serve as a replacement for a footlocker. He starts thinking about what a change this will be, getting rid of those old wooden footlockers. It's as if the New Action Army is truly coming into being right here. It's because he's high that he's thinking this, getting nostalgic and imagining that old soldiers of his generation will one day reminisce about green wooden footlockers in the same way that he hears sergeants yakking about "Those great Ike jackets."

He's fiddling with two tin walls and trying to make a corner out of them, but not having much luck because he's not really trying very hard, when it starts hitting him. A nausea begins to well up inside him, along with a growing ache in his gut because he hadn't bothered ordering a hamburger at the bowling alley because he had been so disgusted. A weariness begins spreading throughout his body, and he recognizes the sensation. He is coming down from his high. Disappointing. He had hoped the buzz would last a couple hours. The other men already have one locker standing upright and are busy fitting the shelves. Palmer's weariness turns into sleepiness, and his eyelids begin to close on their own. He keeps glancing at his wristwatch, but the minute-hand seems glued to seven-fourteen.

He takes off his watch and shoves it into a pocket and really goes to work on the box, stitching the seams together with bolts and trying not to think about his weariness, which is the way to kill time. He had learned this in high school where the clock above the classroom doorway always drew his eyes so that he had to keep them fixed on the babbling nun if he wanted Latin to come to an end.

When he has the last of the bolts and nuts affixed but not wrenched tight, he stands up to find a pair of pliers, and while he's at it he takes out his watch and sees that it's only a quarter to eight, and this finishes him off. Impossible to go on working another two hours without a little sleep. And since they are all the same rank in the room and there's no senior man to exercise any authority, instead of scouting a pair of pliers he climbs onto his bunk and lies on his back and closes his eyes.

Ten minutes and I'll be back on my feet, he thinks, then his thoughts disintegrate, the sounds and light fading like turning off a TV.

"Look who thinks he's finished for the night."

This statement, accompanied by a metallic tapping noise, startles Palmer out of his sleep. He opens his eyes and sees Private Vinton standing at the foot of the bunk hitting the steel frame with a pair of pliers.

"Get off your lazy ass, Palmer."

The rest of the men continue to work, but they watch and grin as Vinton puts on a show. He's in the spotlight and knows it. He hammers the frame until Palmer finally raises his head and says, "Knock it off, Vinton. I don't feel good."

"Medic! Palmer doesn't feel good!"

The laughter of the audience only encourages Vinton. He pockets his pliers and grabs hold of the bunk and starts shaking it. "Up and at 'em, dud!"

Palmer drops his head back onto the pillow and closes his eyes. "Go fuck yourself, Vinton."

The room goes silent. Palmer raises his head. Sgt. Sherman is standing in the doorway, his chin drawn toward his chest, his lips pressed thin. Courtney and two other men are standing behind him looking over his shoulder. All the grab-ass and laughter had brought them down the hall.

"Are you on sick-call, Palmer?"

"No, sergeant."

"Nobody in this platoon has been relieved of duty."

Palmer slips off the bunk and gets down on his knees and starts tightening nuts with his fingers. He doesn't look up but can feel Sgt. Sherman standing over him. So it takes this, rather than sleep, to fill him with energy. He tightens bolts and keeps his head bowed into his work, and when he finally does look up he sees Sgt. Sherman examining the nearly-finished wall locker. Courtney is no longer in the room, no longer gazing at Palmer curiously as he had done out at the rifle range.

When Sgt. Sherman leaves the room, Vinton leans over and says in a stage-whisper, "Hey, Palmer, why didn't you tell the sarge to go fuck himself?"

Palmer ignores him, thinking this is what I get for drinking on duty.

At a quarter to ten Top returns from his quarters in lifer-housing sated with a home-cooked meal and a few hours of gangbuster television and announces that work is finished for the day.

Palmer immediately stands up and takes off his fatigues and tosses them into his locker and climbs onto his bunk while everyone else stands around admiring their handiwork like they just can't get enough of sheet tin. Palmer pulls the blanket over his head to block out the fluorescent lights overhead and closes his eyes. Day One is over, and there is no end in sight. He can't yet calculate how long it's going to take to put six wall lockers together, but he does know one thing — if he has to come right out and say it to the other members of his squad, he will make certain they understand that they must not finish their lockers before everyone else in the company does, otherwise they will be put to work building lockers for the second and third platoons. If he accomplishes nothing else during this detail, he must make it absolutely clear to the members of his squad that they will be punished if they do a good job.

CHAPTER 5

A strained silence hangs over the barracks on Saturday morning as the troops labor at lockers instead of putting on their civilian clothes and heading down into San Francisco to drink beer and chase pussy as Top had said on Wednesday which everyone had thought was so fucking witty. They know they've got a mission to fulfill, but it's Saturday, and even in basic training they were given Saturdays off unless there was a field maneuver scheduled, like bivouac, or else IG-inspection painting of woodwork and scrubbing of urinals for the approval of visiting Generals who never seemed to have time to examine the commodes.

So there isn't much laughter in the halls of Company D this morning. The only thing Palmer can hear is the scrape and warp of manhandled tin and the quiet rattle of bolts being tightened, each man balled up in his own thoughts about the army and the sands of Saturday slipping through his sober fingers.

At eleven A.M. Top shows up and passes the word along that the work on the wall lockers will cease as of now. Palmer puts away his tools and begins changing out of his fatigues along with the rest of the men in his squad whom he's gotten to know better during the past few days. Nothing like the communal oppression of a shit detail to forge a bond between men who under less strenuous circumstances might loathe each other, which is how he feels about Vinton.

Everyone is getting out of the company area as fast as he can because nobody wants to get nabbed for any shit details which might spring up without warning, which is the nature of shit details. Keillor has relatives in Walnut Creek across the bay and is going there for the weekend. Martinez is headed for Candlestick Park and the protracted frenzy of a baseball game, and Vinton and Mallory have decided to pool their money and scour the city in search of someone who might be willing to sell a used car to two GIs with cash-in-hand. At least twenty enlisted men in the company own cars, including Courtney, whom Palmer once saw getting out of a gray 1962 Chevy parked in the enlisted men's lot across the alley behind the barracks.

Palmer opens his wall locker and begins throwing together what amounts to a kind of gag civilian-costume. The only clothing he had brought from home is a pair of blue jeans, so he will be wearing his army low-quarters in lieu of the tennis shoes that everyone else seems to own. For a shirt he will be putting on the khaki dress-blouse that he normally wears under his Class A uniform coat. And to hold up his blue jeans, his military black web-belt with its shiny brass buckle. It's sort of a half-assed get-up but it'll make him feel a little like a civilian for the weekend. He doesn't even own a coat.

Beaudry walks into the room while Palmer is seated on a bunk tying his shoes, and asks if he's going down into San Francisco today. Palmer's only plan is to get drunk at the bowling alley, but visiting the city is something he has wanted to do ever since he arrived here, and so he lies and says yes.

"Mind if *ah* come with ya?"

Beaudry is from west Texas and his accent is thicker than PFC Gunther's thanking place drawl. He's wearing a white

Stetson hat and green Madras shirt with mother-of-pearl buttons, black jeans, and high-heeled tooled-leather shit-kicking cowboy boots. He looks like a pretty good man to have along on a first trip down into the heart of hippie town.

Palmer doesn't know anything about the layout of San Francisco. He does know that it's the home of the hippies, and had once been the home of the beatniks. He knows that Lawrence Ferlinghetti has a bookstore down there some-where because a friend in Denver, a hippie, once showed him a copy of The Coney Island of the Mind which Palmer had thought was cool and wondered if it was possible to make a living writing that kind of stuff. But beyond the occasional anti-war riot viewed on television, this is all he knows about San Francisco.

The walk to main post takes almost an hour. Down a steep brick street through a row of quaint nineteenth-century lifer houses, they come to Lincoln Boulevard which makes a hairpin loop around a wild and wooded part of the Presidio where the chlorophyll stink of trees and dying leaves fills the air like an obnoxious perfume.

The howling of kenneled hounds comes from a valley within the loop. Palmer tells Beaudry about the time a K-9 Corps unit came to his training company at Ft. Gordon to attract new recruits. The German Shepherds were spectacular. They streaked across the parade ground like speedboats and mauled their trainers who were protected by padded clothing, the massive canine jaws going for the crotch again and again. Imagine owning a monster who would obey your slightest command. Palmer had been tempted to sign up, but could see that taking care of a dog would involve a lot of work. You would have to train your animal, and feed it, and take it on runs, and scoop its shit, and give it baths and make sure it was comfortable and secured at night—when would you find time to drink beer?

The hairpin takes them out of the forest and past the Presidio cemetery on a long and gently-sloping sidewalk leading straight down into main post. The glowing pastel hills of San Francisco look like they can't be more than a ten-minute walk away, but after another forty minutes Palmer and Beaudry are still on main post, approaching the Lombard Street gate. Palmer's feet are already starting to ache, and he cannot help but think that if he had gone to the bowling alley he would be on his third beer by now.

A long dull walk up Lombard toward Van Ness a mile away, Beaudry tells Palmer about the time he had worked as a clown in a rodeo back in Texas right after high school. "Ah once got kicked by a Brahma bull." Palmer tells Beaudry a little about Denver but doesn't have much to say, since all he had done after high school was drink beer and work shit jobs and wait for his draft notice in the apartment that he shared with his two brothers, one of whom, Mike, has a lottery number so high that he will never have to worry about Vietnam. The conversation drifts to music, and Beaudry surprises Palmer by saying he has never heard of Bob Dylan. Palmer in turn amazes Beaudry by admitting he has never heard of Loretta Lynn.

"Do y'all ski?" Beaudry says.

"No."

Standing at the top of the hill at Van Ness and Lombard, Palmer can see that this is turning into the sort of trip that will be better to talk about afterwards than to actually do, a thing to write to his brothers about, or to intrigue his friends sitting in their dumps in Denver with their draft deferments and shit jobs. His feet hurt. His worthless low-quarters weren't made for hiking, they were made for standing, as a tailor in the basic-training reception center had said when Palmer had told him that his Class A uniform pants were too tight when he sat down: "Soldiers aren't supposed to sit down."

The bay lies spread around the peninsula, flat and metallic gray with tiny white sails floating among all the islands, Angel and Alcatraz and Terminal, with bridges stretching to the far shores. It occurs to Palmer that he should have brought his movie camera, except it tends to gain weight over time.

Beaudry points at the Embarcadero at the bottom of the hill. "Y'all wanna go down and look 'er over?"

Fisherman's Wharf is all unpainted wood and docks lined with rustic gift shops and restaurants which are too expensive for two soldiers one week short of a payday. They pass the Ripley's Believe-It-Or-Not Museum which delights Palmer because he had always thought Ripley was just paperback book stuff. A crowd is gathered around an exhibit set up to lure customers inside—a four-foot long faucet which appears to be floating unsuspended above the sidewalk and spewing a column of water into a wooden bucket which never overflows.

A woman in the crowd is squealing, "How is this possible! How can this be!" She is truly amazed. People turn to look at her in her white-framed sunglasses and green muumuu.

"How is this possible! How can this be!" she says over and over. She is the star of the boardwalk.

Palmer and Beaudry smirk at each other, smug with their comic-book comprehension of corny gadgets. They start looking for a place to eat, passing gift shops with knickknack souvenirs which look cheap to Palmer even though he wishes he could afford a souvenir of San Francisco. Porcelain mock-up of the Golden Gate Bridge. Felt pennants boosting local teams, tack it to your wall above your bed. Two hours gone out of his drinking day. He could have drunk ten beers by now, in theory. But you need to pace yourself in daylight, because when darkness comes, you stop counting.

They pause outside a sidewalk cafe specializing in fish 'n' chips, a food that Palmer has never tasted. He suggests they go ahead and take a chance and try it, try something new, like his weekends in basic and MP school when he'd left post and gone into Hopkinsville, Tennessee, or Augusta, Georgia, because he thought he ought to get out and see new places while he was in the army and experience new things. He had the mind of a nun. All he saw were hundreds of GIs just like himself stumbling from pawnshops to strip-joints in a Class A daze.

He sits at one of the outdoor tables while Beaudry goes inside for the beers and chips. Beaudry is twenty-one, but Palmer won't come of age for another month. The beer costs one dollar and fifty cents per can. You could buy a six-pack of Old Milwaukee for a dollar-fifty back in Denver. Palmer is stunned. "How is this possible?" he says. "How can this be?" Beaudry gives up a muted, throaty Texas chuckle and pulls out a chair.

The food tastes awful—plus, it isn't a bit filling (three-fifty per bag) and Palmer realizes he should have just ordered a hamburger and quit pretending to be something he's not: worldly. He wants another beer, but doesn't want to pay a buck-fifty for it. He never was very good at mathematics, but he can calculate blood-alcohol content in terms of dollars intuitively, so he knows they won't be partying at the Embarcadero.

No porno theaters on Fisherman's Wharf, no topless/ bottomless all-girl-revue next door to the souvenir shop where pop and the family are buying T-shirts and ready-made transparencies of the city for the slide-projector waiting in the closet back home.

Palmer and Beaudry trash the remains of their food and walk further along the wharf and come to a whaling ship open for touring, one-dollar admission. Pop and the family are walking around on deck taking photographs of each other. A group of noisy little boys are leaning over the bow and spitting into the trash-littered brine. Palmer and Beaudry talk it over. Might be interesting to see how whaling men lived during the nineteenth century cooped up in a hull full of blubber. But Palmer finally breaks down and says, "Let's not do it. It's probably not going to be any better up close and minus a buck."

Beaudry nods. "Y'all wanna head back to the Presidio?"

Palmer is glad he has suggested it.

Where's all the hippies?

Where's all the skin-flicks?

Where's San Francisco?

The sun is on the horizon by the time they get back up the hill to Lombard Street where the green hills of the Presidio look as far away as the Rocky Mountains. Palmer thinks about calling a cab, but is too cheap to suggest it, so it's almost dark by the time they step back through the Presidio gate.

Beaudry hasn't spoken much for the past half-hour, and Palmer assumes he's bored, possibly even regrets teaming up for the afternoon. But then, as they pass Letterman General Hospital just inside the main gate, Beaudry says, "Y'all wanna stop at the enlisted men's club for a beer?"

"Sure!"

Palmer is infused with new energy. During the long walk he hadn't even thought about the EM club on main post. All he had been thinking about was that interminable hike back uphill to the quad to get to the bowling alley. So in spite of his burgeoning blisters, he picks up the pace. The enlisted men's club is only ten minutes away.

Landscaped with flagstone and evergreens to give it a modern look, the club is basically a bunker built for drinking. The double-doors are braced wide open, and seated on a folding chair inside the foyer checking IDs is a black E7, a big man who doesn't smile even though Palmer smiles at him as he approaches. Palmer is everybody's buddy now, and he isn't even drunk.

"No blue jeans allowed inside," the E7 says.

Palmer stops walking and stares at the man, stunned.

Beyond the sergeant's massive head he can see the dim interior of the club, the colorful and brightly-lit beer signs, the bartender polishing glasses, the pool tables and booths, and the empty, waiting, bar stools.

"What about black jeans?" Beaudry asks.

"They're okay," the sergeant replies.

Beaudry glances at Palmer and shrugs as if to say, "Sorry, pardner, see ya later."

He doesn't say this.

Instead he says, "Why don't-cha go on over to the main PX and buy some regular pants?"

CHAPTER 6

It's a like a K-Mart though not as big, but much bigger than the small PXs of basic where all you could buy were toilet articles and strange dull skin magazines of mostly women in not even see-through panties and bras. Palmer walks past shelves stacked with things he'll never need in the army, like spatulas or glue, and finds the men's-clothing department where he tries on a pair of black dress-pants which fit all right around the waist but are a bit short. They're only six bucks though, and he wants to get to that beer.

He pays at the register, which leaves him fourteen dollars for the night, but that should be plenty in a place where the most expensive beers cost sixty-five cents. He hurries back to the EM club and shows his sack of pants to the sergeant, who lets him step into the latrine to change.

As he enters he sees Beaudry sitting at a table on the far side of the room, his white Stetson glowing in the bar darkness resting in the center of the table. Palmer walks behind a partition which hides the restroom doors from the big room. He steps into a stall, unsacks the black pants and strips out of his jeans. The slacks feel a little tighter than they had at the PX, and he's pretty skinny to begin with, but that's all right because this is just a six-dollar Halloween costume to get him into the party.

He's seated on the commode tying his shoes when he hears the surprising click of more than one pair of high-heels coming into the room. Even when he gets the stall door open and steps out with his sack of jeans in his hand he doesn't realize his mistake because he assumes that these two women have walked into the wrong latrine. He is just about to tell them about their mistake when they both stop dead and stare at him. One of them says, "Oh yeah?" and the other goes out and takes quick look at the sign and comes back in and says, "We're in the right place."

Without a word Palmer walks past them and out the door. He turns and looks at the sign above the door which says WOMEN. The MEN sign is above the next door over. The absence of a urinal affixed to a wall might have given it away to a man trained to be a policeman, but it didn't. He goes into the big room and tries to put it out of his mind, hoping Beaudry didn't notice that he had come out of the ladies' room. But Beaudry only looks at his pants and says, "Good enough," and gets up to buy two beers.

Palmer sits down in a chair with his back to the restrooms and slides his sack of jeans beneath the table and waits for his first beer to arrive. When Beaudry brings the bottles, Palmer accepts his with an eager thanks and drinks half of it in one long pull, and is surprised when Beaudry doesn't do the same.

Customers begin drifting into the club, single GIs in civilian clothes, and couples, and the occasional lone woman, possibly WAC, everyone getting started on their off-duty Saturday night in the army. Palmer hears the sounds of cars parking outside, engines shutting off, doors slamming, women laughing. After their second round of beer, Beaudry suggests they play pool.

Palmer doesn't know anything about pool. He had never played much in the basements of friends who owned tables, never cared about that or ping pong or even card games like Hearts or Poker, the things people do to kill time in the way he kills time by drinking. He knows pool only from *The Hustler* where he had learned the moves and idiom of the game, the way you stand with a hip-cocked gait chalking your cue, the way you lean over the table long-backed as you eyeball your next shot muttering "Six in the corner" or better yet just "Six." He knows all that. He just doesn't know how to shoot pool, so Beaudry sinks most of the balls.

Three men on barstools who look like buck sergeants come over and put quarters on the edge of the table to play the winner, and the next time Palmer loses he goes back to his beer. When Beaudry comes over for a sip from his own bottle, Palmer asks how he's doing, just to say something to him, to get him talking, because Beaudry hasn't said much of anything since they had arrived. Maybe he's bored, but also maybe he's just caught up in concentrating on beating his opponent and winning a quarter's worth of pool from the next man. He gives Palmer a nod in answer, and goes back to the table.

The jukebox hadn't been plugged in earlier, but now the bartender hooks it up. The muted lights of its red and blue bubble-panels give the darkened room that satisfying deep-sea ambiance so conducive to serious drinking. There's a wide space on the floor for dancing, but nobody gets out of their chairs.

The bar is packed by the time Beaudry loses the pool table. The sergeants start hoo-hawing and racking up balls, and Beaudry goes into the MEN room. He comes out a few minutes later and goes to the bar, but buys only one beer. He doesn't seem very interested in drinking, which disappoints Palmer, who wants to keep Beaudry here as long as possible because he doesn't want to drink alone, and isn't ready to make that long walk back up to the quad. But he does understand that some people just don't have his capacity for, or interest in, drinking beer. Back in high school he was always the last to leave a party, and he could never understand people who said things like, "No thanks, my back teeth are floating," or the most incomprehensible of all, "I've had enough."

When Beaudry finishes his beer, Palmer offers to buy another round. Beaudry shrugs and says okay. Palmer gets up and works his way through the standing-room-only crowd and pays for two beers at the bar. When he gets back to the table he finds Vinton and Mallory seated with Beaudry. They have returned from their afternoon of browsing OK lots for used cars.

Because he's high, Palmer is only a little annoyed to see Vinton. He sits down and hollers above the music from the jukebox, "Did you buy a car?"

Vinton leans into the middle of the table. "I was just telling Beaudry, we had to go clear to Oakland to get the car, and it cost eight hundred dollars."

"Eight hundred bucks!" Palmer says.

"The place was closing down when we got there, so we signed the papers and paid for it and drove it off the lot and headed for the Bay Bridge." Vinton starts shaking his head. "It was running fine, but after we paid at the toll-booth and got out on the bridge, blue smoke started coming out of the tailpipe."

A grin sprouts across Palmer's face, but he stifles it with a swallow of beer.

"We got halfway across when the engine started losing power."

"Losing power!" Palmer squeals. He can't help it. He slaps the table.

"The fucker quit on us right in the middle of the bridge. We had to walk back to the toll booth and call a tow-truck, and when the mechanic finally showed up, he said the car was a piece of junk. I told him that was impossible because we had just paid eight hundred dollars cash for it. But he said that in his opinion we were shit outta luck. He ended up towing it to a junkyard and we took a cab here. So now we're out four hundred bucks apiece, plus cab fare."

Palmer is delighted that such shit should have happened to someone he doesn't like. He starts laughing, then starts coughing. The other three faces at the table remain somber. Beaudry was raised in the country, had grown up around pickup trucks and sundry internal-combustion vehicles, and probably wishes he could have been there to look under the hood and advised them not to buy the heap in the first place.

Palmer picks up his bottle and has another swig to clear his throat, then sets it down with a punctuating tap. "Christ, Vinton, how could you let a used-car salesman rope you into buying a lemon?"

Vinton gives him a hurt look. "How was I to know it was a lemon? I don't know anything about cars. What would you have done?"

"Well, first of all, I would have taken it out for a test drive."

"I didn't think of that."

Mallory doesn't say anything. He's staring at the tabletop exactly like a man who had just blown four hundred bucks.

"And second," Palmer says, "I wouldn't have forked over a dime until someone who knows about cars had looked it over for me." He's getting hot with his advice now, strutting and smirking like he's got Vinton cornered.

"You must know a lot about cars," Vinton says.

"Well I guess I know my way around an engine," Palmer replies.

"It's outside," Vinton says without inflection, so that Palmer doesn't get it at first.

"What?"

"Our car. It's outside."

And still Palmer doesn't get it, because he is as high from pontificating as he is from booze. It's Beaudry who gets the joke first. "You fucker," Beaudry says, and Palmer sees him grinning with shy rancor at Vinton. Mallory is grinning too, sitting up straight now and scooting his chair forward. Vinton starts laughing, and points a finger at Palmer.

"I had you going, didn't I? We did buy a car in Oakland but it runs great! It's parked right outside!" He looks around the table. "Did you hear what Palmer said? 'I guess I know mah way around a en-jine.' I gotcha, didn't I, Palmer? I gotcha!"

Palmer picks up his beer and takes a drink, and then, because he knows he had better say something, says, "Yeah, you got me."

"Got you? I had your ass over a fucking barrel!"

Even Beaudry is laughing, laughing at himself for being suckered so easily. He can take a ribbing. He's a good sport. He isn't too proud to admit that he had been duped by a practical joke. Palmer, on the other hand, is livid.

He glances at the jukebox to indicate that he has little interest in Vinton's prattle and is considering digging up some quarters and picking out a few tunes to liven up an otherwise uneventful evening.

"Do you guys want to go for a ride?" Vinton says. "Let's head down into the city and hit some bars."

Palmer shakes his head no and lifts his beer and drinks it overlong to show that his interest lies elsewhere.

"Shore," Beaudry says.

"Come on, Palmer, let's go bar-hopping," Vinton says.

"No thanks. I'm not twenty-one anyway."

"We'll find a joint that doesn't check IDs," Vinton says.

"No thanks. I think I'll head back to the barracks."

Vinton and Mallory stand up. Beaudry lifts his Stetson off the table and taps Palmer on the shoulder. "Whyn'tcha come with us, Palmer?" But when Palmer says nah, still choked and fuming, Beaudry says, "Catch you later, buddy," and heads for the exit with the others.

Palmer crushes out his cigarette and lights another and sits for a few minutes finishing his beer, then gets up and goes to the bar. He's not going back to the barracks. That was a lie, like the lies he always uses to avoid doing what he doesn't want to do, or to get people to leave him alone.

He returns to the table with a fresh bottle and sits down, fully aware of the inappropriateness of a lone man hogging a table in a bar packed with standing bodies, but he doesn't care. He takes a long drink and lifts his burning cigarette and takes a puff.

"Excuse me, friend, are those seats taken?"

He looks around. The man is wearing civilian clothes but has a GI haircut. He looks like he might be a sergeant E6. He has his arm around the waist of a pretty woman in a tight red dress. She's looking at Palmer with her eyebrows raised, eager to hear his answer. Alongside her is another couple looking down at those three empty chairs.

"No, they're not taken," Palmer says, gathering his flattened cigarette pack as he speaks, his Zippo, his beer.

"Would it be all right if we asked you to trade places with us?" the man says. "We got one stool at the bar and there's four of us here. You're not waiting for anyone are you?"

Palmer stands up in proper barroom etiquette, and the women sit down fast. The man leads him to the bar and picks up a waiting drink. "I appreciate it, friend." He walks into the crowd, and Palmer sits down on the empty stool and stares at his face in the mirror on the back wall.

He sits there for the rest of the evening, getting up only to go to the MEN'S room. He doesn't talk to anyone, but doesn't mind being alone as long as he can keep on buying beer. He would just as soon sit on this barstool for the next nineteen months.

Being drunk and alone like this reminds him of his two years between high school and getting drafted. After he had left home, all he did was work terrible jobs and drink beer and watch TV. Exhausted from helping carry sofa-beds into the homes of housewives on Monaco Parkway, he would walk back to his basement apartment every night with a six-pack of Budweiser bought at a corner U-Tote-Em store. The furniture-upholstery foreman had never liked him, but then seemed interested when Palmer mentioned that he had received his draft notice. "The biggest mistake I ever made was leaving the army," the foreman said, the only friendly thing he said during the six months Palmer had worked there. Palmer had broken up with his girlfriend so he had no one to kiss goodbye before flying to Ft. Campbell. His high school buddies had avoided the draft, each in his own way. On a week's leave in Denver after basic training Palmer got drunk every night in a favorite 3.2 bar, and was amazed to learn that nobody there even knew he had gone into the army. But then, when he heard that a high-school classmate had been wounded in Vietnam, it didn't interest him, because it didn't involve him.

CHAPTER 7

A few minutes prior to last-call Palmer tells himself, "Go now, while it's still early." He's suddenly fixated by the notion of "beating the crowd," as though the solution to his problem lies in strategic withdrawal. But his only problem is the long walk back up the hill to the quad. A taxi is out of the question because somehow his fourteen dollars has dwindled to two dollars and a pocketful of change that he doesn't think would be enough, though he doesn't know for certain because he has never hired a cab in his life. What's the penalty for not having enough to cover taxi fare? Movie cabbies always take the scenic route, vultures who pick you clean, always on the lookout for rubes. Then the bartender hollers last-call, and Palmer orders another Bud, deciding with a perceptive bit of drunken rationale that one more beer really doesn't matter at this point.

Then he finds himself standing outside the club with his back against the wall, breathing deeply and trying to clear his brain for the hike ahead of him. The cold hard flagstone feels good against his back. Laughing people file out the door past him heading toward their cars. The jukebox is silent, and all the lights inside the club have been turned up full. He's sorry now that he hadn't taken Vinton up on his offer to go down into the city.

He pushes off from the wall and heads for a tree-shaded side street which runs behind the redbrick finance offices toward Lincoln Boulevard. He hears bar-closing sounds behind him, men hollering, engines revving up, the high-pitched laughter of women muted by car doors slamming shut. It would probably take two minutes to get up to the quad on wheels. He turns the corner at Lincoln and keeps his head bowed watching his feet kick out in front of him as he executes a kind of leaning stumble that keeps him upright. The sidewalk rises at its gentle angle toward the cemetery and the last streetlight where the road curves toward the woods that he knows will be as dark as the nineteenth century.

Tombstones begin appearing on his left, planted in the grass beyond a low wrought-iron fence topped with arrow tips to keep no one in or out. How many bodies really lie beneath the ground and how many markers only stand for bodies blown out of existence at Pearl Harbor, Normandy, Khe Sanh? No identification among the remains, dog tags liquefied by heat. There's more than one Unknown Soldier but he had never thought about that until he was in the army and had a reason to think about it. At a basic training jungle-warfare range he had inadvertently stepped on the blunt bullet-tip of a dud 88-millimeter shell poking its nose out of the ground, and the Range NCO smiled at him and said, "You're dead." An instructor passed around a punji stake and told them to take note of the fishhook tip that the Viet Cong customarily dip in human shit to supplement the crippling wound with infection. At the hand-grenade pit the instructor who stood facing him while he pulled the ring on his live grenade looked nervous, and in that moment became the only real person in Ft. Campbell above the rank of private.

When he comes close to the last streetlight on the hill he begins hearing an echo to his footsteps. At first he thinks it's only his hearing distorted by the booze, but then he glances around and sees a man following him at a distance of thirty feet.

This sobers him up a bit. He stops walking and turns completely around and looks right at the man, not feeling especially worried because he is too drunk to worry about anything, but cautious because the Zodiac killer is said to be on the peninsula, and while you wouldn't expect a murderer to be stalking victims on an army base, a Class A uniform would be a pretty good disguise. Then he realizes the man is Thorpe.

Wouldn't talk in battalion supply, wouldn't go along with hiding out from afternoon details, and now the sorry motherfucker is trailing him past the cemetery without having the military courtesy to make his presence known. Then he realizes the man isn't Thorpe at all.

It's a GI skinny like Thorpe but taller, with longish blonde hair falling over one eye. There's an engineering battalion patch on his arm.

"Are you going to the top of the hill?" the man says when he gets closer.

Palmer nods and straightens up, tries to camouflage his drunkenness.

Big teeth, freckles, hollow chest, the man smiles and says, "Mind if I walk with you? It's probably safer with two men walking together in this place."

"Are you with the engineers up at the quad?" Palmer says. "Yes, the 357th."

He comes up alongside Palmer, and together they step out on the left foot and enter the pitch-darkness of the hairpin turn where the wailing of kenneled Shepherds echoes in the valley.

"Where's your coat?" the man says.

"I left it in the barracks," Palmer lies, probably the only person in America who doesn't own a coat. "How long have you been stationed here?" he says to change the subject.

"A week. I just got back from Vietnam."

Palmer is intrigued. He has never had an opportunity to talk to a Vietnam veteran except the Drill Sergeants of basic whom you never had real conversations with anyway. "What did you do over there?"

"I was with the Hundred and First Airborne."

Screaming Eagle. "Airborne," Palmer says aloud because it was the chant of basic where they double-timed singing *"I wanna be an Airborne Ranger, I wanna live a life of danger."* The only thing that falls out of the sky is bird shit and Airborne Rangers, said the Cavalry DI. "Did you go to jump school?"

"No, I graduated from clerk school in Ft. Knox, and when I got to Vietnam they assigned me to an Infantry headquarters company."

"Did you see any combat?"

"Nope. Spent my whole year behind a typewriter."

Even after five months in the army Palmer still has the idea that everyone who goes to Vietnam sees combat. He pictures this man seated in a tent with his fingers working the keys of a Smith-Corona while mortars plaster the concertina-wire perimeter.

"So." Palmer searches for the most diplomatic words he can find. "How did you like it?"

"I didn't like being there, but I'm glad I went. It was a good experience."

Palmer has to take his word for it because the man had served there, but this doesn't sound like the sort of conclusion he himself would ever draw. Nevertheless, he's glad to hear it, glad to hear something good said about the war.

They navigate the moonless loop around the valley past the forest with not a single car coming at them from either direction to offer a bit of light. When they come into the haze of the first streetlamp at the base of the steep road that will take them up through lifer housing to the quad, the engineer says, "What unit are you with?"

"The Military Police battalion."

"You're an MP?"

"I'm with Company D."

The man doesn't say anything for a moment. Then he extends his left arm and lets his bony wrist slide out of his sleeve. He curls his fingers into a ball. "See that scar?"

Palmer looks at the flesh, white where it rounds the knuckles, and sees the ragged thread of a healed wound.

"Yes?"

"I broke that fist on an MP's nose in a bar fight in Vietnam."

Palmer looks at the man's face. He doesn't know how to respond to what the man has just said—which is that he hates MPs, just as the trainees had been told in MP school that ordinary GIs would hate you like the hippies out on the street hate civilian cops and call them pigs, and that you should expect it, and get used to the idea, because when you go out on patrol you can look only to your sidearm and to your partner for help, and should look nowhere else, because everybody hates the MPs.

So he doesn't say anything.

They walk up the hill side by side in silence, and when the small PX comes in sight the engineer peels off and crosses over, so that they are now walking side by side with the distance of a street between them.

Palmer arrives at the narrow sidewalk which bisects the quad. The grass is blanketed by a fog rolling fast between the barracks from the lip of the Pacific. He looks over at the engineer crossing the grass at an angle toward a barracks down near the bowling alley. As the man gets further away the fog hides his feet so that he begins to look like a ghost floating above the ground. It's an odd feeling to be hated by a stranger.

Palmer aims for the rectangle of the lit Company D porch, crossing illegally on the holy lawn where every day a helicopter lands to pick up battalion brass but where no soldier is allowed to walk, like a high-school gymnasium floor guarded by snarling seniors with push brooms. His head and shoulders begin to ache as he moves along hunched into the wind. He's exhausted from all the walking he has done today, and when he enters the heat of the foyer he feels a nausea beginning to sweep through him. He unbuttons his shirt which is damp from fog and sweat, and heads for the latrine. He has to piss badly.

Seated in a stall, he is only vaguely aware of it when he begins vomiting. He does what drunks do, watching the disaster from a detached distance. A chowder-like beer-nut liquid splatters all over his shoes as well as his skivvies which are down around his ankles. But it doesn't really disturb him because he's already formulating what he believes to be a good plan. He will take a shower, and wash and dry his clothes in the twenty-five cent machines next to the shower room.

But by the time he gets his clothes off, he's already forgotten the last part of his plan and steps into the shower remembering only to be careful about the hot water. Give an equal turn of both hot and cold faucets. He feels he has actually accomplished something when he doesn't scald himself.

"Palmer, wake up."

A voice drags him out of a sleep that he wants to crawl right back into. He hears his name being called two more times, and finally opens his eyes and sees that he's lying on the shower room floor beneath a spray of water. He has a vague memory of sitting down at some point because his legs were weary from all that hiking and he had wanted to give them a few moments rest.

"Are you all right, Palmer?"

It's Courtney. Palmer can see the toes of his spit-shined boots as he leans to turn off the hot and cold faucets overhead.

"Are you gonna die on me, Palmer?"

An inch of water covers the shower room floor, enough to drown in if you're as drunk and stupid as Palmer feels. He has no idea how long he's been lying here, but he doesn't want Courtney to know he's drunk. He sits up quickly and works his jaws and says, "I'm fine," except his lower lip fails to touch his upper teeth so that his reply comes out as a nasal honk. His clothes are scattered all across the shower room floor. Little eddies of beer nuts are drifting around his legs and clogging the drain hole.

"Jesus Christ, Palmer, you're a fucking mess."

Courtney gets behind Palmer's head and reaches under his armpits and lifts him like a rag doll and sets him on his feet. Palmer is flabbergasted. Courtney is a strong sonofabitch.

Palmer looks around at the mess he's made in the shower room, then remembers the mess he had made in the toilet stall. "I better clean this place up," he mumbles.

"I'll mop up, Palmer. I'm CQ runner tonight. Why don't you go to bed?"

Palmer is not as drunk now as he had been at the end of the long walk. He's sober enough to be embarrassed. Courtney must think he's a dud, and there isn't much he can say or do to fool him into thinking otherwise. He picks up his PX pants, and realizes that he had left his sack of blue jeans at the EM club.

He staggers into the hallway holding his pants in front of him out of a futile sense of propriety. A wall begins banging into his right shoulder, then he feels a hand gripping his left arm and he looks over and sees Courtney guiding him down the middle of the hallway. Courtney is grinning, but at least he's not laughing aloud. Palmer suddenly wants to apologize for loading that bullet backwards, but can't quite string the words together.

When they get into his room, Palmer drops his pants on the floor and climbs onto his bunk, noticing during his ascent to his mattress that Vinton isn't on the bunk below, isn't yet back from town, and neither are Beaudry or Mallory. He collapses onto his pillow, and doesn't wake up until noon.

When he does wake up he's filled with the hangover horrors. He remembers clearly the events of the night before, and is stunned by the scope of his drunken walk in the darkness up the hill to the quad, the loss of his jeans, and the humiliation of being discovered nude and unconscious in a lake of beer nuts.

His shoes are resting side by side beneath his bed but the rest of his clothes are nowhere in sight. He puts on a pair of fatigue pants and goes looking for them, and finds his clothes neatly stacked and folded on a wooden table in the latrine. They've been washed and dried, even his PX pants. He realizes that Courtney must have done it. Palmer's belt is curled on top of the stack but his billfold isn't there, so his hangover horrors increase and he becomes angry at Courtney for leaving his billfold out where anyone could steal it, blaming him in the way that drunks are always blaming everybody for everything.

He gathers his clothes and hurries back to his room and puts them into his wall locker. But then, as he's making his bunk, he finds his billfold under his pillow where Courtney apparently had slipped it for safekeeping the night before, right beside his comb.

Even though he owes Courtney two quarters, he knows that hunting the man down and paying him back will probably end up costing a lot more than fifty cents, so he chooses instead to remain indebted to Courtney, and leave it at that.

CHAPTER 8

The morning after the shower episode is no different from all the mornings Palmer had awakened after he had first discovered drunkenness and then hangovers, which were funny when he was in high school, when you could brag to your friends about having experienced a hangover like you were bragging about having bagged a Cape Buffalo. So it's not so much the hangover itself as the terrible memory of Saturday night that makes Palmer give up smoking and drinking.

On Sunday he eats alone in the mess hall, then walks toward the bowling alley and turns off and crosses Lincoln Boulevard and heads into the woods to the thinking place. He sits on the ground with his eyes closed because the sun is too bright for his beer-blasted eyes, and the distance to the water makes him dizzy. He remembers his first attempt to quit smoking, just prior to being sworn in, when he was worried that his poor physical condition would prevent him from keeping up with all the other trainees in basic. That routine lasted four weeks before he finally broke down and lit his first cigarette in a bar called "The 32 Club" in Ft. Campbell, and when he did, he felt like a failure, even as he was taking pleasure in the heart-hammering buzz.

When he wakes up on Monday morning he can still feel the effects of Saturday night as a kind of lingering staleness of the brain that makes him feel distracted and distanced from the shit details which last until noon. Captain Weller marches out onto the grass at the one o'clock formation, and because the last time he did this was to announce the arrival of wall lockers, Palmer finds himself listening with a kind of despair for the sound of trucks coming up the alley.

"Men, I've got some good news to pass along to you today," the captain says. "Company D is up to full strength now, which means we're going to begin taking part in the retirement parades down on main post."

Palmer has heard about the retirement parades. Monthly ceremonies where thirty-year men of the officer and enlisted ranks who have given their lives over to the military are honored with a brass band and speeches and troops passing in review.

"So today we are going to devote our time to putting our uniforms in shape. Tomorrow at noon I am going to hold an inspection right here in front of the barracks, and I want you men standing tall and looking good." The captain grins. "I want the General to know that Company D is the best damn outfit in the entire Sixth Army."

It makes you laugh inside, an enlisted man, Palmer anyway, to hear an officer curse. It's like hearing a priest curse to motivate listless basketball boys.

The captain dismisses the formation, and the troops move into the barracks and begin pulling gear out of their lockers. A Presidio parade is something Palmer hasn't done yet, so he's interested in finding out what it's like because he's always liked doing a new thing or learning a new skill, even if he does it only one time, like the M-60 machine-gun, anything to break the monotony of army life. Even the men whom he happens to know from rumor smoke pot downtown on weekends get caught up in the idea of standing tall and looking good for the parade.

He sits on the floor with the rest of his squad sharing cans of Brasso and Kiwi and cotton rags and putting new shines on their brass and boots and buckles. Those who smoke are smoking, and everyone's got a can of pop at his side. Vinton starts making wisecracks about the sexual proclivities of west Texans, and Beaudry calls him a stupid sonofabitch and a donkey-dick motherfucker, but he isn't really mad because this is their thing now. They've become good buddies since Saturday night, but communicate only within the context of bickering, a kind of a show for everyone in the room because Vinton does like to be in that spotlight.

Having a good time like this and cracking jokes with his buddies makes Palmer want to drink beer, and he starts thinking about slipping out of the barracks and heading down to the bowling alley for a couple bottles, except that he has quit drinking, and smoking, the two things that always go hand-in-hand or else lead to one another. The problem with sobriety is that it makes you feel so good that you feel like going out and getting blasted. He tries not to think about it, tries to concentrate on putting a spit-shine on his parade boots, which he hasn't been able to do since he had first begun polishing them in basic training.

Martinez, on the other hand, has the ability to slap a shine like wet ink onto the toes of his boots. He has some kind of dexterity in his wrist and fingertips that Palmer has seen before, some sort of angle of approach like putting English on a cue ball, something that comes only with practice. That afternoon he goes to Martinez and asks him to explain how he gets such a good shine on his boots, but instead of telling him, Martinez takes one of Palmer's boots and a rag and spits on the toe and rubs for half-a-minute, and bam—ink.

He takes the other boot and repeats his performance and hands it back with a smirk as if to say, How come you can't do this simple shit, buddy? But Palmer doesn't care. He's happy to have his boots looking decent for the first time ever.

He goes back to his room and sits on the floor knowing now that he can do it because he had watched Martinez's finger-and-wrist action and is certain he can emulate it. He spits on a toe and rubs for half a minute, and pretty soon he knows the shine is never coming back.

You can always take chances on things that don't matter, things that you can fix by yourself after you screw them up, but he can't fix this and can't go back to Martinez and ask him to do it again. So he gets depressed, and feels like having a beer, and sets his mismatched boots under his bunk and decides to spend the rest of the afternoon fucking up his brass.

When he goes to sleep that night he hopes that by morning the polish on the screwed boot toe might somehow settle and smooth out and take on a shine, but the same mismatched shit and ink toes are standing side by side beneath his bunk when he wakes up at dawn.

The latrine is crowded with men trying to see into the mirrors above the sinks, but Palmer already has his place, having gotten there before the rush in the way he always tries to finesse the drudgery of competition. He puts on the parade helmet-liner that he'd gotten from supply the day before, its bright yellow Company D decal glowing on the front against the lacquered olive-drab surface. He latches his white pistol-belt around his waist and tucks his white scarf into the neck of his Class A coat, and stands at attention and inspects himself in the mirror. Satisfied, he goes around to the back of the barracks and down to the basement arms-room where he checks out his M-14. In his squad room he replaces the olive-drab sling with a white one, then steps out to the front sidewalk and joins the other men standing around stiffly and afraid even to smoke, everyone grinning and posturing like teenage boys at a prom, adjusting the belted back pleats of each other's uniform coats and plucking lint from lapels.

Palmer sees Lt. Norbert standing on the porch talking to an enlisted man, and thinks about going up to him and saying hello, just to see if the lieutenant remembers him from the night of the motor pool. But Sgt. Sherman calls the company to attention and everyone falls in. Captain Weller and Top come out of the foyer and march onto the grass, and the CO puts the formation at ease.

"Men, today Company D will be taking part in its first retirement parade. I'm going to inspect you here in just a minute, but I'm not going to be looking at your rifles, so you won't have to present arms."

This annoys Palmer because he had spent a half-hour ramming rags down his rifle-barrel the previous evening and getting his weapon in shape. But that's the army for you. It isn't always hurry-up-and-wait, sometimes it's hurry-up-and-as-you-were. Top calls the troops to attention, and there's a snappy rumble of boots and the click of rifle butts along the sidewalk. Captain Weller marches up to the first squad of the first platoon, Palmer's squad, and begins looking them over.

Palmer is fifth in line, but already his gut is tightening as it always does whenever someone in authority is going to be examining him for flaws. The captain comes down the line fairly quickly, with Top and Lt. Norbert right behind him, then he's standing in front of Palmer, who looks right through his head toward the white facade of battalion head-quarters. He waits for the captain to get it over with and move on to the next man, but the CO stays right where he is, his head bobbing as he looks Palmer up and down.

"Your boots are atrocious, Palmer," the captain says. He leans in and peers closely at Palmer's neck. "You've got somebody's blood on your scarf."

Two gigs in the bag. Palmer can feel the First Sergeant glaring at him.

"Is that your assigned helmet-liner?"

"Yes, sir," Palmer replies, even though he's at attention. His voice is a bit hoarse.

The captain frowns and mutters, "What are you so nervous about, Palmer?"

"Nothing, sir!"

"Your helmet needs work, Palmer."

"Yes, sir!"

The captain eyes him boot to saucer cap, then points at the barracks. "Go stand on the porch, Palmer."

Palmer carries his rifle at port-arms into the shadow of the porch and stands at attention facing the rear of the company thinking, How is this possible? How can this be? I worked so hard!

When the inspection is over, Palmer is the only man standing on the porch. The captain marches out to the grass and faces the company. "Men, I am extremely pleased with your performance today. You look damn good. In about fifteen minutes the buses will be arriving to take you down to main post." Then he dismisses the formation, but Palmer remains where he is. He knows he hasn't been dismissed. He knows that, for him, it is just beginning.

Out of the corner of his eye he can see the captain talking to Sgt. Sherman and Lt. Norbert. The sidewalk is empty by the time they step onto the porch. "Not a very good showing out there, Palmer," the captain says.

"Yes, sir," Palmer replies. He doesn't try to make an excuse. He equates alibis with griping.

The captain puckers his lips and frowns down at Palmer's boots for a moment, then looks up. "Did you have guard duty last night, Palmer?"

"No, sir."

At this point Lt. Norbert leans in. "Sir, Private Palmer is the man I told you about last week. His performance on guard duty was outstanding."

The captain considers this for a moment, then turns to Sgt. Sherman. "See that this is taken care of, sergeant."

"Will do, sir."

The captain and Lt. Norbert head into the barracks.

Palmer can't believe it. The keys to the kingdom squandered on a passel of gigs.

"Come with me, private," Sgt. Sherman says. "We're going to get you squared away." He takes hold of Palmer's upper arm just like Sgt. Armand did and escorts him to the porch door to his room. Sgt. Sherman doesn't seem very angry though. In fact, he seems a little bit amused, though maybe he's only relieved that the CO didn't jump in his shit.

Sgt. Sherman steers him down the hallway into Tichener's room. Courtney bunks there too. He's sitting on the edge of a folding chair adjusting the white sling of his M-14. Tichener is knotting his tie in front of a small round shaving mirror hanging inside the door of his wall locker. Both of these super troops had aced the inspection.

"Tichener, I want you to take charge of your man here and help straighten out his gear," Sherman says.

"Will do, sarge," Tichener says, turning away from the mirror and looking at Palmer's uniform. Sherman walks out of the room. Tichener reaches up and takes Palmer's helmet-liner off his head and examines it. Palmer notices now that parts of the yellow Company D decal have flaked away, and the OD paint underneath it is dull and cracked in spots.

"I got it that way from supply," he tells Tichener.

Tichener ignores the alibi and reaches to the top shelf of his locker and pulls out an aerosol canister. "You got to spray some of this shiny shit on your helmet to make it look good." He aims the nozzle and shoots a sweet-smelling mist onto the helmet, a lacquer which settles and dries fast into a hard gloss.

Palmer nods, watching closely and listening like a good student who is willing to learn, but he's really trying to ignore the presence of Courtney. "I didn't have time to fix it," he says. "I just wiped it down with a wet rag to get the dust off."

"Naw, that ain't good enough," Tichener says, towering over him and hoisting the helmet high as he fires short, glassy blossoms. "You got to go to the PX and get a can of this shit and spray your helmet good and let it dry overnight, see? This is all right for now, but you got to put it down on some newspaper and spray it all over. Then put it inside your wall locker to dry so the dust won't get to it."

Palmer nods. He hasn't seen a newspaper in weeks.

"Now, I don't know what to tell you about your boots, Palmer, except maybe you ought to try burning some polish into them. You know, use your cigarette lighter and make a few passes across the toe till it melts into the leather, only don't go burning no holes in your boots, okay?"

Courtney finishes tightening his sling and sets his rifle on his bunk and walks over and stands next to Palmer. He's as tall as Tichener. They both look like giant aliens from some unbelievably posh planet. Courtney points at the white dickey around Palmer's throat. "You launder your scarf, don't you?"

It's obvious that Palmer had made the mistake of washing and drying his scarf in the quarter machines in the shower room. He glances once at Courtney but doesn't say anything. The memory of Saturday night, and the fact that Courtney had laundered his vomit-covered clothes, and the fact that he still owes Courtney fifty cents and has never tried to repay him, makes him feel ashamed.

"Let me see it," Courtney says, holding out a hand.

Palmer unsnaps the scarf and gives it to him.

"See how the weave is wrinkled?" Courtney says, rubbing the fabric between his thumb and forefinger. "When you put it through a regular washing-machine, it fucks it up. You should have sent this to the dry-cleaners. They would have gotten the blood out, too."

Palmer doesn't know where that little pink spot came from, but he doesn't really think it's blood. Hawaiian Punch maybe. But there it is, smack in the middle of his shriveled dickey.

He takes the scarf from Courtney's hand. "The Captain can pay to dry-clean it if he's so worried about it."

This is what it has come down to now. He's not only making alibis, he's griping.

"How long have you been in the army?" Courtney says.

"Five months."

"Did you graduate from basic an E1?"

"Yes." An odd turn of questioning. No doubt the confirmation of a suspicion long on Courtney's mind, and this annoys Palmer. "I worked my ass off in basic training. I did everything they told me to do and I did it right, and do you know who got promoted at graduation? The kiss-asses who buddied-up with the Drill Sergeants." His voice is getting a bit shrill, so he quits and waits for Courtney to laugh. But Courtney just stares at him.

"Well in the meantime," Tichener says, "you stuck here for the duration, so you really ought to make an effort. You don't want the Old Man to do a tap dance on your forehead again."

Palmer looks at Tichener. "I'm sorry I made you look bad out there. I mean, as my squad leader and everything."

"Don't worry about it, GI, I'm short. I'll be in Vietnam one of these days soon."

"Did you get orders for Vietnam?" Palmer says.

"Naw, not yet, but I got my ten forty-nine in, so it's just a matter of time."

"Why do you want to go to Vietnam?" Palmer says, and he means it, because he can't understand why anyone would want to go to the war on purpose.

"Because I'm sick of babysitting fools like you," Tichener

says. But he's smiling. "Go on and wash that blood off your scarf."

Palmer picks up his helmet and walks out without looking at Courtney. He goes into his room and sets the damp helmet on top of his locker to dry, then takes a bar of soap to the latrine and begins working on the pink spot.

It occurs to him then that nobody ever really jumps in your shit in the army, and that barring killing someone or going AWOL, they never really do get all that pissed-off about anything. It's as if officers and NCOs are forced to spend half their time sweeping back a relentless tide of EM blunders, when all they ask is that you do what you're told, cooperate with your buddies, and if at all possible, try not to destroy anyone's career.

The buses arrive and chauffeur the troops down to the main post, a five-minute trip, and pull up at the asphalt parade ground just across the street from the redbrick finance offices. Hundreds of men in Class A uniforms and dress-whites are milling around in their designated areas waiting to be told to fall in. A platform has been set up on the far side of the grounds, and high-ranking brass are seated on folding chairs behind a podium where the retiring General will say his last words to the army. Palmer climbs off the bus and carries his rifle to Company D's spot and falls in with the first squad of the first platoon.

The Sixth Army Band is queued up in front of the grand-stand in their white and red uniforms, their brass instruments sending golden flashes of sunlight sweeping across the asphalt into everybody's eyes. The sight of the band reminds Palmer of a man he had known in basic training, a short cocky kid who bragged that he wasn't worried about going to Vietnam because he had enlisted at a recruiting office where he had signed a contract to play with an army band in Washington D.C. Whenever they marched out to the rifle ranges, the kid had to carry his M-14 as well as a bass drum to hammer out a beat while the troops chanted cadence, and when the Drill Sergeants made them double-time down the road, it nearly killed him. Sometimes the other men volunteered to carry his rifle, but most of the time they let him go it alone, him and his Washington D.C.

Palmer sees a Company C bartender from the bowling alley standing at the head of the MP battalion wearing a silver helmet and holding the battalion colors, the sort of prestigious dick-job you get when the CO not only knows your name but likes you.

Whistles begin blowing and sergeants begin hollering at the troops to fall in. The companies snap to attention bringing a sudden silence over the parade grounds like a drop in air pressure. The General (two-star) steps up to the podium and is introduced by a bird colonel. The PA system is inadequate, so when the General begins his speech his voice is tinny and echoes from speakers hung on poles on the far side of the grounds. But Palmer does hear and is struck by one phrase, "thirty-seven years in the service of my country," which means the General had already been in the army eight years before Palmer's father was drafted and shipped to the South Pacific.

When the General steps away from the microphone, a few other officers take their turns, followed by the top ranking enlisted man of the entire Sixth Army, a Command Sergeant-Major whose license plate Palmer happens to know is EM-1 because the cadre once told the troops that when they finally got around to pulling road patrol, "Don't even waste your time ticketing that car."

After the last man gives the last speech, the drum-major takes his place at the head of the band. He stands poised with his back arched, a six-foot silver spear of a baton raised overhead. The band begins belting out something by Sousa which Palmer can't name but recognizes from the Clifton Webb movie. The companies as one execute a right-face and march around the field past the grandstand. The retiring General stands at the edge of the platform at attention, saluting the flag and the colors of each company as they pass in review.

When you're a little kid you think marching is what the army is all about because of the movies, and then you go into the army and find out that marching is just a way to move groups of men from here to there, because the army is really only about war. But then you get roped into pageantry, which is all about marching, and you stand tall and feel proud because that's what marching is all about. Trombones, trumpets, piccolos in your ears. Rin Tin Tin was named after a snare drum. The current joke going around the company asserts that "military music" is an oxymoron, but Palmer doesn't care what anybody thinks—this stuff is dynamite. He can feel the satisfying beat of the bass drums right through the soles of his atrocious boots.

CHAPTER 9

When the buses pull up behind Company D, Palmer goes down to the basement arms room and turns in his weapon. He heads upstairs to change out of his uniform, and as he walks down the hall toward his room Sgt. Sherman steps out of the operations office and tells him to pass the word along to the first platoon that the EM are being given the rest of the afternoon off but have to show up for five o'clock formation.

Palmer strips out of his dress whites fast and puts on his fatigues, and when the rest of the squad comes in he gives them the word, pleased that he will be the first body out the door before sergeants start roaming the halls looking for someone to haul boxes or paint walls or count canteens. If he was still drinking he'd be on his way down to the bowling alley, so he's not unaware of the irony involved here—just when he goes on the wagon the army hands him an unprecedented opportunity for some afternoon boozing.

But the small PX is where he intends to spend part of these free hours, checking out the paperback rack and flipping through the meager collection of rock albums. After that he may wander over to the thinking place or else just walk along Lincoln Boulevard and explore some of the scenery that he's so far seen only from jeeps and buses. Someone said there's supposed to be a bunker serving as some kind of ammo dump off in the woods on the hillside which rises south of the quad, so he might hike over there and take a look at that. But first he goes down to the foyer to check out the bulletin board.

He's familiar with most of the men in the company by now, and can match a face to every name on the roster of men who've been chosen by the Department of the Army to go to Vietnam. Each man on the posted list has been in the company at least two months longer than he has. Tichener's name isn't there, and Palmer wonders again how any man could possibly put in a 1049 transfer out of what is supposedly the most beautiful army base in America just to live in a shit hole like Vietnam. He could understand transferring to Hawaii, possibly even Germany, but never Vietnam.

He's still wondering about this as he steps out onto the porch and sees the Company D honor-guard lining up for an inspection right outside the window where mail-call is always held. The guard is scheduled for funeral details later in the afternoon, and will be firing twenty-one gun salutes over the graves of veterans being buried. Courtney is part of the guard, also Tichener, the two tallest men in the company. Maybe picked for size, each of the seven men is only a bit shorter than the next so that the rank looks flush, looks good, looks professional. After the inspection they will get on a bus which will take them somewhere on the peninsula, maybe South San Francisco, or even across the bay to Oakland. It's one of the jobs like MP duty which they rotate with companies B and C each month, but Palmer doesn't envy them this job, just as he doesn't envy the clerks confined to the staff offices all day. He doesn't want anything to do with funerals. The men in the honor guard like it though because it takes them away from the company on mid-week afternoons, but more importantly, it keeps them off shit details, a big incentive, but it still doesn't appeal to Palmer. He has never been to a funeral in his life. Everybody he ever knew is still alive.

Lieutenant Norbert is the officer in charge of the guard. He's standing out on the sidewalk with Sgt. Sherman going over the list of funerals. The inspection hasn't begun yet, is still a minute or so off, and Palmer suddenly gets an inspiration. He heads back down the hall to his room to dig out his 8mm Bell-and-Howell home-movie camera and see if he can't make a small addition to his cinematic scrapbook of his stretch in the service. Capturing a bona fide stateside garrison mission on film, even if it's just an inspection, would be a major contribution to what so far has amounted to a static and rather dull catalog of pasty faces, white clapboard buildings, and olive-drab vehicles. During basic training he had always meant to take his movie camera along to the rifle ranges, but on top of all the gear they had to lug along on their hikes, the troops were usually kept too busy running around by the Range NCOs for that sort of tourist activity, so he always ended up leaving his camera back in the barracks. He had managed to fill up only two reels of film throughout basic training, mostly on weekends when there wasn't much going on except GIs giving his camera the finger for posterity.

He reaches into the neck of his T-shirt and drags out his dog tag chain with its attached keys. One is for the wall locker and one is for his soon-to-be obsolete footlocker. He stoops to insert the wall-locker key, whose twin resides in a safe in the operations office in case the CO wants to pull a surprise inspection, which nowadays usually amounts to a search for contraband — meaning pot.

His movie camera is stored on the top shelf in a Styrofoam box. Tucked at the rear on the bottom of his locker is his 8mm movie-projector which he had hand-carried from Denver on the day he had flown to the Presidio. He brought it because he had no idea how long his permanent-party status would last in California (nineteen months he'd hoped and still does) and he wasn't about to go a year-and-a-half without watching any of the movies he knew he would be making.

The camera is loaded and ready to shoot. He always keeps a roll of film loaded because he had learned when he was a kid that things happened, the best or most interesting things, when you weren't thinking about taking pictures at all, in the way that people supposedly got shots of flying saucers or the Loch Ness monster with cameras snatched up and jerking so badly that the pictures looked like shit and were probably hoaxes anyway.

He opens the porch door to his room. Lt. Norbert has already called the formation to attention and is getting ready to inspect them. Palmer leans against the door frame to steady the camera and hikes the viewfinder to his eye and begins filming the formation from the side. And since he sometimes likes to play around when he makes movies, he decides to snap the shutter-stop one frame at a time. This will give the finished product a frantic, high-speed, Keystone Cop look that was always a crowd-pleaser back home.

Lt. Norbert marches up to the first man in line and examines the shiny black bill of his saucer cap and the polished brass shield affixed to the front of the crown, his chin dropping as his eyes move down to the man's tie and buttons and medals, his head moving mechanically until he's looking at the man's boots. Then up again for a last look. He reaches out with one hand and tugs the man's white pistol-belt, squaring it away, not a gig but merely an adjustment before moving on to the next man in line.

Then something breaks the lieutenant's concentration. He glances around the porch as if to ascertain what that strange clicking sound might be, that distracting and rhythmic tap-tap-tap echoing in the hollow shell of the porch. He looks to his left, looks directly into the lens of the camera, and says, "What are you doing, Private Palmer?"

Palmer stops taking pictures and lowers the camera and smiles at the lieutenant. "I'm taking a home-movie, sir."

But the lieutenant doesn't smile back as Palmer had hoped he would, doesn't grin with delight at the prospect of being the star of a locally-produced documentary film. He just stares at Palmer.

Stares until Palmer isn't quite certain what he ought to say or do. Then the lieutenant turns back to the job at hand and moves on to the second man in line, his chin dropping and rising as he looks the man over.

Palmer raises the viewfinder to his eye and begins snapping pictures again, though not with the same enthusiasm that had motivated him to begin this project in the first place. In fact he isn't entirely certain that he ought to continue doing this at all, but the lieutenant hadn't ordered him to cut it out, so he continues snapping pictures, and as the inspection slogs along endlessly, the tiny click of the shutter-stop seems to grow louder, begins to irritate even Palmer.

Courtney is the last man in line to be inspected, the tallest of the group. Lt. Norbert reaches out and makes a minor adjustment on his web belt, then marches to the front of the formation. He tells the squad that the bus will be arriving in the parking lot within the next ten minutes and he wants everyone to be out there ready and waiting. He dismisses the troops.

Palmer stops filming. He looks down at the footage meter, a little glass bubble on the side of the camera, and sees that he's taken approximately one minute's worth of film, not very much but not too bad compared with most of the stuff he had ever managed to get on film. And while he's staring at that little bubble he sees out of the corner of his eye the figure of Lt. Norbert strolling toward him with his hands clasped behind his back.

"Private Palmer, don't you think it would have demonstrated military courtesy to have asked my permission to film my inspection?"

Palmer stands at attention, squares his shoulders, and answers quickly. "Yes, sir. I'm sorry, sir. I didn't think you would mind, sir."

"What sort of movie did you take, Private Palmer?"

The subtle and sarcastic lilt in the lieutenant's voice indicates that he knows what Palmer has done. An 8mm home-movie camera is hardly a baffling technological marvel beyond the comprehension of the average person. "Just a regular home-movie, sir," he lies.

"May I see the movie after you get it developed?"

"Certainly, sir."

The lieutenant remains silent for a moment, looking Palmer right in the eye.

"Very good, Private Palmer. You're dismissed."

Palmer stands even straighter and holds his camera in his left hand and salutes. Lt. Norbert returns the courtesy and walks away.

Palmer backs into his room and closes the door and stands staring through the window at the now empty porch. His heart is beating fast, but not because he had been nailed. It's because that was the first time he had ever deliberately and intentionally flat-out lied to an officer. There is no way in hell he is going to get this movie developed.

He touches the tiny latch on the side of the camera which holds the lid shut. He intends to open the camera and yank out the film, exposing to light and thus ruining all the images, an instinctive move born of desperation and adrenaline. But he stops himself, thinking, I've screwed everything else up, I better not screw up my only hope.

All he needs is the lieutenant to walk in and find him standing in fifty feet of celluloid spaghetti. The thing to do is to destroy the evidence in secret, late at night, preferably after the lieutenant has left the company area and gone to his babe's house in Sausalito.

Palmer opens his wall locker and places the camera back in its Styrofoam box on the top shelf, and isn't the least surprised when Courtney walks into the room.

"What did Norbert say to you?" Courtney says with a grinning conspiratorial familiarity that makes Palmer uncomfortable. His shame still grips him.

Palmer closes the locker door. "He told me I don't have any business being in the army."

"What?"

"He said I should have asked his permission to film the inspection."

"That's bullshit," Courtney says, his voice turning hard. "You don't have to ask anybody's permission to take pictures."

Is Courtney a barracks lawyer? The last thing Palmer wants to hear right at this moment is a lecture on his holy and sacred fucking rights as an enlisted man. He shrugs. "Well, you know, they've got a rule for everything in the army, and half of 'em aren't even written down. He told me it would have demonstrated military courtesy to ask his permission first."

Palmer braces himself for a legal harangue, but Courtney surprises him by saying instead, "Can I see the movie after you get it developed?"

"No."

"Why not?"

"Because I'm not going to get it developed."

"But why not? I want to see how I look on film."

"I'm not going to get it developed because I filmed it in fast-motion to make it look funny. If Lt. Norbert ever sees it, I'll probably get busted down to E-nothing."

"Fast-motion?" Courtney says. He steps up close and lowers his voice. "Listen Palmer, you have got to get that film developed. I really want to see it."

Palmer realizes that he should have lied to Courtney about the nature of the movie, because it's not lies, it's the truth that spins webs. He shakes his head no and opens his wall locker and reaches to the top shelf and pulls out a James Bond novel that he has been trying to finish since MP school. "I gotta go take a shit."

He walks past Courtney and goes down the hall and enters the latrine. He steps into a stall and locks the door and sits on the commode with his pants on and reads for ten minutes. He doesn't have to take a shit. He lied.

CHAPTER 10

On Wednesday, one week after the job had begun, the last wall locker in the barracks is completed, and all the activity which had come to seem normal, the sounds of tin warping and bolts scraping and men laughing and bitching, ceases, so that there is a quiet in the barracks which makes the building seem new, as if construction workers have packed their toolboxes and walked off a site. And though he had hated the work while he was doing it, Palmer had known he would miss it when the regular shit details returned to fill the daily schedule, as they do.

Company D is put to work on Thursday morning policing the grounds of the Presidio, and Palmer's squad is assigned a jeep and trailer and sent off to police the trash along a section of cliff road near Baker Beach. Palmer walks a dirt path on the hillside below road level and comes upon a bra tangled in a bush. He picks it up and shakes it out and holds it high. "What the heck is this thing?" he hollers. Everybody laughs. He flings it into the trailer. A few steps further along he spots a pair of men's jockey shorts, but he keeps on walking.

From there they drive to the area around Julius Kahn playground and start policing picnic litter. Lifer kids playing on swing sets wave at the working GIs, but the chaperoning officer-wives reading paperbacks won't even lift their eyes to glance at the enlisted men performing work normally given over to prisoners from the stockade, whom Palmer has seen before, the big white letter P on the backs of their fatigues glowing in the sunlight as they drag-ass with burlap bags in their hands, the stockade guards herding them along pointing out cigarette butts and jockey shorts. The prisoners are killing time that isn't even army time, it's their own time, because once they've served their sentences they will have to finish out the remainder of their original enlistments, drafted or otherwise.

The cleanup detail is called to a halt just before noon. Palmer's squad drives back to the barracks and empties the contents of their trailer into a Dempsey dumpster outside the kitchen. Palmer eats chow, then heads to his room to sleep for half an hour, but doesn't even get to his bunk before Sgt. Sherman hurries in saying, "Palmer, did you write a letter to your congressman?"

"No, sergeant."

"Are you sure?"

"Yes, sergeant." Palmer doesn't even know who his congressman is.

"All right, come with me, troop."

Sgt. Sherman leads him down the hall into the operations office. The First Sergeant is slouched at his desk on the other side of the counter, his hands stuffed into his pockets. He's chewing an unlit cigar and staring at his telephone. His chair squeaks as he swivels around and raises his chin and looks at Palmer as though peering from beneath the brim of a cap. "Private Palmer, did you write a letter to your congressman?"

"No, sergeant."

"Have you been doing anything lately that we ought to know about?"

"No, sergeant."

Top takes the cigar out of his mouth and points it at Palmer. The tip is black with spit. "Colonel Billings just called and told me he wants to talk to you. Do you have any idea what he might want to talk to you about?"

"No, sergeant."

Palmer has said "No, sergeant" three times in a row, which is beginning to sound evasive. He knows he had better start forming more complex sentences. Even if he is innocent of doing something as asinine as writing a letter to his congressman, he doesn't want Top to think him discourteous.

"Well, it's like this, Palmer. The battalion commander wants to see you in his office right now. But if you haven't done anything wrong, we'll back you up." And while Top is speaking, his eyes are searching Palmer's face for a lie. Top's eyes are father eyes. "Sgt. Sherman will accompany you to battalion headquarters."

"Yes, sergeant."

As they walk around the quad, Palmer knows what Sgt. Sherman is thinking: this goddamn private has broken the chain-of-command and gone over everybody's head with some pissant gripe that could have been taken care of on the company level, and now the shit's hit the fan.

They enter battalion headquarters and climb to the second floor. The battalion commander's door is guarded by a SP4 clerk/typist seated at a desk manipulating the keys of a silent electric typewriter.

"The colonel is expecting us," Sgt. Sherman says.

The specialist gets up quickly and tells them to wait. He steps into the colonel's office and closes the door.

Sgt. Sherman then reveals the extent of his lack of faith in Palmer by reminding him to salute the colonel and to answer truthfully every question asked. Palmer says yes sergeant even though he would like to say I've been in the army long enough to know how to talk to a goddamn colonel. The clerk returns. "Go on inside."

Caps in hand, Palmer and Sherman walk into the colonel's office. No linoleum here, the floor is a deep shag, and the walls are covered with paintings of mounted cavalry, foot-soldiers, swords and flags, with cannons generating enormous billows of brown and gray smoke. The colonel stands up from behind his desk, and the men exchange salutes.

"Colonel Billings, this is Private Palmer," Sgt. Sherman says.

"Good afternoon, Private Palmer."

"Good afternoon, sir."

The colonel is a short man, stocky but with a flat stomach like a man who takes good care of himself, lifting weights maybe, handball, perhaps boxing or even judo. He smiles. "Have a seat, gentleman," indicating two chairs upholstered in red velvet which might have been arranged in front of the desk specifically for this meeting.

Palmer sits down but does not lean back against the soft nap. He sits erect on the edge of the seat and waits for the colonel to bust his ass or pin a medal on it.

The colonel picks up a sheet of paper from his desk. "Private Palmer, I received a report this morning which states that you took some home-movies of Lieutenant—" He pauses a moment to glance at the paper. "Norbert's inspection of a funeral guard the other day."

"That is correct, sir."

The colonel sets the paper down and smiles. "Are you a home-movie buff, Palmer?"

"Yes, sir. I own a Bell-and-Howell eight-millimeter home-movie camera."

Palmer is absolutely fucking staggered. Lt. Norbert had squealed on him.

"That's interesting, Palmer. How long have you been making movies?"

"Since I was twelve, sir."

"Do you have plans to pursue film making as a career after you get out of the army?"

"No sir, it's just a hobby." He could go ahead and sketch out his vague plans to be a film maker someday, but he knows better than to waste the colonel's time articulating his elusive dreams.

"I was surprised, and somewhat pleased, to read about your movie camera, Private Palmer. The reason I asked you to come over here is to find out whether you might be willing to do me a little favor."

"Certainly, sir."

"I've been commander of the MP battalion for three years. I'm going to be retiring from the service next month, and I thought it would be nice to have a souvenir film to take with me when I go home to Flagstaff."

"Yes, sir."

"Now, Company D is scheduled to go on road patrol in a week or so, and what I have in mind is a movie of Military Policemen being inspected before they go out on duty. Do you think you could put together something like that for me?"

"Yes, sir. I would be glad to do that for you, sir."

"Well that's good to hear, Palmer." The colonel leans back in his chair. "Now I want you to understand that there's no hurry on this. You can do it whenever you have the time."

The colonel so far has not directed any of his comments toward Sgt. Sherman, but at this point Sherman speaks up. "I will personally see to it that he gets that movie made as soon as possible, Colonel."

Colonel Billings smiles at him, beams at Palmer, and stands up. The meeting is over. "Sgt. Sherman, I would like to speak with you for a moment if I could."

Palmer stands up and salutes, does an about-face and walks out the door. He closes it softly and steps into the hallway and immediately begins wondering what might come of this situation. How will Lt. Norbert react when he finds out that his petty vengeance has transformed Private Palmer into the battalion commander's blue-eyed boy? He extrapolates upon the scenario: after the filming is completed, he cozies up to the colonel and gets invited to his home for a formal showing of the movie. He's charming to the colonel's wife, and to his guest, a brigadier general, and ultimately cops a dick job like Battalion Documentarian and gets the hell out of Company D altogether.

He looks at the clerk by the door manipulating the type-writer. The man is only a Specialist Fourth-Class but has the razor-cut, starch-pressed, fastidious air of an officer. Maybe it wouldn't be such a bad thing after all to have a clerk/typist job. Perhaps this man's.

Sgt. Sherman comes out of the office grinning. "You're going to film the first patrol that gets inspected next week."

There's a definite spring in the sergeant's step as they march back around the quad. Not only did his hand-picked Private Palmer not write his congressman complaining about the conditions of servitude oppressing the candy ass of his mama's boy, Palmer has upped the prestige of Company D, and thus of Captain Weller. It's clear that Sgt. Sherman is eager to get back to the operations office and give Top the lowdown.

The rest of the company has been sent down to the motor pool to pull first-echelon maintenance on the vehicles. When Sgt. Sherman informs Palmer that the CQ runner will have to drive him down to join them, it doesn't bother Palmer at all, even though the motor pool is the worst detail to get stuck on, the most boring and tedious and meaningless detail, if you consider washing a jeep and checking the oil over and over again for three hours to be boring and tedious and meaningless. But Palmer feels too good for this assignment to get him down. Right at this particular hour on this particular day, he doesn't think anything in the world will ever get him down again.

Now that he has quit drinking, Palmer doesn't know what to do with himself in the evenings. On the fourth Saturday of basic training, when he went on the wagon for the first time since high school and had nothing to do, he took a bus into Hopkinsville, Tennessee, just to look around. But he found that Hopkinsville was no more interesting than most parts of Denver would be to a stranger. A hilly sort of town, it had a lot of tree-shaded clapboard houses and redbrick buildings. He hunted down the local USO which turned out to be a bleak room with only Ping-Pong and one wall of paperbacks. He finally went to a movie, which he could just as easily have done back on post. He saw Elvis Presley as a storefront doctor, and Mary Tyler Moore as a nun in mufti. They fell in love, but no can do.

He headed back to Ft. Campbell right after that, walking out of town along a highway filled with hundreds of hitch-hiking soldiers just like himself, GIs bored senseless and incapable of understanding what it was they thought they were trying to do. A 1954 Plymouth pulled up beside him. The two occupants asked if he needed a ride back to the army base: five bucks a ride, an outrageous price that he was glad to pay. After he got in the back seat he realized they were drunk. On the floor lay half a case of Budweiser. When they pulled onto the road, the men told him they were sergeants E5 and made money on weekends hauling men back and forth to Hopkinsville. "Hailp yoursailf," the man riding shotgun said, pointing at the beer on the floor. Palmer declined, then asked whether they had served in Vietnam. The two men looked at each other and broke out laughing, and said, "Fuck no!" in unison.

So drinking, and not tourism, was the thing that finally came to fill Palmer's evenings at the end of each military day in both basic and MP school. And since this was how it had been ever since he had left home at eighteen, he never really did learn what an adult did with his free time that did not involve alcohol. He realizes he has to think things up.

On Friday evening after chow, he gathers his Class A uniform and four new white and green scarves and walks to the dry-cleaners across the street from the small PX. A civilian runs the place, a little World War II-haircut woman who tells him his clothes will be ready on Monday morning.

He crosses the street to the small PX and starts browsing the paperback racks. He wants something to read besides the James Bond novel that he had begun in MP school. The fantasy of living a life of danger had begun to wilt in basic training, so he doesn't enjoy 007 thrillers as much as he did when he was a troubled teen and could hold all the world's evil in the palm of his hand. He ends up buying a copy of *The Painted Bird* by Jerzy Kosinski, intrigued by the surreal cover art.

Back in the barracks he climbs onto his bunk and starts reading. Ten minutes later, bored shitless, he stows the book in his wall locker and digs out the James Bond novel.

———————

Throughout the following week Palmer is in bed by nine o'clock every evening. The first in the squad room to sack out, he's oddly disappointed when nobody questions why he's doing this, nor asks him to join them at the bowling alley, nor suggests an evening trip down into the city. He expects Vinton to say something, to make a wisecrack, or even accuse him of being a snob. But nobody pays any attention to him at all.

On Friday morning, at the end of his second week on the wagon, there is no hint in the air of what's to come at noon. Palmer is assigned to work in the cavernous, whitewashed, arms-room cleaning pistols with four other men under the supervision of the arms clerk, a funny guy who had been a disk-jockey in civilian life and who keeps up a running patter of jokes to entertain the detail while they disassemble .45s and oil them and put them back together. It's amazing some of the jobs men had held before they were drafted. Palmer had known a firefighter in MP school, a lobster fisherman, and a telephone lineman who said he could climb a pole and splice a wire and be back on the ground before you could spit.

He envies anyone who has a skill that will earn him a decent living after he's discharged. All Palmer has is Latin and a driver's license.

At noon he goes to the small PX and picks up his movie. After Lt. Norbert had put him on report he went ahead and dropped the film off to be developed. Like Courtney, he wants to see what the fast-motion pixilation of Lt. Norbert will look like. He expects it to be amusing, but plans to view it only one time and then get rid of it. Like, soak it in gasoline, and light it, and throw it in the ocean.

He steps outside the PX and stuffs the plastic reel into his back pocket and tosses the paper sack into a trash can. When he enters the barracks he feels like he's smuggling in a lid of pot. He hides the reel in the bottom drawer of his locker beneath a stack of skivvies, and decides it would be best to watch the movie on Saturday night between ten and midnight, when all of the officers and most of the cadre will be at home, and everyone else will be out partying.

During noon chow, word goes around that a special formation will be held at thirteen-hundred hours, and everyone has to be there. It sounds like more wall-locker business to Palmer, but when the company forms up on the front sidewalk at one o'clock, nobody seems to know what it's all about, and the sergeants aren't talking.

Sgt. Sherman calls the formation to attention, and Top and the CO march onto the grass. Smiling strangely, Captain Weller puts the troops at ease. "Men, I've got some very good news to share with you this afternoon. Company D has received orders from battalion headquarters to promote twenty-four men to the rank of E3, Private First-Class."

This is amazing news. One-third the men of Company D are E2's just out of MP school. A buzz of pleased murmurs rises from the ranks.

"As you were," the captain says with a grin. "Now, the First Sergeant is going to read off the names of those men being promoted, and you can walk out here and I'll hand you your pips. Specialist Legget, bring out the box."

SP4 Legget, the head clerk in the operations office, comes out of the foyer carrying a small cardboard box and stands alongside the captain, who reaches into the box and pulls out a tiny flat-black metal PFC rank pin and holds it up.

This is Palmer's day. This will cap the good luck he already had with Colonel Billings. In fact, this is his week. He feels so good that the bitterness that he has carried in his heart ever since he was overlooked for promotion at the end of basic training evaporates. He can see now that early promotions are fundamentally meaningless, the carrot-on-the-stick used to motivate young trainees to give it all they've got and do their very best, which he certainly had.

Top begins reading the names off the list. "Anderson! Beaudry! Carney!"

The men double-time out to the captain and salute and receive their pips.

"Keillor! Lawton! Lewis!"

They trot back grinning, working the old tarnished brass mosquito-wing off their collars and pinning on the new rockers.

"Mallory! Martinez! Overman!"

Palmer leans forward in anticipation of hearing his name. He intends to write a letter immediately to his brother Phil in

Ft. Lewis and tell him about this latest promotion, which will include of course a raise in pay.

"Vinton! Youngfeld! Zimmer!"

Top folds the paper in half and lets it dangle at his side.

Palmer is still leaning, which may explain why the world seems to be tilting even further out of kilter than it did at the end of basic training.

He straightens up as the captain announces that since this is Friday, the entire company will be let off duty until Monday morning as a kind of celebration. He calls the troops to attention and tells them to fall out.

Palmer wanders up to the porch and edges past the men gathering around the open window of the staff office where early mail-call is being held. He steps into his room and shuts the door. What makes this situation particularly mortifying is the fact that some of the men who had just been promoted had graduated from MP school after he did.

The thing to do is to get away from the company area as quickly as possible. He goes to his wall locker and opens it, but ends up staring at the E2 chevron on his Class A uniform sleeve. The porch door opens and the men of his squad walk in laughing and punching each other on the shoulders and fingering the new pips on their collars. Beaudry opens his wall locker and pulls out his white Stetson and slaps it onto his head and howls a word which through the thunder of blood in Palmer's ears sounds like "Yeehaw!"

Vinton walks past Palmer, then backs up and looks at his collar. "Didn't you get promoted?"

"No."

The other men gather around to stare at his collar. "Why not?" Mallory says.

"I don't know."

"Jesus Palmer, I'm sorry to hear that," Vinton says.

Palmer looks to see if Vinton is being sarcastic, but he's not. He's only staring at Palmer like someone looking at the victim of a hit-and-run accident.

Beaudry's rolling Texas drawl breaks the silence. "You got a raw deal, buddy." He takes off his cowboy hat and stows it in his locker. "I don't know about y'all, but I'm putting in for a transfer outta here. This place is chickenshit."

Courtney steps through the doorway carrying a letter and glances at Palmer but doesn't say anything. He goes on down the hallway.

The rest of the men start opening their wall lockers and digging out their civilian clothes. Palmer knows they're happy but are keeping quiet about it, fiddling with their shirts and socks and talking about sports or women or anything but their promotions. He knows they'll wait until he leaves the room before they start slapping each other on the back again.

He takes out his ill-fitting black slacks and tosses them onto his bunk and starts unbuttoning his fatigue shirt. Sgt. Sherman walks into the room fast, like a man bearing a message he wants to get rid of fast.

"I'm sorry you didn't make PFC, Palmer. Your name fell at the bottom of the list and we ran out of slots." But Palmer knows he's just giving the official reason, and not the real reason. The commiseration in Sgt. Sherman's voice is strained. Sherman works up a small smile and says, "Your name is at the top of the list for the next promotion."

Barely aware of the words coming out of his own mouth, Palmer says loud enough for everyone in the room to hear, "You can tell Colonel Billings that I'm sorry, but my home-movie camera is broken."

The slack flesh on Sgt. Sherman's jaw tightens. He turns and walks out of the room.

Palmer puts on his PX slacks and khaki dress-shirt and low-quarters, and reaches to the top shelf of his locker for his Zippo and a pack of Camels that he had left there two weeks earlier because he knew all along that he was never going to give up smoking.

He leaves the room by the porch door and goes around to the alley where he lights up and begins chain-smoking. He stares through the fence at all the cars in the parking lot and wishing one of them belonged to him because he feels like getting in a car and driving fast and far. He tosses finished cigarettes across the alley without field-stripping them, and with each butt flicked, he tries to fling from his mind The Truth, that noisy little runt everybody pretends to love, who keeps whispering over and over inside his head, "You brought this on yourself."

PART TWO

CHAPTER 11

Tourists pack the parking lot taking snapshots of their families with the Golden Gate Bridge rising in the background, mom in grass hat and sundress, kids with sticky snack mouths squinting in the afternoon light while pop fiddles with the focus and barks at them to stand the hell still and smile. Palmer stares at the stretch of road-bed touching the Marin shore more than a mile away and wonders how anything as massive as this bridge could have been built before he was born. His vague notion of the past: a nation of drooling idiots staggering around blindly shooting at bears and boiling turnips in log cabins—and wasn't engineering invented just a few minutes prior to World War II? A large and impressive exhibit rests on a pedestal at the edge of the parking lot, a section of bridge cable sliced like a chunk of sausage exposing its bundled guts. Children chase around it screaming. A small boy leans back against the pedestal and acts cool with folded arms.

No hippies here, mostly young couples and families, and older men with hair shorter than Palmer's. He feels naked without his fatigue cap. A GI from the third platoon bought a Beatle wig to blend in with the weekend crowd, but Palmer likes crew cuts because you don't have to fuck with them, even though he carries a comb.

Figuring a steady pace of three miles an hour, it should take him only twenty minutes to get across the bridge. He moves out onto the pedestrian sidewalk and mingles with all the other tourists doing this for the same reason he's doing it, so they can go home and tell their friends, "I walked that fucker."

A hundred feet out he stops to look over the side straight down at Fort Point, a redbrick fortress built literally on the absolute northernmost tip of the San Francisco land-mass, the former guardian of the entrance to the bay, now a toy shrouded in the shadow of the twentieth century.

A Navy ship, maybe a battleship or cruiser, is coming from the direction of the Oakland docks. He watches its slow progress as he approaches the center of the bridge, then stops to wait for it. He peers over the railing at the vertical distance to the surface of the water which makes him giddy. He wonders why looking along the length of a football field doesn't make him feel the same, then the ship is below him and he wishes he had brought his movie camera because he knows that he will never stand on this spot again as long as he lives. Torpedo-shaped body, decks, smokestacks, masts, big guns, all sliding along the wall of the world.

He turns around and looks at the Pacific horizon, the same route his father had traveled in 1942. Slept in the sands of the Solomon Islands, wore radio headphones, and could still remember the Morse code when Palmer was a child, singing dit-dot-dit to the melodies of Glenn Miller. The first troops to arrive in Vietnam disembarked from ships, but now it's Boeing 727s with stewardesses wishing you good luck.

He is thirsty, but expects to find some sort of snack bar on the Marin side of the bridge for all the hiking tourists. He lights a cigarette and tries to smoke while walking, but it makes him wheeze for breath and he ends up tossing it over the railing. He likes littering when he's pissed off.

Forty minutes to the far shore, then there's no place to buy a Coke, not even a gas station. Looking back toward the Presidio he can see the white glint of the quad buildings through the green blanket of trees which makes the hilly army base look like a paradise to anyone who doesn't have to live there. Alcatraz looks scenic from this perspective too.

He climbs down a dirt embankment off the highway and sits in the weeds to have a smoke in private before starting his equally pointless journey back. Strange that he could get used to not having a car. One night in Denver he rode a bicycle to a 7/11 at five minutes to closing and made it in time to buy a six-pack of beer, then came down with a cold the next day from all the unaccustomed exertion. Ft. Cronkite is way down the hill, and Sausalito might as well be in Kansas. Too far to walk. Who are these fools who hitchhike across America wearing backpacks and beards, the women with daisy patches on their asses? Where do they shit? In basic training he once needed to shit badly on the way back from a rifle range at the end of the day, and when they double-timed he was afraid he was going to dump his load into his boots. It took an hour to get back to the barracks, and when he ran into the latrine and unbuckled his pants, his canteen, bayonet, and pistol-belt crashed to the floor.

He smokes three cigarettes, then gets up sorry he had started this trip, but had wanted to experience the illusion that he could walk away from the army, illusions so necessary to get through the days, and especially the nights, which is why he drinks beer and is planning to go to the bowling alley as soon as he gets back to the Presidio.

He climbs up over the railing and starts the return trip. Demoralizing to see the quad getting closer with each step.

Twenty-four promotions. Does this mean that twenty-four PFCs died in Vietnam, forcing the Pentagon to pick at random twenty-four new GIs to rise in rank? Every week thousands of trainees enter the army and thousands of veterans go home, not including lingering lifers. A trainee from Jamaica bragged that he planned to stay in the army twenty-years. "Ah am a lifah, mon." He smiled when he said this, showing a gold-capped tooth with a hollow crescent moon. A trainee from Panama said he would receive American citizenship for serving in the army, and an MP trainee also looking for citizenship said that when he was a child he had escaped from Czechoslovakia with his family. He said he remembered running across fields at night and climbing fences with his mother and father, and hiding under bushes in the daytime. Hearing a buddy tell a story like this sort of pissed you off at communists.

Then he sees Thorpe coming his way.

Familiar slouch, arms held strangely and slightly away from his sides, he's still a ways off and doesn't seem to have noticed Palmer, who has no interest in talking to the sorry prick. He watches Thorpe carefully, keeping the bodies of passing tourists between them, then Thorpe turns off and goes to the railing to look over the side.

When Palmer passes behind him, Thorpe doesn't notice, or maybe is snubbing Palmer on purpose, which is what Palmer is doing to him.

It's annoying to have encountered Thorpe at all, like the cap to a particularly half-assed day. He crosses the highway near the toll booths and passes through the Presidio gate at Merchant Road, thinking, now I have something to tell my grandchildren: "I walked that fucker."

But then, when the bowling alley comes into view, he feels too weary to begin drinking, too tired from all this stupid hiking, and there's nothing quite as irritating as boozing when you're sleepy. He decides to go back to the barracks — an hour in the rack and he'll have all of Friday night to sit in the bowling alley. And fuck the sergeants if they come around scouting shit-detail bodies. He'll pretend to be asleep. In fact, the thing to do is to not care about anything for the next eighteen months. Just do what he's told on duty, and speak to people only as required by the job. And at noon and evening eat at the bowling alley instead of the mess hall, and if he feels the need to get away from the company, go to the movie theater down on main post, or to the library. He'll put in his time and keep to himself, and if Sgt. Sherman ever offers him a promotion to PFC, he'll tell the lifer to shove those pips up his olive-drab ass. "I'm short," he'll say. "Eighteen months and a wake-up, and I'll be home."

The notion of turning down a promotion doesn't strike Palmer as ludicrous until he wakes up well-rested and clear-headed enough to realize that he would turn his back on every ideal he has ever possessed in exchange for a promotion.

The pop of a muffler in the parking lot wakes him. When he opens his eyes to the darkness, a panic grips his heart, the panic of drinking-time lost. But then he remembers he had given up drinking. He had given up smoking too, though he had smoked on the bridge, a thought that now depresses him.

He lies on his bunk for a few minutes staring at the patterns of light cast briefly on the ceiling by cars passing in the alley, and he considers his idea of refusing to speak to anyone for the next eighteen months. He decides it would be too much work.

On top of the energy it would take to successfully ignore them, he would have a lot of people mad at him all the time. And he won't be roaming down to the theater on main post either, though he likes the idea of checking out books from the library and staying in the barracks every night and catching up on all those novels that he knows he will never in his life under any other circumstances read, like Wuthering Heights or Bleak House, books you think you're supposed to read if you want people to think your brain is worth a shit.

The barracks is silent. Everyone else is down in the city, or boozing at the EM club. Palmer gets out of bed and switches on the overhead lights and goes down to the latrine. When he gets back he digs out his James Bond novel and climbs onto his bunk and lies on his back and starts reading. But at the end of every paragraph he raises his eyes and stares at the ceiling. He knows he'll never be able to do this every night for the next eighteen months. He could easily drink beer every night for the next eighteen months, but he couldn't do this. Then he hears footsteps coming toward his room, and he gets up on one elbow with his back to the door and pretends to be reading.

The scuff of shoe leather stops in the doorway, an indication that it's a sergeant looking for a volunteer. Palmer waits for a voice to order him to hop to, but the man doesn't say anything. Strange how you truly can feel eyes on the back of your head. He finally twists around to ask what it is the sergeant wants him to haul or sweep or scrub or paint or assemble. But it isn't a sergeant. It's SP4 Courtney.

"Are you going to hang around in the barracks all Friday night?" Courtney says.

He's wearing a wrinkled blue windbreaker, threadbare white Levis, brown loafers. He looks like a lean first-string center on a championship basketball team. If it had been anyone else, Palmer would have slipped off the bunk and gone down to the latrine to avoid him. But Courtney has been present at just about every one of his fuck-ups, so there isn't much point in trying to hide anything from him. Maybe he just wants his fifty cents back.

"Yeah," Palmer says.

Courtney strolls over to the porch door and opens it letting in a cool breeze. Palmer assumes he's just passing through. Relieved, he turns back to his book. But he doesn't hear the door shut. He hears only muffled foghorns bawling warnings in the bay.

"When I was in operations today I heard Sgt. Sherman tell Top that your movie camera is broken," Courtney says.

"So what?"

"Everybody knows you lied."

"Good." Palmer closes his book and sits up. "Did you come here just to tell me that?"

"No." Courtney shuts the door and leans against Beaudry's bunk. "I had a pizza with Lee and Earle this after-noon at the bowling alley. They told me they went to MP school with you."

Palmer nods.

Lee and Earle are both from The South. They recently pooled their money to buy a motorcycle and are probably right at this moment bird-dogging poontang in Sausalito. They're friendly fellows, but the sort of men who get into fistfights with strangers in bars. Palmer has never drunk with them.

"They told me you were the best shot with the .45 in your training company."

Palmer nods. He was as amazed as everyone else when he made the highest score at the target range that afternoon in Ft. Gordon. But he ultimately credited it to the fact that he had spent half his life aiming a movie camera.

"Tell me something," Courtney says. "How can the best shot in an MP training company load a bullet backwards into a magazine?"

Palmer slips off his bunk and opens his wall locker and puts the paperback into the bottom drawer. "Accidents like that happen to me," he says. "I don't plan on becoming a brain surgeon or anything."

The fact that people have been talking about him behind his back confirms what he has always suspected, that he is the subject of warranted gossip.

"Is that the movie?" Courtney says.

The edge of the Norbert reel is sticking out from beneath a stack of skivvies. Palmer shoves it back under and closes the drawer.

"You got fucked," Courtney says.

Courtney doesn't seem inclined to take hints, and the situation suddenly reminds Palmer of his own inability to make Thorpe talk in the battalion supply room that day, and this makes him start to smile, but he doesn't want to smile, so he channels it into bitterness and breaks his personal vow.

"Did you see who got promoted?" and doesn't wait for an answer, "Devlin and Potter. They both came here after I did."

"Devlin's father is a bird-colonel."

"I know it."

Everyone knows it.

"Do you want to go to the bowling alley and get drunk?" Courtney says.

Braced for an insipid argument, Palmer is surprised by the suggestion, and doesn't say anything.

"I'm buying," Courtney says.

"Okay."

Palmer grabs his cigarette pack off the top shelf, shuts his wall locker, and heads for the door.

"Don't you have a coat?" Courtney says.

Palmer looks down at his shirt and shakes his head no.

"Jesus, Palmer, you really oughta buy a coat."

CHAPTER 12

The walk to the bowling alley takes two minutes, enough time to complete the ritual that forges all new duty-station acquaintances. Courtney tells Palmer he's from Iowa, and when Palmer says he's from Colorado, the Standard Denver Dialogue ensues:

"Do you ski?"

"No."

The bowling alley foyer is packed with men crowded around the pinball machines. Courtney and Palmer edge through the packed bodies and look around the snack bar for an empty table. There's a small one vacant at the far end of the bar up against the wall, and Palmer goes to claim it while Courtney goes for the beers.

When he gets hold of his first bottle of Budweiser, Palmer doesn't swig down half of it right off, his usual method of speeding things up. He sips at it slowly but steadily while they discuss each other's training background. Courtney had graduated from Ft. Gordon nine months earlier, which means six months before Palmer arrived in Georgia. In army time, as perceived by Palmer, this makes Courtney a relic, a veteran of ancient campaigns.

"My brother Phil is taking Infantry AIT in Ft. Lewis," he says, and Courtney replies, "Vietnam," meaning that as soon as Phil graduates he will be sent into combat.

The casual, almost glib, manner with which he says this annoys Palmer. He discovers that he doesn't particularly like hearing anyone, a stranger or a buddy, talking about his brother's potential death in such a nonchalant tone of voice. A minor pall falls over his side of the conversation.

"Maybe I'll run into your brother when I get over there," Courtney says.

"Did you get orders?"

"No, but I put my transfer in the same time Tichener did. It'll come down one of these days."

Another choice opportunity—Palmer at last can grill a man who is willing to do something he himself would never do under any circumstances. "Why do you want to transfer to Vietnam?"

"MP duty is supposed to be great over there."

"You can get shot over there too, you know."

Courtney grins. "In the Infantry maybe. MPs don't die in Vietnam."

Palmer's annoyance increases. He doesn't have access to statistics, but he does know that MPs escort convoys, and that MPs fought the Viet Cong at the American Embassy during Tet. "Of course MPs die in Vietnam."

Courtney dismisses this with a flip of the hand not gripping his Bud. "Have you talked to Melrose?"

Palmer knows about Melrose, a Vietnam veteran in the second platoon who has three months left in the army.

"No."

"Talk to him."

"What do you mean, 'talk to him'? He didn't die in Vietnam, so MPs don't die in Vietnam?"

Courtney thinks this is funny. "Melrose spent his whole year working the blotter in an MP station in Danang. He said it was the best duty he ever had."

"What—there's no VC in Danang because they didn't kill Melrose?"

"What are you worried about, Palmer? You probably have a better chance of getting shot right here in San Francisco."

The conversation is drifting toward a kind of hostility, and Palmer decides that coming here might have been a mistake. He lights a fresh cigarette without responding to Courtney's wisecrack and looks out at the lifers flinging their polished balls down the lanes.

"Did you really get Lt. Norbert's film developed?"

It's suddenly clear what this drinking session is all about. Courtney just wants to see the movie, he isn't interested in being buddies. He is using Palmer to get what he wants. Palmer recognizes the technique—he practically invented it.

"You saw it there in my locker."

"How about showing it to me when we get back to the barracks?"

"Okay. Let's go look at it right now." Palmer stands up, prepared to call Courtney's bluff and get this pretense over with.

"Are you kidding?" Courtney says. "If Lt. Norbert caught us we'd probably both go to the stockade. Sit down. We came here to drink."

Palmer sits down. A rash move anyway, to walk away from free beer. He finishes his bottle, and Courtney goes to the bar for another round and a bag of potato chips which he tears open and places in the middle of the table as he sits back down. "What's the deal with your film making anyway?" he says. "Are you going to Hollywood after you get out of the army, or what?"

Palmer is surprised. Doesn't Courtney know that people don't go to Hollywood anymore to make movies? They drive around the country in trucks. Hollywood is dead. He thought everybody knew that. But as with Colonel Billings, though for different reasons, he decides not to go too deeply into the subject. It would take at least twelve beers for him to throw in the towel and admit that he will probably end up the Orson Welles of Vehicular Cinema.

"No, I don't plan to go to Hollywood. I just want to make independent films. You know, underground movies."

"How do you plan to finance them?"

Nonplused, Palmer is silent for a moment. He has never considered money to be an obstacle. He has always felt that, should he ever decide to make a feature film, the money would somehow just be there. "I don't worry about things like money," he says, though in fact he has never possessed more than two hundred dollars cash in his entire life, and that only after his second army payday

"You know what you ought to do," Courtney says. "You ought to go to Universal Studios and take their tour. I went there with my parents when I was in high school. It was great."

"I'm not interested in making commercial movies."

"No really, Palmer, you ought to take their tour. You can see how stuntmen work, and how makeup artists do stuff, and all that."

Laymen are always loaded with advice. What does Courtney know about film making? Palmer has never used stuntmen or makeup in his home movies. Nor has he ever used sound, or built sets, or even written screenplays. And now that he thinks about it, the only thing relating to conventional film production that he has ever actually used is a Bell-and-Howell spring-driven 8mm home-movie camera, an obvious though previously undeliberated fact. "So what's your ambition in life?" Palmer says. "What are you going to be when you grow up?"

"A security guard," Courtney replies.

"A security guard?"

"Sure. With my MP background I'll be able to get a good job with a civilian outfit back home."

Is he serious? Palmer had intended to find out what Courtney wanted to do, and then mock it, because Courtney seems like the kind of person who would go to college and become an engineer, or a lawyer maybe, or a doctor, and it's easy to make fun of good jobs, easy for the broke to mock the flush. But all of the sudden Courtney seems to him like the men he had known on all the jobs he had ever worked as a civilian, delivering flowers, delivering furniture, delivering ice cream, sweeping floors, picking lint—men with families to support and children to feed and bills to pay, men who didn't go out and try to find a better job than the kind Palmer was perfectly happy to have, a pointless job that paid shit.

So he only nods at Courtney's answer and drinks his beer in silence and watches the lifer wives bend down to pick up their balls and hoist them aloft and eyeball the duckpins and let fly. When Palmer empties his bottle, Courtney goes for another round.

It's not until Palmer is handed his fifth beer (he always keeps careful count of his drinks at the beginning, like someone jotting down the odometer mileage before setting out on a car trip, and then never referring to it again) that it occurs to him he ought to buy a round. But he squelches the thought.

The noise in the building seems to be getting louder, which is probably true because even the bowlers are getting drunk. He had become fairly adapted to this noise the first night he drank here, but now realizes how hard it is to have a conversation in a bowling alley, because this is the first time he has tried to have one.

"This place is too noisy," he says. "I wish we had an enlisted men's club up here on the hill."

"Be grateful you've got a bowling alley to drink in, Palmer."

"It's too bright in here."

Courtney nods, agreeing with something at last.

"We had an EM club at Ft. Campbell called the 32 Club," Palmer says. "It was like a cafeteria. The lights were bright all the time, and the beer was never cold enough, and the only thing I ever heard on the jukebox was 'Crimson and Clover.' It was a terrible place to drink, but it was all we had."

"There you go, Palmer," Courtney says. "All you need is a warm bottle of Bud and a really bad song and you've got your own enlisted men's club."

Palmer smiles. At least supertroop has a sense of humor. Palmer can't stand to be around people who want to fucking argue all the time. He picks up his bottle and drains it. "Want to play pinball?" he says. Then adds generously, "I'm buying."

You play pinball the same way you play pool: place a quarter on the edge of the glass to let the current player know that when all five balls have gone down the chute he has to turn over the flippers—an etiquette not written down anywhere, just civilization in action.

They hang out in the pinball foyer for an hour, during which Courtney buys two more rounds. There aren't very many players waiting in line by then, but Palmer prefers to play when there's nobody at all around so he can hog the machine and feed it quarters until his craving is slaked. He's enjoying this. It reminds him of his two months at Ft. Gordon where the discipline was unbelievably lax compared to basic training. The MP trainees were completely on their own after five P.M. There was a movie theater right across the street from his barracks, and a small enlisted men's club just down the block where he and his buddy Gilchrest played pinball every night. Gilchrest was a pinball addict, and once told Palmer that he could live his whole life in a game room. The best memory Palmer has of the army so far: two months in lax Georgia playing pinball in the enlisted men's club until closing time—the beer was ice-cold and the jukebox played the Beatles.

When the last ball drops down the chute Palmer and Courtney return to the snack bar where Palmer finally offers to buy a round, the eighth, he can still count. He looks at the clock on the wall next to an elevated TV where John Wayne is getting ready to die on Iwo Jima (as a kid he had believed it was against the law for John Wayne to die in a movie). An hour-and-a-half left of drinking time, but suddenly he wants to see his movie. He considers trying sneak outside with a few beer bottles and smuggling them into the barracks, but the bartender, the SP4 from the Company C color guard, watches things too closely.

"Let's finish these and go look at the Norbert film," Palmer says.

The squad room is dark. His caution exaggerated by booze, Palmer peers through the door window to determine how many men might be in the room, but can see nothing because, as he had only just determined, the squad room is dark.

He opens the door slowly and hears the sound of Keillor snoring on his bunk. He supposes Vinton and Mallory, and possibly Beaudry, are out making the scene in Vinton's piece of shit Ford Falcon, which is what Palmer had thought the first time he saw it parked in the lot behind the barracks, a judgment based on simmering envy rather than his nonexistent knowledge of cars.

He silently crosses the room to his locker. Losing and regaining his balance with a teetering ebb and flow, he removes his dog tag chain and fumbles with the locker-key, drops the chain, stoops to pick it up and bumps his shoulder against the locker, then spends a few seconds trying to insert the key upside down.

Maintaining a lookout by the door at Palmer's whispered insistence, Courtney observes this pantomime stealth in silence. He breaks it only after Palmer bangs the movie projector against the tin locker making a sound like a snare-drum chucked off a roof. "I thought you wanted us to be quiet."

Ignoring him, Palmer carries the projector to the electrical outlet on the wall furthest from the hallway door. He sets it on the floor. A minute to set up and thread by-feel the reel of 8mm film, he aims the lens so that the picture will be projected on a blank patch of white wall near the baseboard. When he turns the machine on, the chattering of sprockets, the whine of the belt-driven motor, and the glare of the 300-watt light bulb render moot all his prudent skulking. "Shut the door!" he hisses.

Courtney shuts the hallway door and crosses the room and takes a front-row seat on Mallory's bunk and leans down to look at the foot-square rectangle of light on the wall.

Palmer's earliest Presidio efforts flicker onto the screen: a panoramic scene of the Pacific Ocean, hand-held and unsteady as the camera moves a bit too fast across a landscape of waves and boats. The scene ends with a poorly-framed shot of the Golden Gate Bridge, which becomes the central motif of this lifeless, brief, and authentic home-movie. Another angle on the twin spires of the bridge, concentric in arrangement, the smaller-appearing Marin-shore tower contained within the hollow frame of the closer tower, a shot Palmer had seen on a picture-postcard in an airport gift-shop on the day he arrived in San Francisco.

This is followed by an overlong shot of the ICBM missile displayed in the park near the thinking place, then an inordinately shaky shot of a jeep approaching along Lincoln Boulevard, which he had seen coming like a UFO and had quickly raised the camera to capture—a disappointing but earnest attempt to get some motion into his motionless-picture.

Then the real show begins.

A few seconds of total blackness on the jury-rigged silver-screen, then the funeral guard appears, standing at attention as Lt. Norbert begins the inspection. The nature of the rendered special-effect (Keystone Cops) reveals something anatomically-incorrect about a man walking at attention. Head erect, shoulders squared, back rigid, arms hanging straight down with his fists held severely along the seams of his pants, Lt. Norbert waddles like a penguin toward the first man in line and stands with his head bobbing up and down, chin chopping the air as he inspects boots, brass, and saucer cap. And then, from where Palmer and Courtney are seated, the lieutenant appears to reach out and touch the man's crotch.

It's a tough minute for the audience, with fists pressed against mouths to stifle laughter as again and again Lt. Norbert appears to reach out and tweak the cock of this man or that as he moves down the line, in fact merely pointing out a wrinkled pleat or adjusting a web belt. Lt. Norbert approaches the last and tallest man in line and touches the dick of Funeral-Guardsman Courtney, who bears the insult without flinching. Norbert waddles back to the front of the formation and whacks himself on the forehead with a vicious judo-chop that can only be interpreted as a salute.

The End.

"Show it again," Courtney gasps.

Palmer had intended to show the movie only one time and then pack things safely away, but not only has his audience response been too gratifying to stop now, he also wants to see a rerun of what he now thinks of as The Lieutenant Pervert Show.

Awakened by their poorly-muffled laughter, Keillor sits up on his bunk and puts on his glasses and asks if they're watching porno movies.

"Come look," Courtney says. "It's better than porno."

Keillor stands beside Courtney in his T-shirt and skivvies and watches with folded arms as Palmer rethreads the film and runs the movie again. Keillor's laughter is not quite as manic since he hasn't been drinking, but he does appreciate the performance, the volume of his chuckling rising appropriately in response to the crotch-grabbing thrusts of Lt. Pervert's right arm.

The hallway door opens. "What's going on in here?"

Adrenaline skates up Palmer's spine and he yanks the plug from the wall. Courtney looks around. "Hey guys, check this out."

Three men are silhouetted in the lit rectangle of the doorway. When they step into the room, Palmer recognizes them clearly in the after wash of his newfound sobriety: Tichener and two men from the fourth squad.

"Skin flicks?" Tichener says in a whisper.

"Nah, check this out, man," Courtney says.

Hands shaking, breath a bit short, Palmer plugs in the machine and rethreads the film, uncertain of the wisdom of showing the movie to "outsiders." Then it occurs to him that he ought to run the film in reverse rather than wasting time rethreading it—another by-product of his sobriety.

"Close the door, okay?" he says to Tichener, who quietly shuts the hall door.

The laughter this time isn't quite as satisfying to Palmer, even though it's equally robust, particularly Tichener's. His original plan in ruins, Palmer doesn't know why he even bothers to make plans.

"Show it again," someone whispers, and Palmer reluctantly switches the gears into reverse. This gives the lieutenant's performance a saltier edge as he waddles backwards along the rank of men, pawing their peckers.

Torn between his fear of getting caught and the satisfaction of having produced an authentic crowd-pleaser, Palmer runs the one-minute spectacle twice more, then says that's all folks and unplugs the machine.

But the crowd has been pleased. Tichener carries his deep and muffled chuckling into the hallway followed by the fourth-squad men, one of whom whispers, "That was pretty good, Palmer." By the time the movie equipment and reel have been stored away, Keillor is snoring on his pillow.

"You don't trust people much, do you?" Courtney says.

"Why should I?"

"Your secret is safe with those guys."

Palmer shuts the door to his locker but doesn't say anything.

Courtney stands up and throws his windbreaker over his shoulder. "Listen. Hudson's discharge is coming up in two weeks and they're going to be looking for someone to replace him on the honor guard. Let's get you on it."

"No thanks."

"Why not? It's good duty. It'll get you out of here on weekdays."

Palmer shakes his head no and waves Courtney off with both hands. "I don't want anything to do with dead people."

"We don't have anything to do with dead people. All we do is fire salutes over their graves."

"Anyway," Palmer says, "Lt. Norbert is in charge of the honor guard, and I don't want to, you know, get involved with him again."

Courtney apparently understands because he doesn't say anything more about it. "Okay. But when we start MP duty next week, let's see if Sgt. Sherman will let us patrol together."

"All right."

"And don't take a shower tonight," Courtney says as he walks out of the room. "You're plastered."

CHAPTER 13

Palmer fully expects to be left off the MP duty roster because he does not believe that anyone vindictive enough to deny him a promotion could be satisfied with only that. He expects Sgt. Sherman to concoct an excuse to prevent him from putting the MP brassard on his arm and going out on the road with the rest of Company D, so when word goes around the barracks that the duty rosters for the first week's patrol assignments have been posted, Palmer goes down the hall prepared for disappointment, knowing that after he sees his name has been left off the list he will have to go to Sgt. Sherman and ask for an explanation, and a bad scene will ensue, and the situation will deteriorate, and everything will just go to hell.

The rosters for all three platoons are tacked to the cork bulletin board in the foyer, but it's the first sheet Palmer strains to see over the heads of all the eager men gathered around like college students checking posted grades. When he sees his name typed between those of Keillor and Vinton, it comes as a surprise which has a peculiar undercurrent of disappointment, as though he has been denied a particularly satisfying form of outrage. But that disappears when he realizes that he is at last going to be allowed to do the job he has been trained to do, which is the only thing he's wanted to do since arriving at the Presidio, which is to be a Military Policeman.

At 1450 hours on Monday, Courtney comes into Palmer's room and inspects his uniform. "Tighten your belt," he says. "It's starting to droop."

This from the weight of a nightstick, holster, ammo pouch, and handcuff-case encircling his skinny frame. It will droop even more when he puts a .45 into the holster and tucks two magazines containing seven fat bullets apiece into the ammo pouch.

They go down to the arms room and check out their .45s. Palmer takes his back up to his room to practice unsnapping the button on his holster flap and drawing his weapon and locking the slide open and presenting arms all in one smooth motion, because Lt. Norbert will be inspecting the swing-shift and Palmer doesn't want to invoke the proven wrath of the company XO and find himself gigged out of a job. But when the lieutenant finally does inspect the swing-shift, he doesn't indicate through word, gesture, or eye-contact that he has ever met Private Palmer.

———————

A bus delivers the swing-shift to the small stucco red-roofed Provost Marshall's Office situated across the street from Letterman General Hospital. Strangely, the main thing on Palmer's mind is not the day's work ahead of him but rather how hard it would be, how hard it must be, for a cherry-boy in the Infantry in Vietnam to go out on his first combat patrol in the jungle, to jump from a helicopter for the first time into elephant-grass clutching his M-16, and holding down his helmet in the prop breeze, and looking for his squad leader, and waiting for that first spray of VC bullets to hit his eyes or teeth or testicles. Nothing Palmer will be doing today could even begin to compare with that, so he knows he shouldn't be so fucking apprehensive about going out on the road for the first time, but he is anyway.

When the swing-shift walks inside, the desk sergeant smiles down at them from his six-foot high platform. He knows they are newbies fresh out of MP school, and wet-behind-the-ears, and don't know shit, and carry loaded guns. He nods at the two veterans, Courtney and Tichener, and tells everyone to step on through to the back room to wait for the Provost Marshal.

The back room is small, only a table and two chairs for writing reports, and a row of hat-hooks on the wall. As soon as the troops are assembled in the room, the Provost Marshal strides in grinning, a lean, red-haired young officer who places his fists on his hips and introduces himself as Captain Hoover, and tells the troops to form up in two ranks.

Palmer maneuvers himself into first place in line, as in basic training where he had always wanted to be the first to do the new thing and was never reluctant to look like a fool and make the first mistake because that's how you learned best. He unsnaps the holster flap and pulls out his .45 and jacks the slide back and performs present-arms, but the Captain merely gives him a quick once-over and moves on to the next man, and finishes the inspection quickly.

The Captain stands in front of the men and gives the mandatory cherry-boy MP speech. "Do not, I repeat, do not put a bullet into the chamber of your weapon. If I find a man carrying a weapon with a bullet in the chamber, he will be taken off duty and given an Article 15. Last month we had a man accidentally fire his .45 into the clearing barrel outside the front door because he didn't listen up, and now he's pushing a broom in Company C."

It's the-last-man-to-do-that again. He's everywhere.

The Provost Marshal implores the new men to listen to their senior partners. "And you senior partners, cut your trainees a little slack. Try to remember when you were trainees."

That's it. There's nothing left for the army to tell them. They're MPs now. At some point the army has to let its soldiers go out and do whatever it is they have been trained to do: write a ticket, cook a chicken, patrol the Mekong Delta.

Unable to mask their giddiness, the men march outside grinning and straightening their pistol belts and squaring their white saucer-caps, and waiting for their vehicles which are already beginning to pull into the parking lot. MPs climb out of the cars buzzed like kids climbing off a carnival ride, their uniforms rumpled, their web-gear askew, their fists crammed with traffic tickets. They immediately begin telling war stories to anyone who will listen, tales about the civilian they busted for speeding past the PX, or the three-star General they chauffeured from Sixth Army Headquarters to the officer's club, or the mysterious jimmied lock they investigated on a quartermaster warehouse down near the marina, lightweight adventures that make Palmer eager to get out on the road.

Courtney comes out of the MP station with a clipboard containing blank incident reports and traffic accident forms. He hands Palmer a virgin ticket book and says, "Don't lose this." Then says, "You'll do most of the driving today."

The first thing Palmer learns about MP duty: it's difficult to sit in a car with a nightstick on your left hip and a holster on your right. When he gets seated behind the steering wheel he looks at the radio and microphone, at the dashboard switches for red light and siren—there's also a plastic screen like a windshield separating the front seat from the back seat to protect the MPs from violent prisoners

"You're going to write your first speeding ticket today," Courtney says.

They drive to the motor pool where Palmer checks the oil and windshield-wiper fluid and fills the gas tank, careful not to soil his uniform. Courtney doesn't help. He believes in on-the-job training. He won't do anything for a trainee except nitpick and carp, the privilege not of rank but experience.

When they get back on the road, Courtney tells him to drive up into the hills overlooking main post so he can start learning the back roads and side streets, and especially the one-way alleys which are usually good for a traffic ticket.

"One-one, Presidio." A call on the radio from the desk.

Palmer glances at Courtney.

"Well?" Courtney says.

Palmer picks up the mike. "Presidio, one-one."

"Ten-one-six."

Return to the PMO. He hangs a U and heads back to the MP station.

The desk sergeant has two prisoners awaiting transfer up to the stockade. They're in the detention cell, a long narrow room behind the desk, no beds, just a bench to sit on while a man waits for his commanding officer to send someone to pick him up after he has violated a military law, or to wait for an MP unit to take him on that winding road up to the Presidio stockade at the far corner of the quad.

The turnkey unlocks the cell door and two prisoners shuffle out shackled at the ankles. They're just kids, faces dirty, red-eyed, their fatigues torn and stained and reeking of month-old armpit-and-shit smells so obnoxious that when they move past Palmer he has to take two steps backward. One of the kids is wearing a leather hat with a bright red band encircling the crown, an incongruous and almost insulting article of clothing in concert with his military fatigues.

"Have you ever put handcuffs on a man before?" Courtney says to Palmer.

"Only in training."

"Do what I do."

Palmer had cuffed men in MP school during one hour of training, like all the inadequate single hours of training for each aspect of an MP's job. Plus, his prisoner was another trainee and was cooperative, not like a collared or cornered criminal might be. Courtney approaches the taller of the men and tells him to turn around. He crosses the man's hands behind his back and snaps the cuffs on with a swift click.

"You don't have to make them so tight," the prisoner says.

Courtney turns the prisoner around and leans into his face. "Shut your goddamn mouth! Nobody told you to talk! You speak when spoken to, prisoner. Do you understand me?"

The kid drops his head and stares at his shoes.

"I said do you understand me, prisoner?"

"Yes, sergeant."

Courtney's field-promotion makes the desk crew laugh. "Handcuff your prisoner," he says to Palmer.

Palmer removes the cuffs from his pouch, approaches his prisoner and tells him to turn around. The kid turns, the chains on his ankles ringing against the floor, and he crosses his arms behind his back. Palmer applies the cuffs. The kid's hands are warm. They feel like dead birds.

"All right, Courtney," the desk sergeant says, "these two shit-heads went AWOL from basic training in Fort Ord thirty days ago. SFPD found them in a hippie hovel down in the Fillmore district. They've been hiding out with hippie girls. I want you to take 'em up to the stockade where they're gonna wash all the hippie lipstick off 'em, and kill all the hippie fleas, and check their dicks for hippie clap."

"Frisk them," Courtney tells Palmer.

Palmer runs his hands down their arms and up their legs remembering the MP instructor saying don't be afraid to check his crotch because your prisoner might be hiding a razor blade under his balls. Not likely. The shit-stench of their clothing makes him gag.

"Put them in the car," Courtney says. "I'll get the paperwork."

It feels strange to be ordering human beings around for the first time in his life. When Palmer says, "Outside," he hears his own father's voice come from his throat. He herds them out the door and into the backseat of the car. After he and Courtney climb into the front seat, one of the prisoners leans toward the plastic screen. "Can you hear us?"

"Shut up," Courtney says.

The prisoners whisper and giggle as Palmer drives onto Lincoln Boulevard and follows the road up past the cemetery and around the hairpin forest and up through lifer housing toward the quad. He takes a right at the dry-cleaners, drives one block to the stockade, and pulls up in front of the sally-port.

A stranger wouldn't know it was a stockade except for the barbed-wire draped around everything in sight, and concertina wire, spring-loaded curls of razor-laden wire also strung around perimeters in Vietnam but which VC sappers are said to be able to slip through like eels. At the other end of the parking lot stands a tin garage and wash rack where prisoners are hosing down battalion vehicles under the eyes of three Company A guards holding what look like sawed-off shotguns. The guards are wearing plastic riot helmets with yellow visors. Attached to their pistol belts are long white wooden riot-batons. A black guard with a shotgun cradled in his arms walks up to the driver's side and leans into the window. "How's it going, Courtney?"

"Hey, Specialist Withers," Courtney says, opening his door.

"Leave the keys and I'll have my prisoners wash your vehicle while you're inside," SP4 Withers says, his head cocked back a bit so he can see Courtney through his visor.

Courtney and Palmer guide the prisoners through a fenced walkway. The door to the stockade opens before they get there and a big man in a Class A uniform peers out at them. "Specialist Courtney, what this?"

"AWOLS."

"Don't be bringing no AWOLs into my jail." He smiles and stands back to let them in. "Right on down the hallway. Sgt. O'Bannon will be with you di-rectly."

This is the first time Palmer has ever been inside a prison. He's seen them only in movies, expects to hear shouting or the rattling of tin cups on bars, but hears none of these things. When the door to the world closes behind him, all sounds cease except the sniffling of one prisoner who seems to have caught a cold on the ride up.

The receiving room is small like the back room of the PMO, a table and two chairs, two doors. "Face the wall and don't move," Courtney tells them.

"Could you please loosen my handcuffs?" the taller prisoner says. "They hurt."

A door opens and two guards walk in, an E6 and an E5.

"Specialist Fourth-Class Courtney, back on the road— outstanding," the E6 says. "What have you got for me today?"

"Staff Sergeant O'Bannon," Courtney replies, "one of your prisoners just complained that his handcuffs are too tight."

"Which one?"

"The tall one."

"This one?" O'Bannon says, walking over to the prisoner. "He asked me to loosen his cuffs."

"Why did he do that, Specialist Courtney? Is he a pussy?"

"I don't know, sergeant."

"He smells like a pussy. What are these pussies in for?"

"AWOL from basic training."

"Uh oh. Do you know what we do to AWOLs in this place?"

"I don't want to know, sergeant."

"Why not, Specialist Courtney? Are you a pussy?"

"That's an affirmative, sergeant."

The E6 leans into the tall prisoner's face. "My name is Sergeant O'Bannon. I'm in charge of the motivational platoon. Do you know how to do pushups?"

No reply.

Sgt. O'Bannon returns to the table and takes the paperwork from Courtney. He looks at Palmer's name-tag. "Private Palmer?"

"Yes, sergeant?"

"Private E2 Palmer, would you be so kind as to strip search these prisoners for me?"

"Yes, sergeant."

Shit. Palmer knows all about the strip search. The instructors devoted an hour to it one afternoon in MP school, and while they didn't take it to its logical conclusion, he does know that the process ultimately involves rectums.

He steps into the stench of the AWOL's bodies and removes their handcuffs. "Listen up, prisoners. Take off all your clothes and put them in a pile next to your feet." He backs away.

They go at it slowly, in the way of prisoners. When they're naked he tells them to raise their hands and lean against the wall. He searches their clothing for hidden contraband, turning the pockets inside-out and ruffling along the seams but doing it slowly to avoid sticking himself with the diseased end of a hypodermic needle as warned in training.

A few coins, crumpled bills, crushed cigarette packs. He sets these on the table under the eyes of his grinning superiors.

He gropes through the prisoners' long unwashed hair for razor blades or anything else the AWOLs might have been able to secrete under the greasy mats, then checks inside their mouths and under their tongues, and peers down their throats. Then he tells them to turn around and bend over and spread the cheeks of their buttocks.

Who knows what might be hidden up there? Balloons maybe, filled with heroin or cocaine or pot or whatever the hell else a man might stick up his ass that he thinks he might need later on in jail when the lights are out and he's got plenty of time and darkness to go poking around in his anus.

A quick glance and he's pretty certain he doesn't see anything suspicious in or around the general area of either knotted brown orifice staring back at him in the bright receiving-room light.

"All clear," he says to Sgt. O'Bannon, who seems to be getting a kick out of Palmer's amateur proctology. The sergeant laughs aloud and signs the transfer papers and hands Courtney his copies, then tells Palmer to bring him the leather hat.

The E5 tells the naked men to pick up their clothes and step through the door which, when it opens, gives Palmer a brief glimpse of a hallway leading to the prisoner quarters, and a view through a barred window of the grassy courtyard where the prisoners are brought out for PT every morning— and beyond the perimeter fence, a view of the bowling alley, his enlisted men's club, where prisoners cannot go.

"Come here, Private Palmer," Sgt. O'Bannon says, examining the leather hat. "I want you to see something."

He points at the red hatband, then peels it back revealing a long fish line wrapped around the crown. He yanks it off and holds it up. "You have to look everywhere when you strip-search a prisoner, Palmer. A prisoner could use this fish line to strangle a guard. You've got to check in every possible place where a prisoner might be able to hide some kind of weapon."

The sergeant isn't angry. He knows this is OJT for Palmer, who nods and tries not to look as inept as he feels.

After he and Courtney leave the building they wait for their vehicle which is still in the tin shed being scrubbed by a sullen prisoner dragging a sponge in slow circles around the hood. No laces in his boots, no belt, no hat. He's a kid like the

AWOLs, his face frozen without expression except that of enduring what he has brought upon himself.

"You get a move on there," SP4 Withers says. The prisoner speeds up momentarily, then goes back to lethargic scrubbing, all the while seeming to watch the guard out of a corner of a fixed and hood-staring eye. "I try to cut these prisoners some slack 'cause I know I could just as easy be in their place," the guard says. "But sometimes they ask for it."

When the car is ready, Palmer and Courtney get in and drive toward the intersection near the dry-cleaners. When Palmer pulls up at the stop sign, Courtney looks over at him. "You felt sorry for those AWOLs, didn't you?"

Palmer doesn't answer. All he can think about is how utterly fucking miserable it would be to get stuck inside that stockade.

"I could tell you felt sorry for them," Courtney says. "But let me tell you something, Palmer, I don't have any sympathy for those duds. They didn't have to go through anything in basic training that I didn't have to go through."

It's true. Those AWOLs are just duds and pussies. They will hate the stockade even more than the basic training that they ran away from and which Palmer had liked, and they will probably never be smart enough to understand why every move they make is so fucking stupid. Empathy is the word Palmer would use, but doesn't.

Ft. Cronkite is part of their designated zone which has to be patrolled twice-daily, so one half-hour before sunset Palmer drives out of the Presidio gate at Merchant Road to the toll-booth of the Golden Gate Bridge and passes a white-haired toll-taker in a civilian/military saucer cap who smiles, he likes soldiers, had probably served in WWII.

They drive past the spot where Palmer had seen Thorpe leaning over the railing, and he thinks about mentioning this to Courtney, except he would have to explain what he himself was doing all alone out on the bridge that afternoon, the illusion-of-running-away business. He takes the road down to Ft. Cronkite past the scene of his debacle and cruises into the rolling deeply-weeded countryside on a two-lane asphalt road and through a tunnel which feeds out into the Marin Headlands.

On this part of the reservation war games are played every week by GIs assigned to Vietnam. Palmer can see a group of them as he drives past a dirt road, three-dozen men holding M-16s and standing near two parked buses. One kilometer beyond that spot is a small wooden shack designated as a Vietnamese ville, their target for today.

He slows the car as they approach a cluster of lifer housing where the road dead-ends.

"All right, Palmer, we're going to get you a moving violation. Drive back up the road. We're going to set up a speed trap."

Palmer hangs a U and heads back slowly, searching the shoulder for a good place to hide in the weeds. He pulls off near a curve and parks far enough in so that no one will see them until it's too late. He shuts off the engine.

They wait.

Most of the MP work he has performed so far has been for show, driving around and talking on the radio, but he hasn't really done anything because he hasn't yet done it in front of a person violating the law. You can't hide in a car all day and call yourself an MP, which is his instinct. You have to confront a culprit, have to be real and not be like someone who just talks about being a film maker someday or is good with a pistol but never shoots at anything which is no different from not being good with a pistol at all.

The driver of the Mustang doesn't see them. A blue blur sweeping around the curve, Courtney says go get him and Palmer starts the engine and pulls out onto the road. He trails the car for a quarter mile with Courtney leaning over to watch the speedometer and finally telling Palmer to flip on the red lights. The Mustang takes its time pulling onto the shoulder of the road. Palmer parks behind it and gathers his ticket book and makes sure he has a pen. He and Courtney get out of the car.

The driver rolls his window down. He's wearing Air Force sunglasses. The rank on his collar indicates that he's a Specialist Sixth Class, which Palmer finds interesting because he never actually knew there was such a thing.

It's time to talk now, but just before Palmer begins, something inside him says, You're not a cop, Palmer, you can't bust people, you're a drunk and a fraud and the driver is going to laugh in your face.

"Good evening, Specialist. May I see your driver's license and military ID?"

The Spec Six seems miffed at being stopped, or more precisely, ambushed. Riding shotgun is another GI, a buck-sergeant in sunglasses. The humiliation of being stopped by a cop. Palmer knows that stinko feeling.

He examines the license.

The man is thirty-one years old, which means he's a lifer, and lifers don't like to get tickets. Traffic tickets are for E4 and below. The man is fuming now, his jaws clamped rigid at the insult as Palmer informs him that he was clocked doing thirty-five miles-an-hour in a twenty-five mile-an-hour zone.

His buddy is smirking. (Aren't MPs assholes? We drive this fast every day. We own Marin County you dumb cop.)

But neither man says anything except the driver fuming as he replies, "Yes, that's correct. Yes. Uh huh," then grimacing as Palmer begins to write in his ticket book.

But he fucks it up, writing information in the wrong boxes, and has to flip the page over and start a new ticket. He hears Courtney chuckle. He looks over at Courtney and says, "Go sit in the car."

Courtney walks away grinning.

He gets it written and hands it to the driver, and then, because he's pissed at himself for fucking up his very first traffic ticket, not to mention his first body search, and because he's annoyed by the groovy Air Force shades on both men, he leans down and says, "Let's try to drive a little slower, Specialist."

The man doesn't say anything, just rolls up the window, starts the car, and pulls onto the road. Palmer walks back to his vehicle and gets in. After the Mustang disappears around the curve, he tells Courtney what he had told the driver.

"Did you really say that?" Courtney says.

"Yeah."

"Jesus, I can't believe it."

But Courtney likes it. He's grinning.

Palmer feels good, and is already looking forward to writing his next ticket. Power is far more interesting than he had ever expected it to be, having never possessed any power before. He makes a U-turn and heads back to the Presidio.

At eleven-thirty P.M., one half-hour before shift change, Courtney is at the wheel taking them through main post. Palmer is riding shotgun and smoking a cigarette which he had thought he would never do on MP duty, taking it more seriously eight hours previously than he does now.

There is nothing going on, the radio is silent, and there are no cars on Lincoln Boulevard. He can see that, come next week, the graveyard-shift is going to be dull until dawn. Day-shift is where the real action is, eight in the morning until four in the afternoon. His platoon will pull a week of day-shift only once, and swing-shift twice during the next month. He's thinking about this when Courtney makes a U and flips on the red light. A black '64 Ford had passed them headed for the Lombard gate, and Courtney gets on its tail.

When the car pulls over, Palmer says, "What did he do?"

"Wait here," Courtney replies.

Palmer doesn't like this. MP partners are supposed to do things in pairs, including watch each other's back when they approach cars. But Courtney is the senior partner, and Palmer has to trust him. He watches as Courtney goes up to the car and starts talking. Courtney takes the driver's ID, says a few more words, then comes back and climbs in. "Look at this." He holds out a driver's license with a bad photograph of a blonde woman staring into the camera.

"What did she do?"

"She didn't do anything."

"Why did you stop her?"

"Jesus Palmer, don't you know anything about picking up women?"

Courtney copies her address into his notebook. "I'll be right back."

He gets out and goes up to the woman's car and leans in the window and starts talking. Palmer can see his jawbone flapping. The woman nods, shakes her head no, yes, no, yes. After a few minutes the Ford takes off toward the Lombard gate, and Courtney gets back in.

"What took you so long?" Palmer says.

"Was I gone long?"

"Did you ask her for a date?"

"Do you know how long it's been since I've had a woman?"

"You've never had a woman."

Courtney glances in the rear-view mirror to see how dazzling he had looked while talking to the culprit. He glances at Palmer. "So you want me to find a date for you before we sign out?"

"What's her name?" Palmer says.

"Cheryl."

"So—when are you and Cheryl getting married?"

Courtney tucks his notebook into his breast pocket, grins at Palmer, and starts the engine.

CHAPTER 14

There's a surprising number of cars in the Baker Beach parking lot for a Wednesday midnight. Beaudry is at the wheel. Seated shotgun, Palmer looks at sleeping seagulls huddled on the cliffs overlooking the civilians strolling the beach in the moonlight or camping out in tents pitched near the rocks. Beaudry makes a circuit of the parking lot and slows for a yellow Chevy backing out of a space. Neither of MPs pay much attention to the Chevy until the driver floors it and burns rubber headed for the cliff road. Palmer and Beaudry are taken by surprise, startled in fact, though not so much by the screech of tortured tires as the blast of sand ricocheting off their windshield.

Beaudry floors it, but by the time they're halfway up the cliff road the MP vehicle is actually slowing down. He picks up the microphone and tells the desk that they're in "hot-pursuit." It doesn't matter though because by the time they make the hilltop the Chevy is gone.

Beaudry hammers the steering wheel with a fist. "Goddamn this fuck bucket! They oughta give us four-twenty-sevens instead of this slant-six shit!"

This is interesting to Palmer because he's never seen Beaudry mad before.

Palmer radios the desk and tells them that the chase is over and the vehicle got away. Shot with adrenaline, Palmer and Beaudry head back to their patrol zone looking for someone to pull over for any reason at all and a convertible comes barreling

down the cliff road toward Baker Beach. They fall in behind it with the red lights flashing.

The driver pulls over and hops out and grins at them. He looks like a rock star in his shiny yellow silk shirt, tight purple pants and curly blond hair, almost an Afro. They're pretty sure he's a civilian. When they tell him why they had pulled him over (excessive speed for road conditions) he seems delighted and says, "Is this really an army base?"

They take his driver's license and go back to their car and stand by the headlights to talk it over. The driver is so jolly that Beaudry suspects he might be high on drugs. They discuss giving him a roadside sobriety-test, except that he is being cordial and cooperative, and isn't hassling them at all, plus he's kind of amusing. They decide to let him go with a warning.

"Thanks a million, fellas!" he chirps, then hops into his ragtop and splits the scene.

Letting him go makes them both feel good enough to finally start laughing about their low-speed chase up the cliff road. When they get back to the barracks at the end of the graveyard-shift and start trading war stories with other MPs, their hot-pursuit lasts a little bit longer in the telling, and Beaudry adds, "We had our holsters unbuttoned."

This is the first job Palmer ever had that he doesn't want to stop doing it. Time passes too quickly during each shift and doesn't pass quickly enough between shifts. He stops going to the bowling alley on week nights, and spends his evenings working on his gear and getting things ready for the next day. He goes to bed early and doesn't miss the beer at all, because he's got something he likes even better. He would be willing to work seven days a week if they would let him.

He wants to do this every day for the rest of his time-in-service because it is the best job an enlisted man could possibly have. He is his own boss eight hours a day, he carries a loaded pistol, and best of all, he can bust officers.

On Saturday evening at the end of the second week, Courtney walks into Palmer's room and finds him sitting on the floor polishing a boot. "The army doesn't pay you extra to work on your own time."

Palmer ignores him.

"Put your gear away," Courtney says. "We've got plans for tonight."

"What plans?"

"We're going to my girlfriend's apartment. I told Cheryl about you."

Palmer stops polishing. This pleases him. He likes being the sort of person other people tell their friends about. "What did you say to her?"

"I told her you make movies. She thought that was interesting."

"Yeah?" He continues polishing his boot.

"She works in a graphic-art shop downtown. She draws pictures for ads in magazines and newspapers. But there's this one thing about her you won't believe. I want you to meet her tonight."

Palmer stops again and looks up at Courtney. The thought of meeting a woman who has "heard about him" makes him uneasy.

"Well, I don't know—"

"You don't know? What—are you having dinner with the battalion commander tonight?"

Palmer examines the toe of his boot, then begins putting things away. "No, I'm not doing anything."

"Okay. I told her we would show up around eight."

"Is she like—an anti-war type?"

"No. She digs soldiers, but she does smoke pot. And she paints these freak-out posters and hangs them on her walls. But there's this one thing about her you will not believe. You have got to see this for yourself."

Pot. Palmer knows all about pot. He had smelled it at the Underground Cinema 12 in Denver but had to ask his brother Mike what that sweet stink was. The nuns had taught him that pot will physically rot your brain and cause you to commit mortal sins involving genital phenomena. Palmer pictures Courtney and himself in Cheryl's apartment sucking on super bomber joints with their faces smeared in Day-Glo paints as they wallow in a cesspool of acid-rock and free-love. This is how the narcs will find them when they bust down the door and handcuff them for a trip to the Presidio stockade.

"Where exactly does she live?" he says, as if the answer might put the kibosh on the whole deal.

"Parnassus Avenue, on a hill above Golden Gate Park. Wait'll you see her apartment. She's got strobe lights. And the only thing she eats is vegetables."

Vegetables.

This is starting to sound like Charles Manson stuff.

Palmer stands up and opens his wall locker and starts fiddling with the new civilian clothes that he had recently purchased.

"Let's hit the road," Courtney says.

Palmer finally decides that if things gets completely out of hand, he can always dive out a window and take a bus back to the Presidio.

A quick stop at a liquor store on Stanyan Street for a six-pack of Budweiser, Palmer opens a can and begins sipping at it. "Haight-Ashbury," Courtney says, pointing to their left as they drive past the Panhandle. Palmer and his brother went to the Vogue Theater drunk on beer and sat in the pot stink and watched Golden Gate Park summer-of-love movies and felt like they were part of the radical underground. Their hair was long, they listened to Moby Grape, they talked about how cool it would be to "score some maryjane" but didn't quite know how to go about it. They never missed an episode of *The Smothers Brothers Comedy Hour*, and were outraged when CBS canceled it. But at least they still had *Laugh-In*. Rumors began to spread that Paul McCartney was dead, then Palmer got drafted and had to get a haircut.

Cheryl's apartment building is at the top of a steep brick street which intersects with Parnassus Avenue which rises past the University of California Medical Center a few blocks farther up the hill. Courtney parks at the curb and points at a bay window. "That's her place."

Palmer rolls down his window and listens for the bass beat of hard-rock but hears only the hiss of rubber trolley tires coming up Parnassus. A quick chug to kill the beer and he's ready. They get out and walk around the corner to the front door where Courtney rings a bell on a brass plate full of buttons. There's an intercom but Cheryl doesn't ask who it is. The door buzzes and they open it and pass through a small foyer into a building which is nicely-kept for a hippie hovel.

Clean red carpeting and varnished woodwork. A single yellow light hangs above each of the five doorways along the hall. And in the air, the odor of evergreen disinfectant.

"Now don't embarrass me by saying anything uncool," Courtney says, heading for the door farthest down the hall, a long sprint in an emergency, Palmer notes. He wants to pull out another beer but only holds tighter to the cans inside the crackling sack as Courtney knocks on the door.

It opens, and a woman with blonde hair peeks out and says, "Hi Courtney," in a breathy, shy voice.

"This is Palmer," Courtney says, leading him into her apartment.

Couch, chair, desk, coffee table with wine-bottle candle-holder and unlit wick. No pillows, no strobe lights, no vegetables. Paintings on the walls, but only mountain landscapes.

Courtney takes off his jacket and sits on the couch. Palmer looks back at Cheryl because he had walked in too fast to get a good look at her, but gets one now. Pink sweater, white pants, tennis shoes, hair short though not Mia Farrow, with natural curls. Her blue eyes take on a watery sheen as she smiles and says, "Let me take your coat, Palmer."

He removes it and hands it to her.

"Why don't you two shake hands?" Courtney says.

They shake hands. Her flesh is cool. Palmer can't recall ever shaking hands with a woman before. "How do you do?" she says, and he hears the faintest trace of a Southern accent as she says "do"—deyoo.

"Palmer's been in the army six months," Courtney says.

Cheryl puts both their coats into the closet. She turns and smiles. "I've been looking forward to meeting you, Palmer. Courtney has told me a lot about you."

Palmer smiles, nods, holds up his paper sack. "He told me about you, too. Would you like a beer?"

"For Chrissakes, Palmer," Courtney says. "Can't you forget about drinking for two seconds?"

Cheryl accepts a beer. Palmer takes one for himself, and as Cheryl carries the rest into the kitchen Palmer sits down on a chair near the far end of the couch.

"Nice place, isn't it?" Courtney says.

"Asshole."

When Cheryl comes back into the room, Courtney points at Palmer. "My buddy tells me he thinks your place is swell."

"Thank you very much, Palmer."

"He thinks you're swell, too."

"Well thank you, Palmer," she says, smiling. "Would either of you gentlemen like something to eat? My daddy once told me that soldiers are always hungry."

"No thanks," Palmer says. "I ate at the mess hall." A woman who likes to cook for men. But he's always hated eating in the homes of strangers.

"I'll take a hamburger," Courtney says.

"What would you like on it?"

"The usual."

When she goes into the kitchen, Courtney says, "This you have got to see." He gets up and crosses the room to the stereo. "Come here and look at her record collection." He kneels beside a peach crate full of LPs. "Look at the kind of music she listens to."

Palmer squats and looks at the titles: Buddy Holly, The Beach Boys, Elvis. "What's wrong with these?" Palmer says.

"What's wrong is she doesn't have anything recorded since sixty-five. No Beatles, no Stones."

"Get away from there." Palmer looks around. Cheryl is standing in the doorway holding a spatula. "Don't look at my records," she says with a frown, but Palmer can tell it's some sort of joke between them. "Courtney thinks my record collection is inadequate."

Palmer lets the albums flop in the box and goes back to his beer.

"You just sit down and wait for your hamburger," she tells Courtney.

When Courtney stands up, Palmer can see how much taller he is than Cheryl, a head taller. Whereas if Cheryl and Palmer stood face-to-face, his lips would reach her hairline. She turns and goes back into the kitchen.

"She listens to Chad and Jeremy for crying out loud," Courtney says.

"Is that the unbelievable thing I had to see for myself?"

"Not by a long shot." Courtney points at the paintings on the walls. "Nice artwork, huh?"

Palmer knows nothing about art. He shrugs. "Did she do them?"

"Hey Cheryl!" Courtney hollers. "Palmer the art critic wants to know if you did these paintings!"

The only sound that comes from the kitchen is the sizzle of meat. Courtney chuckles. "I think not."

Cheryl walks in balancing a plate on her fingertips like a waitress and sets it down in front of Courtney but doesn't sit next to him. She comes down to Palmer's end of the couch and sits so that her knees are almost touching his. Palmer glances at her knees, then pretends to be interested in the meat monstrosity Courtney is examining which smells good:

steaming beef, ketchup, onions, with mustard dripping down the side of the bun as Courtney takes a bite. Palmer now wishes he had asked for one, and feels a tug of hunger in his stomach which he kills with a swallow of beer.

"Thanks, Cheryl," Courtney says, setting the burger back on the plate. "By the way, Palmer loves your paintings."

"They are not mine," she says. "I should never have told you about them."

Another love game that Palmer has no interest in hearing. He starts looking around for the bathroom.

"Tell ol' Palmer here where you got these paintings."

Cheryl turns to Palmer. "You see, I like to have nice pictures in my apartment." This is as far as she gets before Courtney interrupts her.

"She checks them out of the library! Can you believe that!" He chokes on a wad of bun and starts stomping his feet on the hardwood floor.

Palmer gazes at a painting above the stereo. "I didn't know you could check paintings out of a library."

Cheryl nods. She hasn't moved to help Courtney as he gags on his cadged meal, hasn't dashed to his side the way a girlfriend would to pat him on the back to dislodge the food hampering his guffaws. She sits with her arms folded and her pink lips pursed.

"Can I use your bathroom?" Palmer says.

She points. He crosses the room and steps into the bathroom and shuts out all the intolerable heckle-nonsense and love-play that Courtney is getting such a bang out of.

It's been a long time since he has been inside a human bathroom. The cold tile and porcelain is camouflaged with

the femininity of rug things and perfumed knickknacks. A
thick fuzzy butt-warmer on the toilet-seat. Racks of fresh
towels and washcloths which smell of rose. A clean odor
rising from used hand-soaps gathered in pink netting resting
in a wicker basket on the top of the toilet tank. He feels
guilty unzipping and whipping it out in such a fancy crapper.
Afterwards he spends a minute looking at his face in the
mirror. He has been drinking only twenty minutes and feels
barely a buzz, hardly enough to take part in Courtney's
asshole games. He once mixed a single Budweiser with a
single Colt. 45 Malt Liquor and got sicker faster than the time
he mixed tequila with crème de cacao at a friend's house.

He comes out of the bathroom and finds them sitting up
on the couch straightening their clothes and pretending they
weren't groping.

"Did you fall in?" Courtney says.

Palmer picks up his empty and asks where Cheryl put the
beers.

"They're probably in the refrigerator," Courtney says.
"You know, that cold white tall metal machine thing." He looks
at Cheryl and shakes his head. "Palmer is from Denver."

Palmer steps into the kitchen where the light is blinding,
a Forties kitchen of white porcelain and white sink and stove
and walls, everything more brilliant and blinding than the
bowling alley. He opens the refrigerator, and sees the beer
and a bottle of pink Chablis.

"Why don't you show us your drawings?" Courtney says
when Palmer comes back in.

Cheryl is shy at first and doesn't want to display the product
of her craft tucked away inside her portfolio secreted in the

closet, but after a minute of urging she gets up to retrieve it because it's no harder to talk an artist into showing off her talent than it is to talk Palmer into showing his home-movies. She drags out a black briefcase the size of a card table and lays it on the floor. She crawls around unzipping the edges and spreads the cover open like a book.

Courtney and Palmer get down on the floor beside her and start leafing through Bristol board covered with pictures rendered in the mediums of charcoal and pen-and-ink and even Crayola. A pencil-drawn sports-car with bulbous liquid fenders, a woman's hat and veil stark in black ink, charcoal-drawn scowling or laughing faces, nudes, still-lifes, landscapes, boats, flowers, cows. Palmer is speechless, as he always is in the presence of anything capable of generating money.

"These are good," he says, wary though because, after all, maybe they're crap.

"Thank you, Palmer."

"Did you do these for ads in local newspapers?"

"No. I did most of them back in North Carolina when I was a student. I used them to get my job here."

Palmer can't help but feel that if he could draw as well as this he wouldn't be in the army. If he could do anything at all he wouldn't be in the army.

"You oughta see Palmer's movies," Courtney says, moving back to the couch. "They're awful."

"I was hoping you would bring your movies tonight, Palmer," Cheryl says, collecting the artwork and putting it back into the briefcase.

"I didn't ask him to," Courtney says. "I didn't want to ruin the party."

"But I did so want to see them."

"They're good enough to show to soldiers," Courtney says, "but I wouldn't show them to real people."

Palmer gets up and goes back to his chair. Cheryl stores the briefcase in the closet, then comes to his end of the couch and sits down and places her right hand on his left thigh. "I want very much to see your films, Palmer, and I do hope you will bring them next time."

"What next time?" Courtney says. "You two have met and gawked at each other, and that's that."

Cheryl turns to him and folds her arms. "Palmer is welcome to visit me any time he wishes. I think he is a very fine gentleman, and I do sorely miss the company of gentlemen."

Courtney rolls his eyes, which makes Cheryl giggle with one hand raised in genteel politeness in front of her open mouth.

Courtney stands up. "Put on your coats. We're going to buy some records."

———————

The fog is so thick that when a trolley comes toward them from the bottom of Parnassus hill all they can see at first are squares of light floating above the rubber-tire rumble which passes with a metallic power-pole clatter. The record store is two blocks down and one block over on Irving Street which is bright with bars and the lights of Greek corner grocery-stores. Courtney buys two early Beatle albums, "Please Please Me" and "Beatles For Sale." Then they walked to a grocery where Cheryl buys two six-packs of Bud. Palmer buys another pack of Camels, worried about running out.

Back in the apartment they sit on the floor and listen to the brand-new without-a-scratch albums. Is Paul really dead? During sophomore year the class hippie came to school bummed out, and when Palmer asked why, he said he had heard on the radio that The Fab Four were breaking up, which Palmer scoffed at, believing that the Beatles would never break up if only because they were making so much money.

He lies on his back on the living room floor by the stereo with his eyes closed and listens to the records, and later on to Courtney and Cheryl seated in the kitchen drinking coffee which he can smell and it smells good but he doesn't want coffee, he doesn't want to sober up, he wants to lie here and get even higher. Cold beer and Beatles, he's found his enlisted men's club. Then Courtney is lifting him off the floor and Cheryl is laughing and stuffing his arms into his new wind-breaker which Courtney had talked him into buying—but Palmer doesn't want to leave because there's one last thing that hasn't been said, only he can't think of what it is, except it's the thing that never gets said when you're partying and trying to say everything and then it's time to go and you say, wait a minute, wait a minute, there's something else, but you can't remember what it is, and all it is: I don't want the party to end.

He finds himself seated shotgun in the car with Courtney cranking the stubborn ignition. The fog has lifted above the street which is arc-lit gold. He should have asked Cheryl if he could take the beer with him, a fantasy of sitting in his skivvies on his bunk with a six-pack, boozing in the barracks until dawn, a very bad fantasy. But people never let you take the beer.

He has something else though, something that keeps him warm even as Courtney pumps the accelerator, something more potent than gas explosions inside a frigid engine block: the perfect skeletal imprint of Cheryl's palm on his left thigh, as tangible as a drawing of the human hand rendered in the medium of heat.

CHAPTER 15

Sunday morning, the least likely day of the week an enlisted man would expect to be hassled by the cadre, Palmer is awakened by the sound of someone repeating his name, raising him notch by notch from the depths of a hard beer sleep.

"Palmer, wake up."

He recognizes the voice of Legget, and is astounded that another enlisted man, a clerk/typist, would violate the unwritten code of Sunday morning. Blinking to part his sleep-encrusted eyelashes, Palmer rolls over and looks at the head-clerk of operations standing beside the bunk displaying an appropriately wary expression.

"Palmer, I've got a message for you."

"What is it?" Palmer croaks, his vocal chords dry from last night's cigarettes and beer.

"The Provost Marshal called this morning and wants you to come down to the MP station."

Palmer raises himself on his elbows. "What for?"

"He didn't say. But Top—" Legget pauses a moment. "Top asked everybody if you screwed up last week."

"Shit." Palmer drops onto his mattress. "What time is it?"

"Nine o'clock."

"This is my day off, Legget."

"That's what I told Top when he was in here this morning. He wanted me to drag you out of bed at seven, but I talked him into waiting until you woke up."

"Is Top here?"

"No, he went home."

"Then I didn't wake up, okay?"

"That's okay with me, Palmer. Except the Provost Marshal called back a few minutes ago asking if you were going to show up soon. He's leaving for Ft. Ord today and won't be back until Tuesday, and he wants to get something settled."

"Get what settled?"

"He didn't say. But listen, and I don't mean anything by this, but did you screw up last week?"

"Probably."

"I really think you ought to go see the Provost Marshal right now, Palmer. Top might even come back here and wake you up himself. Ever since—that business with the battalion commander."

"All right, I'm getting up." Palmer throws the blanket down the length of his overheated body. He gives Legget a resigned smile. He's not mad at Legget and wants him to know it. Someone once said you should never make enemies of cooks or supply sergeants, and Palmer includes head-clerks on that list.

"Take a quick shower," Legget says. "Don't even shave. I'll drive you to the PMO myself."

But Palmer does shave, and as Legget drives him down to main post Palmer holds his cap in his hand and sits at an angle on the padded canvas seat with his head thrust out the right side of the jeep to let the wind blow the hangover off his face.

The desk sergeant nods when he walks in and says the Provost Marshal is waiting. Palmer makes his way to the rear of the silent Sunday building and stops at the captain's door. He runs his fingers over his pockets to make sure all the flaps are buttoned. He squares his shoulders, takes two deep and ineffective breaths, and clears his throat. He knocks on the door and waits for permission to enter.

"Come in."

Cap in hand, Palmer steps into the office and marches up to the Provost Marshal's desk and salutes. "Sir, Private Palmer reports."

The Provost Marshal is seated behind his desk smiling, grinning in fact, obviously pleased that a mere two phone calls to Company D has brought Private Palmer here. He gives an abbreviated salute in return. "Thanks for coming down here, Palmer. I know this is your day off but I've got something here I'd like to get taken care of."

"Yes, sir."

The captain lifts a traffic ticket out of a drawer and places it on top of his desk. He rotates the slip of paper so Palmer can read it—the first traffic ticket Palmer ever wrote, the blue Mustang at Ft. Cronkite.

"I have a few questions about this ticket, Palmer. Now, the thing is, I'm sure you clocked this man correctly doing thirty-five miles-per-hour in a twenty-five mile-per-hour zone, but when a Military Policeman writes a traffic ticket, he has to take a number of things into consideration, the time of day, the traffic congestion, the weather conditions, and so forth."

He asks what the conditions were like that day, and Palmer tells him it was evening, the sky was clear, the road was dry, there were no other automobiles in the vicinity and no pedestrians, and the traffic-stop had taken place out in the countryside at least one mile from the nearest military housing—he almost says "lifer" housing.

"So basically," the Provost Marshal says, "except for violating the speed limit, it's clear that this man was not putting anyone's life in jeopardy. So a question arises, Palmer, as to whether or not this ticket was really justified."

Palmer understands immediately what the captain is up to. The utilization of serpentine logic is familiar, the indirect method of elaborating upon a touchy point, which in this case involves the pulling of a traffic ticket.

"So what I would like you to do, Private Palmer, is take this ticket with you and think about whether or not you feel it was justified. And if later on you decide that it was, you can come back here and we can discuss this further."

Hardly worth a Sunday morning roust from bed, but Palmer is nevertheless enjoying this dialogue, just as he had enjoyed talking to Lt. Norbert on the night of the motor pool, and Colonel Billings on the afternoon of the Battalion Documentarian. The Provost Marshall wants something from him, something only he can give, and he's willing to give it because you never know what might come from doing a special favor for an officer, especially a Provost Marshal (a man along with cooks and clerks whom you do not want to alienate), although he does know what comes of these things, which is always nothing.

He picks up the ticket. "I understand, sir."

The captain beams at him and stands up with military courtesy. "Thank you for coming in on your day off, Palmer. I want you to know that I really do appreciate this."

They exchange salutes, and Palmer does an about-face and walks out with the ticket in his hand, his hangover now lessened by this latest delusion of having the inside-track with a man of influence.

Legget is sitting in the jeep reading a paperback book which he stuffs into his back pocket the moment Palmer walks out the door. He watches Palmer with his eyebrows raised, but Palmer only strolls up to the jeep and climbs in and sits back with a sigh.

Palmer knows what Legget wants—The Lowdown. The Scoop. The Buzz. Why in the name of God was Private Palmer called to the PMO on a Sunday dawn? Top is probably seated in front of his TV in lifer housing right at this moment chewing an unlit cigar to shreds and wondering the same thing: who is this Private Palmer who is always getting called on-the-rug for things that could harm the reputation of Company D but somehow never do?

Palmer toys with Legget, a clerk/typist and thus a gossip-hound dying to learn not only the verdict, but what the trial was about in the first place. Palmer says nothing as the engine kicks over and the jeep rolls onto Lincoln Boulevard. He sits in silence, yawning and scratching the itchy underside of his shave-reddened chin and squinting with feigned interest at the passing landscape. Timing is everything. He finally plucks the traffic ticket from his pocket and glances over at Legget, who eyes the thin slip of paper as he makes the hairpin turn near the cemetery.

Legget is mildly disappointed at Palmer's explanation, a pulled ticket not the juicy item he had hoped for. Sundays are a slow-go in operations.

Palmer returns to his bunk and sleeps for three hours. When he awakens he feels only a bit fuzzy as he rolls out of bed to catch the end of noon chow, a hangover-pleasing feed of chicken, mashed potatoes and gravy. When he gets back to his room and sets about remaking his bunk properly, Courtney walks in smelling of Cheryl's perfume.

"What did the Provost Marshall want?" Courtney says, though the look on his face indicates that he already knows, and had probably just finished talking with Legget.

"Nothing," Palmer replies, digging into his shirt pocket and pulling out the crumpled ticket. "He wanted to talk to me about this." He hands it to Courtney.

"What about it?"

"He asked me to decide whether I really think I was justified in writing it."

"You bet your ass you were justified."

Palmer shrugs.

"What are you going to do about it?" Courtney says.

"Nothing."

"Nothing? Do you know what the Provost Marshal is trying to do?"

"Yes. He wants me to pull the ticket."

"That's bullshit, Palmer."

Palmer realizes too late that it was a mistake to have shown the ticket to Courtney, the straight-arrow, the STRAC soldier, the super troop. He takes it out of Courtney's hand and stuffs it into his pocket. "Did you just get back from Cheryl's?"

"You and I are going down to the Provost Marshal's office and hand that ticket back. I was there when you wrote it, and that ticket was justified."

"No we're not," Palmer says. "I don't care about the ticket."

"What do you mean, you don't care? That ticket was justified. The man was speeding."

"I know, but I don't care."

"Well why don't you care?"

"I don't know. I just don't."

Courtney's face mimics an expression that Palmer has seen many times before, on the faces of his parents, nuns, priests, gym coaches, and all of his Denver friends at one time or another, the lower lids of the eyes slightly puffed out.

"All right, Palmer," Courtney says. "Okay. But if the Provost Marshal ever tries to pull one of my tickets, I'll take it clear to the fucking Inspector General if I have to." He turns and walks out of the room.

Palmer leans face-forward against his bunk and rests his head on the mattress, wearied by his tendency to piss people off by doing absolutely nothing. Courtney is just the kind of person who really would take it all the way to the IG's office. He believes in this army shit.

Palmer steps outside to the porch to have his first smoke of the day. He opens the un-cracked pack of Camels which he had bought the night before out of smoker's panic but hadn't even touched. Lighting up, he sees a lone man coming this way across the narrow sidewalk which bisects the quad. He peers at him because he can tell even from this distance that the man is wearing a robe, a blue one. When the wind blows, the robe flaps open revealing pale green clothing which looks like pajamas. The man isn't even wearing shoes, just some kind of low-cut slippers which expose the fish-belly white of his ankles.

It's Thorpe. Just the sort of stupid fucking thing Thorpe would do, wear his robe to the PX to buy toothpaste or a pack of Winston or some goddamn thing. When Thorpe gets close to the porch, Palmer makes a big production out of turning his back on him at the very moment when he might have been saying, "Hi, Thorpe," had they been friends or at least speaking acquaintances.

Thorpe steps up onto the porch as Palmer begins his turn while blowing a long cloud of smoke as a kind of signal to Thorpe that he is getting as big a snub as he had dealt Palmer during that detail-dodging noon a few weeks earlier. Prior to beginning his turn though, Palmer tries to make eye-contact so that Thorpe will fully comprehend the depth of the snub. But Thorpe doesn't look at him. He just keeps staring straight ahead at whatever it is he always seems to be staring at.

Nevertheless, Palmer feels good after Thorpe has gone into the building, feels good for having shit on him. When he finishes his cigarette he is no longer annoyed at Courtney because he has given it all to Thorpe, even if Thorpe didn't know he was getting it, which he may not have because he had walked into the foyer without even glancing at Palmer, which was kind of annoying.

Palmer field-strips his cigarette, then goes into the latrine and steps into a stall and sits on the commode. He takes out the traffic ticket and studies it for a bit, trying to decide whether or not to flush it away. He knows that he is not going to return it to the PMO and risk pissing-off the Provost Marshal, whom he decides is either a buddy of the SP6 who had been driving the Mustang, or else a buddy of a high-ranking personage who knows the driver.

He decides not to flush it away. He might need it someday in someone's court martial, probably his own. He folds it neatly and puts it into his billfold. If nothing else, he will have a unique souvenir of his stretch in the service: the first traffic ticket he ever wrote. Someday he will be able to tell his grand-children, "I pulled that fucker."

He leaves the stall and washes his hands at a sink. When he turns the flow of water off he hears a sound like men hurrying up the stairs, the thud of running feet and voices raised. He doesn't pay much attention to it, although he does think it is odd because men never run and yell in the barracks.

When he steps into the hallway he finds a crowd of men standing at the bottom of the stairs talking in muted voices and looking up at the landing, that tight and difficult spot which had given the troops trouble when they were hauling crates up to the second floor.

He crosses to the bulletin board and looks up the stairs to see what's going on. The landing is empty. Nothing at all is going on as far as he can see. He spots Courtney near the exit from the mess hall and is about to ask him what the attraction is, when the foyer goes silent but for the sound of footsteps descending from the second floor.

Four men are coming down, three dressed in the white fatigues of hospital orderlies, and the fourth wearing a famil-iar blue robe. It's Thorpe again, now surrounded by the men in white who look like they're not so much escorting him as herding him down the stairs, one man on each side and one behind who looks like he's ready to jump on Thorpe's back if he tries to run. Balled up in Thorpe's fists are a pair of blue jeans and a shirt, his nervous hands packing the wad of clothing like a snowball as he shouts "I want to go home!"

He doesn't seem to be directing this comment toward anyone in particular. He continues staring straight ahead as his feet negotiate the steps one by one in a kind of jarring slow descent, his escorts holding their hands up prepared to catch him if he falls but not touching him. When he reaches the bottom of the stairs, the audience parts to let him pass.

"I'm going home!" Thorpe shouts, his voice ragged and mournful and even frustrated because it looks like he had been interrupted while packing. It is only now that Palmer realizes he's wearing a Letterman General Hospital robe and pajamas.

The crowd moves outside to watch as Thorpe and the orderlies shuffle along the sidewalk toward the parking lot where an ambulance is waiting with its rear doors wide open. The orderlies help Thorpe climb in. Two get in with him, and the third shuts the doors and runs around to the cab and hops in and starts the engine, but drives out of the lot slowly. No red light or siren, indicating that speed will not be a critical factor in this emergency, will not facilitate the cure.

Palmer looks at Courtney. Their disagreement forgotten in the wake of this peculiar moment, they don't know what to say. Nobody knows what to say. The men begin drifting away, to go on about their business and to wait for the explanation that everyone knows will surface eventually.

The explanation comes predictably from Legget, who has only to tell one person, so that within an hour the entire barracks has heard various correct and incorrect versions of the story which begins with an incident that took place at two in the morning. Thorpe had walked into the operations office wearing his Class A uniform and used the company phone to call a taxi for a trip to the airport. The CQ runner, an enlisted man, overheard this and went to find Sgt. Weigand to tell him about it, because nobody was scheduled to sign out of the company at two in the morning. Sgt. Weigand went upstairs to Thorpe's room to see what it was all about, and came down five minutes later and got on the phone to Letterman General Hospital. Ten minutes later, an ambulance came and took Thorpe away.

This is the first part of Legget's story.

The second part begins when Thorpe walked out of the psychiatric ward of Letterman General Hospital without anyone trying to stop him or apparently even noticing that he was leaving. He walked all the way across main post in his hospital clothes and up the hill to the quad. He went into his room on the second floor and opened his wall locker and started gathering his things to go home. That's when Palmer came out of the latrine and found everyone looking up the stairs.

So Palmer had been a witness to the third and last part of Legget's story, the return of the men in white.

But after hearing parts one and two, all he can think about is the long walk Thorpe had taken from the hospital up to the quad, the same route he and Beaudry had once walked, except that Thorpe wasn't even wearing low-quarters but cheap, thin-soled, disposable hospital slippers. And with all that walking, the soles of his feet might have been blistered, might even have been bruised or bloodied, but Palmer doesn't know because when Thorpe had gotten close to him, Palmer had been too busy perfecting the blatant gestures of his snub to look at the man's feet. He had been too busy turning his back on Thorpe.

CHAPTER 16

Palmer will turn twenty-one at midnight, but he keeps this fact to himself, the third and last of the most significant birthdays—sixteen meant a driver's license, eighteen meant 3.2 beer and a draft card, but he knows that the biggest change now will be only that he can get bombed in strip joints.

He has already made his plans for his private celebration on Saturday. No more long marches in the drunk dark, he will take a taxi down into San Francisco like other troops do on weekends, and get out at Market Street and walk into bars at random and order boilermakers, though in each bar he will drink only one scotch and a beer to toast the party he won't have but had long looked forward to celebrating in Denver with his high-school friends, a kind of disappointment.

Courtney is his road partner on the last day-shift before they go back to the swing-shift. Palmer can't believe that three weeks have already passed by. One more week on the road, and then they start the training cycle for a month, then detail month, then back on the road again. He hates the way his army duty has turned out. He wants to pull MP duty all the time. Then Courtney mentions that he and Cheryl had their first fight the previous evening.

"What about?" Palmer asks, not that he wants to know. He doesn't want to know anything about anybody, but he knows it's expected of him.

"She wants to get a roommate."

This is interesting. It could make them a foursome. "How come?"

"Money. She isn't making enough at the shop to live on decently."

Decently. Palmer had lived two years after high school on fifty-dollar weekly paychecks. There were no parents or priests in his life, just a senile landlord and a door with a lock on it. That was pretty decent.

"Before we met she was thinking about finding a roommate, but then she put it on hold," Courtney says. He steers the car onto a descending dirt road skirting a stone wall, the south perimeter of the Presidio.

"So now that she's had her fill of you, she wants a roommate?" Palmer says.

Courtney doesn't laugh. But after a moment says, "Fill of me is right."

They're both chuckling as they come to the bottom of the hill, the end of the road not far from the flat oval of a putting green. Flagpole still in the cup. No vandals on a military golf course. Courtney makes a U-turn and drives back up to Arguello Boulevard.

"Shit, Palmer, a roommate!" He bashes the steering wheel with a fist. "She has a Murphy bed for crying out loud. I can't date a woman who has a Murphy bed and a roommate."

Palmer doesn't know what to say. He doesn't have enough experience with beds and women to offer an insight— not nearly enough, if none at all can be defined as "nearly."

Courtney stops the car at the intersection and lets the engine idle. "I offered her a deal. I said I would pay half her rent. Then I would have a key."

"What did she say?"

"No. She said she isn't ready for that. I told her it would

only mean she could quit worrying about having to find a roommate. It's not like I'd live there."

"Well maybe." Palmer stops because he doesn't really want to get involved, doesn't want to start offering unsolicited opinions, or especially, bad advice.

"Maybe what?"

"Maybe she just wants another woman around so, you know, she'll feel safe."

"She said that. She did say she'd feel safer with another woman around. She's had roommates before. Her last one got married four months ago. She thought she wanted to live alone, but now she's not so sure."

Palmer thinks of the things he might say to Courtney, like, dump her, or learn to live with it. Just then a car filled with GIs enters the Arguello gate at a high rate of speed and Courtney pulls in behind them. He clocks the car doing forty-five in a twenty-five, and flips on the red light. The driver is a PFC. One of the three passengers is a buck sergeant, and all are engineers from none other than the home of the bitter Screaming Eagle, just down the block from Company D.

Courtney has a personal rule that he lives by: he won't ticket anyone below the rank of sergeant, will give them only warnings, whereas he always tickets sergeants and officers. But Palmer hasn't bought into that, not yet, so he writes up the driver himself, then waits for Courtney to bitch about it, but Courtney doesn't say a word.

On Saturday morning Palmer can't sleep past ten A.M. because the thought of going to his first legal wet-bar awakens him prematurely. He goes down to the latrine and showers, shaves, and smiles at his crew cut in the mirror. He knows he will be tagged for a soldier in the hippie bars because every civilian his age has hair down to his ass—this has become Sgt. Sherman's thing: "Palmer. Barbershop." It happens every ten days. Palmer once saw Sgt. Sherman hand a reluctant GI a dollar after the man claimed he was too broke to pay for a haircut.

His wardrobe has grown since the night of the PX slacks. In his locker hangs three new short-sleeved shirts, two pair of blue jeans, a coat and a windbreaker. He still hasn't bought tennis shoes because he feels uneasy about having everything right all at once. He's thinking about wearing his combat boots into town when Courtney walks into the room and gapes at him.

"You're awake!"

Palmer doesn't want to reveal what he's up to. He doesn't want Courtney—though not just him but anybody—to be a part of his melancholy celebration.

"Are you busy today?" Courtney says.

Palmer points his thumb in the direction of the city and mumbles, "I'm going downtown."

"Well listen. Cheryl and I are going to the beach this afternoon, and you're invited."

"The beach?"

"Sunset Beach. We're going to have a picnic. Drink a little wine, get a little sunburn. Are you with us?"

This sounds good, and thus annoys Palmer because he's been looking forward to holding his birthday party alone in the cloying gloom of darkened bars in the heart of an indifferent metropolis. But Cheryl might wear a bikini.

"Okay."

Palmer brings his projector and movies along because, Courtney tells him, Cheryl insisted she wanted to see them. When Cheryl lets them into her apartment, Courtney sets the box of films on the coffee table and says, "This bastard almost got away from us."

Cheryl goes into the kitchen and brings out a cake with lit candles poked into the frosting. Palmer doesn't like surprise parties, doesn't even like to go to them for other people, but smiles and stands there feeling stupid as Cheryl sets the cake down on the coffee table and says, "Happy Birthday, Palmer." She stands on her tiptoes and kisses him on the lips. Unprepared, unbraced, his lips pucker but hers are no longer there. "Blow out the candles," she says.

He leans over, then feels incompetent when the twenty-first doesn't go out. No wish.

"The sonofabitch was leaving the barracks when I found him," Courtney says. "I didn't think the lazy bastard would get up until noon. The next thing I know he's headed down-town to get shit-faced."

"How did you know this was my birthday?" Palmer says.

They both stare at him. "Remember the last time you were here?" Courtney says. "You must have told us fifty times that today was your birthday."

"I did?"

"At least fifty times," Cheryl says.

Palmer wants to call them liars, except Cheryl did bake a cake. He had been under the impression that he always remembered everything he ever said or did when he was drunk, so this is a revelation. He starts taking off his wind-breaker and talking fast to mask his embarrassment. "So are we really going to the beach today or what's the story here anyway?"

"Put your coat back on," Cheryl says, picking up the cake and returning it to the kitchen. "We're having a birthday picnic for you at Sunset Beach."

"Tonight we'll watch your movies," Courtney says.

Cheryl already has a basket packed with food. She cuts some cake and wraps it in cellophane, and puts three bottles of red wine in with it.

They don't take Courtney's car because Cheryl doesn't want him to drink and drive. They walk down the block to Irving and wait for the Judah trolley. It takes them on a straight shot across low rolling hills three miles west to Sunset Beach. End of track is a cul-de-sac surrounded by sand hills.

They get off and hike to the top of a dune and look out at the last straight-edge of America, white sandy beach running without a curve in both directions. Gulls levitate in the breeze. Tiny birds with stick legs skitter along the surf toeing scrimshaw into the sand.

"Let's set up below the bluff," Courtney says.

Palmer follows behind them, watching Cheryl's butt cupped in the tight fade of her jean cutoffs. He knows she's wearing an orange bikini top beneath her T-shirt because he'd seen it through the white cotton fabric back in the apartment.

They find a cove, a half-moon carved into a fifteen-foot high cliff where a fallen tree trunk lies barkless and sanded silver by the wind. It serves as Palmer's chair back.

Courtney begins collecting driftwood for a fire, and Cheryl pulls things from the basket: blanket, paper plates, Dixie cups for wine. Fine wine for his birthday, the bottles have corks. Palmer fiddles with a corkscrew and shatters the cork and has to push it down into the neck where it bobs among the flotsam. He pours the fragments into a cup and tosses them onto the sand, then pours himself a drink which tastes exactly like all the illegal wine he has ever swallowed.

Courtney and Cheryl strip, stacking their shirts and pants neatly on the smooth swayback of the log. Cheryl stands exposed in the complete orange bikini, and Palmer gives her body a furtive, deliberate, all-encompassing quick study. Breasts bulging half-revealed at the top. Flesh pale just above the bikini bottom. Navel drawing muscles toward itself. White flesh of thighs and ribs. Blonde sheen of fine body-hair highlighted by the sun as she turns to look at the ocean.

Courtney has on a pair of purple trunks. Tanned, he's a runner and has no body fat. His limbs look like a detailed medical drawing of the human muscular-system, the brawn that had plucked Palmer like a rag doll from the shower room floor.

Palmer doesn't take off any clothes, but he might do it if he gets drunk enough to not care if Cheryl sees his fish-belly white chest and stringy arms and legs.

"How many hotdogs would you like?" Cheryl says.

None, but he asks for one.

He refills his drink and watches Courtney break kindling over his knee, using split sticks to build a small cathedral of wood in a scooped sand pit. Palmer digs out his Zippo and hands it to Courtney, who lights a twig, holding his palms around the fragile flame and working it into a blaze like the Boy Scout he probably once was: Eagle. Palmer never got past Tenderfoot even though he was in the Scouts for two years.

Cheryl holds a skewered hotdog above the flames, and Palmer stares at its bubbling skin and considers the fact that he would have been on Market Street by now if they had not invited him here. Eventually he would have started talking to older men, to find out if they had served in WWII like his father had. He would have made certain to mention that he was in the army and that this was his twenty-first birthday. None of the men would be impressed or offer to buy him a drink, and eventually he would walk out embarrassed.

Cheryl and Courtney each have a cup of wine, but drinking does not seem central to their moment. Palmer pours himself another cup full which dribbles onto his lap because a strong and erratic breeze is coming off the ocean, blowing smoke into his face. Cheryl hands him the first hotdog. He squeezes ketchup onto the bun and holds the paper plate tight in the wind and forces himself to eat it even though he's not hungry. Should have brought beer to wash down the food. Planning is everything. But the potato chips go down fine.

Cheryl puts a thin slice of cake onto his plate, then fixes two more plates. She and Courtney sit together against the log and chew and stare at the ocean. The solemnity of repast descends on the party, and no one talks. The air is filled with the endless crush of breakers, and seagulls crying in the sun. A single white sail moves along the horizon. Are there sharks in the water? Palmer sips at his wine and considers taking off his clothes.

"Would you like another hotdog?" Cheryl asks. Her Southern accent emerges in the word "like" so that she says "lack." Palmer smiles and says yes. He doesn't really want another but wants to get along with everybody today, and knows that some people take eating as seriously as grammar, or the proper way to parallel park.

After Cheryl hands him the hotdog, she and Courtney get up and walk down to the water's edge to stick their toes in the brine. Their backs are to Palmer, so he buries the hotdog in the sand beside his left thigh. Cheryl and Courtney begin walking along the waterline with their arms around each other's waists, and Palmer speculates upon how many seconds will pass before Courtney drops his hand and squeezes her ass.

"Mister, do you know any place around here that rents metal detectors?"

The voice of a child coming from behind the log, Palmer looks around and sees a little girl maybe eight years old with black bangs and dark brown eyes. Did she see him bury the hotdog? And more importantly, will she tell?

"What did you say?" Palmer says.

"Do you know any place around here that rents metal detectors?"

He can hardly comprehend what she is saying. Where did she come from? She steps around the log, her sandaled feet frosted with dirt rather than sand. Asian maybe, or Mexican, her voice is clear and unaccented as she puts her hands on her hips and begins explaining. "My little brother lost the keys to our car in the sand, so I thought that we could rent a metal detector to find them. Do you know any place around here that rents metal detectors?"

"Metal detectors," Palmer says as he sits up straight and looks around at the top of the bluff to see whether an entire family of brown-eyed Okies might be standing up there waiting for their little girl to talk to the crew cut bum drinking wine on the beach. He doesn't see anyone, but imagines a father asleep on the front seat of a beat-up station wagon, it would be red with white trim, the chrome-stripping rusted by salt air.

"I don't know," he says. He visualizes the landscape he had passed coming from the bus stop. Mostly apartment buildings across the boulevard which runs the length of the beach. He can't recall seeing even a grocery store. "I don't think there are any places that rent metal detectors around here."

The girl takes a deep breath that lifts her whole body. She sighs. She's exasperated, but Palmer can see she's a take-charge sort of kid, and he wonders why she's doing this without any grownup supervision.

"Are you alone?" he says, then regrets it immediately because it sounds wrong.

"Yes," she says, then she too regrets it. Something in her eyes recedes, and she takes a step back from him verbally. "Except for my brothers are with me and my father and my mother." Her voice fades, as it will when children try to lie to grownups they don't know well enough to fool.

"I really don't think there are any stores close by here at all where you could rent a metal detector," Palmer says. He hasn't had a conversation with a child in years. He wants to go with her to the spot where her little brother ruined their day and dig around in the sand until they find the keys. Get Courtney and Cheryl to help.

The girl takes another deep breath and sighs. "Well, I guess the only thing to do is just keep on looking."

Always the only thing to do. Palmer nods and purses his lips and says good luck, talking to her like she's a grownup because she's out here all alone acting like one even though he knows she doesn't stand a chance of finding those keys.

The girl trudges off down the beach, and Palmer watches her heels kicking up the soft sand which impedes her progress. Beaches are strange, things slow down. She heads toward a low fogbank which is drifting onto the shore a bit further down.

He looks in the other direction, and sees Cheryl and Courtney walking side by side but no longer embracing. He senses they are having an argument as they walk head-bowed along the edge of the water. He takes a drink from the bottle, no Dixie cup, and decides to make jokes when they return. He will tell them about the little girl. He looks to see how much distance she has made, but the fog has already taken her, leaving only a trail of tiny footprints marking a gentle sweep toward the cloud. She will never find a metal detector, will never find those keys, and will probably end up losing her way back home.

The wind shifts, and smoke from the dying fire blows into his face and stings his eyes. He lets the drawn tears run unimpeded to wash away the smoke which is a hell of a lot stronger than cigarette smoke. He takes a tube from the pack which is already half-empty and lights up. Inhale. Exhale. Smoke it down to the butt and crush it out in the giant ashtray upon which he sits. More wine. If he could stop time, he would do it. If he could resign from the army he would do it. If he was a civilian in Denver he would be drinking beer and watching The Bowery Boys on Channel 2 right now. He would be hungover, and in despair over the shit job he would have to go back to on Monday morning.

Cheryl and Courtney aren't talking when they get back, but he senses that they are determined not to let their problems ruin the party. Courtney pops the cork on the second bottle and takes a large swallow and hands it to Cheryl, who takes a large swallow too. Palmer likes that. He takes it from her and has a drink.

"Is anybody hungry?" Cheryl says.

Palmer shakes his head no and pats his shirted belly. He glances down at the sand next to his thigh and is horrified to see flies crawling all over the spot where the hotdog is hidden. He sweeps them away and presses his hand flat against the evidence.

"I'll take a hotdog," Courtney says, but when Cheryl pulls one out of the plastic wrap he grabs it out of her hand.

"Let me cook it for you," she says.

"No thanks." He bites it in half.

Cheryl begins clearing away the windblown blanket for a sunbath, lifting it by a corner and giving it a deft snap sending sand flying. She does not invite Courtney to lie next to her. She stretches out face-down, and Palmer examines her with his peripheral vision. Long back. Ivory thighs. Can't bring himself to glance at the tight place where the bathing-suit bunches between her buttocks with Courtney nearby, so he busies himself lighting another cigarette. Courtney fiddles with the dying coals of the fire, as if undecided about bringing them back to life.

The sunlight fuses with the alcohol and begins to lull Palmer's brain, and he lets his head tap back against the log to get a Colorado suntan: red face and white chest. Sitting absolutely motionless, he feels himself drift into a doze. He hears the breakers, the occasional seagull, and grows so motionless that he can't even sense his arms or legs unless he twitches a muscle. The strange occasional buzz of a bee hovers near his nose and keeps him from sinking fully into unconsciousness. The bee flies up his nose and he abruptly sits up and realizes it was his snoring.

Eyes damp and matted when he opens them, he begins licking his sticky mouth. He looks to his left and sees Courtney and Cheryl seated against the log wrapped in the blanket, watching him and grinning.

"You were snoring," Courtney says. "It sounded like a bear killing a horse in a wind tunnel."

Cheryl, too ladylike to laugh, smiles at the ocean.

Palmer looks at his watch and is surprised and then annoyed to see that he was asleep forty-five minutes. Almost an hour stolen from his drinking time, although he does feel pretty good, his body tingling, his brain clear. The fog bank which had taken the little girl is almost upon the campsite, though not nearly as thick as it had appeared from the distance.

"I thought you were a drinker, Palmer," Courtney says.

His mouth a bit numb, Palmer has to work it to shape his words. "What do you mean?"

"One bottle of wine and you pass out."

"I didn't pass out, I fell asleep."

Cheryl and Courtney start giggling, which is irritating, but then Palmer starts giggling too. The log shudders against their backs and rocks in its bed.

"I had a visitor while you guys were gone," Palmer says.

They squint at him in the failing sunlight. He tells them about the little girl, and points toward her footprints, but they've been erased by the wind.

Courtney nods. "Probably the Ghost of Sunset Beach."

"It was a little Mexican girl," Palmer says.

"Lots of people have seen her," Courtney says. "In nineteen fifty-five a tidal wave hit the beach right here and washed away a family having a picnic. Every year on the anniversary someone runs into this girl who claims to be searching for the keys to her family's car—and it's always the same little girl."

Palmer stands up and peers at the horizon. "Bite me," he says.

He picks up the wine bottle and tips it back, then passes it to Cheryl who takes a swig and hands it to Courtney, who takes a swig too. Palmer is pleased. The afternoon is coming to an end, but his friends aren't quitting on him.

He takes the bottle down to the shore and hears at his back the crackle of cellophane and the soft cleansing snap of the blanket as Cheryl and Courtney begin policing up the picnic site. The heels of Palmer's shoes sink into the sand soaked by the tide. He looks at the water as it recedes leaving seaweed and tiny scuttling critters seeking shelter. He stares at the horizon. He could get into a boat and sail straight across the water to a shell-pocked beach in Vietnam. Cheryl and Courtney join him, the picnic basket gripped in Courtney's fist.

"I should have brought my movie camera," Palmer says.

"Next time," Courtney says.

Palmer looks at him, then at Cheryl. She's dressed. If he had brought his camera, he could have had a movie of her almost nude forever.

"Next time," he says.

They walk the shore as far as a public restroom not far from the cul-de-sac. They make a brief stop to use the concrete facilities which smell like AWOL soldiers. The trolley has only just arrived, so they have to sit in it for fifteen minutes until it goes back on schedule.

Palmer wants to open the third bottle of wine. He'll step off the trolley out of sight of the driver and pop the cork, hide the bottle up the sleeve of his windbreaker, and sip surreptitiously on the trip back. But he doesn't do it. The trolley is full by the time they reach the stop at Irving. Can other passengers smell the booze on his breath? They get off and go into a corner grocery where Cheryl buys a gallon jug of red wine and Palmer buys two packs of Camels. Courtney buys a twenty-five cent cigar, which Palmer thinks is a pose, but a pretty good one, so he buys one too.

They carry the stogies unlit between their lips like Top as they climb the hill to the apartment. When they get inside, Cheryl tells them not to worry about getting sand on the floor, then she goes to take quick shower. While she's in the bathroom, Palmer sets the movie projector up on the coffee table. He aims the lens below one of Cheryl's library paintings, and when she comes out dressed in shorts and a blouse and smelling of Zest, they pour wine and watch the main feature: The Lieutenant Pervert Show.

"There I am," Courtney says, the giant shadow of his finger pointing at his image.

"You look very handsome," Cheryl says. She laughs at the cock-poking ballet, but doesn't ask to see it again.

Then Palmer shows what he calls The Bird Films. Here's a man giving him the finger at the quick-kill range in basic training. Here are five men seated on the back porch of a barracks, flipping him off. Here's an entire chow line giving him the bird. Because Courtney had trained at Ft. Gordon, he has an interest in what are fundamentally dull home-movies, the faces of strangers in someone else's high-school yearbook. Bald pimpled heads, lackluster eyes, Palmer can still match a name to every face. "That guy there got the clap in Hopkinsville," is the only war story he tells.

Cheryl brings out the cake with the candles relit and melting onto the frosting. Palmer blows them all out keeping his wish to himself, then has to force himself to accept another slice, but finds he's hungry after all. Cheryl gives him a present, a small gift-wrapped package which fits into the palm of his hand like a box which could contain an engagement ring. He rattles it, listens, wants to make a wisecrack but can't think of one, then tears open the paper exposing the familiar Kodak yellow of a box of eight-millimeter home-movie film.

"Now I really do wish I'd brought my camera."

"I wish you had too," Cheryl says.

"We've had this conversation," Courtney says.

I'll bring it next time, Palmer tells himself, fingering the smooth aluminum puck in his hand. He expects to spend a lot of weekends in this apartment during the next seventeen months, as many weekends as Courtney will tolerate anyway.

The birthday party ends before nine o'clock, the longest party Palmer has ever left so early. When they put on their coats to leave, Cheryl gives him another kiss.

Outside, Palmer climbs into Courtney's car and decides he will go to the bowling alley as soon as they get back to the Presidio, but then he can barely walk when they get to the Company D parking lot. Courtney escorts him inside and warns him not to take a shower ha ha then hangs around while Palmer climbs onto his bunk.

"I'm going back to Cheryl's," Courtney says. "See you tomorrow night."

Thanks for the beach party, Palmer says, and as soon as the porch door shuts he realizes that he had left his birthday present at Cheryl's. But that's all right. He can drop by and get it any time, Cheryl said so, and this thought makes him feel so good that he considers getting dressed and slipping out to the bowling alley for a nightcap, three or four nightcaps even. But the idea only makes him laugh—his least favorite thing in the world: the party is over and he knows it.

PART THREE

CHAPTER 17

Palmer wakes up from his birthday party at noon dehydrated, which is good in its way because he doesn't have to piss, the curse of beer. When he makes it into the mess hall in time for late lunch he is balled up in the happy pain of this particular celebration and so does not notice the peculiar silence in the room, broken only by occasional whispers that he notices only after he has swallowed a glass of milk and eaten a piece of chicken.

There aren't that many men in a noon mess hall on a Sunday to begin with, but the three men seated at the table next to his aren't even clowning or cracking jokes about the food or discussing their Saturday night in town. "Why did he do it?" one man says, and another says, "I saw him sitting on his bunk at midnight polishing his boots with the lights off."

So Palmer becomes aware that something odd has happened in the way that you can smell smoke before you see it or the fire. Even the KPs are sweeping and refilling salt-shakers without the smiles or the wisecracks working KPs always utilize to mask the misery and embarrassment of the job.

Palmer finishes half his food, returns the tray to the stack in the kitchen window, then goes to the latrine where he rinses his mouth without benefit of Crest or Listerine. He looks at his face in the mirror. Puffy from wine. Now that he can buy hard liquor he supposes things will take a downturn. He sits in a stall four doors away from the stall where he once threw up and waits indifferently for the hangover purge of his guts wrought by hot chicken and ice-cold milk.

Four men are standing by the Coke machine talking quietly when he comes out. He doesn't know them, or he would ask what's going on. They're from the platoons upstairs, and are also new in the company, which makes him feel like a veteran even though he has been here only seven weeks.

As he walks past the door to the operations office, Sgt. Weigand comes out. Palmer slows down and says, "Sergeant," loud enough for Weigand but no one else to hear. "What happened?"

Weigand glances at him. "Thorpe jumped off the Golden Gate Bridge last night and killed himself." The sergeant goes on down the hall and knocks on the door to Captain Weller's office.

Palmer looks into the operations office and sees Top and Sgt. Sherman, and two men in civilian clothing who might be CID gathered around the desk of SP4 Legget, who is talking quietly on a telephone.

Palmer walks on down the hall toward his room, thinking about the moment three weeks earlier when he had seen Thorpe looking over the railing of the bridge. Then he hears his name called. He turns around and sees Sgt. Sherman standing outside the operations door.

"Palmer, come here. I want to talk to you."

There's no edge in his voice as there always is when Palmer has done something wrong or needs a haircut or some brass wants to talk to him and no one knows what about. "Yes, sergeant?"

"Did you hear about Thorpe?"

"Yes, sergeant."

"Battalion asked us to assign a man for an escort to accompany Thorpe's body to Wichita, Kansas. That's his hometown. I'm offering you the detail."

Palmer doesn't want it, and so doesn't answer.

"You should take it, Palmer," Sgt. Sherman says. "It's good duty. Five days TDY, and the army picks up all expenses. You leave Tuesday afternoon and fly to Wichita, and you don't have to be back until Saturday night."

Five days away from the Presidio. Six, if he takes the mythical day-of-grace which everyone knows does not really exist, except this one will because it falls on a Sunday. If he accepts the mission he will miss out on his fourth and last week of MP duty, and he doesn't want to miss out on that because it will be another two months before Company D goes on the road again. But in basic training he had made a vow that he would never refuse any assignment the army gave him, and he still believes in the vow and always will. He also understands that Sgt. Sherman is handing him a kind of peace offering. The sergeant had exercised his prerogative as platoon leader to deny Palmer a promotion which he felt Palmer did not deserve, and now he is attempting to balance that by offering a detail which, under most circumstances, would be considered a plum job: five days TDY, all expenses paid. He also understands that Sgt. Sherman has no interest in being friends, he just wants everybody to get along.

Palmer nods, and tells Sgt. Sherman he will do it.

On Monday morning Sgt. Sherman gives Palmer the keys to the CQ jeep. He drives down to the redbrick finance offices across from the parade grounds and picks up some advance travel pay. The SP4 clerk in charge tells him to get receipts for everything so he can be reimbursed when he gets back. He drives down to the marina to a white clapboard WWII building housing Graves Registration and meets with a civilian, an elderly man who hands him paperwork to be signed by the mortician whom he will meet at the Wichita airport. From a desk drawer the man pulls out an American flag folded tri-corner, and tells Palmer to drape it over the coffin as soon as he arrives in Kansas.

Palmer drives to battalion headquarters and talks to a SP4 clerk/typist named Croner who gives him a copy of his travel orders and an envelope containing a round-trip plane ticket for a Tuesday United flight. Palmer asks questions about everything and take notes, intimidated by the magnitude of the assignment. What if he loses the coffin in-transit? But SP4 Croner assures him that there's nothing to the assignment at all. He will get on a plane in San Francisco and get off in Wichita. A mortician will be there to meet him and sign for Thorpe's body. In all probability the mission will be finished within an hour after he arrives.

This sounds all right. Five days to lie around in a Holiday Inn and drink beer and forget that he's in the army. "Remember to get receipts for everything," Croner tells him just before he leaves.

Finished with his official business, Palmer decides to drive down to the main post PX. He is fucking-off a bit because he is unsupervised, but he wants to buy some sort of briefcase large enough to carry both his orders and the tri-cornered flag. After looking over the merchandise he decides it probably would be more proper to hand-carry the flag, and he ends up buying a cheap thin black-plastic briefcase for the paperwork alone.

When he gets back to barracks, the first platoon rooms are empty. Back on swing-shift, the off-duty troops are not hanging around the barracks until it's time to go to work. He spends an hour preparing his Class A uniform and polishing the brass shield on his saucer cap and putting a shine on his dress shoes, then decides to get a haircut even though Sgt. Sherman had made him get one less than a week earlier.

At eleven A.M. on Tuesday he goes to the operations office and calls a cab to take him to San Francisco International Airport. Company D is quiet, as it has been ever since the news of Thorpe's suicide was officially passed along to the troops. The previous evening there had been no shouting in the showers, no evening laughter and grab-ass in the hallways. Nobody seems to have known Thorpe very well, not even the men in his squad. Palmer is glad to be getting away from this peculiar silence, even if he is not especially glad to be going to Wichita.

At the airport ticket counter he talks to a clerk, who tells him where the coffin will be loaded, and allows him to go through a security door to the plane after Palmer tells him he wants to see it loaded for himself, to make sure nothing goes wrong.

The coffin is resting in the sunlight on a gurney among baggage carts stacked with luggage. Two handlers wheel the coffin to a conveyor belt and slide it on. The coffin rises toward the dark doorway in the belly of the plane, where two gloved hands reach out to drag it in.

Palmer hates flying. The alarming thrust of the takeoff and the extreme tilt of the cabin has always made him uneasy, so he considers buying a mixed-drink to calm himself as the flight attendants begin wheeling carts down the aisle. He likes the idea that his very first legal mixed-drink would be purchased ty-thousand feet above the earth, but he is concerned about getting drunk and losing his orders and missing the connection and screwing up the whole funeral, so he orders a 7-Up instead.

The flag is resting on his lap, and the briefcase is tucked into the overhead rack. His concern is mostly for the flag, which is why he decides not to smoke, afraid of getting ashes on it, or burning a hole in the fabric. When turbulence jostles the plane, he worries about spilling his soft drink on the flag, and drinks the pop quickly.

He makes himself sleep as much as possible, though it's mostly a doze, the annoying hydraulic sounds of the plane continually pulling him back to consciousness. When the air-pressure begins popping his eardrums he wakes up and looks out the window and sees the scattered nighttime lights of Wichita below. He lifts the flag from his lap and brushes at it and begins going over the few things he has to do next. SP4 Croner was right. There is nothing to this. Once off the plane he will find the loading dock and sign the coffin over to the mortician, and after that he will go outside and find a cab and tell the driver to take him to the nearest Holiday Inn.

Palmer is the last passenger off the plane, waiting with military courtesy while the civilians shuffle down the crowded aisle. At the gate he explains his mission to a clerk and asks directions to the loading dock. He picks up his duffel bag at a carousel and walks down a long empty corridor and through a set of double-doors onto a covered loading-dock which looks just like all the warehouse docks he had ever worked on during his shit jobs in Denver. The air is hot here, thick, and feels damp.

Thorpe's coffin is resting on a lone gurney in the middle of the otherwise empty dock. An American flag has already been draped over it. Surprised, Palmer wonders who could have done that. The baggage handlers further along the dock? What is he supposed to do with the flag under his arm?

A shining gray hearse arrives and makes a circle on the concrete driveway outside the building and begins backing up to the dock. When it stops, the driver's door opens and an elderly man gets out, skinny in a gray suit which flaps in a Wichita wind coming through the open garage doors. He climbs a concrete staircase and looks at Palmer through his wire-rim glasses. He grins, showing gold bridgework. "Private Palmer? I'm Walter Gerlach, owner of the Hillside Mortuary."

A quick handshake and Palmer unzips his briefcase and digs out the paperwork, but Mr. Gerlach doesn't even look at it. He smiles and raises his eyebrows, his whole face going into rubbery motion as he speaks. "Now listen, it's just you and me here, those bastards won't lift a finger," pointing at the baggage handlers. "We're going to have to slide the coffin into the car ourselves."

Palmer drops the papers back into his briefcase and holds up the tri-cornered flag. "I was told to drape this over the coffin as soon as I got here."

"Oh—well." Mr. Gerlach rubs his chin and looks at the coffin. "It already has a flag."

Palmer decides that it would probably be best to do as he was told rather than pretend to know what he is doing. "I have orders to put this on the coffin, so I would like to do that."

"Well all right, let's do it," Mr. Gerlach says. They unfold the flag and stand at each end of the coffin and lower it squarely on top of the first flag. A minor snafu, but it annoys Palmer.

Mr. Gerlach grabs the handle and guides the gurney to the edge of the dock, putting a bit of English on it by swinging his bony hips so that it rolls squarely up to the door of the hearse. He has done this before. "Give it a shove," he says, hopping to the floor.

Palmer puts his hands on the coffin above Thorpe's head or else feet and pushes it smoothly into the hearse. Mr. Gerlach leans inside to lock it down, then closes the door.

"All right," Mr. Gerlach says, clapping his hands once and raising his eyebrows, "let's hit the road. I'll be dropping you off at the Chautauqua Motel. That's where all our body-escorts stay. It's no palace, but it's darn comfortable, and it's real close to the shop."

Palmer pulls out the paperwork again but Mr. Gerlach doesn't even look at it. He goes to the driver's door and says, "Hop in," which Palmer not only does not want to do, but did not imagine he would have to do. He picks up his duffel bag and climbs down off the dock. He opens the passenger door and puts his duffel bag on the floor and slides in.

Mr. Gerlach guides the hearse out of the loading dock and heads toward a gate shack. The air-conditioning is not on, but the interior of the hearse is cool, with a scent of rose in the air. The engine is surprisingly silent. This is the first time Palmer has ever ridden in a Cadillac. Mr. Gerlach waves at the guard who waves him on through. As they head toward the road which will take them into Wichita, Mr. Gerlach looks over at Palmer and says, "You're a Military Policeman, is that right?"

"Yes, sir."

"You don't look very tough for an MP."

An appalling observation, but Palmer knows it's true. Six-foot one, one hundred and sixty pounds, he has the face of a teenage boy. But he has to say something, so he says, "When you have a forty-five caliber pistol on your hip, you don't need to be very tough."

Mr. Gerlach raises his chin, peels back his lips, and laughs aloud.

They pass through a residential neighborhood like the neighborhoods of North Denver, heavy trees, houses of white clapboard or redbrick, the lawns burned yellow. A group of kids playing on the sidewalk stop to watch the hearse pass by.

"I don't know what your commanding officer told you," Mr. Gerlach says as they turn onto Douglas Avenue, the main drag, "but apparently the family doesn't have very much information about how their boy died. Now the thing is, the family is coming at nine o'clock tomorrow morning to view the body, so you might want to show up around eight. That way you can be there when they arrive. When I talked to Mrs. Thorpe on the phone this afternoon she still hadn't gotten many details from the army, so I guess they're expecting you to fill them in." He points through the windshield. "There's the shop."

Palmer sees a two-story white-brick building with a walled-in parking lot. Behind the plate-glass window hangs the flickering blue curls of a neon logo spelling "Hillside Mortuary."

Three blocks further along they turn into the driveway of a motel, the Chautauqua, its vacancy sign dark.

"You'll have the corner room at the rear of the building," Mr. Gerlach says. "That's where all our escorts stay. You won't hear any street traffic at all."

They enter the office where a middle-aged woman wearing purple slacks and a Hawaiian shirt is sipping pop and watching a TV behind a counter.

"Mrs. Ingersoll, this is Private Palmer."

She smiles and says hello and moves to the counter and spins the registration book around. Palmer scribbles his name. Interesting, the financial relationship between the military, mortuaries, and motels. He asks for a receipt.

"You're in number twenty," she says, handing him a key.

Mr. Gerlach drives him up to his room but Palmer doesn't get out. He opens his briefcase and asks Mr. Gerlach to sign for Thorpe's body, three copies. Mr. Gerlach smiles at the formality and makes three quick scribbles.

"I could send my assistant Kyle to pick you up in the morning," Mr. Gerlach says, "although it is just a three-block walk."

"That's all right, I don't mind walking," Palmer lies with a smile, climbing out with his duffel bag. "I could use the exercise." Mr. Gerlach grins and waves, and puts the hearse into gear.

Palmer unlocks the door to his room and steps inside. Musty odor like a shower stall. There's no tub in the bathroom, which disappoints him because he hasn't sat in a tub in months. The bed is soft, the bedspread cold to the touch. At least there is a TV, but it's black-and-white when he turns it on. The question is, should he go right now to the liquor store which he had seen on the corner when they drove in? He wants to go, just as he had wanted to order scotch on the airplane, but decides he had better not. He doesn't want to show up at the mortuary in the morning hungover and smelling like booze. He decides not to stink up his uniform by smoking tonight either. When he meets the Thorpe family he doesn't want to smell like he's having a good time.

CHAPTER 18

Palmer is awake before his alarm is even close to going off. Throughout the night he had kept waking up worried that he would miss the alarm. He would look at the green glowing hands of his folding travel-clock and then fall asleep forgetting immediately what time it was. But when he sees the gray morning light beyond the curtains he knows he won't be going back to sleep. He lies in bed listening to the street traffic which he can hear clearly. He doesn't want to get up. He isn't looking forward to meeting the Thorpe family at nine o'clock. Still disappointed that this mission hadn't ended at the airport, he is at least glad he hadn't gone to the liquor store the night before. He has two hours until the meeting, but he wants to get this day over with, and this is what finally gets him out of bed.

He takes a shower and decides that when the meeting is over he will go to the liquor store and buy a six-pack. He won't even stop to change out of his uniform, he'll just walk right down to the corner and make his purchase. Later on he might buy some scotch, but he is certain he will want a beer very badly after the meeting.

He dresses in front of the mirror and takes a long time inspecting himself, adjusting his tie and squaring away his cap and straightening his .45 medal and the rectangled red-and-yellow striped ribbon which everyone gets in basic training for having served in the military during a time of war and which everyone refers to as a "KP ribbon." He is glad he had decided to go to the barber shop.

There is nothing important in his briefcase but he takes it along just to have something in his hands. He leaves the room and walks up Douglas Avenue toward the mortuary. He passes a cafe, but decides not to eat breakfast right away even though he is hungry. He will eat after the meeting is over but before he goes to the liquor store.

He stops on a corner to wait for a red light, and a souped-up coupe, possibly a '32 Ford, wheels around the corner past him. The hot-rod is occupied by four teenagers, probably on their way to high school because he can see at least one letter-jacket. He wouldn't even have looked at the car if one of them hadn't stuck his head out the window as they made the turn and yelled, "Pig!" at the top of his voice. The car races down the street with two grinning faces watching him through the rear window.

That was something even he might have done in high school if he had three buddies along to give him the courage. But he doesn't want to hate those kids because he knows they are Future Enlisted Men of America. They look the way he and his buddies had looked in high school, long hair and pimples in a customized car. One of his buddies owned a blue '47 Dodge with baby moons and white pinstripes, and another owned a '59 Chevy with a four-barrel carburetor which could take it from zero to eighty in one second or something. He knows that in a few years those four Wichita plough jockeys in the '32 Ford will be going down to the Selective Service Office just like he did and sign up for the draft. Two of them will be taken by the army. A third, the letter-jacket athlete, will be given a medical deferment. And the fourth will be given enough money by his daddy to go to college where he will dabble in the radical politics of the New Left before he obtains his degree in business administration and buys a gray flannel suit.

So Palmer doesn't want to hate those kids, but he hates them anyway. Their volley gives him a shot of adrenaline which leaves him completely wide awake, and when the light turns green he steps off on the left foot and walks to the Hillside Mortuary feeling ready now to face the Thorpe family and deal with any questions they have, questions that, as he enters the silence of the funeral home, he actually believes he is prepared to answer.

It's like walking into a church. A Protestant church. Muted organ music and a thin odor of incense mingle in the air. The carpeting is the same beige hue as the walls. There is a reception desk in the foyer but nobody is seated behind it. He waits, peering down the hallway for someone to come, but no one comes. He stays where he is though because he doesn't want to start nosing around inside a mortuary.

After a minute Mr. Gerlach comes down the hall fast, all rubbery smiles and eyebrows, his shoulders hunched and his fingers spread as if he's getting ready to demonstrate something. "I'm glad you're here," he says. "Mrs. Thorpe arrived fifteen minutes ago. The rest of the family will be showing up soon, so it's good you got here early because things are moving along. If you want to come on up the hall with me, I'll introduce you to Mrs. Thorpe."

"All right," Palmer says, his voice a bit hollow because things are moving faster than he had expected. He follows Mr. Gerlach up the hall toward an open doorway. They enter a room where a woman is standing with her back to them, looking down at an open coffin.

In a soft and consoling tone of voice Mr. Gerlach says, "Mrs. Thorpe, this is Private Palmer, the young man who escorted your son from the Presidio."

She turns. She's old. No makeup on her face, her hair is blonde but fading to gray and not well-combed. Her gray eyes are magnified by the thick lenses of her glasses. She is wearing a coat too heavy for the weather, and Palmer suddenly notices how cold it is in the building. Thorpe is lying in the coffin, his face waxy, shining.

Mr. Gerlach discreetly backs out of the room.

"How do you do, Mrs. Thorpe?" Palmer says, mimicking Mr. Gerlach's consoling voice.

The woman offers her hand. Palmer can feel the bones beneath her flesh which is papery and cool. After she releases his hand she puts a finger to her lips and says, "How did Lee die?"

Palmer had never known Thorpe's first name, which is Leland, which he had learned only when he had seen it printed on the escort orders.

"Did he drown, or did he die when he hit the water?" she says. She is shorter than Palmer, and bowed a bit so that she has to turn her head slightly to look up at him, as if peering into the branches of a tree.

"I'm sorry, ma'am, I do not know," he says. "I will try to get that information for you."

"Would you? I couldn't learn anything from the army representative whom I spoke to on the phone."

She seems more perplexed than saddened about her son's death. There is nothing Palmer can tell her that she doesn't already know. Neither of them knows anything, and Palmer is suddenly angry that Sgt. Sherman had sent him here without any information.

"It all happened so fast," Mrs. Thorpe says. She opens her purse and pulls out a wad of Kleenex. "We got the phone call on Sunday morning, and they said they would be sending Lee's body on Tuesday. It's been hectic. I was so relieved when they told me they would be sending a soldier along to answer our questions."

An odd mechanical rustle at his back, Palmer turns and sees an elderly man in a wheelchair entering the room with a young man pushing him along. The man in the wheelchair has Thorpe's features, skull shape, same tight skin, but especially the eyes, which are slitted a bit. The man behind him bears no resemblance to Thorpe at all. Thick head of longish hair, not quite hippie, clear brown eyes, thick dark mustache. He is wearing a sweater, slacks, black shoes. He is dressed for church.

"Martin, this is Private Palmer," Mrs. Thorpe says. "He brought Leland home from California." She turns to Palmer. "This is my son Martin, and this is my husband Edward."

Palmer shakes hands with both men. The old man seems dazed, his lips moving silently and continuously as if he might be praying. Mrs. Thorpe gets behind the wheelchair and pushes her husband up to the coffin.

Palmer glances at the door. "Excuse me, Mr. and Mrs. Thorpe, I will be right outside if you need me."

He walks out without looking back and goes up to the reception desk and just stands there. Thorpe's face had looked like a varnished rubber mask.

Mr. Gerlach hurries down the hall toward him. "How's it going?"

"Fine."

"As well as can be expected, eh?" Mr. Gerlach says, his eyebrows hopping. "It won't be much longer."

Palmer is glad to hear this. After they leave he plans to check out of the Chautauqua and find a Holiday Inn near a liquor store. "Is this the entire family, or do you expect others to come later?" Palmer asks.

Mr. Gerlach's face plunges into a frown. "I don't believe anyone else is coming. I expect a lot of people at the funeral though. You'll be there for that, won't you?"

"When is the funeral?"

"Tomorrow afternoon at two o'clock. I'm sure the family would want you to be there. I can ask for you."

Palmer doesn't say anything, doesn't even nod because that would be like a commitment. But it doesn't matter because when the Thorpes come out of the room Mr. Gerlach goes up to them and in a crooning tone of voice begins mixing consolation with business. He glances at Palmer, and when Mrs. Thorpe nods, Palmer knows he will be going to the funeral.

Mrs. Thorpe and Martin approach Palmer and thank him for his help. Palmer fixes a smile on his lips and moves his eyebrows, and again mimics Mr. Gerlach's voice saying, "I will see you tomorrow afternoon."

Mrs. Thorpe steps outside and holds the door while Martin maneuvers the wheelchair onto the sidewalk. After the door closes, Mr. Gerlach claps his hands once and says, "I bet you're glad that's over with."

Palmer smiles. He is unused to such honesty.

"The church service will be at two o'clock tomorrow afternoon," Mr. Gerlach says, "so you might want to show up here about one-thirty. We'll give you a ride to St. Benedict's."

"All right."

"Why don't you come on back and meet Kyle."

Palmer follows him to the rear of the building, the beige decor giving way to linoleum and fluorescents. They enter a small room, a kitchenette.

Kyle is fiddling with a coffee machine. Except for the lavish haircut, he could pass for an army officer. Closely-shaven, broad-shouldered, his suit finely tailored, when he offers his hand Palmer notes that his fingernails are impeccably manicured. The hands of a man who prepares the dead for burial.

"Kyle, this is Private Palmer. He brought the Thorpe boy."

"How do you do," Kyle says, his voice as deep and smooth as that of a disk-jockey. "You look like a man who knows how to make coffee."

"I don't know anything about making coffee."

"That's too bad. Neither do we." Kyle opens a cupboard door above the percolator and looks inside. "We're out of filters."

"I've got some in my desk," Mr. Gerlach says.

"That's a hell of a place for 'em."

"Listen, the Thorpes have gone home. We're going to have to move Lee out this afternoon to make room for the Sanderson woman."

Kyle plucks a stale filter from the machine, shakes the residue flake and scum into the sink, and smiles at Palmer. "I can probably squeeze three more cups out of this if you don't mind waiting."

"Actually, if I'm not needed here, I'd like to get back to the motel," Palmer says.

"Oh that's fine, that's fine, don't let us keep you here," Mr. Gerlach says. "Why don't you hold off on that coffee, Kyle?"

"Why don't you bring me those filters?"

"They're in the office, but hold on a minute, let's walk Private Palmer to the door."

They lead him back to the foyer where he makes the mistake of glancing into an adjacent room graced by an arched doorway. He sees coffins.

"Our display room," Mr. Gerlach says. "Would you like to see it?"

It's like an auto showroom, lavish carpeting and drapes, the air shot with the cleansing odor of rose. Each coffin is perched on a pedestal with the lid open at waist-level to show the pleated white satin or silk pillow where somebody's head will rest. The coffins are shiny like new cars too, silver and copper, and fine woods, and pearl.

"Now this section over here holds our most expensive models," Mr. Gerlach says, crossing to a corner of the room and placing a palm on the glassy surface of a coffin either wood or imitation.

Palmer holds his briefcase with both hands and listens and nods and waits for Mr. Gerlach to finish explaining how long the casket will last underground—he refers to the box as a casket and not a coffin. He describes the fine quality of the upholstery and the fabric of the pillows where scalps will fester and rot until Palmer is not listening anymore but wandering around apparently admiring the merchandise but really making his way toward the front door because he wants to get out of there.

"You're probably the first person who was ever in this room who didn't come to buy something," Kyle says.

Mr. Gerlach chuckles. It gets him started. "Tell him about the Louisiana oil man."

Kyle grins. "This oil man came in one afternoon and told us he wanted the most expensive casket we had. It was for his wife who had just died in an auto accident." He glances at Mr. Gerlach, and both men grin. "So we sold him a casket that cost twenty-five thousand dollars."

Palmer tries to smile bigger because he's been smiling the whole time. He raises his eyebrows to give them what they want, which he assumes is astonishment.

Mr. Gerlach breaks in on cue. "Well! We found out later that he wanted the most expensive casket available on the market, not just in our showroom. Why, we have caskets in our catalog that run higher than fifty thousand dollars!"

Palmer can't smile any bigger or raise his eyebrows any higher, so he starts shaking his head. He tries to chuckle, but it isn't in him. He looks toward the front door. "I guess I had better be getting back to the motel."

They've had their fun though, telling their favorite anecdote, and aren't bothered at all by his eagerness to get going. They know all about schedules and deadlines and taking care of business. They are businessmen. This is their vocation. When Palmer was in grade school the nuns told the children, "God will reveal your vocation in life to you." They encouraged the children to listen hard to learn whether God wanted the boys to become priests. Or the girls nuns. Palmer listened hard. He would have liked to go to a seminary to become a holy person. Even when he was looking at dirty magazines in the drugstore or watching for the bumps of women's nipples at the swimming pool, he wanted God to tell him that his vocation would be to one day put on a robe and go help poor people in places with names like Santiago or Mombasa and never want anything material, not money, or liquor, or pussy, he would just be a holy man, doing holy things for all the poor people of the world. So he listened hard all through grade school and the first year of high school, but God never said a word.

The Wichita sun is so bright it makes his eyes water when he steps out onto the sidewalk. He heads for the motel waiting to be called a pig again but all the teens are in school. He steps into the cafe and orders a BLT to go. When he gets back to the motel he buys a Coke from the machine outside the office and goes into his room.

He strips out of his Class A uniform, sits on the bed in his skivvies and eats his breakfast watching a noon newscast in black-and-white. Thursday's one-thirty appointment means he has to be awake by twelve-thirty at the latest, so if he starts drinking now and quits by midnight it will give him a good twelve hours sleep to kill his hangover so that he will show up at the church only slightly ill. Three hours after the funeral he ought to be back here with a fresh bottle and can get started on the rest of his TDY. This is his best-case scenario, where everything will work out the way he always wants things to work out when he drinks heavily, the way things never work out.

But before deciding what to do he takes a shower, because it may be only imaginary but he thinks he reeks of formaldehyde. He washes his hands and face, and the inside of his nose, getting his soapy finger up in there and really twisting it around because he has the idea that formaldehyde molecules are clinging to his nose hairs. Thorpe's forehead and cheeks and chin had reflected the light in a way that made the flesh look like glass. Palmer wouldn't have recognized him if he hadn't already known it was Thorpe. Thirty-two feet per second/per second—the length of a football field. Surely Thorpe had died the moment he hit the water.

Palmer is tired after he finishes his shower, so he lies on the bed intending to sleep for only an hour, but sleeps almost four hours, partly from jet-lag and partly from just being in the army. When he sits up and looks out the curtain and sees the light turning everything golden, he feels cheated out of drinking time even though he hasn't decided yet whether to do any drinking or not. He knows he shouldn't drink anything at all, that he should finish this mission before he starts partying, but at the same time he wants to get drunk to take his mind off the mission.

He turns on the TV and watches the news and a repeat of *Laugh-In*, and decides to go ahead and light up a cigarette because it might satisfy his need to indulge in a goddamn vice. But it only makes him want to drink beer, as smoking always does, and when it finally gets dark outside he turns off the TV and sits on the edge of the bed and smokes another cigarette and thinks about buying a six-pack. All this indecision is making him edgy.

He gets dressed in civilian clothes and puts on the windbreaker Courtney had made him buy at the main PX because it was driving Courtney crazy to see him going around without a coat. He puts on his new belt too, though he had never worn a belt when he was a civilian because it wasn't the groovy teen style back in Denver. He had told Courtney he would buy tennis shoes on the next payday, just to get the guy off his back.

He leaves the motel room and walks along Douglas Avenue in the darkness, heading in the opposite direction from the mortuary, listening to cicadas buzzing in the massive cottonwood trees which seem to grow on the front lawns of all the houses along this boulevard. He comes to the liquor store with its red neon signs buzzing and flickering behind the windows, but he keeps on walking.

He stops on a corner one block down from the liquor store and looks at his watch. He adds up all the hours he will have left to drink during the three days ahead of him, plenty of time, although time always seems to evaporate the moment he opens a bottle. The house he is standing in front of has two cottonwoods growing on the front lawn. Chunks of white fiber are falling from the branches like snow, shaken loose by a soft breeze. It had been windy out at the airport, but in this part of town the currents seem to stay at treetop level, leaving everything surprisingly humid and murky near the ground. He has never felt such humidity as this.

The wind picks up. He has to close his mouth to keep from choking on all the cotton blowing past. He's never seen anything quite so odd, and it reminds him of a day in MP school in Georgia when it had snowed for the first time in that part of the country in a decade. Half the men in the training company had never seen snow before because they were from the Deep South. When the snow began falling, training was called off for the day. The city of Augusta went on red-alert, and schools and businesses were shut down. Highways were closed. The entire state ground to a halt because a quarter-inch of snow had accumulated on the ground. The trainees from the northern states had laughed at all the panic, and the trainees who had never seen snow before in their lives walked around trying to catch flakes on their tongues, then tried to scrape enough off the ground to make snowballs.

What if he got drunk and missed the funeral? Thorpe would still get buried, but would his family call the Presidio to complain or ask why Private Palmer had never shown up? Would Mr. Gerlach and Kyle come to his motel room and knock on the door? The motel manager would unlock the door with a pass-key and let them into the smoky stink of a bender where the unconscious carcass of a snoring GI lay wrapped in a sweat-stained sheet oblivious to the meaning of duty or even common decency.

He turns and walks back the way he had come. He passes through the flickering red liquor lights and goes on to the motel. He buys a Coke at the machine and goes into his room. He knows he will have trouble getting to sleep, which is what he always thinks when he wants to drink but doesn't, which isn't often, but often enough for him to believe he has to have it or he won't be able to do anything.

He wakes up at dawn with the TV still tuned to the same channel that he had been watching when he fell asleep waiting for *The Late Show* to begin.

CHAPTER 19

Palmer is glad again that he doesn't have the pain of a hangover when he gets out of bed in the morning. He showers and shaves and thinks about the two free days ahead of him. Thursday night and Friday and half of Saturday—all of Saturday if he wants to fashion his own day-of-grace and return Sunday night, or even Monday morning just prior to reveille, though he wouldn't risk that. It occurs to him that he ought to pack his duffel bag and bring it with him to the mortuary so he won't have to return to the motel after the funeral. He can go straight to an airport motel where no one will be able to track him down.

Having a plan makes him feel better because the moment he awoke there had been a tightening in his gut that hasn't gone away. He puts on his civilian clothes and walks two blocks to the cafe for a breakfast of eggs, bacon, coffee, orange juice and Texas toast, then decides not to go back to the motel right away. As he had done at Ft. Campbell and Ft. Gordon and the Presidio, he decides to walk around and see a part of the country he knows he will never see again.

He walks back toward the motel, passes it, and comes to the cottonwood corner and crosses over. He continues walking past residential homes, the same white clapboard he had seen in Hopkinsville and Augusta, the spoor of pioneer carpenters. When he comes to a Safeway store he knows there is nothing to see in Wichita, or at least this part of Wichita. What could there be to see in Kansas anyway? A sod house built by retired whalers, step inside and look around for a buck.

An hour has gone by. He returns to the Chautauqua and sets his alarm for one P.M. and takes off his shoes and lies on the bed. He dozes but hears the passing of cars on Douglas throughout his sleep, and when he wakes up, it's only eleven.

He switches off the alarm and starts putting his uniform on. He takes his time. He looks at himself in the mirror as he knots his tie and unloosens it and knots it again. It takes him half an hour to get dressed. In basic training he had five minutes. He overslept three minutes one morning and went into an almost psychotic panic trying to lace his boots. When there's nothing left to do he decides to go to the mortuary earlier than scheduled.

He packs his duffel bag, padlocks it, and leaves the key to the room on the dresser. He shoulders the bag and walks up the street listening for the sound of approaching teens. When he gets close to the mortuary he realizes that a member of the Thorpe family might see him carrying his duffel bag and will know that he is packed and is ready to haul ass. The knot in his stomach tightens.

He lowers the duffel bag and holds it like a suitcase and opens the door and peers in. Nobody around. He steps inside quickly and sets the bag behind the reception desk and goes looking for Mr. Gerlach, since he knows where to look. He walks past the open doors of rooms where caskets are raised on biers, but he doesn't look to see if they are occupied.

The two morticians are laughing when he walks into the kitchen. They are surprised to see him this early, and tell him so. "I have to be back in San Francisco on Friday," he lies. "So I thought I would just leave from here after the funeral." He explains about his duffel bag, watching their faces for disapproval that never comes because they are both business-men who understand about watching the clock and keeping tight schedules. He goes and gets his duffel bag and sets it in a corner of the kitchen.

Kyle offers him a cup of coffee and he takes it. Mr. Gerlach fills him in on what they will be doing today: a service at two P.M. at St. Benedict's Catholic Church, a trip to Mt. Calvary cemetery, then they will bring him back here. They tell him that Thorpe's body has already been transferred to St. Benedict's, then they leave him alone to attend to their business.

Palmer sips at the coffee which he didn't want, and waits for the arrival of the Thorpe family, and only now does it occur to him that he should have brought his James Bond novel along on this trip to pass the time. He would have packed it in his duffel bag, but he hadn't expected to be doing any reading in his imaginary Holiday Inn.

St. Benedict's is like all the churches of his childhood, high-ceilinged and hollow like a cathedral, the odors of varnish and beeswax in the air. Mass is at the midway point. Most of the mourners are seated in the front rows, but Palmer is seated alone in a pew at the rear of the church where he stares at the backs of the heads of the friends and relatives of the man whom he more than once had shown contempt for. He looks at the altar, at the carpeted steps with the cluster of silver bells which will ring at the transubstantiation. Along the side aisles are stair-stepped tables of candles which you can light for a dime, or could when he was a child. He never ate before going to Mass in those days. He would go alone to the noon service because his parents and brothers and sisters always went early at seven or eight while he slept or searched the channels of dull Sunday TV for cartoons. During Mass he would stand with his knees locked so long that he sometimes fainted. It would begin with a cloud of dark spots boiling in front his eyes. The voice of the priest would fade away. Then, depending on whether he was in a pew or in the standing-room-only crowd at the rear of the church, he would find himself seated on wood or tile, his sight and hearing returning like the approach of a distant train. This went on for years. It never occurred to him to tell his parents about it.

Thorpe's father is in his wheelchair alongside the front pew where the family is sitting with their heads bowed. The priest is a young man. He steps up to the podium and begins his sermon by saying that though he had never known Leland Thorpe personally, "Every man's death diminishes me." Palmer sits with his head bowed too, and when everyone stands to go to communion he stays where he is and watches the procession. When he was a teenager he always went to communion even if he hadn't gone to confession the night before because if you didn't go to communion it was a blatant admission: you were guilty of sex sins and everybody knew it. The true spirit of Catholicism had been incomprehensible, and ultimately lost on him.

The Mass ends, and five young men step onto the altar with Martin Thorpe. They surround the casket. Pallbearers, the men look like jocks, awkward in tight-fitting suits, their hair longish, with bristles and patches of mustaches or beards. The priest's lips move as he gives quiet instructions. The pallbearers bend at the knees, take hold of the metal handles, lift the casket, begin shuffling toward a side door where Palmer knows the hearse is parked because he had ridden in it to the church with Kyle.

He waits until they go out the door, then he leaves through the front and stands at the end of the driveway until the hearse is loaded. He is surprised by all the cars in the parking lot, by all the people who have come for the service. Thorpe didn't have any friends that he knew of at the Presidio. He counts nineteen cars in the lot.

After the casket is loaded, Palmer walks up the driveway and climbs into the passenger seat of the hearse. Kyle hops into the driver's seat and grins. "Almost over," he says. He puts on sunglasses which make him look rather cool as he leads the funeral procession through the bright Wichita sunlight toward Mt. Calvary.

Motorcycle cops escort the cars, playing leap-frog at each intersection, stopping the green-light traffic. Palmer looks at the faces of the people in the waiting cars. Some of the people look at the hearse, and some of them look at the sky, but not one of them looks at him.

Two tall brick pillars stand at the entrance to the cemetery. The cars pass between the pillars and enter the grounds and climb a gentle slope toward the top of a hill where a dark green tent has been set up. It has only one wall, its roof peaked like a circus tent above rows of chairs and a podium.

Kyle parks at the curb. Palmer gets out and stands by the hearse and waits for the mourners to make the short climb to the tent. They take their time. There is no hurry. The pallbearers pull the casket from the rear and transport it up the hill, and Palmer follows at the back of the crowd. The chairs fill with elderly women and men, with girls, with young women holding infants.

Palmer can feel their eyes whenever people glance his way, but he keeps his eyes on the bier above its earthen hole hidden by a carpet of artificial turf like a Putt-Putt green. The priest steps up to the podium carrying an enormous Bible with both hands. He sets it down and opens it, and looks at the people seated in the front row, Mr. and Mrs. Thorpe, Martin, a few others.

"Let us pray," he says, and begins reciting the Our Father.

Heads bow, but because but he is at the rear and no one can see him, Palmer keeps his head up and stares at the casket. He notices sunlight making shadows on the back wall of the tent, the shadows of two men. One of the men is smoking a cigarette. A shadow of smoke shoots from his mouth. The shadow of his other hand is resting on the shadow of an upright shovel.

The priest finishes the prayer and raises his head. He says he is speaking for the entire family who would like to thank everyone for attending the service. The ceremony is brief. The priest says a few more things, and when he finishes, the people begin standing up. The shadow of the man behind the tent throws down the cigarette and steps on it.

Palmer had thought there would be some kind of drawn-out eulogy, possibly hymns, speeches, weeping. He thought it would be like in the movies. Women turn to look down at their chairs for purses or sweaters. People begin walking past him on the left and right, but he stays where he is, looking at the casket. The two men come around from behind the tent wall.

They are young. They are gravediggers in T-shirts and blue jeans and boots. One bends down and grabs the artificial turf and drags it out from under the bier, and the other flips a switch on the framework. Thorpe's casket begins descending into the hole, jerking a bit as the supporting straps feed out with a sound of clicking gears. Palmer watches until he can't see the lid of the casket anymore, then he turns and walks down the hill to the hearse.

Mr. Gerlach approaches him. "Martin Thorpe would like to speak with you." He points at a station wagon parked behind the gray Cadillac sedan which had brought the family. Martin is standing beside it. Mr. Gerlach pats Palmer once on the shoulder. A little shove. Go.

Martin smiles at him. "My mother wanted me to tell you that we're having some friends and family over for coffee and cake at the house, and she'd like to know if you would care to join us?"

"I would be happy to join you," Palmer says in his borrowed voice.

Martin opens the door to the station-wagon, and Palmer climbs in next to Mr. Thorpe, whose wheelchair is folded up in the luggage space in the rear, and who doesn't look at Palmer once during the ride to his home.

Cars are parked at the curb in front of the house, but the driveway has been left empty. Martin pulls into the driveway and gets out and goes to the rear to remove the wheelchair. Palmer asks if he needs any help, but Martin smiles and says no. He helps his father out of the car and onto the chair, and begins wheeling him toward the front steps. Mrs. Thorpe comes up to Palmer and takes his arm and pats his hand gently and says, "You're our son now."

They walk together to the front porch, and wait while Martin works the wheelchair backwards up a short ramp. The front door is being held open by an elderly woman, who smiles at Martin and then at Palmer as they enter the house.

Kitchen chairs have been set up around the living room filling the spaces between overstuffed chairs and a couch already filled with elderly people. It's warmer inside the house than outside, Palmer can feel the humidity weighing on his Class A uniform. Martin offers him a seat, and asks if he would like some cake and punch.

"Yes, thank you," Palmer says. Then, "May I use your bathroom?"

It's off the dining room where women are supervising the cutting of flat cakes in long pans. He goes into the bathroom and shuts the door and locks it, and stands for a moment listening to the muted voices beyond the door.

The air is cooler in the bathroom though there is no window, or maybe because of it. He undoes his tie and un-buttons his shirt to get some air against his skin. He looks at himself in the mirror but doesn't really see his face because he is listening to the voices of the guests, and wondering if anyone out there feels that the army is somehow responsible for Leland Thorpe's death, and maybe holds it against him too.

He removes his coat and drapes it on the doorknob, loosens his web-belt and sits on the lidded toilet. Young people out there with long hair and mustaches, will any of them call him a pig? But Thorpe had been a soldier, had been in the army, and these are his friends. Thorpe's father had probably served in WWII like everybody's father. Palmer stays in the bathroom five minutes, the longest he thinks he can stay away before people start wondering. He's convinced that everyone in this house is thinking about him and only him, and not their grief.

He is handed a small plate with a slice of white cake and a plastic fork. Another middle-aged woman hands him a small cup of punch. He says thank you. She smiles. He is seated on a kitchen chair in the living room with empty chairs on either side of him. He concentrates on eating his cake and sipping at his punch, and it finally occurs to him that this is no different than being among strangers at a wedding party, like the ones he had attended when friends from high school had gotten married before they had even turned twenty-one. He had never understood why they didn't want to get out and see the world a little or at least have more than one girlfriend before they got tied down forever. Two of them already have children. When he was home on leave from basic they were always too tired to party.

He starts looking directly at the elderly men and women seated on the couch, the people of WWII who had lived through Hitler and would have nothing against soldiers, and maybe had been soldiers themselves or had been married to soldiers. Bulbous, bi-focaled eyes, men clutching the tops of canes, women with strangely-painted faces, their hands battling arthritic shakes as they nibble at crackers. Here and there he catches an eye, a smile, a friendly nod, but nobody comes over to talk to him. He hears references to football in the conversations among the jock pallbearers. He could break the ice by joining their talk but he knows nothing about football except that the Denver Broncos are the worst team in the NFL.

Martin sits down next him. "I understand you're a Military Policeman in the same company my brother was in, is that right?"

"That's correct. I'm in the first platoon of Company D. You're brother was in the third platoon."

Martin knows this of course. A stupid thing to have said, but not as stupid as the thing he is about to say. He will say it because he is talking too fast because he is glad to have someone to talk to. He knows that Martin is making a generous effort to be a good host, since it is obvious by now that Palmer is being ignored by everyone in the room.

"Do you like being an MP?"

"Yes, I do."

"We're you drafted?"

"Yes, I was."

"Where are you from originally?"

"Denver."

"Oh? Do you ski?"

"No."

Martin nods. "Lee always seemed to like the Presidio." His eyes drop as he says this. "In the letters he wrote to us, he seemed to be enjoying his work."

Palmer wants to lie and tell him that he had known Lee well, that they had pulled a lot of details together and had gotten along fine, but he doesn't say that. Instead he says, "It's a good place to pull MP duty. The Presidio is headquarters for the Sixth Army. It's supposed to be the most beautiful army base in America. It's an open post, you know, so there aren't any gates or guards at the entrances."

Then he says:

"Tourists can drive right through the Presidio to get to the Golden Gate Bridge."

CHAPTER 20

A silence falls over the room which he will later decide he only imagined. Martin doesn't react in any particular way. Palmer continues talking, but will never remember what he said after that. He keeps a smile fixed on his face and keeps his vocal chords churning sentences, aware only of a chill in his spine, deep in the marrow like a vein of freshly-manufactured Freon.

Martin asks if he would like another cup of punch, and takes the empty into the dining room. Palmer sits up straight, and slowly and consciously and deliberately looks at each person in the room. Nobody is looking back. Nobody seems to have heard what he had said, although he knows from personal experience that Catholics often respond to awkward or intolerable events by simply pretending they didn't happen.

Martin brings the refill. After a few minutes Palmer works the conversation around to the fact that he will have to be getting back to the motel soon. When he stands up to leave, people he hadn't spoken to begin nodding and saying goodbye. Everyone is extremely cordial as Martin and Mrs. Thorpe walk him outside.

"I wasn't able to get very much information at all about Leland's death from the man I spoke to on the phone," Mrs. Thorpe says, her voice sounding frail and importunate. "There was just so much going on."

Palmer turns to her and says in his own voice, "I'll do my best to get that information to you, Mrs. Thorpe," and he means it, because fulfilling such a promise seems to him the only thing left on earth that can redeem him, if such a thing is possible.

Martin drops him off in front of the Chautauqua Motel. Palmer waits until the station wagon is out of sight before he turns to the door to his room. Only then does he remember that he doesn't have a room.

The three-block walk to the mortuary is made in an unnecessary and exhausting hurry, because when he gets there the door is locked and the lights are out. He is over-heated in his Class A uniform coat, but not from the humidity or the recent quick march. It is the heat of flesh infused with blood. He is certain that his face had been a bruised shade of crimson when he said goodbye to the Thorpes.

He looks down the dark block in the direction of the motel. He had learned long ago that the only two things a soldier really has to worry about on leave is money and a copy of his travel orders. He has money, but his orders are locked inside the mortuary. There is nothing to do but return to the Chautauqua and get the room back and wait until dawn. But in desperation he starts making a circuit of the building with a vague notion of looking for an open window and climbing through and searching among the dead for his duffel bag. Then he sees a light in a window at the side of the building.

It's next to the service door where caskets are brought in and out. He rings the bell and waits, and after a minute Kyle shoots the lock and opens the door. No longer looking like a disk-jockey, he's dressed for manual labor. "Private Palmer! How you doing, buddy? I'll bet you came back for your duffel bag."

Palmer is asleep when the pilot announces their approach to Stapleton International Airport in Denver. He had not drank the previous night, had gone right to bed and slept hard and sober in an airport motel, but was still tired when he got on the Friday noon plane for San Francisco. A brief layover in Denver, he sits up and looks out his window at the familiar lie of the white-peaked Rockies twenty miles away obscured a bit by a brown haze dulling the afternoon sunlight. It feels peculiar to be sitting on a plane in Denver knowing he can't get off and go home, although in fact he doesn't really have to be back in San Francisco until Sunday, which means he could get off the plane and take a cab to his brother's apartment, the same basement apartment where he had lived for two years before getting drafted. He could spend Friday and Saturday night there. He imagines himself showing up without warning and knocking on the door. Mike would come up the stairs wearing only blue jeans, would be half-asleep and hungover, just like Palmer himself had been for those two years of bachelor living. Mike would be shocked to see him, and even more shocked when Palmer hissed, "Mike! You've got to hide me! I've gone AWOL!"

It would be a good joke, and there is nothing to stop him from doing it, not even common sense. But he stays on the plane. He wants to get back to Company D and sign in and get this mission over with, the only thing he has wanted since he walked out of the Thorpe house.

He doesn't drink any alcohol during the flight. He makes himself sleep as much as possible, and even when he can't sleep he keeps his eyes closed.

As soon as the plane arrives at San Francisco International he forgets a plan he had made during the flight. The plan had been to head straight to an airport bar and drink a few scotch-and-sodas, but once off the plane he is caught up in the momentum of the crowd headed for the carousel. He doesn't want to lose the bag again, and in the end he goes outside and gets into the first cab in line.

When he arrives at Company D, he tips the driver two dollars and asks for a receipt. He gets out and carries his duffel bag around the front and enters through the porch door to his room.

Mission completed, although he still has to sign in, but not for another twenty-four hours. Officially he is not even at Company D, he is in Kansas. His only plan now is to change into civvies and head for the bowling alley even though he's tired. But it's Friday night, and he can still get in three hours of drinking, and he knows theoretically how many beers he can drink in three hours: fifteen.

He puts his duffel bag into his wall locker without unpacking and hangs up his coat and tie. He goes down to the latrine, and afterwards stops at the bulletin board to check his name on the new KP roster, but it hasn't been posted yet.

Then he sees his name printed on a bulletin from the Department of the Army, the most recent roster of men who have been reassigned from Company D to the Republic of South Vietnam. Courtney's name is on there too, and judging by the date at the top of the page, the bulletin was posted on the same day that Palmer was browsing caskets in the showroom of the Wichita mortician.

PART FOUR

CHAPTER 21

Palmer sips the last bit of scotch from the shot glass and sets it on the bar with an unintentionally loud click. The bartender looks his way, but Palmer shakes his head no. It's three o'clock in the afternoon and this is only the fourth bar he has been in today, having barely made two blocks on this bar-hop which originally he had planned to make on his birthday exactly one week earlier. The bartender in this particular place had asked for his ID, and Palmer had expected him to remark on the fact that the license is expired, or that it had been issued in Colorado, but the man only glanced at his face to match the photo taken in Denver two years earlier when Palmer had long hair and weedy sideburns which he had shaved off soon after growing them because they had looked ridiculous.

Before leaving the bar he checks his pocket where his money is secured by a rubber band to both his Colorado driver's license and his military ID. His billfold is secreted safely on the top shelf of his wall locker where he had put it before leaving post in a cab because he wasn't entirely certain how this day was going to turn out. Reassured by the bulge of his stash, he slides off the barstool.

He stops in the doorway to light a cigarette and to let his eyes adjust to the glare of Market Street because being drunk in the light of day is not something he's used to. After a minute he steps out to the sidewalk and starts looking for another bar but stays close to the storefronts, peering through open doorways and hoping for something different or at least interesting. A surprising dull sameness to saloons. He can see the marquees of two Market Street movie theaters on the next block up, legitimate theaters and not porno like the ones on this block. Patton is featured at the theater nearest, and half a block further along, Woodstock.

Coming toward him also keeping close to the storefronts is a hippie with hair down to his ass. Sandals, blue jeans, a blue work-shirt with sleeves rolled to the elbows, "Wanna buy some pot?" a breathy whisper as he brushes past. The thing Palmer had once wanted to write home to his friends about: "I saw hippies and one of them offered to sell me marijuana." Back when there was no reality, back when he was in the army stationed in, of all places, San Francisco, California.

He turns and looks at the back of the man's head, and says, "No thanks," loudly enough for nearby pedestrians to hear him. A very uncool thing to do, which makes him feel good—sorry, man, my drug is brewed not harvested. Then it occurs to him that he should have talked to the guy, even if just to bullshit him into thinking he was going to buy some pot. He hasn't talked to anybody all day. He hasn't seen Courtney since before Wichita. Probably at Cheryl's. Courtney's bad luck to fall in love and get sent to war. Palmer's bad luck not to fall in love and get sent to war.

"Whoah!"

His fear realized, the collision is all texture and mass and shadow and sound as Palmer reaches out off-balance and touches the cool surface of a pane of glass. The man he just plowed into tries to help him keep his balance, a young slick-looking guy in what Palmer immediately thinks of as a sharkskin suit but doesn't really know, a kind of shimmer emanating from the gray, almost silver, threads.

"Whaddya say there, friend?"

The man is smiling, not at all disturbed that a drunk has careened into him. Palmer is delighted that a clean-shaven, well-dressed, well-groomed stranger has started a conversation with him.

"Thinking of buying an engagement ring for that special gal?"

His hand still planted firmly on the glass, Palmer looks through it and sees a sun-struck arrangement of gold rings, wristwatches, and diamond necklaces. He's leaning against the display window of a jewelry store. The man in the sharkskin suit is a street-barker salesman.

Balance regained, it's a delicate moment. Now that he has someone to talk to, he doesn't want to lose him. True of both of them. "Just looking," Palmer says, as though he in fact had been browsing, as though this is the reason he had crashed into the salesman and not alcohol.

"Why don't you step inside and take a look around, soldier?" The man knows he's a soldier, and it's not only the cut of his hair, it's his black army-issue low-quarters. Salesmen on Market Street look at people's shoes.

There's a musty smell inside the store, which is little more than a big bleak hollow room with a wooden floor and wooden shelves and a long display case with green-tinted glass lit from the inside showing off wristwatches and rings.

"What's your name?" the salesman says, slipping behind the counter and taking up a position not far from the cash register.

"Al."

Palmer says this because he knows the salesman is not going to talk him into buying anything, thus assuring that his lie will be successful. He will string anyone along when he's drunk, and when he's drunk, his money is good for one thing only.

"How ya doing, Al? My name's Bob." He jabs a hand at Palmer, and they both squeeze hard.

"Army or navy?"

"Army."

"Where are you stationed?"

"The Presidio."

"Right here in town? That's great. What do you do there?"

"I'm a Military Policeman."

"Whoah," Bob says, raising his hands and backing away, "I didn't do it." He laughs. Palmer smiles. Must think I'm an idiot, but then he probably knows his business.

"So what's it like to be a Military Policeman, Al? Do you investigate a lot of crimes?"

"Every now and then," Palmer lies. "But you don't see many crimes in a place where everybody has a gun."

The salesman gives up a small smile at this, but it's real.

Only a few minutes since his last drink, yet Palmer has the annoying sensation that he's sobering up. There are bars waiting, and it seems the salesman wants only to talk. Can Bob smell the booze on his breath? Of course. Thus assuring himself of a sale.

"Do you have a girlfriend, Al?"

"Back home."

"Where's home?"

"Denver."

"Hey, you must ski."

"No."

"Man oh man, if I lived in Colorado you couldn't keep me off the slopes."

"It's too much work."

Bob hangs a U without losing a beat. "Are you two engaged?"

"Not yet," Palmer says. "But we've talked about it." Lying comes so easily, though it's acting really, and he's enjoying it because there are few things as satisfying as bullshitting a bullshitter.

"Do you love her, Al?"

This surprises Palmer. How could a salesman have the nerve to ask something so fucking personal? "I don't know what's going on between us," he replies.

With a smoothness that Palmer is aware of and even admires to a certain degree—the sly aplomb of the sales persona—Bob changes tack and leans toward him. "Can I ask you something, Al?"

"Sure."

"When was the last time you saw your mother?"

"Six months ago."

"Can I ask you something else?"

"Sure."

"When was the last time you told your mother you love her?"

Palmer alters his voice slightly to the high-pitched resonance of a mixed-up teen. "I always sign my letters with love."

Bob nods. Bob the Businessman lids his eyes. "What I mean is, when was the last time you did something for your mother to show her that you loved her?"

I left home ha ha. "What do you mean?"

"Let me show you something, Al." Bob does a knee-dip and opens a drawer beneath the counter. When he stands up he's holding a purple-velvet jewelry box in the palm of his hand.

"I don't think so," Palmer says, "I gotta get going."

"Fair enough, Al, but before you shove off, I just want you to take a quick look at something."

Annoyed, mostly at himself, Palmer stays to listen.

"What do you think would happen if one week from today your mother received a package in the mail and found this inside it?" He raises his eyebrows as he raises the hinged lid of the box. Planted inside is a golden four-leaf clover. Studded in its heart is a small diamond. It looks like something you would wear on St. Patrick's Day as a joke.

Bob removes the item from the box and holds it out. "Here, feel the weight. That there is solid gold."

Palmer doesn't take it.

"It's the price you're worried about, isn't it, Al?"

Strangely, he's right. If it sold for a buck he might buy it just to show to his mother who had worked in a jewelry store during her Omaha youth. Look Mom, look at the crap Market Street jewelers foist off on Our Boys In Uniform. Has anything changed since World War Two?

"How much is it?"

"To be frank with you, Al, I've always found that when a young man is purchasing a symbol of love for his mother, the price is never a large consideration. I can see that you've got a business head on your shoulders, so I'll tell you what I'll do." He mounts the piece back in the box. "We have military financing. We can arrange to take a small payment out of your paycheck every month, and you won't even miss the money because you'll never see it. You'll have this item paid off in less than a year.

"How much are the payments?"

"All right, here's the deal I'm going to set up for you, Al. Now if the payments are too large, we can make a special arrangement to lower them and extend your billing period to eighteen months, but we'd prefer not to do that because it really screws up our accounting system."

"How much are the payments?"

"Minimal. And we can do that because we finance our customers ourselves and cut out the middle man."

"How much are the payments?"

"I can see that you're worried about the money, Al, so I'm going to do something out of the ordinary here. I'm going to bend the rules a little and give you a discount even though that's something the boss doesn't like us to do. But I can make up the difference out of my own pocket which I'd certainly be willing to do for you because I think you're serious about buying."

"How much are the payments?"

"For you, only fourteen dollars a month and that does include the entire financing package plus taxes. We also require a ten percent down payment up front."

"Oh I can't afford that." Palmer turns and heads for the door.

Bob intercepts him before he gets there. He's relentless, and Palmer can appreciate that too, though mostly he's amused. The man has no idea what he is up against, and what he is up against is Palmer's next drink.

"Did you see our display?" Bob says, pointing at a setup next to the door. It's a bulletin board resting on an easel, covered with Polaroid pictures of soldiers and sailors and Marines. Some are wearing civilian clothes, and all of them have crew cuts. A few black-framed army-issue glasses toss back the light of flashbulbs, the eyes of the men not wearing glasses a stark red. Each man is holding up a golden four-leaf clover.

"These are some of our customers who bought the gold brooch," Bob says. He steps up close to Palmer and lowers his voice. "What's the matter, Al? Don't you get along with your mother?"

As he walks out of the store Palmer hears at his back a smacking sound like someone hitting a palm with a fist. Bob the Businessman, skunked.

Fifteen minutes gone forever out of all the hours left before Vietnam. Four weeks left at the Presidio plus four weeks leave in Denver. Fifty-six days times twenty-four hours, minus the past fifteen minutes. Does all this add up to the rest of his life?

He crosses to the next block and goes into a bar filled with civilians who look like they might have just gotten off work. Suits and ties and briefcases. He sits on a stool and looks at the clock. Three forty-five. He orders a shot and a beer and drinks the shot right off to burn the smell of the jewelry store out of his sinuses. There's that tang in the air of rotting wood, like the stockroom of his dad's Woolworth when he was a kid. His father was drafted at twenty-seven and discharged at thirty-one. He was employed at the F.W. Woolworth in Cheyenne, Wyoming, when Pearl Harbor was bombed. Living alone in a rooming house, he didn't hear the news until he went to a movie that afternoon. The woman in the ticket booth told him that all servicemen were required to report to their military installations. He told her he wasn't in the service and to sell him a ticket.

The rejuvenating power of hot scotch and cold beer. Palmer had been getting tired standing there listening to that jewelry salesman flap his jaws. How can anybody drink standing up at a bar? Westerns are horseshit. He wishes Courtney were here, and thinks about calling Cheryl. The two of them would be surprised, thinking he was still in Wichita at the funeral. But they'd had their party. The only person Palmer had talked to in the company after getting back was a man from the second platoon also on the Vietnam roster who had approached him in the mess hall at noon and said he and a few others were trying to get as many men as possible to fly over to Vietnam together. He wanted to know if Palmer had decided when he was going to sign out of the company. A strange bit of army acquiescence, the men going to Vietnam have thirty days to sign out, and the choice of date is theirs.

But the idea struck Palmer as obnoxious, as if the man was talking about a tour of Yellowstone. He told the guy he hadn't decided yet but would let him know when he made up his mind, another dull lie. Flying over with Courtney would be all right, but they probably wouldn't get the same duty station anyway. Danang, Pleiku, Nha Trang, Qui Nhon, Cam Ranh Bay, the names of places where Company D veterans already had served. He has never looked closely at a map of Vietnam and doesn't know where any of those places are, even though Vietnam maps had been plastered on the walls of classrooms

from Ft. Campbell to Ft. Gordon. It occurs to him now that
he ought to take a look at a map, to sort of get to know the
place where he is going to spend the next year and probably
die. Learn the terrain. Be prepared. Don't put your homework off until Sunday night. He will always have the mind
of a nun.

He orders another boilermaker.

The sun is gone by the time he walks out of the bar into a
darkness held at bay by birthday-cake marquee bulb light
shining on all the young people, not really hippies, just
young, waiting in line outside Woodstock. Nobody is waiting
outside Patton. The Woodstock Theater raised its admission
price to five dollars, a genuine gouge and rip leading to
angry calls on talk-radio, miffed commentary by TV anchor-
men and letters-to-the-editor. Mallory went to see it and said
long-haired kids sitting in the aisles sang along with the
performances. Sounds corny to Palmer, who doesn't like
acid-rock. Early Beatles forever. He crosses Market Street and
walks toward the F.W. Woolworth store and realizes that he
has been on the San Francisco peninsula for more than two
months and has seen almost nothing of it.

A trolley is rotating on a circular platform beside the
Woolworth before starting its journey back up Powell Street,
conductors in uniform doing it manually, like push-starting
a car in a Denver winter dawn. Street vendors hawk jewelry
to mom and pop who have stopped to take pictures of the
trolley. Sidewalk musicians play guitars or saxophones, or

else hammer tambourines, their hats upturned on the sidewalk. Kids Palmer's age are hanging out listening to the music or panhandling, or else just sitting on the sidewalk in circles wearing ponchos, leather hats, granny glasses. They're blue-jean hippies, and remind him of the first AWOLs he and Courtney had transferred to the stockade. Probably no AWOLs here, just boys waiting for their draft notices, the girls just waiting. When he had arrived at basic training on the bus, half the men still had long hair, and a few had mustaches, though he didn't see any beards. One white inductee had an interesting overblown red Afro. Palmer had supposed they were trying to show the army that it couldn't push them around and intimidate them into getting their hair cut before they showed up for induction, but after the recruits left the barber shop you couldn't tell the rebels from a crate of cantaloupes. If there's one thing the army knows how to do, it's push people around.

He looks at his watch. Six-thirty. He's been drinking for six hours and can still stand up. He had seen his name on the Vietnam roster not quite twenty-four hours ago. On the day that he had received orders for MP school his worries had dwindled considerably because even if he got sent to Vietnam he wouldn't be humping the boonies with a rucksack and a rifle. But that was when two months of MP school stood between himself and Vietnam. Now he's worried again, and his only consolation is that his brother Phil no longer has to worry about going to Vietnam as a combat rifleman because the army by law can't send two brothers into a combat zone at the same time. The Sullivan Law. Palmer had seen the movie about the Sullivans when he was a kid. Bobby Driscoll was in the movie, but died in 1968, his corpse found in a tenement in Greenwich Village.

The thing to do, now that he has had his afternoon on Market Street, his twenty-one drunk in real bars though no striptease, no topless or especially bottomless, is take a cab back to the Presidio and get on the phone and call his brother Phil. It's the sort of news that an Infantry trainee would want to hear as soon as possible.

When the taxi pulls into the parking lot, Palmer makes a slow show of tipping the driver two dollars and almost asks for a receipt, but worries he might get nailed for faking a trip on his reimbursement.

He goes into the barracks with the assumption that Courtney is at Cheryl's apartment, but when he looks into Courtney's room he sees him lying on his bunk with one arm flung across his eyes. The overhead lights are off and the room is dark.

Courtney drops his arm a notch and looks at him. "When did you get back?"

"Last night."

"Someone told me they saw you in the barracks today but I didn't believe him."

"We're going to Vietnam."

Courtney nods. "I did something stupid last night."

"What?"

"I asked Cheryl to marry me."

"What did she say?"

"No."

Palmer doesn't say anything. This news doesn't seem very important. Nothing seems very important anymore.

"She said we should wait," Courtney says.

"For what?"

"Until I get back from Vietnam."

Palmer pulls out a flattened pack of cigarettes and knocks one out and sticks it in his mouth.

"Don't light that," Courtney says. He's a runner and doesn't like people smoking in his room.

"So what's the problem?" Palmer says, annoyed. "You wait until you come home, and then you get married."

"The problem is," he says, rising on an elbow and eyeing the unlit cigarette, "I'll be gone a year."

Palmer wants to say, there's no point in marrying her now because you're going to die in Vietnam just like I am. We're two dead men having a conversation in a dark room.

But says only, "When are you signing out of the company?"

"I don't know."

"I'm waiting until the last day. Some of the men upstairs are trying to get a group together to fly over at the same time." He doesn't know why he even brought that up. Now he's one of them.

"How was the funeral?" Courtney says.

"Sort of depressing."

"Did you meet Thorpe's family?"

"Yeah."

"What were they like?"

"They were nice. The father uses a wheelchair. He must have been pretty old when Thorpe was born." Palmer pauses a moment, then says, "Did you ever know Thorpe's first name?"

"No. What was it?"

"Leland."

Courtney nods, slides his arm over his eyes.

It's almost eight o'clock. Palmer is tired, and realizes he's not going to call Phil after all. His brother is probably at a Ft. Lewis EM club anyway, and there would be no way of finding him. "I've been downtown all day drinking."

"You smell like it."

Palmer puts the cigarette back into the pack. "I'm turning in." He would like to take a shower before he goes to bed but decides not to risk it. He knows he's as loaded now as on the night of the bitter Screaming Eagle, but not as weary and worn out and exhausted. The magic of taxis, a lesson learned too late.

CHAPTER 22

The sound goes muddy, and the hatched-faced child of the old west can no longer be understood. At the back of the room the sergeant flips switches and curses at the movie projector, but Palmer just sits and listens. There was a time when he might have stood up and volunteered his esoteric knowledge of movie equipment with, always at the back of his mind, the idea that helping out might be to his benefit at some point in the future. But now he just sits, waiting for the class to end, waiting for the day to end so he can get over to the bowling alley for his first beer of the evening. He already had his first beer of the day at noon, three of them along with an oven-warmed hamburger. He had learned from his mistake on the night of the wall lockers to get something in his belly when he drinks, illicitly or not.

The speaker squeaks and Johnny Crawford's voice resumes describing his time in the army. As with all the movies shown so far during training month, Palmer had seen this one in basic, though then he had been charmed to see the son of The Rifleman decked out in fatigue green, tall and filled out, a man with broad shoulders, though his face still that of the kid Mark McCain. A brief singing career, then drafted to make training films. Mickey Dolenz had been Circus Boy, then a Monkee, and a friend of Palmer once claimed that Mickey Dolenz was serving at Ft. Ord, like Elvis in Germany—imagine pulling KP alongside the King of rock 'n' roll. Gerry Lewis drafted too, and last year in a 3.2 bar someone had told him that the Beaver was killed in Vietnam.

"Palmer, wake up!"

He opens his eyes, surprised that the sound of the rewinding projector and the brightness of the switched-on overhead lights didn't wake him first. Asleep erect in his seat, something that hasn't happened since basic training. Sgt. Logan is looking right at him, trying to be a hard-assed sarge. Promoted from Specialist Fourth-Class to Sergeant E5 three weeks earlier, he has trouble getting anyone to take him seriously. It's hard to be a sergeant when everyone knew you as a dud EM. Usually newby buck-sergeants get transferred to another unit, but for some reason Logan is still here.

Palmer sits up straight and smiles at Sgt. Logan. He's embarrassed at getting caught asleep, but more than that, is worried that Logan might come over and smell the beer on his breath.

One more film to sit through, and when it comes on, Palmer is disappointed because he has seen this one too. Some of the repeats are interesting and grotesque—the traffic accident films, or the man's toes turning black because he was standing motionless in his snowy Germany foxhole. The doctors pull off his dead toes like a funny little hat. But this film is about a GI who won't bathe. Shot on an obvious Hollywood set in black-and-white, the man's buddies gather around him in the barracks and sing "What Do You Do With A Dirty Soldier?" while the plough jockey with the cruddy neck hangs his head in shame.

Palmer has come to prefer shit-detail month over training month. Repetitious daily classrooms weigh heavily on his heart, though getting out on the parking lot of the bowling alley with a four-foot billy club to practice riot-control isn't too bad. The sergeants once talked about an anti-war riot down at the Lombard gate a year earlier. "I got spit on by so many protesters that my fatigues turned black," said one grinning sergeant. Another sergeant diddled the tip of his nightstick and said, "I can't wait to get a little hippie blood on this thing." All the draftees looked at each other, then looked at the sky. The proximity to the bowling alley had made Palmer thirsty, as does his proximity to Vietnam.

———————

On Friday night he goes down the hall to see if Courtney might be interested in going to the bowling alley, but Courtney is gone, he's always at Cheryl's, Palmer hasn't seen him in the barracks during the evening since Sunday.

The bowling alley is crowded, so he can't sit in what he has come to think of as "my spot," the table at the far end of the bar up against the wall where he and Courtney had drunk together the first time. He steps up to the counter but has to wait to order because the crowd is heavy, a Friday night crowd, and when he finally gets his beer there's no place to sit down. He goes to the railing and watches the lifer families bowl, and wonders why it had never occurred to him to play a game. He buys a second beer and goes into the pinball foyer and stands with the crowd around his favorite machine and considers putting a quarter on the glass, but decides not to. Cheering strangers only want you to lose so they can take over the flippers.

When he goes for another beer he sees SP4 Glasgow, a Vietnam veteran with two months left in the army, seated at his own favorite spot near the railing. Sometimes Glasgow drinks with other men, and sometimes he drinks alone, but he always drinks. Sometimes he shows up at morning formation hungover and wearing fatigues that look like they have been slept in, but none of the sergeants ever gives him any shit, other than telling him to go take a shower and put on fresh fatigues.

Palmer would like to go up to Glasgow and ask him what it was like in Vietnam, or more specifically, how did he manage to come home alive? But Glasgow might not want to talk about the war. And since Palmer has never made any attempt to talk to Glasgow before, a pretense at friendship now might be a little too transparent, which is the basic problem with making friends with people only when you want something from them.

He hasn't called Phil yet. A peculiar kind of lethargy comes over him whenever he thinks about making the call. It's only when he drinks that he feels guilty about not letting his brother know he won't be dying in Vietnam. Sober, the knowledge makes Palmer strangely indifferent, the way a "given" often affects him—which is to say, what's the rush? But he decides to try and get in touch with Phil later on in the evening, and at nine-thirty he leaves the bowling alley high but not killer drunk. Phil is probably out drinking too, a convenient excuse not to call him, but then maybe Phil's CQ would try to track him down in the company area.

A heavy fog is drifting across the quad—Palmer can feel a sheen of moisture clinging to his face which he wipes off with his fingers which glisten like Thorpe's wax face in the porch light of the building he's passing, the engineering barracks of the bitter Screaming Eagle.

When he walks into Company D, a new buck sergeant named Lyttle is standing in the foyer changing notices on the bulletin board. He does a double-take, and says, "Private Palmer! Where've you been?"

This pisses Palmer off because it's none of this newby-sergeant's business what he does when he's off-duty, and it's only out of military courtesy that he replies, "I was down at the bowling alley, sergeant."

"You got a phone call twenty minutes ago."

A death in the family of course. Why else anyone would call him? "Who was it?"

"A girl. I wrote her number down in the office."

One of his sisters. Someone must have died. He can think only along this line, he doesn't think about Cheryl at all, who also has the company number, but that's who had called.

Lyttle shows him the number on a note pad in the office, and Palmer asks if he can use the phone. The sergeant says yes, then hangs around to listen in. There's not much Palmer can do about that, so he dials, and when Cheryl answers, she sounds upset.

"I'm glad you called. They told me you were gone."

"I was at the bowling alley."

"Palmer, I hate to ask this of you, but could you come over to my apartment? Courtney is here and he's drunk, and I want you to take him back to the barracks."

"What's the matter?"

"I just want him out of here. Can you come and get him? He has his car here, but he's too drunk to drive."

Palmer tells her it will take at least an hour to get over there. He hangs up and tells Lyttle that Courtney is drunk down in the city and needs someone to come get him. Could the CQ runner drive him as far as the Lombard gate? From there he'll try to flag a taxi coming from the EM club. But the asshole buck-sergeant says no, so Palmer ends up phoning for a cab.

He sits in the slightly oily-smelling backseat of the Yellow Cab and watches a familiar landscape passing, the same route he had followed to Cheryl's on the first night he had gone there with Courtney. Golden Gate Park is empty. His brother Mike had talked about moving to San Francisco during the summer-of-love, but had gotten a job in a garage instead. Palmers never do anything. He considers asking the driver to stop at the liquor store on Stanyan, but decides it would probably be better to do that on the way back to the barracks, fulfilling his fantasy of sitting on his bunk and drinking beer until dawn, although the current fantasy involves a pint of scotch, and later on perhaps wandering upstairs to watch one of the two TVs rented by two different groups of men in the second platoon. San Francisco has good late-night TV. Vinton had tried to talk the squad into getting a TV from a rental place downtown, only five bucks apiece, but Palmer wouldn't part with even that small amount for something as important in his life as TV once had been, and he has since regretted it.

One hour after he had spoken to Cheryl on the phone he arrives at her building. When he presses the button, the security door immediately buzzes with its incredibly annoying electric growl. Cheryl comes out of her apartment before he's even halfway down the hallway.

"Thank you for coming, Palmer," she says. Her face is drawn and tight, she's been crying, her eyes rimmed red, her cheeks flushed. Palmer enters the apartment and sees

Courtney lying on the couch wearing his windbreaker. One arm across his eyes, he looks like he was getting ready to leave and then passed out.

"Please take him out of here," Cheryl says.

"What happened?"

"Please don't ask. Just take him out of here. I don't ever want to see him again."

Palmer walks over to the couch. "Wake up, Courtney." He leans down and taps Courtney's shoulder, but doesn't get any response. He decides that Courtney is faking it—sleeping people wake up when you touch them.

"Get up, Courtney. Give me your car keys, I'm driving you back to the barracks."

The stirring begins: arm moving slowly away from the face, eyelids flickering, a protracted inhalation of breath. Palmer recognizes the moves. Courtney is pretending to wake up.

"Give me your keys."

Courtney closes his eyes and guides his hand to the pocket of his windbreaker, pulls the keys out and holds them up, then drops them to the floor. Palmer recognizes this too—drunk stuff, drunk tricks, drunk jokes, and later on there will probably be drunk talk.

He picks up the keys and reaches for his arm, "Come on, Courtney," but Courtney bats at his hand. To speed things up, Palmer grabs his shoulder and rolls him onto the floor.

Courtney starts laughing, which is good, then starts mumbling, "All right, all right," and it occurs to Palmer that Courtney might be pulling this act because he's embarrassed that Cheryl had to call for help. He tries to move Courtney along, helping him up off the floor and sort of aiming him at the door. Embarrassed for everybody, Palmer tries to make light of it, but when he smiles at Cheryl, she's weeping and dabbing at her face with a Kleenex. None of this is funny to her. She wants him out of here.

He guides Courtney into the hallway and tells him to wait. Courtney leans back against the wall and closes his eyes, and Palmer goes back into the apartment and shuts the door. He puts his arms around Cheryl, and she leans her head on his shoulder.

"If you want to talk, I can come back here after I drop Courtney off," he says quietly so that Courtney won't hear.

Cheryl doesn't say anything, but shakes her head yes with her lips clamped tight and her eyes squeezed shut leaking tears.

Courtney is gone. But Palmer finds him outdoors on the sidewalk standing with his face raised to a night sky hidden by a fog so thick that it's almost a rain. His mouth is wide open and he's breathing deeply.

"Are you okay?" Palmer says, wanting to get this chore over with quickly.

His hair matted, his face wet and sparkling in the light of the foyer, Courtney looks down at him but doesn't say anything.

"Come on, Courtney. Let's go back to the barracks."

Courtney tucks his hands into his pockets and walks so steadily to the car that Palmer wonders if he's drunk at all. Courtney climbs in shotgun, and Palmer gets behind the wheel and starts the engine. He maneuvers the car out onto the steep slick brick street and coasts downhill and turns right past Kezar Stadium. He turns left onto Stanyan Street, drives past the panhandle lawn which points like a finger toward the peace/love Haight now invisible in the fog. They pass the liquor store and come to a red light at Geary, where Palmer stops the car.

"Do you know why I came back to the barracks that night?" Courtney says, his voice so thick that Palmer knows he's been drinking something.

"What night?"

"The night you didn't get promoted to PFC. The night I came back to the barracks and found you lying on your bunk feeling sorry for yourself."

Palmer nods but doesn't look at him.

"Do you know why I came back?"

"No." Palmer keeps his eyes fixed on the red light.

"I came back to see if you had packed your bags and run home to mama."

When Palmer doesn't say anything, Courtney adds, "You always seemed like the AWOL type to me, Palmer."

The light turns green.

"So you were wrong," Palmer says dryly, stepping on the gas. When Courtney doesn't say anything, Palmer glances over at him. "You know something, Courtney? Everybody thinks they've got me all figured out. Everybody thinks they can see right through me. You're just like everybody I ever knew."

Up Geary and turning right onto Arguello, he drives through the Presidio gate past the golf course and up the hill toward Company D.

Courtney looks over at him. "You're right, Palmer. I was wrong about you." Then says, "Thanks for coming to get me."

"What did you do to Cheryl?" Palmer says, not a bit mollified. "She was really mad at you. You didn't hit her did you?"

"No. I just drank too much. Then I got sarcastic." He clears his throat and wipes at the moisture dripping from his hair. "I made a crack about her drawings, and she got mad."

"What kind of crack?"

"Just that she wouldn't have to waste her time drawing pictures if we got married."

"Is that why she called me? Is that why she was mad?"

"We had an argument after that."

"Did you ask her to marry you again?"

"I shouldn't have gone over to her place drunk. That was where I messed up."

Palmer slows the car and makes the turn into the Company D parking lot. He laughs softly and shakes his head. "You know something, Courtney? You just might be right about that."

He parks in a space behind the barracks, and they get out. Palmer follows Courtney all the way into his room and waits while he drags his clothes off and falls into bed.

"I'll close the door," Palmer says as he backs out of the room even though doors are supposed to stay open in the barracks. A feeble pretense at consideration, but he's hoping that the closed door might help muffle the sound of Courtney's car pulling out of the parking lot.

CHAPTER 23

Retracing the route, Palmer makes a stop at the liquor store even though he knows he can't drink an entire pint of Johnny Walker and expect to be able to drive back to the barracks. But he has a plan. Two swallows before he rings Cheryl's doorbell, and after the night is over, one swallow in the car for that satisfying hazy drive back to the barracks where he can toss the pint into a dumpster or else finish it on his bunk, the sort of decision that can't be made until it's time to surrender to the inevitable.

He doesn't open the bottle until he's parked safely outside Cheryl's in the same space he had vacated almost an hour earlier, an omen in his view, miraculous in a city where people park on the sidewalk in non-emergencies. The question is, should he bring the pint in with him?

He decides to leave it on the front seat where it will be easily available if he needs it. He gets out and goes to the front door, rings the bell, and peers through the flimsy lace curtains covering the glass. In his fantasy scenario, Cheryl hurries out of the apartment and greets him with silent kisses and takes his hand and leads him to the Murphy bed to show her gratitude to him for removing Courtney from her life. He assumes that Courtney is gone forever because he could not imagine any woman ever wanting to see himself again if he had come to her place drunk and made her that angry.

He rings the doorbell a second time, then has to wait almost a minute before Cheryl finally steps out of the apartment. She doesn't hurry as she comes down the hall. She had changed out of the clothes she had been wearing earlier, now it's baggy paint-stained khakis and a bulky sweater frayed at the cuffs. Her arms are folded across her breasts, and she isn't smiling although she no longer looks angry.

"Thank you for coming back, Palmer," she says as she opens the door. She doesn't open it wide. She blocks the way with her body.

Palmer is no stranger to this message. "Is it all right if I come in?"

She stands back. He edges past her and walks down the hall and enters her apartment. Every light bulb in the place is burning, even in the bathroom.

Cheryl steps inside and closes the door. "Thank you for helping out, Palmer." She doesn't make a move toward the couch, or to the kitchen as he had hoped, to mix him a drink. She just stands there with her arms folded like she doesn't want him to know she has tits.

It's cold in the room. The unsyncopated clank of the radiator pipes which he had become accustomed to in the background is missing. Cheryl is from the South so he would think she would always want the heat turned on, but maybe the cold is a novelty. At any rate, it doesn't look like it's going to get any warmer in the apartment. "Would you mind if I had a drink?" he says.

She surprises him by hurrying into the kitchen as if glad to be doing something other than what he doubtless wants to do. He sits on the couch but keeps his windbreaker on as a signal to her that things are going to work out the way she wants, that he will not be staying long enough to take off his coat.

He feels better when she brings out a bottle of scotch instead of the beer he had been expecting. She hands him a shot glass. She will not be drinking, and when she sits down on the only chair in the room, he is not surprised.

He pours a shot and drinks it off, and sets the glass down. "What happened tonight?"

Cheryl answers matter-of-factly, as though she had been rehearsing this conversation the whole time he had been gone. "Courtney came over around six. He was drunk. I shouldn't have let him in but he said he just wanted to talk." She pauses and looks him in the eye. "I suppose he told you he asked me to marry him."

"Yes."

She looks at the floor and her voice goes hard. "I don't want to get married right now. Getting married is what the women of my family do." She looks up at Palmer. "I came to San Francisco to get away from my family."

This is not the conversation Palmer had been looking forward to having during the drive over. He looks at the scotch bottle. But he's had his drink. "I'm sorry this happened, Cheryl."

She looks up at him. "I'm sorry you and Courtney received orders for Vietnam."

"I sort of expected it all along," he says, which is only a half-lie. "When I came here from MP school, I knew they could still send me over there."

"My daddy served overseas in World War Two," she says. "In France."

"My father served in New Guinea."

The conversation has now moved halfway around the world. He considers going ahead and pouring another drink, then realizes that his Colorado driver's license had expired on his birthday, and if he gets stopped by the San Francisco police on the way back to the barracks he could be arrested for drunk driving with an expired license in a stolen vehicle. But still, he thinks about having another drink.

"I plan to sign out of the company in three weeks," he says. "I'd like to see you again before I go home."

"You can come see me any time," she says. "I do want to say goodbye to you before you leave."

"I just came over to make sure you're all right," he lies. "Thanks for the drink. I better get Courtney's car back to the barracks."

She looks relieved when he stands up, as he knew she would—she doesn't have to deal with two assholes on the same night. Then she surprises him by putting her arms around him and kissing him on the lips, which, because he has been thinking about it, he is able to take brief but expert advantage of. Her lips are unbelievably soft, not like the rigid puckers of former Denver girlfriends who were always irked at him for taking them nowhere except drive-in movies, the only memory he has for comparison.

"Thank you for coming back here," she says, dragging a tangle of hair from her face and smiling as though there had been no problem earlier in the evening. He can tell that she is absolutely delighted to see him leave.

Three drinks within the past twenty minutes, yet he feels more sober now than when he had dropped Courtney off. As he starts the car he feels slightly appalled at what he had attempted to do, now that he has failed to do it.

He drives around the block and down to Irving and gets out and carries the pint to the curb. He sets the bottle gently upright next to a mailbox where someone who needs it a lot less than he does might find it and make good use of it, a middle-aged bum perhaps, since hippies drink and smoke only tea.

No longer concerned about getting stopped by SFPD with an open bottle in his possession, he feels good as he drives back to the Presidio, feels relieved, like he has just been allowed to take back a bad move in chess. To help cover his tracks, he parks in the same spot behind the barracks that he had parked in earlier. He gets out and locks the door, walks around to the front of the barracks and opens the door to his room. "You went to see her, didn't you?"

Palmer's hand is still on the doorknob, and he almost steps back onto the porch. It's Courtney's voice, but he can't see him because the fluorescent light coming in from the hallway makes the rest of the room black.

Courtney comes toward him out of the shadow of a wall locker. "You took my car, didn't you?"

Palmer starts to answer but finds he has to clear his throat first. "Yes, I took your car. I went back to make sure Cheryl was okay." This sounds so lame that he adds quickly, "You scared the hell out of her." Courtney's fists are balled in the pockets of his fatigues. Palmer can see the ridge of each knuckle in the poor light. "I took your keys without asking because I knew you wouldn't let me use your car."

Courtney stares at him.

Palmer glances from Courtney's eyes to his pocketed fists, but can't really see them very well. "Let's go into the hall," he says. He steps around Courtney into the glare of the fluorescents and turns so he can see everything if anything happens. Courtney follows at a slow stroll. His eyes are red, but they're hard, so Palmer knows he's angry, and expects Courtney to swing on him.

"Did you kiss her?" Courtney says.

"I went back to see if she was all right. We talked and when I left she thanked me for coming and kissed me goodnight."

Courtney eyes are on Palmer's face, but at least his hands are still in his pockets. He drags one out and runs his fingers through his hair. "You should have asked me if you could take my car, Palmer." He doesn't sound angry now. He just sounds resigned to the sort of friend Palmer has turned out to be.

"I know," Palmer says. "I'm sorry, but I knew you wouldn't—" He reaches into his pocket and pulls out the keys. "Here."

Courtney takes them and turns away and shuffles back to his room. Palmer stands in the glare of the fluorescents feeling the slow remission of a steady adrenaline flow leaving a hot ache in his muscles. He looks down at his hands. They're starting to shake as though they had been flexed for a long time.

He steps into his room and leans against his bunk in the darkness. He feels as he sometimes had felt back when he was a civilian between jobs and had been drinking for days on end and would finally wake up sober one morning engulfed by the awful sensation that he had committed some terrible crime. He would go out to buy food, and would feel as if everyone in the neighborhood was watching him from their windows and commenting on how fucked-up he was. He could usually get rid of the feeling by getting drunk as soon as possible, but if he stayed sober, it took days for the feeling to fade away.

CHAPTER 24

"Well buddy, Ah've decided to reenlist."

Palmer and Beaudry are on the same sort of shit detail in the Company D supply room which Palmer and Thorpe had once pulled in battalion supply, make-work to fill a body-roster devoid of meaning. They had been talking about Palmer's orders for Vietnam, then had Beaudry dropped his bomb.

The only other person Palmer had ever known to reenlist was a trainee in the reception station prior to basic who was told by his temporary platoon-sergeant that if he signed up and added another year to his drafted enlistment he would receive a re-up bonus, but he had to do it right now or he would never get the opportunity again. The kid ran to a phone booth to call his wife and tell her about this once-in-a-lifetime offer. It was embarrassing.

"Where do you want to go?" Palmer asks, because when a man reenlists, he transfers.

"Korea."

"I have a buddy from MP school in Korea. He's a stockade guard in Seoul."

"Well, shit, give me his name, and if Ah see him Ah'll say howdy for ya."

But it's inconceivable to Palmer that anybody would add a year to his enlistment. How could anybody not think the way he thinks? How could Beaudry not hate the army enough to reenlist?

"Beaudry?"

"Yeah?"

"You're not a lifer are you?"

"Hail no."

"That's the real reason you're reenlisting, isn't it? You're a lifer."

"Whyn'tchoo go fuck yourself, Palmer."

"You want that re-up bonus, don't you? You want to buy a new car."

"Kiss mah ass, you donkey-dick motherfucker," Beaudry the grinning Texan says.

"Well, when you get to Korea, don't forget to write."

"Ah won't," Beaudry says, completing the ritual of the Mandatory Buddy Lie which is performed by every enlisted man during his stretch in the service. A man says it for the first time at the end of basic when he believes he has made friendships that will last a lifetime, and that when he's seventy years-old he'll still be writing letters to these kids with whom he suffered and endured eight weeks of training. He also says the Mandatory Buddy Lie at the end of advanced individual training: MP school, Infantry, signal corps, artillery—and, Palmer assumes, a man says it at the onset of his discharge.

Lifers, of course, never say it.

————

At noon the supply sergeant lets them go. When they get downstairs Beaudry walks right up to Sgt. Sherman and says, "Sarge, I wanna re-enlist."

Sgt. Sherman's weary lifer face lights up, and he smiles. "Where do you want to go, Beaudry?"

"Korea."

Sherman's face falls. "Germany," he says, tapping Beaudry on the shoulder. "That's the place to be an MP in this man's army."

"Naw sarge, I wanna go to Korea."

Sgt. Sherman puts a hand on Beaudry's shoulder and guides him into the operations office. "Let's talk this over, troop."

Palmer steps out onto the porch grinning because this is like hearing one of your friends announce that he's getting married, or that his wife of two months is pregnant, when it seems like only yesterday you were sitting in his car in the senior parking-lot smoking cigarettes out of sight of the nuns and talking philosophically about The Future, that fuzzy and abstract series of events which you assumed was going to kick-in the moment you received your high-school diploma.

Mail-call is being held at one of the open windows on the porch, so Palmer walks over to the rear of the crowd and listens for his name. He isn't expecting anything because none of his worthless Denver friends ever writes, nor does anyone in his family except his brother Phil in Ft. Lewis. Palmer writes to Phil on occasion because he remembers how disconnected from the world he himself had felt during training and how great it was to get a letter, but until recently he rarely ever thought of Phil, and when he did write, it always took an effort because he couldn't think of anything to say.

So he's pleased when he hears his name hollered by the mail clerk, a man who was once a member of his training platoon at Ft. Gordon and who is now entrenched in an office job. Palmer takes the letter and walks into his room looking at the neatly squared and easily recognizable handwriting of his brother Phil. He tears the end off and slides the letter out and is surprised that it's only one page long, because trainees tend to ramble.

He reads the letter, and then, instead of putting it on the top shelf of his wall locker where he puts all his letters before accumulating enough of them to throw away en masse, and instead of getting into the chow line forming up at the screen door to the mess hall, he puts the letter into his shirt pocket and leaves his room and heads down the sidewalk with a kind of mechanical inevitability toward the bowling alley where he had thought he might stop going during the noon hours, following the near-debacle of last Saturday night.

A surprising number of GIs are in the snack bar this noon. You can never tell about Fridays. He edges toward the counter and dispenses with pretense and asks for two bottled Buds which the bartender, the color-guard member of Company C whom Palmer had recognized at the retirement parade, sets on the counter with a sharp tap which Palmer interprets as disapproval.

He takes his beers to his spot against the wall and drinks half of the first bottle before he removes the letter from his shirt pocket and smooths it out on the Formica and rereads it.

Just a short note from Phil saying that he will graduate from Infantry AIT on Friday (today—which means he will be in Denver by this evening) and that he had already received his orders for his next assignment, and that following his allotted fourteen-day leave from Ft. Lewis, he will report to the Army Replacement Depot at Oakland, California, for further reassignment to the Republic of South Vietnam.

Palmer doesn't let Cheryl know he's coming. A little before noon on Saturday he calls a taxi, and at one P.M. he has the driver let him off at a bus stop on Irving Street one block down the hill from her apartment. Barely buzzed by his lunch beers he steps into a bar which he and Cheryl and Courtney had passed on the day they had gone to the beach. He wants a shot of hard liquor before making the uphill trek.

A shaft of stark sunlight coming through the front window guides him to the bar, but the room beyond is so dark that until his pupils dilate he doesn't realize he has entered what appears to be a biker bar. The bartender is a big man, bearded and heavy-set in a black T-shirt, with tattoos up and down both arms. He smiles and asks what Palmer would like.

"A shot of Johnny Walker Red."

Frowning, the man does a slow turn toward the shelves, then looks back and says he's out of Johnny Walker—what else would you like?

Palmer doesn't want to say bar scotch because he's heard that's supposed to be the cheapest stuff. "What have you got?"

The bartender eases back to let Palmer see the selection of dusty bottles lined up against the mirror. When Palmer doesn't say anything right away, the bartender points with a thumb and says, "Wild Turkey?"

Palmer nods, sensitive to the diplomacy of letting this man make the choice. But he has never drank Wild Turkey before, has never tasted bourbon, and is extremely disappointed by the flavor as he knocks it back and pays and walks out. Bikers. The only thing he knows about motorcycle gangs comes from Roger Corman movies and Marlon Brando.

He walks up the hill toward Cheryl's apartment past a Victorian building where long-haired kids are seated on a stoop playing guitars. Freedom hovers like an aura around them, and their mere presence makes Palmer feel momentarily like a civilian again, thus enhancing his own giddy sense of freedom.

He looks up at Cheryl's window as he passes, hoping she might glance out and see him. But her shades are drawn, which means she might not be home, and if she isn't, he will just go to a bar and make calls until she does show up. When he rings the bell to her apartment though, her voice answers sharply through the speaker, "Who is it!" which surprises him.

"It's Palmer."

"What do you want?"

Her irritation is both obvious and incomprehensible. He leans toward the speaker. "I came over to tell you some good news."

"Did Courtney send you?"

He pauses a moment to look around at all the cars parked at the curb up and down Parnassus hill. He leans closer to the speaker. "No, Courtney didn't send me. I came over to tell you something."

He waits for the terrible electric noise of the door buzzer, but it doesn't come. Instead, Cheryl steps outside her door at the far end of the hall and stands looking at him. Then she strolls down the hall with her arms folded, and when she gets close to the door she looks above his head. "Is Courtney with you?"

He shakes his head no and pulls the envelope out of his pocket and holds it up. "Courtney's not with me. I have some good news to tell you."

"What news?"

She isn't going to open the door. Palmer doesn't want to explain all this through a window, but there is nothing else to do. He removes the letter and unfolds it and places it against the glass.

She looks at it, then raises her eyes and looks over his head.

"My brother Phil got orders to go to Vietnam," he says.

Cheryl reaches down and unlocks the door, pulls it open fast and hisses at him to get inside. She leads him down the hall into her apartment where the odor of paint is heavy in the air. An easel is standing in the middle of the floor supporting a stretched and framed canvas. All around the easel, on the chair and coffee table and couch, are the utensils and clutter of her art.

"Excuse the way the place looks," she says with a shy smile.

Palmer walks up to the easel and looks at the picture. Two kittens side-by-side, one sleeping and one awake licking its paw. Some kind of ad. "This is good."

"Thank you." She crosses the room, raises a curtain and opens a window. "Stinks in here, doesn't it?"

"I like the smell," he says. "My mother studied painting when she was a girl. She still has her palette and brushes. I like the smell of oil paint."

"I'm working with acrylic," she says. "I'm doing a job for the shop."

Palmer doesn't know oil from acrylic. He looks around for a place to sit down, but everything is covered with paint-stained newspapers and rags.

"Did Courtney send you here with a message?" she says.

"No. I got this letter from my brother Phil, and I wanted to show it to you." He holds it up. "He wrote to tell me he got orders to go to Vietnam."

She nods. She doesn't understand.

"There's a rule in the army that says two brothers can't be sent to a combat zone at the same time." He begins waving the paper as he speaks. "It's a rule from World War Two. And since my brother and I both got orders for Vietnam, only one of us has to go over there."

"Which one?"

"Well. My brother. He's supposed to be there in two weeks, and I'm not supposed to go over there for almost six weeks."

Cheryl nods, understanding now, but she doesn't seem impressed. Somehow the scene isn't playing out the way Palmer had imagined it would. He imagined that she would be happy for him, would demonstrate her joy with hugs and kisses. Then he stops thinking about himself long enough to take a good look at Cheryl. Baggy blue-jeans, shirt dotted with brightly-colored fingerprints, her hair is swept back and held with braids. A fine spray of speckles colors her forehead at the hairline. "Why are you working at home?" he says.

"Didn't Courtney tell you?"

"No. I haven't talked to him all week."

"He came by my shop at noon two days ago. I wasn't there. He got into an argument with my boss, and my boss told him he'd call the police if he ever came back. Then my boss suggested I work at home."

"Has Courtney been coming around here?"

"Yes."

Now Palmer knows why it had been so easy to avoid Courtney around the company all week. But it amazes him. How could Courtney be doing such a thing?

"When you see Courtney, tell him to stop coming over here," she says. "I don't ever want to see him again."

Palmer folds the letter and tucks it into his pocket

"There's something else," she says. "I'm glad you came by. You left this here on your birthday."

She goes to her desk and picks up the silver hockey-puck of eight-millimeter film and hands it to him. He takes it and rubs the slippery metal surface with his thumb. He starts to say I wish I had brought my movie camera with me that day, but says only, "Thanks," and stuffs it into the pocket of his windbreaker.

The odor of acrylic is in his clothing and hair, is an aura around him as he steps out to the sidewalk and looks downhill and sees Courtney's car coming up the hill toward him. He turns and walks up to the intersection and considers going down to Irving and catching a bus and ignoring Courtney altogether, except that ignoring a man sometimes can be like running away. So he waits at the intersection and watches Courtney bring the car around the corner and pull up at the far curb.

It's difficult to tell through the window whether he's mad, but Palmer doesn't care because he is pissed at what Courtney has been doing to Cheryl, is pissed at what he is doing right at this very moment.

Courtney rolls down his window and hollers, "Do you need a ride to the barracks?" as if he just happened to be passing by.

Palmer crosses the street but goes to the driver's door to look at Courtney up close. "Hop in," Courtney says. He doesn't look mad. Palmer walks around and climbs in shotgun.

Courtney glances once at Cheryl's window, then drops the shift into gear and guides the car down the hill. "Did she say anything about me?"

"Yes, she did. She said you came around the shop and argued with her boss."

Courtney nods. "I just wanted to talk to her." He gives Palmer a quick look. "Listen, I don't care why you went to see her this afternoon."

That's fine with Palmer, but he wants Courtney to know the reason. He pulls the letter out of his pocket and slaps it lightly against the dashboard.

"I went to her place to show her this letter from my brother Phil. He got orders for Vietnam. He'll be there in two weeks."

Courtney keeps his eyes on the road but raises his chin a bit as if thinking things over. He understands clearly, and states his understanding. "You have to go," he says.

"No I don't."

Courtney glances at him and smiles. "You would do that to your brother, wouldn't you?"

"I'm not doing anything to him. The army is doing it to him."

"He's Infantry. If he goes over there he'll probably get killed. Do you want to go to another funeral?"

Palmer doesn't say anything.

"He could step on a land mine and come back with no legs," Courtney says. "He could come back blind. Do you want that to happen to your brother?"

Palmer remains silent. Courtney glances at him again, then looks at the road. "Don't worry, Palmer. If you go in his place you won't be laying down your life for anybody. MPs don't die in Vietnam."

But Palmer knows that they are not really talking about his brother. In basic training the Drill Sergeants had told them that while they were doing the low-crawl through mud pits wearing thirty-pound rucksacks, Jody was back home diddling their girlfriends. The Drill Sergeants told them that when they got to Vietnam and stood toe-to-toe with Charlie, Jody would be lying face-to-face with their girlfriends in the backseat of his Cadillac convertible. Jody was a 4-F, a draft-dodger, and a college boy. Then the Drill Sergeants would yell, "What is the spirit of the bayonet?" and the troops would shout, "To kill!"

If Palmer doesn't go to Vietnam, he will remain in San Francisco for at least another year—Courtney has been saying as much for the past few minutes, in a voice subtly losing its steady timbre.

When they arrive at the Company D parking-lot, Courtney pulls into a vacant slot, the same slot where the car had been parked on the night Palmer stole the car. As the two men walk side-by-side toward the barracks Palmer reaches into his pocket and pulls out the reel of film. "Look at this. I left it at Cheryl's on my birthday."

In one smooth motion Courtney snatches the canister from his hand and chucks it into the air above the red tile roof of Company D. Palmer is stunned. He watches the rising arc of the projectile as it disappears over the barracks.

But then Courtney holds his open hand in front of Palmer's nose. The canister is lying on his palm.

"Asshole," Palmer says. He grabs the film and stuffs it into his pocket, his anger now replaced by a lesser kind of anger, that of being the butt of a rather good prank. He has no idea what he saw flying into the air. Perhaps only his belief that Courtney would do such a shitty thing.

When they enter the building Courtney steps into the foyer to read the bulletin board and Palmer enters through the porch door to his room. He has a depressing sense that from now on he will be either embarrassed in Courtney's presence or else angry. He puts the canister of unexposed film on the top shelf of his wall locker and looks at his khaki uniforms.

Never worn before, they have never been cleaned or dirtied, and the odor of warehouses still clings to the fabric. He supposes he will wear his green Class A uniform to Oakland, and will bring along one pair of khakis in his duffel bag for the theoretical trip home from Vietnam at the end of his tour. Courtney is right. Palmer had known it even when he was drinking bourbon in the biker bar on Irving Street. He had known it when he was walking up the hill past the happy hippies sitting on the stoop playing their acoustic guitars. He had known it even when he was denying it to Cheryl. He had known since mail-call on Friday afternoon that he would be the brother who would end up going to the war, because MPs don't die in Vietnam.

CHAPTER 25

Palmer eats chow in the bowling alley that night, as he will try to do every night from here on out in a desire to distance himself as much as possible from Company D, now that he is only technically a member of it. He still hasn't called Phil to tell him the good news, a thing he intends to do this very evening, now that he knows for certain that he is going to Vietnam, that there is no realistic way out of it.

Phil will arrive at the Army Replacement Depot on a Friday, and Palmer plans to take a bus to Oakland the day after, and together they will talk to whoever is in charge of these things and formally request that Phil's orders to Vietnam be canceled. But the more he thinks about it, the more half-assed the plan seems. It could be a mistake to assume that anyone at Oakland knows about, or even cares about, the intricacies of an army regulation that Palmer has never actually seen in print.

A kind of dread sprouts in his gut when he thinks about this, and he takes a drink of beer to stifle it. A man in MP school had said that a cousin of his had arrived in Vietnam and stepped off the plane at Tan Son Nuit and was killed by a bullet in the head. Phil could be in the boonies for weeks before his orders could be changed. So it might be best to go back to the company right now and make that call to Denver and get things started, even though Phil is probably right at this moment drinking with his college buddies somewhere in Denver. There is no phone in the basement apartment which Palmer had shared with his brothers, so he knows he might have to leave a message with their slightly senile landlord, a man born in 1890 who can still remember when most of North Denver was orchards and truck-gardens. But when Palmer enters the operations office to see if it's possible to make a collect phone call to Denver (will his landlord even remember him?) the CQ tells him that he had received a phone call an hour earlier.

Not a death in the family this time. Palmer knows what it is and doesn't care. He doesn't want anything more to do with Courtney's stupid devastated love affair. He has devastation of his own to think about. But still, he knows he has to return Cheryl's call.

He dials her number and she picks up the phone on the first ring and tells him that Courtney had left an hour earlier but that she wants Palmer to come over anyway. If he doesn't, she's going to call the police and have them arrest Courtney.

Palmer hangs up, and decides it would probably be better to call Phil in the morning, when the news that he isn't going to Vietnam will be the cure for the hangover that Phil is probably going to wake up with, and what better cure could a man ask for?

Seated in the back of a darkened cab, Palmer wonders why Courtney keeps doing this. Is any woman worth this much heartache? Probably yes, but he has never met her. He likes Cheryl, but why beat up your own heart over a woman who doesn't want you around and has actually said so to your face? Maybe this is the first time Courtney has ever been dumped by a woman, which is Palmer's area of personal expertise: angry blonde behind a closed screen door, brunettes he now thinks of as frowzy, a car-hop, a waitress, a telephone operator. He would be willing to give Courtney the benefit of his hard-earned insights, but Courtney isn't around when the driver pulls up in front of the medical center.

There's a still fog on Parnassus, no wind at all, and walking down the hill Palmer hears only the sounds of retreating trolleys and the scuff of his army shoes on the damp sidewalk. Cheryl's bay window is lit, the kitchen window too. He looks at the drawn curtains and watches for silhouettes moving back and forth, and when he doesn't see any he can't decide whether this is good or bad. He listens for shouts or the sounds of things breaking, but hears nothing. No SFPD cars around. He crosses the street and goes to the front door and presses the bell, and is surprised when the security lock buzzes right away.

He looks around the street before stepping inside, and as he walks up the hallway he keeps looking back expecting to see Courtney's silhouette pressed against the lace curtains on the foyer door.

Cheryl steps into the hall, her lips pressed tight, her eyes red from crying. She doesn't say anything, doesn't thank him for coming, but leads him into the apartment where the floor is cluttered with open cardboard boxes and stacks of folded clothing.

"Has Courtney been back since you called?" Palmer says.

"No."

He sees now, in the brighter light, that her face is blotchy from weeping, her nose pink from dabbing at it with Kleenex and blowing uselessly. Her eyes encircled with shadow, she is exhausted. Palmer looks around at the boxes, which he at first thought had to do with her art. "You're moving out," he says.

She nods, and crosses the room and sits on the couch. She draws her legs up and, like a child, wraps her arms around her knees. "I'm moving out tomorrow morning. Courtney doesn't know. Some men from the shop are bringing a truck over to move my things. I have a friend who lives across town who's going to let me stay with her for a while." She pauses. "I may go back to North Carolina." She begins weeping. "I am so sorry to be acting this way, Palmer. Do you have to go back to your barracks tonight?"

"No."

"I don't believe Courtney will come back here, because I told him I was going to call the police. But could you stay with me until morning? Until my friends arrive? I would so appreciate it. I don't want to have to call the police."

Palmer nods, even though he has no desire to be in the middle of something going on between two people who once liked or even loved each other but don't anymore. "I can stay."

He wants a drink badly. He tells her that he needs to use the bathroom, and goes inside and shuts the door and sits on the lidded toilet and puts his face in his hands. You make friends, and you end up with your face in your hands.

After a few minutes he finds he has to piss after all, so he hurries it. When he comes out, Cheryl calls from the kitchen asking if he would like something to drink. He replies loudly that he'll take a beer. He removes his windbreaker and sits on the couch.

When she brings it out she's smiling, obviously making the best of things. She had washed her face in the kitchen, and the pink from her crying is now a glow. She sits on the chair by the couch and folds her hands in her lap and leans forward. "There is something else I would like you to do for me, Palmer."

"Whatever you want."

"The next time you see Courtney, I want you to tell him not to try to find out where I am going."

"All right."

"I know that he will be able to find me if he really wants to, but I want you to make it clear to him that if I have to, I will personally speak to his commanding officer about this situation."

This is a good threat. Involving Captain Weller would be a terrible thing for Courtney.

"You and Courtney are friends," she says. "I'm sure he will listen to you."

Palmer nods, keeps quiet.

"Have you had dinner yet?" she says.

"I ate at the bowling alley." But when she offers to fix him a hamburger, he accepts.

She returns to the kitchen and begins opening cupboard doors. Palmer looks around at the cardboard boxes. They are filled mostly with clothing but also paint supplies, brushes, rolled canvases. She must have begun packing the moment Courtney left. He looks at the double-doors against the wall where the Murphy Bed is raised out of sight, then looks at the library paintings on the walls, different now from the ones he had seen the first night he had come here.

She brings out his meal, a hamburger on a plate crowded with potato chips. He eats slowly, thinking how truly different this is from mess hall food which everyone makes jokes about but which he likes anyway, especially the army roast beef.

Cheryl waits until he finishes the hamburger, then says, "I still have some scotch if you would care for any."

He nods, wiping the ketchup from his lips casually and not looking her in the eye so she won't see how eager he is. Another beer would actually go better with this wad of food in his now-full belly, but he keeps quiet, afraid of snapping the delicate thread of this pure and unexpected moment. Cheryl comes out of the kitchen carrying two shot-glasses and a bottle of Johnny Walker Red.

"I bought these at the Embarcadero," she says with a giggle, sitting on the couch so close to Palmer that her body heat feels like sunlight. She sets the glasses and bottle down on the coffee table. Palmer picks up a shot glass and studies the embossed picture: a man wearing a green-and-red plaid kilt, squeezing a tucked bag and wheezing into pipes, all this set against a sketchy background of highland hills. "I do not normally drink scotch straight," Cheryl says with Southern-belle modesty, "but tonight I feel that I need it."

She uncaps the bottle and fills both glasses, then picks hers up and drinks it off in one swallow. Palmer would prefer to sip his scotch slowly for the flavor, but knocks it back.

"That was good," Cheryl says. "That was just what I needed."

Courtney was right to have asked Cheryl to marry him. She is beautiful and talented and drinks scotch straight. Courtney couldn't have planned things better.

"Would you like another?" she says.

After they drink those off, Cheryl places her hand on Palmer's knee. "Thank you so much for coming here tonight."

She lifts her hand and tells him that she has more packing to do, and asks if he would like to listen to any records. "Play Chad and Jeremy," he says, knowing that she likes them and Courtney doesn't.

She puts the record on the turntable and sets the needle, then bends over and starts sorting through things in a box. Palmer studies her ass, and recalls a former girlfriend who once told him that women always know when they're being watched.

He offers to help but she says no, she knows where everything is and how to pack it. He pours another tumbler of scotch and starts thinking about all the times he had packed to move to different army bases, or just out of barracks where he had been quartered temporarily. Throw everything into your duffel bag, check your billfold, and go. He had left home with a small cardboard suitcase which his mother had bought during WWII and which he had packed in less than five minutes. He had saved seventy-five dollars out of two months' work as a dishwasher at his father's Woolworth store, just long enough to earn what he had thought was stash enough to go out on his own, which it was.

When the record ends he chooses the next album, but doesn't play either of the Beatles albums that Courtney had bought that first night, though he would like to. Is Paul really dead? When Palmer was in high school one of his younger sisters won a radio phone-in contest to watch a sneak-preview of *Help!* at a Denver movie theater. She was escorted by a disk-jockey from 95 Fabulous KIMN "The Denver Tiger" who pulled up in front of their house in a red sports-car looking like a Mafioso in his tortoise-shell shades and high jock pompadour. Everybody on the block came out to watch her ride away, and for five minutes the Palmers were the coolest family in the neighborhood.

Cheryl closes the flaps on the last box and stands up. "I ought to go to bed now, Palmer. I would so much like to stay up with you awhile longer, but I really am very tired. You are more than welcome to eat and drink anything you find in the kitchen."

He gets up off the couch. "All right, thanks."

"I hope you will forgive me for not staying up," she says, tugging the hem of her sweater bringing the fabric down around her hips, "but I guess I had better get my bed out now."

"Do you need any help?"

"No, you just stay right there. I do this by myself every night." She opens the big double-doors revealing the ugly industrial undercarriage of the bed, and when she pulls it down the springs creak and twang, the bed making a soft booming sound against the floor.

"I don't expect you to sit up all night," she says, going to the closet and pulling out a robe and nightgown. "You are perfectly welcome to sleep on the other side of the bed if you wish. I really don't believe you would be very comfortable sleeping on that couch."

She carries her things into the bathroom and closes the door. Palmer steps over to the bed and sits on it. Not much bounce, firmer than his barracks bunk. Has Courtney ever slept here? Of course. Is he out in the fog right now watching the living room windows? Of course.

The bathroom doorknob rattles and Palmer slides off the bed and goes into the kitchen and starts making noises, opening an ice-cube tray and filling a glass and keeping busy so that Cheryl can climb into bed in private.

When Palmer comes back into the living room, Cheryl is sitting on the bed with the covers drawn up to her waist. "My friends will be coming over around seven tomorrow morning," she says. "You don't have to help load the truck, but I would like you to stay here until they arrive."

He nods and sits on the couch and pours a shot of scotch over ice, then uncontrollably begins to smile. This is the first time he has ever been in a woman's bedroom with a woman actually in the bed.

"There's plenty more to drink in the cupboard," she says, even though the bottle of scotch is in plain view and half full. "If you get hungry, there is a plate of sliced ham in the refrigerator."

"Thanks, Cheryl. I'll be fine."

Cheryl curls onto her side facing away from him and pulls the covers up to her neck. Palmer gets up and goes into the bathroom and inhales the clean and refreshing rosy odor of Mr. Gerlach's hearse for five minutes, time enough, he hopes, for Cheryl to fall asleep. He takes a weak piss. You don't have to piss much when you drink scotch.

He comes out and turns off the living room lights. The implication is that he may sit in the living room and listen to records if he wants. No TV around to watch—what's the deal with artists anyway? But he takes his bottle and glass into the kitchen. It's a terrible place to drink, the white tin and porcelain shrinking his pupils as he looks around for an ashtray. They've all been packed, so he uses a beer can.

He sits in a chair by the kitchen window and lifts the lace curtain and looks out into the foggy night and sees a face looking in at him, his own face reflected in the glass. He decides it would probably be best to stay seated right here for the rest of the night so that Courtney will know he is not in the living room with Cheryl.

But later on, because he is drinking scotch, he forgets the reason and gets up and turns off the kitchen light so that he can see outside better.

He sits down and lights a cigarette and pours another shot of scotch into the tumbler. He spreads the curtains wide and looks down at the steep street below, peers through the fog at a flat-fronted redbrick building directly across the street, and watches the lights of a rubber-tired trolley rumbling up the asphalt strip of Parnassus. He knows that he will remember this scene always. Knows that regardless of anything that might happen later on tonight, or tomorrow, the street below, and the fog, and the redbrick building, and the passing of trolley lights, will remain forever his memory of this night and of these times which are moving fast but without momentum toward the war in Vietnam.

CHAPTER 26

The soft clink of a plate being set on the kitchen table startles Palmer awake. He is immediately filled with the hangover horror of finding himself in someone else's place at dawn. He remembers what is supposed to go on today, the move, and is certain that Cheryl's friends are going to ring the doorbell at any second. He has only a vague memory of putting on his windbreaker for a blanket just before collapsing onto the couch in the middle of the night. Apparently he had slept on his left side without moving because his hip and ribs and ear on that side are sore from having pressed for hours against the poorly-padded wooden frame. He sits up slowly, gauging the intensity of his hangover.

Hearing his rising sounds, Cheryl looks in from the kitchen. "I was afraid I was going to have to wake you up," she says, "and I would hate to wake a sleeping soldier."

He would like to respond to her charming dawn concern but is simply too hungover, and this makes him feel rude. He gets up and goes into the bathroom, locks the door, and stands in front of the sink for a long time splashing cold water onto his face and breathing deeply. He wants to get out of here. Wants to leave without even saying goodbye and hurry back to the Presidio and climb onto his bunk and pull the covers over his head.

But Cheryl is cooking breakfast for him, bacon and fried eggs, he can smell them when he comes out of the bathroom. He feels better now, and is beginning to experience the onrush of that strange energy that sometimes comes after heavy drinking and little sleep, as though his body is calling upon all its reserves to pull itself through the next few hours.

"Are you a coffee drinker?" she says.

He nods. He never had been, but became a coffee drinker in the army. He sits down at his plate and looks at the two egg yellows which do smell good. There's a glass of orange juice, and he drinks it all.

The doorbell rings before he finishes eating. A dread comes over him which he can't control but which he knows is only the booze. Cheryl has already washed the frying pan and is sticking it into a cardboard box, which means he's having the last breakfast Cheryl will ever cook in this place. As she walks toward the door, Palmer says, "It could be Courtney."

She looks back at him. "It's my friends. They honked."

He had heard the honk outside the window but hadn't paid any attention. How awful when people have to start sneaking around and sending secret safety signals to each other. It only makes him sicker about everything that's happening, makes him wish he was already in Denver and all this shit was over.

Three men and one woman come in, the men with long hair and paisley or tie-dyed shirts. They bring a tangible animosity into the room but Cheryl introduces Palmer right away and tells them that he's a friend. The men give him limp handshakes and set to work picking up boxes. They ignore him after that.

There is no reason to stay any longer, it's time to go, but Palmer sits on the couch thinking about the trip back to the Presidio, and trying to get up the energy to start. It's like being in the enlisted men's club on the night of the bitter Screaming Eagle, except for the blinding sunlight waiting outside like a mugger.

He waits on the couch until everyone has gone down the hall carrying boxes, then he gets up and follows, steps outside into a hazy California glare. Cheryl is standing beside the truck with her arms akimbo. She's shivering, though it's not cold out. There is only a breeze from far away Sunset Beach. Palmer waits until her friends have gone back into the apartment, then he says, "I'm going home now," meaning the barracks. "I'll give Courtney your message."

"Thank you for staying with me, Palmer."

When she doesn't make a move to embrace him, he makes the move, stepping up and putting his arms around her. "Goodbye Cheryl."

"Take care of yourself in Vietnam, Palmer."

He knows that she is in a hurry to get moved and is probably afraid that Courtney will show up and there will be blood on Parnassus. It would probably take a minimum of three graphic-artists to subdue Courtney in a street brawl.

He turns away and goes around the corner and down the hill toward the Irving bus stop. Halfway down the hill he begins to feel dizzy. He stops and leans against the wall of a building beneath a bay window and breathes deeply with his eyes closed. It would be all right now if Courtney were to drive by and offer him a lift. He would tell Courtney anything he wanted to know. Then he realizes that Cheryl didn't give him her new address. He looks back up the hill, but it's painful to look up at that mist in the air, not quite an overcast, which collects the light and holds it. He closes his eyes and waits until the dizziness has lessened, then he goes down the hill and sits on a bus bench across the street from the biker bar, which appears to be open.

When his trolley comes he climbs on and rides past the stop where he would have transferred to the Geary bus which would have taken him to the Arguello gate at the Presidio, but instead he takes the trolley all the way into downtown San Francisco, his hangover feeling like a cold wind blowing through his skull.

He gets off at a Market Street stop, and realizes he has stepped off in front of the jewelry store where Bob the Businessman had tried to sell him a gilded clover. He walks away fast, then remembers that it's Sunday and Bob probably isn't there. Are any more bars open at this hour on a Sunday? What he really needs is food. The eggs weren't enough, and anyway he wants hangover food, spaghetti or chile, which they don't serve on Sunday mornings in the mess hall. He comes to a cafeteria and stops to peer through the steamed picture-window. The place is crowded. He wonders how there could be so many people awake on a Sunday morning.

He goes inside and gets a tray and walks down the line looking for spaghetti or chile but all they have in that genre is macaroni. He buys a bowl and a Coke and carries his tray over near the picture-window, the only empty spot in the place. He sits down at a table across from an old man eating soup.

Palmer stares into his bowl of macaroni, then spoons the yellow noodles onto his tongue, savoring the stomach-pleasing hangover-cleaving heat and tangy flavor, supplemented by icy swallows of Coke.

"Thought you was gonna throw rocks at me," the old man says.

Palmer has no interest in a conversation, but the man is seated directly across from him. "Pardon me?"

"When you sat down there, I thought you was gonna throw rocks at me."

The man's face is pitted, the flesh wrinkled and tanned. He looks like a bum, though maybe a dockworker. But his eyes are clear and white, the irises stark blue.

"No, sir," Palmer replies.

The man's hands are big, the fingers of his left hand curled completely around the small soup bowl. "Thought you was ganging up on me."

"No, sir," Palmer replies. "I'm a Military Policeman at the Presidio. We don't do that."

"Army, huh?"

"Yes, sir."

The man lifts a spoonful of soup, sucks the juice and alphabet bits, and swallows. He stabs the spoon into the bowl making it ring. "I was in the Navy in World War Two."

My father was in World War Two. He was in the Signal Corps in New Guinea."

"I worked on a ship."

"What kind of job did you do?"

"I was a belly robber."

"What's that?"

"Cook."

The old man guides the spoon to his mouth and doesn't say anything more. Palmer finishes his bowl, drains his Coke, and gets up from the table. The lump of macaroni in his gut feels like a cache of energy. He steps out onto the sidewalk ready now to find a place which will sell him the cure for what ails him, and what ails him is the desire for a drink. And maybe after that, he will think about returning to the Presidio.

Then he encounters something that interests him even more than alcohol—a Market Street porno theater open for business featuring a movie called *The Passion of Loreen*. He stops to study the eight-by-ten black-and-white stills serving as posters. Naked tits on a Sunday dawn. He pays five dollars for a ticket and goes inside.

Fewer people in here than in the cafeteria, possibly left over from the previous night. He takes a seat in an island of empty seats and looks at the screen expectantly. He expects triple-X, but sees only men and women playing in a pond in the mountains, the men clothed, the women in bikini bottoms but no tops. Big tits, big nipples. The women and men splash in the water and shout and laugh, then chase each other through the woods. When the men finally catch the women, Palmer assumes he will finally get to see what he has never seen in a movie theater before. But the men just hold the women on their laps and bobble their tits and laugh and talk and talk and talk he doesn't know what about. He realizes this isn't an X-rated movie theater. It's something else. It's nothing. Then he falls asleep.

A soundtrack of xylophone music drifts in and out of his dreams, and when he wakes up he sees a naked woman sitting on the lap of a doctor who is playing with her tits. This is a tit theater. He looks at his watch. Eleven o'clock. He has been sleeping for two hours. Did he snore? When he gets out of his seat and walks up the aisle he can see clearly the faces of men in the audience in the light reflected from the screen. He doesn't look anyone in the eye though—might be a secret signal to follow.

Patton is still playing at the theater down the block from *Woodstock* but there are no customers at either ticket booth even though both theaters are open. Too early for the passion that drives those fables. He goes into a bar where there is no TV, no sports audience barking and hooting, only silent men seated alone in booths. Older men, they all look like the belly robber.

It's Sunday, and even when he was eighteen he had tried not to get drunk on Sunday because of work Monday. He has never had a Monday military hangover yet, but what does it matter if six weeks from now he is killed in Vietnam? He will die regretting only not getting drunk on that Sunday in San Francisco. He orders a shot of scotch to get some alcohol into his system quickly, but after that he orders beer. He is glad he had fallen asleep in the theater. Two hours of hard sleep can do wonders for your ability to start in again.

At two in the afternoon he gets into a taxi parked at the curb beside the F.W. Woolworth and tells the driver to take him to the Presidio. He is drunk, but not as drunk as he thought he would feel after nine beers and a scotch, but this has happened to him before—the peculiar inability of beer to affect him as strongly as he had expected. When the taxi arrives at the quad, he has the driver drop him off at the bowling alley.

He is certain that Courtney knows he was at Cheryl's the previous night, and will want to know everything that happened, and will pester him with questions like did she say anything about me and what did you two talk about, but he wants to tell Courtney as little as possible, and does not want to mention at all that Captain Weller could be brought into this situation.

A slow hike up the gentle slope of the sidewalk, when he gets close to his barracks he can see through the window on the porch door to his room. Vinton and Mallory are standing by their open lockers changing out of civilian clothes. Palmer steps up to the porch and opens the door. "Did you sleep with her?"

Courtney is standing in the hallway wearing fatigue pants and a T-shirt. He is barefoot, his fists balled in his pockets exactly the way they had been on the night Palmer had stolen his car. Courtney has been waiting, probably all day and maybe even part of last night, and Palmer realizes that he could have skipped his trip into San Francisco and come here at dawn and Courtney would have been standing in the hallway just like this, red-eyed and angry and saying, "Did you sleep with her?" Could have skipped those drinks and gotten it all over with a lot sooner, except that if he had come here sober he might not have started laughing at the sight of Courtney standing exactly as he had expected him to be standing. From the moment he had awakened at dawn he knew that Courtney would be waiting for him and would look exactly like this, standing in the room red-eyed and barefoot and angry, his fists balled in his pockets. The whole scene makes Palmer feel like an olive-drab seer filled with the wisdom of beer. He feels like a fucking genius.

He is still laughing when things begin to happen slowly the way they do in a traffic accident which can be remembered later in detail as if viewing a slow-motion movie. Courtney's right fist comes out of his pocket. He jacks his elbow back. He launches his fist at Palmer's face, and as the knuckles approach, Palmer can see them getting bigger, can see the skin stretched thin and white where it curls around the knuckles, can see blonde hairs lying flat against the tanned flesh of each finger, sees all this while turning his head to the left so that Courtney's fist glances off the right side of his jaw and slides along his neck. The back of Palmer's head hits the door accompanied by the pop of a flashbulb. His knees buckle and he slides to a sitting position on the floor.

Interesting that the punch didn't really hurt. Palmer has never been in a fistfight before in his life. In grade school the fights had never evolved further than shoving matches because nobody would ever take the first swing, although he did once see two eighth-graders trade punches until their noses spewed blood, the fight finally broken up by a raging nun. He looks up at all the faces looking down at him, and sees Vinton run at Courtney and jump on his back and throw an arm around his throat in a choke-hold.

But Courtney is a strong sonofabitch. He leans forward and adjusts his stance and wears Vinton like a cape. He looks down at Palmer with both fists clenched, as if waiting for him to get up so he can knock him down again.

Palmer now realizes that he should not have laughed. It's always afterwards that he clearly sees what he should not have done.

"The CQ's coming," someone says.

Then Sgt. Weigand is peering into his face. "Are you all right, Palmer?"

"He tripped and hit his head on the door coming in," Vinton says. "He's drunk."

Weigand looks at the door frame, then puts his fingers under Palmer's jaw and tilts his face up. "We better get you to the hospital."

"No," Palmer says, standing up and bracing himself against the door. Courtney is no longer in the room. "I'm all right."

"Are you sure? A head injury can be a serious thing."

Palmer steps out to the porch and shuts the door. He shuts everyone away and goes to the railing and digs out his pack of cigarettes which has somehow been smashed flat, with most of the cigarettes cracked open. He finds a whole one and straightens it and lights it. The door opens. He supposes it's Courtney coming for him again, then hears Vinton say, "Are you all right?"

He doesn't look at Vinton. "I'm okay."

"Weigand doesn't know what happened. I told him you tripped. I knew you'd get in trouble for fighting in the barracks."

Palmer has no desire to talk to Vinton, but he looks over at him. "Thanks for jumping on Courtney." He sucks on his cigarette and gazes out across the silent Sunday afternoon quad and waits for Vinton to go away. He doesn't want to talk to anybody.

"When do you leave for Vietnam?" Vinton says.

"Two weeks," Palmer replies. "I've got thirty-days leave in Denver before I go over."

"That's a pretty good deal."

Palmer flicks ashes toward the sidewalk and doesn't say anything more, but Vinton doesn't seem to get the hint. He keeps hanging around as though there is something important that has been left unsaid. But, "You're not going to faint or anything are you?" is all he says.

"No."

"Courtney hit you pretty hard."

"I know."

Maybe Vinton came out to watch him fall down again. Then he realizes that Vinton came out to learn what the fight had been about, to hear the details of how Palmer had been messing around with Courtney's girlfriend. Vinton is a gossip-hound. He would make a good clerk/typist. But Palmer doesn't say anything.

"Well, take it easy, Palmer."

"I'll try."

Vinton goes inside and shuts the door. Palmer steps off the porch and goes around to the parking lot and tosses his cigarette to the ground and lights another and starts thinking about all the people he had ever made angry at him in his life. The list is long. A girlfriend who had gotten mad when he came over to her house with a six-pack when her parents weren't home. Other girls. The fathers of other girls. The foremen of shit jobs. Co-workers. Friends. Strangers. Priests. He looks up at the window of the second-floor room where Thorpe used to bunk. A new man already has taken his place, so the third platoon is back up to full-strength. There are four hundred seventy-five thousand GIs in Vietnam, and soon there will be four hundred seventy-five thousand and one. He wants to sign out of the company right now but he can't do that until Phil arrives at Oakland. Can't do anything until Phil's orders are changed. And there is still a day of jungle training at Ft. Cronkite that all men shipping to Vietnam have to take, and he has to go through out-processing at the finance office and the hospital and battalion, all this petty shit, he can't just pack up and leave, he's not a civilian, not yet, and may never be again.

But the one thing he can do is call his brother and let him know that he is not going to die in Vietnam. At six o'clock that evening he finally gets Phil on the phone.

PART FIVE

CHAPTER 27

Flak-jacket; pistol belt; steel helmet w/camouflage cover; canteen; the dull blue blade of a virgin bayonet to stuff into the sheath hitched to his hip; the sterile bundle of a First-Aid kit tucked into a canvas pouch—a cotton-padded bandage to stay the bleeding of flesh shot through-and-through; and the lightweight fabric of a bandoleer to drape across his chest, its pockets empty and flat. The range personnel will provide the weight of full magazines after the troops cross the Golden Gate Bridge and enter the brown hilly Vietnamese terrain, though not much weight because they will be firing blanks.

Palmer bundles his armload of gear and carries it downstairs from supply to his room and begins putting it on like a costume that will make him look like an Infantryman, though he will never wear the Combat Rifleman's Badge.

Seven other men from Company D including Courtney are gathered in the parking lot in their helmets and flak jackets, waiting for the bus which will take them to the range at Ft. Cronkite. Palmer keeps the distance of six men between himself and Courtney, who keeps his own face averted. The rest of the men, most of whom have heard about "the fight," smoke cigarettes and pretend the two are not even there.

Lieutenant Norbert arrives, looking much as Palmer imagines a cherry-boy lieutenant might look upon arrival in Vietnam: brand-new dark green fatigues starched-pressed and creased, the pant legs bloused neatly above spit-shined combat boots. A newly-blued .45 tucked into a handsome hand-crafted black-dyed leather holster slung low on his hip. And to complete the picture, the Air Force shades which all officers wear seemingly without embarrassment.

A bus arrives and opens its door, the seats half-filled with men from other Presidio units who also have orders to go to Vietnam: Infantry, engineer, signal corps, artillery, medic, cook, clerk. Palmer waits until Courtney takes a seat at the rear, then climbs on and sits directly behind the driver. Lt. Norbert mounts the steps with an energetic hop and stands bent at the waist peering out the front window to help the driver see the road.

Everyone hates MPs, so there isn't any conversation as the bus makes the circuit of Ralston Avenue and heads for the Presidio gate which will take them to the Golden Gate Bridge. But once off the reservation voices begin to rise, and everyone except Palmer begins talking, some of them even with the MPs, because now it's like basic training where everybody is your buddy and it no longer matters who you are or where you're from, or what your race or creed or brains or wealth, because you're all in the same shit.

Staring out a window with an easterly view as they cross the bridge, Palmer looks for the spot where he had seen Thorpe leaning over the railing. Probably picking his spot, but Palmer hadn't paid enough attention to the location to be able to pinpoint the exact place where he had first snubbed Thorpe.

The bus comes off the bridge and makes a right turn onto the road which takes them down past his bullet blunder and into the rolling high-weeded countryside toward the place where he had written his very first traffic ticket, which had been invalidated on the same day that Thorpe had escaped from the hospital for the first time.

Turning left onto a dirt road, the bus travels a hundred meters into the wilderness and stops at a dead-end. Another blue bus is already parked waiting for them, men standing around smoking, most of them with weapons slung over their shoulders. Forty or so troops will be taking part in the exercise. When the men on Palmer's bus dismount they're told to take a smoke break because the ammo truck hasn't yet arrived.

Palmer wanders down the road to smoke alone, and to look at the terrain, a bowl of low naked hills two kilometers across. Somewhere down at the bottom of that rounded valley stands a wooden hut representing a Vietnamese village where farmer families have worked the same rice paddies for hundreds of years. Now the communists want the government to own the paddies. It's a war over pink slips. He takes his canteen out of its pouch and drinks a mouthful of the cold water which will be warm before training is over. It's only a three-hour exercise so they will be finished by noon, if the blank ammo ever arrives. Lieutenants are standing around with their fists on their hips, grinning at each other's sunglasses and saying, "Did anybody actually inform brigade that we would be meeting here today?"

The deuce-and-a-half eventually arrives, and the ammo crates are opened. Palmer takes ten magazines and squats by the side of the road and tucks them into his bandoleer. Officers begin double-timing from one group to another explaining that the blank ammo cannot be fired on automatic. "Everyone set your weapon on single-shot! Got that? Set your weapon on single-shot!"

Palmer likes this now. He likes being told what to do like a mindless puppet as the hippies say, and going where someone points him, and doing what they tell him to do. He sets his weapon on single-shot and stands up and pokes his arm through the sling, letting the M-16 dangle from his shoulder so his hands will be free for smoking.

"All right, fall in!"

A captain stalks back and forth behind the silvered lenses of his Air Force shades trying to get this show on the road. Most of the troops are strangers to each other but they fall into a tight formation with that small personal pride that enlisted men always seem to take in close-order drill.

The captain stands facing the formation with his fists on his hips and begins reciting the rules of weapons safety. Do the troops in Vietnam get such speeches before marching into the bush? The primary rule of safety on jungle patrol: Don't shoot your buddy in the back.

"An M-16 cannot fire on full-automatic with blanks, so make sure your weapon is set on single-shot." Hands caress firing-mechanisms to please him. "When you're out on patrol, I want you to keep ten feet between yourself and the man in front of you, and make sure your weapons are locked on safety. Do not, I say again, do not fire your weapon directly at the enemy. A blank round discharges a wad of paper that can put a man's eye out. It could penetrate his brain and kill him, so fire into the air when the time comes."

Palmer listens for another last-man-to-do-that story: the last man who did not keep ten feet between himself and the man in front of him, the last man who did not keep his weapon locked on safety, the last man who penetrated someone's brain with a wad of paper and got fined and busted down to E1. But the-last-man-to-do-that apparently isn't present today.

The captain stoops and opens a metal ammo case at his feet and takes out a smoke-bomb, long like a can of spray-paint.

"Simulation hand-grenade!" he shouts. "The men pulling ambush will be throwing these at the patrols!" He pulls the ring and chucks the can across the road where it rolls and hisses and spits red smoke. "You can get a nasty burn from these things, so I don't want to see anybody getting hit with a canister. When it's your turn to pull ambush, don't throw it any closer than five meters from the men on the trail." Then he orders the front rank to fall out and collect their grenades and prepare to move out and set up ambushes.

Courtney is among the men in the front rank. Palmer watches him from the rear rank as he goes to the ammo truck and picks up a tin crate and takes his place in the ambush squad. A second lieutenant from an engineering battalion is put in charge of the ambush. He calls them to attention, left-face and forward-march, and they move out along the dirt road. They veer into the weeds off trail, and the officer gives them a route-step march and they find their own footing along a well-trammeled trail which leads toward a hillside a hundred meters off. Courtney is the tallest man in the squad and easiest to keep track of. Palmer watches his helmet as he marches downslope toward a massive growth of tangled bushes, and after the helmet disappears, he hears sounds of branches being kicked aside, the clink of metal on metal, and the occasional laugh.

"Smoke if you got 'em," the captain says. "It'll be fifteen minutes before they get set up."

Palmer walks to the edge of the road and lights up and stares at the hillside where the ambushes will take place. He can still feel the bruise on the back of his head where it had hit the door. In the barracks the next day he had looked right through everyone he passed in order to avoid inadvertently looking at Courtney, whom he would just as soon never see again.

After a few minutes, he sees him, recognizes his stride as he runs up a hillside, visible for only a moment as he crosses a barren patch of ground. Palmer envies the athletic ease of his ascent. Until he had met Courtney he had never known anyone, not even in Colorado, who could wind-sprint up a hill. Courtney is headed toward a spot marked by the silhouette of a tree whose windblown naked branches grow on one side of the trunk.

"Fall in!"

The captain studies the landscape through a pair of binoculars and talks into a field-phone while the men douse butts and gather into a new formation. There will be two patrols of approximately fifteen grunts each moving out at ten-minute intervals. Palmer joins the first rank, taking his place at what will become the rear, on the theory that, during an ambush, he will be the last man killed.

The captain assigns the first patrol to Lt. Norbert, who is standing off to the side of the formation in a trio of square-jawed young brass whose grins have been replaced by businesslike field-frowns. Lt. Norbert strides forward to take command, his holster bouncing against his right hip.

"Tin-*hut!* Left-*hace!*" The rank pivots left as one, and becomes a file facing the trail which will take them into the valley. "Forward...*hotch!*"

Once off the road the footing becomes difficult, and each man sets his own speed descending toward the high bushes. Palmer looks above the helmets of the men in front of him, searching for the tree where he knows Courtney will be waiting. They move silently along the trail for a few minutes, then the man walking point turns and runs toward the patrol screaming, "Ambush! Ambush!" The soft popping of M-16s up ahead, the patrol stops but not as one, the troops squeezing together like an accordion. Safeties come off and faces turn skyward as a single canister draws a red line across the sky. Lt. Norbert grabs the point-man as he runs past. "Goddamnit! You don't yell ambush when you see the enemy! You signal me and I come up to see what the problem is. You don't yell anything. You're the point-man for godsake!"

Palmer touches his shirt pocket for a cigarette, then drops his hand. The smoking lamp isn't lit. Do real grunts smoke on patrol? The point-man has an incomprehensible look of panic on his face. Lt. Norbert turns him around by the shoulders and shoves him back toward his position. Can patrols in Vietnam be as half-assed as this? Palmer knows he could very well end up in the Infantry and that he is not guaranteed to remain an MP once he arrives in a combat zone, though maybe that's just Army Apocrypha. He will never be able to separate his illusions from his ignorance. When he was inducted he had expected everyone to end up with nicknames, like Bookworm, Lefty, or Ace. His nickname would be Colorado, as in, "Colorado bought the farm last night, Ace." Everyone would look like Bart Maverick, Bret's less-interesting brother. When they got into arguments, they would raise their chins and say things like, "Back off, buddy boy."

The mock grenade empties itself spewing a thick and bitter-smelling red ground-fog which clings like trailing web to weeds and dissipates slowly in the windless air. Lt. Norbert shouts, "Fall in!" allowing the enemy to pinpoint their position. As the troops get ready to move out, Palmer hops once on his toes and looks for the naked tree.

Up ahead there is a sort of briar patch, a quarter acre growth of thick bushes split by the trail, and to Palmer's eyes, the perfect spot for an ambush. He lets a distance of fifteen feet grow between himself and the man in front of him. The foliage rises two feet above the head of the tallest man in the patrol, it's like a canyon, and after Palmer enters the passage he stops every now and then to look behind him, listening for footsteps or the hissing of a smoke-grenade. He wants to foil an ambush before it gets started, or else shoot a man trying to sneak up from behind, or roust a mock VC from a spider hole. But it's impossible to set up an ambush in here because the branches off-trail are too thick. So the enemy waits until the troops file into a clearing on the far side where they can be picked off like ducks waddling out of a lake.

Palmer is still in the briar patch when he sees the first canister sail across the sky. Enemy M-16s open up, and for the first two seconds everyone just stands there taking imaginary hits from all sides. Palmer can see quite clearly that Vietnam is going to be a crock of shit. Lt. Norbert tries to organize a line of defense. Men start firing into the weeds on the right side of the trail and toward the hill on the left, but it's obvious that the patrol has been mowed down.

Someone shouts cease fire, and from the bushes emerge two range officers, second lieutenants whose job it is to judge who among the patrol is dead, and who is wounded, and who is unscathed, and because Palmer had been the last man to come out of the weed patch they decide he wasn't hit. This makes him laugh. They're blind. He's Swiss cheese. He pulls out a cigarette and lights up.

Other men see him smoking and they light up too. The range officers run around designating the dead, and after a few minutes Lt. Norbert says, "Put 'em out and fall in," and the crock of shit is made whole again.

There is one more firefight before they get within range of the naked tree. When the point-man screams "Ambush!" at the top of his lungs, completely rattled by his job, Palmer steps off the trail and squats in the weeds so nobody can see him and he won't have to do anything. But he does fire three rounds straight into the air. The blank-ammo kick is nothing at all, it's like firing a b-b gun.

Red mock mustard-gas creeps along the ground. Palmer holds his breath. From his hidden spot he hears Lt. Norbert directing fire, hears the sizzle of canisters flying overhead, hears men coughing and cussing and laughing. He touches the selector switch on his M-16. Too bad it can't fired on full-automatic. He fires three more rounds at the sky. He likes doing this. He could fire bullets all day long and never get tired of it.

"Cease fire!"

Two new range officers step out of the bushes and start counting casualties. Lt. Norbert is dissatisfied with the perform-ance of his men, particularly the dead. One grenade got three of them. "Don't bunch up!" he reminds everyone, but it's hard not to bunch up when you're walking on rough terrain and the point-man is an idiot. Palmer has heard that the newbies, the cherry boys, the FNGs in Vietnam are always given the job of walking point, since it's one of the most dangerous jobs and the in-country veterans would rather risk the life of a stranger than a buddy, which means that walking point might have become one of Phil's first jobs when he finally got assigned to a firebase. But would the short-timers in Vietnam really trust a cherry boy who might lead them into a VC ambush? Sooner or later though, a man has to walk his first point.

The dead are raised, and the patrol steps out again. Closer to the hillside now, Palmer sees the naked tree which, with every turn and dip and rise in the trail, has grown from a tiny black cardboard cutout to a wind-bent sylvan flag.

He slows, letting the distance to the man in front of him grow again, his eyes glancing from the rutted trail to the hillside and back to the trail. No longer so confident about his earlier observation, he finally stops altogether and stares at the hillside, his eyes scanning the sloping blanket of heavy bushes and tall grass and low scrub pine.

Courtney is a good soldier. He doesn't open fire until most of the patrol has passed his position, enabling him to pick them off from the rear. Palmer sees a single canister launched from behind the tree, the arc of its flight drawing a trail of red smoke across the blue sky like an arrow pointing directly at Courtney's otherwise well-concealed position.

Palmer steps off the left side of the trail where a shallow ditch runs along the base of the hill. He uses this for his path as the firefight erupts. His steel pot rattling on his head, he reaches up and slaps his left hand down on the camouflage cover and runs at a crouch, keeping an eye out for mock VC or even range officers who might give him away.

The noise of the battle as it shapes up—Lt. Norbert hollering orders, the aerosol flight of grenades, the firing of M-16s, the troops yelling at each other and bitching and laughing—serves to muffle the noise he is making as he shoves branches out of his face and trips on rocks searching for the spot where Courtney had climbed the hill. Then he sees boot prints, fresh and damp rising beside a rivulet of hillside erosion which had served as Courtney's path. He stops for a moment to catch his breath, then leans in and starts crawling uphill as fast as he can, hidden by tall weeds and wind-warped pine.

As fast as he can turns out to be the wrong tactic. His decisions are being made now by adrenaline, and consequently he is exhausted by the time he makes fifteen meters. All the cigarettes he has ever smoked and all the beers he has ever drunk press down on him like an invisible hand. He collapses onto the angled bed of earth, gasping with his eyes closed, unable to go on, infuriated that the kid from Colorado can't even climb a California hill. How do drunks ever make it through a war? Then the shooting stops.

The ambush has ended.

He didn't make it.

He failed to execute a successful assault on Courtney's position, and now it's too late. The firefight is over.

With the stink of damp earth clogging his nostrils, he relaxes and lets his body slide downhill slowly and unimpeded like a corpse. When he lifts his helmet to judge the distance he had made toward Courtney's position, sweat runs into his eyes stinging and blurring the vertical panorama of his most recent defeat. The heat of the rising sun penetrates a camouflage of leafy bushes overhead and makes his skin itch where the light touches the backs of his sweaty hands. Too tired to sit up, to even move, he lies flat swallowing spit and gently hammering the earth with his chest as he coughs up light sprays of phlegm.

The close and noisy sizzle of a canister passing overhead interrupts his coughing. He raises his head and hears M-16s opening up again.

Only a lull in the fighting, time which he could have used for climbing, though probably no more than thirty seconds. The hill is like a beach, things are slowing down, but he takes a lesson from this and rises to his knees and cradles the rifle in the crooks of his elbows and crawls uphill at a slow and manageable rate. He tries not very successfully to ignore the agony in his calves and thighs in the way he had successfully ignored it in basic training when he was in good shape and had low-crawled for the record during his final week, his legs even then turning into wooden stumps, and then he is there, lying below a clearing behind a thin hedge of weeds.

Sitting cross-legged in profile with his M-16 lying across his lap, Courtney is methodically reaching into his ammo box and pulling out canisters and yanking rings and tossing smoke without even looking where he is throwing, but throwing hard enough to send them across the trail.

The firing of weapons and the shouts of the men below sound far away. Palmer eases his rifle up, then stops as Courtney picks up his M-16 and points the muzzle to the sky and tugs the trigger eighteen times—Palmer counts—until the magazine is empty.

Palmer's legs are numb, the rifle is heavy in his hands, so

it is adrenaline alone which lifts him to his feet. He kicks his way through the weeds and steps into the clearing.

Courtney turns his head at the sound and looks at the weapon braced against Palmer's hip, looks at the dark hole of the muzzle pointing directly at his chest.

After the first shot, Palmer doesn't hear the others. It is only what he sees that stays with him — the blue cloud of gunsmoke pumped larger by successive shots, the bits of spinning paper flung from the muzzle, the look on Courtney's face as his eyes widen and his jaw drops and his lips peel back in a snarl, his eyes squinting closed as he turns his face away and throws a hand up to protect his ear, his whole body bending and twisting away from the smoke and bits of paper and barking of the weapon which Palmer doesn't hear until the very last round goes off and his finger taps uselessly on the trigger and the clearing goes silent.

Through a curl like cigarette smoke rising from the muzzle of his weapon, he sees Courtney lower his hand in small jerks, turning his body a bit at a time until the two men are staring at each other.

"You're dead," Palmer says.

He turns away and steps through the weeds and skis awkwardly downhill on the heels of his boots with his right hand braced on the ground and his left holding the M-16 overhead. When he gets to the ditch at the bottom and stumbles through the bushes onto the trail, he finds Lt. Norbert and the rest of the patrol staring at him curiously.

"I wiped him out, sir."

"Outstanding, Private Palmer," the lieutenant says. He is proud of his man. He grins and claps his hands once and hollers at the troops to form up and prepare to move out.

Palmer ejects the empty magazine from his weapon. After inserting a fresh one he rubs his face as if applying lather until all the sweat is rubbed off onto his palm, then wipes his palm on his thigh and falls in at the rear of the patrol. As they step out and proceed into the valley toward the mock ville where there will be more ambushes and more firefights, Palmer begins listening for the sounds of Courtney's footsteps.

For the rest of the morning's exercise, and on the ride back to the barracks, and in the mess hall at noon, and on shit details the next day and the day after that, and even when he is getting ready to go to Oakland to try to get Phil's orders changed, Palmer will be listening for the sounds of Courtney's footsteps coming at him from behind.

CHAPTER 28

Beaudry is gone. On Friday evening he had come into the squad room wearing his Class A uniform and carrying his duffel bag and shook hands with everyone and said good-bye. His transfer had come through that quickly because lifers are always willing to accommodate anyone who is willing to become a part of the Regular Army. The Mandatory Buddy Lie was recited by all the members of his now ex-squad, and then a taxi showed up and took him to Korea.

You make buddies in basic training, and you believe you will know them for the rest of your life. Then they're gone out of your life in a military instant, like sudden death, and you find yourself in advanced training marching with men whose names you are now beginning to have difficulty remembering. Yet you still can't believe that you won't meet them again someday, that you won't be friends with them always. You are beginning to learn that life is vast, that your discharge is the least of your uncertainties, and the only one you can count on.

After Saturday morning chow, while everyone else in the barracks is pulling civilian clothing from their lockers and hurrying to escape shit details, Palmer puts on his Class A uniform and goes into the latrine and stands in front of a mirror and inspects himself. KP ribbon and .45 medal properly pinned at the breast pocket, the shield of his saucer cap Brassoed and shining, he wants to look his best when he approaches the personnel at Oakland and asks them to alter his brother's orders. He wants very much to do better than he had done with Top, whom he had approached in the operations office on Friday at noon.

The only other man in the office had been Legget, who was busy with paperwork at his desk. Everyone else was in the mess hall, so Palmer had decided that this would be a good opportunity to have a private meeting with a man who had made the army his life, who had been a soldier in Korea, and who probably understood not only the ins and outs of army regulations but how to manipulate them effectively to attain a desired goal.

It's easy to see now that this was a mistake—the assumption that Top would give a shit about a draftee's problems.

"Sergeant, can I talk to you for a minute?"

Top's chair creaked as he swiveled around and looked at Palmer, the unlit cigar working itself from one corner of his mouth to the other. He didn't say anything.

"My older brother just graduated from Infantry AIT in Ft. Lewis and he received orders to go to Vietnam," Palmer began. "But I've got orders to go to Vietnam too." He paused, as though the momentum of these two statements alone might sufficiently clarify the dilemma.

The cigar in Top's mouth ceased its progress, protruding from the center of his puckered lips. Just before Palmer spoke again it occurred to him that Top's wife doesn't let him light that thing.

"There's an army regulation that says two members of the same family can't be required to serve in a combat zone at the same time," Palmer said. "So my brother arrived at the Oakland Army Replacement Depot, and I need to find out what the process is for getting his orders changed. Can you help me with this?"

Top reached up and removed the unlit cigar from his mouth and pointed the wet tip at Palmer. "You are going to Vietnam, troop," he said. "And there's nothing you can do to get out of it."

Mortified, Palmer tried to control the disgust creeping into his voice. "I understand that, sergeant. I'm not trying to get my orders changed." He glanced over at Legget, who was sitting erect and motionless in his chair firing frantic warning messages with his eyes.

Top eased himself up and strolled across the floor and stood at the counter. He put his cigar between his lips and talked around it. "I've got two brothers laid up in VA hospitals with rubber tubes stuck up their noses because of cowards like you."

Palmer tries not to think about his encounter with Top as he leans close to the mirror, careful to avoid touching the porcelain edge of the sink and painting a wet horizontal stripe across his coat at the crotch. He examines his chin where his beard grows thickest when it grows at all. He has to shave only once every two days. A man in the third squad is growing a mustache but Sgt. Sherman has told him to shave it off. "According to army regulations I have a right to grow a mustache," the man had said with nervous anger in formation one noon hour. Mustaches are considered hippie garbage, and Sgt. Sherman is pissed that one of his troops is giving him this grief. "You have the right to wear a mustache, not to grow one," Sgt. Sherman had replied. The debate is currently at a stand-off, but even Palmer knows that the army will lose this one. Enlisted men always win the meaningless shit.

He returns to his room. Tucked inside his black plastic funeral briefcase are two copies of his orders for Vietnam, and some paperwork which he had requested from battalion headquarters not long after Top had humiliated him in front of SP4 Legget. Thank God no one else had been in operations. Fearing with good reason his own ineptitude, he removes each sheet of paper and places it on his bunk, looks it over, then carefully reinserts each page individually. He zips the case closed, intending to leave it closed until the moment at Oakland when he will be required to open it again, although in fact he will peer into the briefcase at least one more time while on the bus ride across the Bay.

He avoids another encounter with Top by going up to the second floor day-room to call Yellow Cab on the pay-phone. Then he exits the building by the front door following the same route taken by Thorpe on his last day at Company D under a white-coated unarmed escort into the parking lot.

Hippies are hanging around outside the downtown bus depot panhandling quarters and playing guitars, or else handing out anti-war leaflets for a demonstration to be held in Golden Gate Park. A wisp of a girl, a hippie with long stringy but clean blonde hair approaches Palmer as he stands outside the depot listening for the call to board his bus.

He is standing off by himself, away from all the other servicemen, the soldiers and sailors and Marines and even one Coastguardsman, lugging their duffel bags in and out the front doors of the terminal. The girl approaches him with a shy smile, looking so happy to be doing her work for The Cause, her seventeen-year-old eyes sparkling as she pulls a single flyer from a stack cradled in her left arm. Barefoot, she does the sort of tiptoe maneuver that Cheryl had once done, though not for a kiss but to hold up a flyer, smiling and saying in the high-pitched, sweet, and musical voice of an eighth-grader, "Will you be able to make it to our rally?" in spite of the fact that Palmer is wearing an army uniform.

He takes the paper and interprets the psychedelic hand-lettering done by someone who was not very good at it, and thinks again of Cheryl. The leaflet gives the time and a mapped location where everyone will gather to stop the war. He hands it back and smiles. "I won't be able to make it."

"Why not?" she says, apparently not at all insulted and even seemingly happy to have her stack of leaflets returned to their original quota.

"I'll be on my way to Vietnam," Palmer says.

The sparkle in her voice and eyes dims only a bit. She gives him a soft little, "Oh," and a shrug and turns back to the door of the bus station where there are plenty of men Palmer's age dressed in civilian threads who probably will not be too busy two weeks from now to take time out from their panhandling to sing a few songs and smoke a little dope for peace.

The front door of a bar across the street is open and dark. The pale green paint and flat red border of its overhead sign beckon to Palmer. It probably doesn't matter one way or the other whether he walks onto the Oakland Army Base smelling like a brewery because the paperwork theoretically will be doing all the talking today. But he might miss his bus, and this is probably the only bus that he will ever take in his life that he cannot afford to miss, although he could take a taxi across the bay—his brother's life now reduced to so-many-cents-per-mile, a price Palmer would rather not pay unless his back is absolutely against the wall.

He sits in the middle of the bus, not too close to the old ladies in the front who might engage him in conversation, and not too close to the hippies in the back who might engage him in conversation. Out of the city, onto the cantilevered bridge and out over the water, the bus enters the darkness of the tunnel on Treasure Island. When it emerges into the light Palmer gets his first good look at the embarkation point for soldiers headed just about any place on the globe. From this distance the army base is a clot of buildings at the edge of the Bay beyond small black crane-shapes lining the docks. Palmer wonders if this is the spot where his father had boarded a troop ship to go to the South Pacific.

He knows that his father had sailed out of San Francisco Bay, but beyond that he knows very little about his father's trip. It had never occurred to him to ask his father to describe the ordinary details of his WWII experience, the ports he had sailed from, what the living conditions were like on the ships, the poor quality of the food, and how well or badly the enlisted men of his day were treated by the officer corps. And what did they do hour after hour to kill time in the weeks it took to arrive at the Solomon Islands? His father had sailed into the South Pacific a private and came home a Staff Sergeant E6, three stripes and a rocker. What was his trip home like? Did his happiness diminish for even one second as his ship moved eastward toward the Golden Gate Bridge?

September 1945. Palmer's mother was enduring a train ride from Omaha to San Francisco. His parents-to-be had not seen each other in four years. Twenty-four hours after their reunion, they were married, and nine months later there was Phil, the first baby-boomer Palmer.

The bus comes off the bridge and takes the interchange south. Palmer had assumed he would end up in downtown Oakland and would have to take a bus or cab to the base, but the driver begins letting people off at stops, and when they get close to the army depot Palmer pulls the cord and steps off one block from the main gate.

There is something industrial about the look of the place, big parking lots in front of long buildings spread over thousands of acres, something civilian and factory-like and not-quite-military. Unlike the Presidio though, Oakland has a gate shack with guards—the MPs wear white gloves. As he approaches, it occurs to him that he might not be allowed to enter, that he might need some sort of travel orders to pass through the gate, a thought that only increases his dread that today's trip will end in failure and, irrelevantly enough, fresh humiliation, given his reckless promise to Phil.

But the MPs merely point out the entrance to a long building, a door halfway along the walk, so obscure that without instructions from the MPs it might have been mistaken for a door to a janitor's closet. But it is, in fact, the first step on the road to Vietnam.

A black E5 acting as a receptionist is seated behind a desk inside the entrance, and when Palmer asks how he might get in touch with his brother, the E5 tells him to try the operations office.

Palmer walks down a long hallway past men wearing new green jungle-fatigues. He looks at the rank on men's collars, searching for a sergeant E6 or above, a man whose fatigues will be stateside, faded, and tailored. He ends up asking a major, a friendly older man in wire-rim glasses who listens closely as he explains what he's trying to do. "You'll probably find your brother out on the tarmac," the major says. "They're going to hold afternoon formation in a few minutes."

A long walk to the far end of the building, Palmer passes through a set of double doors into a brick transient-barracks. It's like a college dormitory with big bays filled with double-bunks arranged in military rank-and-file. Half the bunks are empty and half are marked as occupied with locked duffel bags hanging from the frames.

There is no one around. He crosses to a window and looks out upon a panoramic view of an asphalt parade-ground like an abandoned landing-strip where hundreds, perhaps thousands, of GIs wearing jungle fatigues are waiting to be called to attention. On the far side of the grounds stands the same white wooden tower which he has seen on every rifle range from Georgia to California, occupied by the same NCO with his face in shadow. The man's tinny electrical voice barks from a PA speaker calling the formation to attention. He puts the troops at ease and begins reading off the names of the men who will be segregated overnight and then bussed to Travis Air Force Base in the morning for their flight to Vietnam.

Beginning to worry, Palmer starts looking for a door which will take him out to the tarmac. Phil has been here only one day, so it's improbable that his name will be called so soon, but a lot of things about the army are improbable, like lifers pulling guard duty, which is what an E8 and other men of his rank are doing stationed in a kind of perimeter around the formation to prevent the enlisted men from slipping away.

The E8 is standing at the rear of the formation. Tall and silver-haired, he looks older than Palmer's father and had probably served in WWII, probably Korea and even Vietnam. Painfully conscious of his knack for pissing-off NCOs, Palmer thinks carefully not only about what he is going to say but how to say it with the utmost military courtesy.

He walks up to the E8 and stands not quite at attention, and says, "Excuse me, sergeant. I'm a Military Policeman at the Presidio of San Francisco. I came here to visit my brother who is going to Vietnam. He arrived here yesterday, and I was told that he might be in this formation. Is there any way I can get in touch with him right now, or should I wait until the formation is dismissed?"

As Palmer speaks, the sergeant's head turns quickly toward him, his body remaining motionless. He listens with his eyebrows raised. He smiles, the ruddy tropic-tanned flesh of his face lifting into wrinkles. "What's his name, private?"

"PFC Philip Palmer, sergeant."

The E8 takes a few steps forward and makes a megaphone out of his bony hands. "Palmer! Philip Palmer!" His voice is as loud and sure as a Drill Sergeant's skimming across the capped heads of the formation. "PFC Philip Palmer!"

A hand goes up in the middle of the crowd and a faraway voice shouts, "Here sergeant!" Palmer sees a head hopping above the formation, then traveling toward the side. Phil exits the formation and begins double-timing toward them.

"Palmer!" the sergeant hollers. "Your brother's here to see you!"

He should have expected it, but Palmer is surprised at Phil's appearance. All his beer fat is gone, and his face is gaunt from the rigors of not only basic but Infantry AIT. His baggy jungle fatigues are flapping on his lean frame, and strangely he's tanned even though he had spent his four months in Washington State where, according to his generally dreary letters, "it rains all the time." New black PFC pips are attached to his collars. Only now does it occur to Palmer that his older brother outranks him.

They grin as they shake hands, and the sergeant grins with them, which is good, because a delicate moment is approaching. Palmer wants to get his brother away from the formation but isn't sure of the protocol, isn't sure how far the E8 might be willing to accommodate them, though he suspects that the sergeant won't interfere with the reunion of two brothers, one of whom is going off to war.

Palmer reaches into his briefcase and pulls out a sheet of paper and says loud enough for the sergeant to hear, "I brought the paperwork," then begins a brief recital of his visit to battalion headquarters, and as he speaks, he begins strolling one slow step at a time away from the formation with Phil at his side. He listens for the E8 to holler at them to stop, but the man doesn't say a word.

When Palmer judges that they are far enough away, he says, "Let's double-time," and takes off at a trot, leading his brother up into the barracks and through the building and out the other side. He lets Phil take over as guide here, leading the way through a maze of bleak warehouse buildings and narrow asphalt side streets which bring them to the Oakland Army Depot enlisted men's club.

The only other person in the place is a bartender who, in his civilian clothes, looks like he might be a sergeant E6. He checks their ID cards but doesn't ask why they're in here instead of out at the formation. Palmer pays for two draughts and leads Phil to a booth where he pulls out all the paperwork and begins explaining things in detail, unlike the tactical sham-conversation out on the tarmac in the presence of the E8.

He leaves out the part where Top had called him a coward and thus a traitor to his country and blamed him for the wounds received by his brothers during the Korean War.

"Now get the hell out of my sight, Palmer," Top said, turning away and going back to his desk. He sat down hard in his creaking chair and slammed a desk drawer shut and picked up a notebook and slapped it down hard on his blotter.

Palmer stood at the counter astonished at his inability to make himself clear. He looked at Legget, hoping to draft an ally to his cause, but Legget was now staring at a piece of paper on his desk, refusing to look at Palmer who had committed the cardinal sin of ignoring the head clerk's subtle but sincere warnings.

Palmer turned and walked out of the operations office. He left the barracks, went around behind the building to his smoking place, and lit a cigarette. His dread now complete, he would be going to Oakland unarmed and dependent solely upon the whim of a clerk behind a desk, probably another First Sergeant with a brother laid up in a VA hospital, a lifer who would probably be as sympathetic to Palmer's request as he would be to the long-range goals of global communism.

He now regretted the things that had gone on between himself and Courtney. If there was one man around here who would know what to do, it would be his ex-buddy, the straight-arrow, the supertroop. This was just the sort of Inspector General bullshit that was right up Courtney's alley. He loved a fight, obviously.

And then, while lighting his third cigarette with his hands cupped around his Zippo to protect the flame from a breeze, Palmer's unoccupied eyes settled on the glowing white facade of battalion headquarters. He took two puffs from the cigarette, then flicked it over the parking-lot fence where it rolled next to a car belonging to a third-platoon man. He walked around the quad to battalion headquarters.

The clerk/typist bay was empty except for SP4 Croner. Everyone else was out to lunch. Croner didn't seem to recognize him, though there was no reason that he should, so Palmer reintroduced himself as the man who had escorted Leland Thorpe's body to Wichita. Croner said, "Oh yes. How did that go?"

"Fine. But I need some help."

Croner sat back in his chair and tapped the center of his glasses and folded his arms and listened while Palmer explained the situation, stating it more concisely now than when he had spoken to Top. When he finished, Croner nodded and sat forward. "Well, the thing is, Palmer, that regulation may not apply to you and your brother."

This was not what Palmer wanted to hear, but he couldn't tell whether his disappointment derived from the fear that his brother might end up dead, or embarrassment that his brother would ridicule him for presuming to have a solution.

Croner crossed the room to a bookshelf containing volumes of green-bound loose-leaf notebooks, the entire library of regulations pertaining to every aspect of a soldier's life. He looked up the relevant regulation, then showed it to Palmer: AR 614-30. "The problem is this, Palmer. You don't really have a choice. The man who goes to Vietnam is the man whose orders were cut first. Do you have a copy of your orders on you?"

"No."

"All right. Why don't you run back to your barracks and get me a copy." He handed Palmer a tablet and a pen. "Write down your brother's name and unit at Ft. Lewis, and I'll get in touch with the Pentagon and find out whose orders were cut first."

A tedious and familiar ache that came from never quite being able to make himself clear sprouted in Palmer's heart. "How long is this going to take? My brother is in Oakland right now."

Croner looked at his watch. "Come back at five."

As Palmer turned to go, Croner added, "By the way, does your First Sergeant know you're here doing this?"

"No."

"Well if I were you, I would let him know you're talking to me about this, just to cover your ass."

Palmer smiled. "You bet."

The clerks were covering their Smith-Coronas when Palmer returned a few minutes before five o'clock. Croner got up from his desk and waved him over. "I've got something to show you." He handed Palmer a sheet of green-and-white striped computer paper filled with tele-typed ink, a printout of Phil's orders.

"These orders were cut at Department of the Army two weeks after yours were cut," Croner said. "Now this is good, because technically Phil doesn't have to go to Vietnam. But the thing is, if he's already at Oakland, he might get shipped overseas before you can get his orders changed."

He handed Palmer another sheet of paper. "I typed this up for you this afternoon. There is nothing official about it, but it might help you to cut through some red tape. Show it to everyone you talk to at Oakland, and if they hassle you about it, tell them to call me."

It was a letter of introduction addressed To Whom It May Concern, printed on the battalion letterhead with a phone number in one corner. It did look official, but was only a note explaining the relevance of AR 614-30 to the Palmer brothers and their orders for Vietnam.

Palmer thanked Croner for his help and promised to let him know what happened. After he got back to the barracks and put the paperwork into his briefcase, it occurred to him that the battalion letterhead was in fact a message from one clerk/typist to another clerk/typist, because Croner already knew what Palmer was only beginning to understand: if you want to get anything accomplished in the army, talk to a Spec Four.

Phil examines the letterhead as he listens to Palmer's story. He doesn't seem quite as gloomy now as he sounded when they had spoken on the phone one week earlier. When Palmer finishes, Phil offers to go buy a second round.

When he returns with the beers, Palmer asks him what it's like here at Oakland.

"They're hardass," Phil says. "If you show up one day late they jump in your shit. A buddy of mine named Neuhouse was supposed to show up yesterday but he didn't get here until this morning, and they sent him straight to the CO's office. He got busted from PFC to E2."

The mythical day-of-grace and the-last-man-to-do-that, going into action as one.

"They're a bear on haircuts too," Phil says. "Yesterday morning when I got in line to sign in, the NCO kicked a man out of line and told him to go to the barbershop, and when he got back the sergeant told him to go the rear of the line."

This doesn't surprise Palmer. Lifers are dully predictable.

"But they don't hassle us much the rest of the time," Phil says. "There's three formations a day, and after they call the names of the men going to Vietnam they pick guys for shit details. They take your ID card away from you so you can't bug out. I already had to sweep up the operations building."

The door to the club opens and GIs start filing in and lining up on the stools at the bar and filling the short row of vacant booths, which means the formation is over and these are the lucky ones who hadn't gotten assigned to shit details. Palmer sees here and there a head shorn closely to the scalp, but can't tell if those men are victims of the dogmatic NCO or just Future Lifers of America who wear their baldness proudly.

When their glasses are empty, the brothers get up from the booth and step outside into the sunlight which is blinding even after only a couple beers. Palmer doesn't feel at all high from his two, but can sense something chemical trying to take place inside his brain, something that feels good and helps ease the dread that, from the moment he had met his brother out on the parade ground, had begun fading so that it exists now as merely a nagging impatience to hurry up and fail, or else succeed.

They walk back through the labyrinth of warehouse buildings to the door which takes them into the operations building and past the sign-in station where everyone's trip to Vietnam officially begins. Phil points out the hardass NCO, a young, chubby, pasty-fleshed E5 in a Class A uniform seated behind a desk. Did this buck sergeant ever serve in Vietnam? Palmer prefers to doubt it, but can't read the skimpy fruit-salad on his chest with any accuracy.

Phil leads him into the operations office. They take their places at the end of a line and wait to talk to a weary, balding E6 taking care of business one GI at a time.

After they get up to the counter, Palmer goes into his explanation, fully expecting the sergeant to explode like Top at the invocation of AR 614-30, but the man probably has heard this story before. "Go to the end of the hall and through that door," he says. "You got to talk to Captain Lewellyn."

They pass through the door into what appears to be the heart of Oakland, where officers and only officers are seated at desks in small rooms working at typewriters or computer terminals. There is not one single enlisted man in sight, the paperwork here so highly-classified that it can be entrusted only to gentlemen.

Captain Lewellyn is seated at a desk in a small office working at the keyboard of a computer terminal. When

Palmer knocks on the door, the man stops typing and looks up. His hair is short, though not quite a military crew-cut. His eyes are gray, his lips thin, he looks like a man who in civilian life would be a lawyer. "What can I do for you men?" he says, his chin drawn toward his neck giving his voice a rounded quality.

They walk in and stand in front of his desk but don't salute. Palmer holds his briefcase at the ready and tells the same story that he had told to Top and Croner. The captain sits motionless at his desk, with only his eyes moving to look at Palmer or his brother as they speak in turn.

"May I see copies of both your orders?" the captain says.

Palmer pulls out his accumulated paperwork, and Phil hands over a copy of his DA orders. "When did you arrive here?" the captain says to Phil.

"Yesterday, sir."

The captain nods, glances down at the papers, and frowns. "There may be a problem. We're going to have to go down the hall."

Another trip to another location, but something seems to be getting done, even if only more in an endless circuit of leg-work. At least the captain, unlike Top, had not flat-out refused to listen.

They enter a room lined with filing cabinets. A black E8 with a white meerschaum pipe clamped between his teeth is seated at a desk reading a paperback book. He looks up when they walk in but doesn't leap to his feet in the presence of the officer. "Good afternoon, captain," he says, closing the book and smiling.

"Sergeant Edmond," Captain Lewellyn says, "we need your help here."

Sgt. Edmond is a big man, like Tichener, like a Drill Sergeant. When he stands to his full height he's looking down at his visitors.

"I need you to pull a card," the captain says, handing him the copy of Phil's orders.

The sergeant examines the orders, then strolls over to a filing cabinet and opens a drawer and starts flicking through racks of cards, IBM by the look of the clipped corners. He plucks a card from the drawer. "Here he is, sir."

"When is this man scheduled to ship out?"

"Three days from now, sir."

"All right, Sgt. Edmond, this man is due for a change of orders. Put his card on hold."

"Yes, sir."

When Sgt. Edmond places the IBM card on his desk, Palmer realizes that this is the defining moment of the past six weeks: his brother has stopped going to Vietnam. He is no longer in the pipeline. He is lying on Sgt. Edmond's desk.

Captain Lewellyn thanks Sgt. Edmond, and leads the Palmer brothers back to his office. After he is seated at his desk, the captain smiles at Phil and says, "Where would you like to be stationed, private?"

Phil doesn't know what to say. But Palmer has a suggestion, a duty station that he had fantasized about on the day he hadn't gotten promoted, when he had very briefly considered reenlisting just to get out of the Presidio but decided instead to walk across the Golden Gate Bridge. "How about Hawaii?"

Captain Lewellyn works at the keyboard of his computer terminal for a minute, then leans toward the monitor and squints at the bright electric letters. "There is one opening for a PFC in an Infantry unit at Schofield Barracks."

Palmer's happiness at this victory ultimately is alloyed with melancholy, so unused is he to success. During the bus ride back to the Presidio he finds it difficult to believe that he had worked so hard to achieve such an appalling goal, and had succeeded in spite of his efforts. In six weeks he will be arriving in Long Bien, the Oakland of Vietnam.

CHAPTER 29

At noon on Tuesday Palmer is lying on his bunk trying to sleep off a hangover from the previous evening in violation of a barracks protocol that he hadn't been able to take seriously even when he was not a short-timer. Legget enters the squad room and tells him that he has a phone call.

Palmer cannot discern whether there is any antipathy in Legget's voice, but he does imagine it, imagines that Legget is disgusted with him for not having taken seriously his warnings in the operations office on the previous Friday.

The phone call could not be a death in the family because there are no Palmer-family deaths projected for the immediate future, so this could only be another call from Cheryl. But even the prospect of hearing her voice fails to motivate him to leap off his bunk and hurry into the operations office where he would have to spend a few minutes in the presence of Top.

Then Legget tells him the call is from his brother.

As it turns out, Top is not in the office. Phil is calling from Oakland to say that he will be leaving for Hawaii on a three o'clock flight out of Travis Air Force Base. There is no trace whatsoever of gloom in his voice, and he says thanks, says it again, thanks, and Palmer promises that as soon as he arrives in Vietnam and is assigned to his permanent duty-station he will write to let Phil know where he is and the APO address where he can be reached. After Palmer puts the phone back on the cradle and returns to his room and climbs on top of his bunk and closes his eyes, he realizes that things are really no different now than they would have been if Phil had never received orders for Vietnam in the first place. A flurry of activity, hopes raised, then lowered, the dust settles, the townsfolk turn away and go back about their business, and Johnny Crawford lopes over a Kansas horizon with his legs wrapped in chaps of rip-stop olive-drab. Then the porch door opens and Sergeant E5 Lyttle startles him awake hollering at everyone to fall out for noon formation.

That evening Palmer sorts through his wall locker looking for things to pack, but there is nothing left to stuff into his bulging duffel bag which stands erect on the bottom shelf waiting for his shaving kit, a last set of dirty fatigues, and his combat boots. His schedule for Friday morning: put on his Class A uniform, sign out in the operations office, and call a cab to take him to the airport. He will make a point of ordering hard liquor on the flight home. He will call ahead and demand that his brother Mike get off his lazy ass and pick him up at Stapleton Airport. Just two days and a wake-up, and he will be home.

He closes his wall locker, tucks his dog tags and keys beneath his T-shirt, pats them flat, and heads for the bowling alley.

On Wednesday morning the entire company falls out on the front sidewalk with no clue as to what the cadre has in mind, except that it will be tedious and meaningless like everything else that everyone except Palmer will be doing until road patrol begins again. Lt. Norbert comes out of the foyer wearing a white T-shirt in lieu of a fatigue jacket, an obvious clue which Palmer fails to read, due to the fairly mild and oddly pleasant dizziness bought last night at the snack bar, as well as his lack of interest in anything pertaining to the company XO.

"You're a bunch of pussies," the lieutenant says, putting a bit of gravel into his voice, a clue which alarms Palmer, as it always does whenever an officer steps out of character and starts acting manly.

"You're flabby! You're out of shape!" the lieutenant snarls as a kind of preface to the verbal thunderbolt he is about to heave into the formation. "Gentlemen, we are going to remedy this situation. I say again — we are going to remedy this situation. Starting tomorrow morning, and every morning thereafter, Company D is going to fall out at oh-seven-hundred hours for PT."

Dead silence.

"That's right, gentlemen. The Daily Dozen. The annual PT test is coming up next month and Captain Weller wants this company standing tall and looking good. He wants us to make the best showing in battalion, and I'm here to make sure that every one of you swinging Richards gets the message.

"But for now, gentlemen, I have something special lined up. Three buses are going to be arriving here in a few minutes, and the entire company is going down to the gymnasium on main post to see if we can't revitalize those judo skills which I'm sure all of you graduates of Ft. Gordon have doubtless forgotten."

Palmer groans, but does so quietly, inwardly, the vibrations tickling the Listerine-soaked surfaces of his wisdom teeth. But it's not so much Lt. Norbert's announcement as Palmer's failure to plan his last days in the company a little better that demoralizes him. He is due to begin out-processing, and could just as easily have begun it this morning as tomorrow morning because it is only a one-day chore, the dismantling of his permanent-party status at the Presidio by going to Letterman General Hospital, the finance office, even the RE-UP office, getting signatures on various official documents and bringing things to a close. But to instigate the out-processing he will have to go to the First Sergeant for clearance, which he had planned to put off until the last possible moment, like homework on Sunday night, and now, as always, he finds himself paying for his not very original sin.

"I've never seen a sorrier group of men in my life," the lieutenant says.

This remark makes Palmer smile, and lessens the despair engulfing him at the thought of judo with a hangover.

"You are Military Policemen!" the lieutenant shouts, striding back and forth with his naked arms swinging like long white Richards. "That green scarf you wear around your neck commands respect at the Presidio. It signifies that each and every one of you is a member of an elite corps. The army expects a lot more out of MPs than it expects out of average soldiers."

The buses arrive and begin idling in the alley, drowning out the lieutenant's voice. He calls the formation to attention and tells the troops to fall out, and as they begin drifting toward the buses Palmer knows exactly what's on everybody's mind: pushups at dawn. Basic training shit, which probably explains why there is so little talk and no laughter as the buses fill. Courtney climbs onto the first bus in line, and Palmer climbs onto the second bus and takes a seat behind the driver.

The convoy creeps around the narrow strip of Ralston Avenue past the small PX and turns down the steep asphalt street through lifer housing. It comes to a halt at the lamppost of the bitter Screaming Eagle, then turns right. A quick run around the valley of the howling hounds, the bus comes out of the forest into a sunlight which seems unusually bright this day, enhanced by the hillside of white tombstones. At the bottom of the hill Palmer looks for the EM club but it's hidden by heavy trees which line the road which runs behind the row of redbrick finance offices. On the night of the long walk he had assumed that the flagstone bunker would become one of his hangouts, but he had never gone back. Even now the memory is painful. Courtney saving him from drowning.

The bus enters main post and turns down a side street into the older section of the reservation, white wooden buildings built before WWII. The peculiar narrowness of the streets has always been a mystery to Palmer, who now supposes that they simply had been laid out by the army corps of engineers back when horses were the primary engines of transportation. The buses pull up in front of the gymnasium.

The building is as large as the bowling alley but never so inviting. The troops are talking now as the buses begin to unload. Mass transportation always improves the mood of GIs who do not have to march the distances they are required to travel. They dismount hooting and laughing like trainees gathering to practice bullshit karate in the sawdust pits of basic.

The interior of the building looks exactly like a high school gymnasium: wrestling mats strung along the walls, floor shiny and varnished so that boots squeak as the men cross toward a set of bleachers which already has been pulled out from the wall. Overhead, grayish light enters through a row of high screened windows. Palmer remembers from grade school: the gymnasium was the place that made him feel afraid.

He climbs above the crowd with his cap in his hand and sits alone in the tenth row, which gives him a good view of two men standing at the far end of the gym beneath a basketball hoop, a black man and a white man. Whistles strung around their necks, they look like jocks, their pecks bulging beneath white T-shirts, their legs slim and muscular in tight gray warm-up pants

"Take your seats and quiet down and listen up!" Lt. Norbert chants. "I want to introduce to you Staff Sergeant McConnel and Staff Sergeant Perry from Company A." Which means they are guards at the Presidio stockade. "They were kind enough to volunteer their time today to act as your instructors."

The Company A guards begin strolling toward the bleachers incorporating the universal jock walk: cocky, flexed, their heads bowed in athlete humility. The white sergeant stands at parade-rest while the black sergeant explains the judo throws which most of the men in the bleachers doubtless have forgotten. As the instructor's voice echoes in the steel rafters Palmer begins looking over the heads of the crowd to find Courtney. He sees him seated directly in the front row, nine bleachers down, leaning forward with his elbows on his knees and listening to the instructor like a star center listening to his basketball coach. He is in his element now. He comes here with Tichener to lift barbells.

"We need ten men to set up mats!" the instructor hollers, and twenty men hop off the bleachers and run across the floor. They spread the mats out in uneven, unmilitary rows. The two instructors take turns tossing each other across their hips, demonstrating the throws that the troops will be doing this morning.

The black sergeant steps up to the bleachers and hollers, "Everyone on this side, move out to the mats," meaning everyone on Palmer's side.

The men rise cheering and hop down the seats and out onto the floor so fast that there is no chance for Palmer to slide over to the other end of the bleachers. When he does not rise immediately, the instructor glares at him like a miffed high-school coach. Palmer sets his cap on the bleacher and rises and plods with an obvious lack of enthusiasm down to the floor and off toward the far end of the court as far away from Courtney as he can get.

"Remove your fatigue shirts and dog tags!" the white instructor hollers.

Palmer wanders around looking for a partner, and spots a PFC from the third platoon standing alone at one end of a mat. Palmer takes his place at the other end and removes his dog tags and scarf and sets them on the floor. He starts to unbutton his shirt, then sees Courtney approach his opponent from behind, taking his arm and gently pulling him away. "This is my mat, GI," Courtney says.

The PFC looks at SP4 Courtney with confusion, then snatches his gear off the floor and starts looking for a new partner.

With the tips of his fingers clamped on the third button of his shirt, Palmer stares at Courtney. A single option runs through his mind: walk away. If Lt. Norbert or one of the instructors asks what the hell he thinks he is doing, he will say he has a sprained ankle or something—the substance of a lie isn't important. Faces in the bleachers begin turning his way. He sees one man elbow another and point. Everyone in the barracks has heard the story about the fight. But does anyone know about the blank-ammo incident at Ft. Cronkite? Only if Courtney told, and Palmer doubts it.

He continues unbuttoning. He removes his shirt and wads it in his right hand, and chucks it to the floor the way he would bounce a basketball hard.

"We are going to begin this morning with the hip throw," the black sergeant says, strutting among the mats, rolling his whistle between thumb and forefinger. "You and your partner will take turns throwing each other. All right, gentlemen—positions!"

Courtney and Palmer step to the middle of the mat and stand face-to-face though neither looks at the other. Palmer stares at Vinton and Mallory on a mat ten feet away. What is Beaudry doing right at this moment? "You can throw me first," Courtney says quietly.

Crouching, Palmer places his right hand on Courtney's side just above the hip bone, and takes Courtney's right wrist in his left hand. Courtney's T-shirt smells of sweat and laundry detergent. He is all muscle and bone and more muscle, and weighs thirty pounds more than Palmer. When the whistle blows, Palmer pivots and swings his hip into Courtney's belly and straightens his knees and throws him. Courtney goes over easy, not resisting the way a drunk GI in a barroom brawl would fight back, all that brawn slithering over Palmer's hip and going down with a clean smack as Courtney's shock-absorbing arm slaps the mat.

The ceiling reflects the grunts and booms and canvas slaps, reflects the laughter too, and the mock groans, and the applause from the clowns in the bleachers. Palmer hears all this above a thin ringing in his ears, the result of a mixture, he supposes, of adrenaline, unaccustomed exertion, and a residue of last night's booze.

The instructors prowl among the students handing out compliments and critical evaluations, then they blow their whistles and tell everyone to get up and assume the position.

It is Courtney's turn now. Palmer reminds himself to stay loose, this is the key, don't go rigid—and remember to slap the goddamn mat. He never could get it right in MP school. The harder and louder you slapped the mat, the less likely you would be hassled by the instructors. But there were not enough training hours, only twelve, to get used to, much less master, this violent manual labor, so he was glad when he had learned that he was a good shot with the .45, the best in the company.

"I'll bet you were worried."

Courtney says this quietly as he crouches and places his right hand on Palmer's hip and takes hold of Palmer's right wrist. Palmer doesn't respond. He is thinking only that Courtney can bench-press more than either of them weighs. Courtney once tried to talk him into coming to the gym for a workout with the barbells, which Palmer might have agreed to except Courtney wanted to run down to the gym and run back up to the quad afterwards. But Palmer knows what he is referring to. He is betting Palmer has been worried that Courtney would report him to Captain Weller for assaulting him with blank ammunition in blatant disregard for, and probably criminal violation of, the rules of range safety.

The instructor blows his whistle, a short pop, a bleat.

The mat drops out from under Palmer's feet and hits his back in less than a half-second. His instinct is to keep his head up, but he can't—and you're not supposed to anyway—so the back of his head bounces off the mat with a painful thud. A brief headache travels the diameter his skull as he gazes at the gray-painted steel rafters in the ceiling and hears the sounds of bodies hitting the mats, the groans and gasps, and the bleacher laughter which is somewhat thinner than before.

He wants to, but cannot, hop to his feet the way Courtney had. He rolls over and does a sort of arm-and-leg pushup bringing himself erect, tugging at his T-shirt and looking toward the instructor, who is trotting around with his whistle clamped between his lips to free his hands to point and clap, or to ball his disgusted fists on his hips.

Palmer is beginning to breathe hard. His eyes are watering a bit from the impact, but he doesn't wipe at them. The bleachers are blurred, so he can't tell if anyone is still looking his way. The joke applause has withered along with the laughter, probably because the men in the bleachers know that they are going to be doing this—Palmer hopes—soon.

"Positions!"

Palmer grabs Courtney's wrist and clamps his right hand on Courtney's side and waits for the whistle.

"I know where Cheryl lives," Courtney says.

When the whistle blows Palmer pivots and throws his hip into Courtney's belly and straightens his knees, but nothing happens. Courtney is refusing to let it happen. Palmer squats and again jams his hip into Courtney's gut and straightens his knees, and this time Courtney lets him do it. He rolls across Palmer's hip and slaps the mat and lies there looking right into Palmer's eyes. He is smiling, almost laughing.

"Who cares?" Palmer says, swallowing hard from the rage at what Courtney has just shown him that he can do whenever he feels like it.

Palmer walks to his end of the mat and experiences a brief and vivid fantasy, that of walking straight across the floor and out the door. He is breathing harder now but cannot get any oxygen. The gym is beginning to stink. The air-conditioners in the rafters have not been turned on.

"Positions!"

Palmer steps to the center of the mat and crouches with his head bowed and looks down at his drops of sweat making dark coins on the canvas. He feels Courtney's hand resting solidly on his hip, feels Courtney's grip tightening around his wrist. "She told me you didn't have the guts to sleep with her that night."

Palmer hears clearly the breathing of other men as they assume the position. Hears individual voices coming from the bleachers. Hears the silence as everyone waits for the bleat of the whistle. Hears the sounds of automobiles passing outside. Hears the last thing he will ever hear Courtney say in his life. "This is only way you'll ever get a woman into bed."

Palmer's feet leave the mat. He sees the flashing gray glow of windows, sees the rafters, sees individual rivets in the rafters, sees jagged-edged, rust-colored patches of metal where battleship-gray paint has flaked off the heads of the rivets, and hears a sound like a broomstick breaking in two.

EPILOGUE

OAKLAND

The enlisted men's club was closing for the night. The bartender unplugged the jukebox and turned the lights up. Their pitchers empty, Palmer and his three new buddies got up from the booth and stumbled outside cracking jokes and laughing. They stopped for a moment to light cigarettes, then began strolling toward the transient barracks, but because Palmer was bunked in a different building from theirs he said I'll see you later, even though he knew he would never see them again. An abbreviated version of the Mandatory Buddy Lie.

One pitcher of his own, plus three more shared with those men, he had gotten as drunk as he had wanted to be. He began moving toward his barracks with a kind of self-propelled and easy robotic walk which beer inebriation permits and which is sometimes difficult to pull off on hard liquor. But he was not so drunk that he was unable to take a shower. In the lights-out darkness of the big bay he unlocked his duffel bag which was hanging from the end of his bunk, and pulled out his shaving kit and a towel.

A few other men were soaping up in the shower room, lone GIs lost in private thoughts about the upcoming war and their place in it. It wasn't until Palmer had started to scrub his left arm that he realized he had forgotten to take off his wristwatch. He felt not only stupid—the other men must have seen it—but badly, because it wasn't his watch. It belonged to

Phil, who had left it in Denver believing he would be spending a year patrolling the jungles and rice paddies of Vietnam. Palmer had taken it from a chest of drawers the day before he flew to Oakland because he had lost his own watch somewhere between the judo accident and the hospital, and all things considered, he did not think Phil would object.

He put the ruined watch into his shaving kit and continued with his shower, soaping the stitches which the doctor at Fitzsimmons had assured him would disappear eventually and which Palmer doubted. Army surgery. You expect a kind of amateurishness even if that's just a myth, but why should an army doctor give a shit about doing an impeccable job on an enlisted man? He had lain in bed for a two weeks in Letterman General Hospital, his left arm held motionless in a fretwork of stainless steel. The doctors had wanted to make certain the bone set properly, and so did the lawyers. It wasn't the doctors but the lawyers who told him that his injury wasn't serious enough to warrant a medical discharge. The lawyers were civilians. This did not surprise Palmer. Whenever the army wanted to accomplish something dangerous, or difficult, or a bit ticklish, it drafted civilians to do its dirty work.

At the end of formation the following morning Palmer was picked with six other men to sweep the operations building, an hour of pushing a broom on a concrete floor which wasn't a bit dirty. The E5 in charge of the detail had been meticulous about taking each man's ID card. He had everyone by the balls then, but most significantly, a man could not get into the EM club without his ID card, so there was no point in even thinking about slipping away from the detail.

He worked his broom over to the same part of the building where the new men signed in, where the E5 had told him to get his hair cut. On his final trip to Fitzsimmons Army Hospital in Denver, when his outpatient care was discontinued and his orders for Vietnam were reinstated, he had thought about going to the barbershop on post. He still had seven days left of his original leave and medical leave combined, and had gotten a haircut on the first day he had reported in at Fitzsimmons. But in the end he decided not to get one, like the guys at the start of basic with their Afros and mustaches and hippie locks. His hair wasn't long by any standard except the army's, but when he got up to the desk that first morning, the chubby E5 told him to go get a haircut and return to the end of the line when he got back. Palmer walked away from the desk feeling both bitter and smug. He had known all along that it was going to happen, and when he got to the barbershop he told the man with the clippers to take it all off. He now looked like a basic trainee.

His name was not called for Vietnam at either the noon or evening formation, though at noon he did get chosen for a detail, sorting discarded uniforms into bins in a warehouse. He spent an hour picking through jungle fatigues with the unit patches of the 82nd Airborne, the 173rd Airborne, the 101st Airborne, the 25th Infantry Division, and the 1st Infantry Division—the Big Red One—sweat-stained and ragged fatigue jackets which had been bleached by the jungle sun and discarded by returnees now dressed in clean khakis for the last leg of their journey home from Vietnam.

At each formation Palmer looked for men from Company D who might have gotten orders for Vietnam. He looked for

Tichener. He hadn't thought he would ever be glad to see anyone from the Presidio again, but now knew that if he recognized a man from his old company he would feel good, would not feel so alone, and would go right up to him and say hello. They might even end up flying over together, which would be all right. Maybe the man would know something about Courtney.

Courtney did not visit him in the hospital. When Vinton dropped by he told Palmer what had happened at the gymnasium. Palmer didn't know what had taken place after his arm broke because he fainted. Vinton said it sounded like a gunshot, a sickening sound. He said Palmer hopped up from the mat holding his left forearm with his right hand and started walking toward the door, but made only ten feet before he walked into the back of a second-platoon man and fell down. Lt. Norbert called an ambulance, which arrived in two minutes. Judo training was called off for the rest of the day, and it did not look to Vinton like it was ever going to start up again.

Vinton visited him twice. It was only after the first visit that Palmer realized Vinton liked him, and had always thought of them as buddies, and had probably never realized Palmer did not like him. Vinton was just a kidder and, unlike Palmer, did not have a shred of malevolence in him.

On his second visit, Vinton brought Palmer's duffel bag and shaving kit, and gave Palmer the lowdown on the latest scandal: Sgt. Weigand had gone AWOL from Company D with only thirty days left of his enlistment. An M-16 was missing from the arms room, and the word around the barracks said that Weigand had stolen it. The CID was asking everyone questions. An M-16 would be worth a lot on the black market. And not only that, Captain Weller was going to be relieved of his command at Company D. "The Weigand thing," Vinton assured him. Vinton figured a woman was behind the whole mess.

You go away, and everything changes. Palmer finally asked about Courtney. Where was he? Why hadn't he come to visit? And though he did not ask, what he really wanted to know was whether or not Courtney had broken his arm on purpose. When Courtney threw him that day, Palmer had for one moment felt like a kite on a string—then his forearm felt like kindling coming down across the sawhorse of Courtney's left knee.

But the only thing Vinton knew for certain was that Courtney had signed out of the company on Friday afternoon and was probably at home right now in Illinois or Indiana or whatever state he lived in.

Iowa. Signed out and went home without coming to apologize, or to explain, or to at least say goodbye.

After Vinton said goodbye for the last time and walked out, Palmer wondered if Courtney really did know where Cheryl lived, and whether he really had talked to her, and if so, had he gotten around to telling Cheryl about the judo class? He wondered if Cheryl would call on the phone which sat next to his hospital bed. He wondered if Cheryl might suddenly show up at the hospital, a fantasy that sustained him right up to the day he signed out of Letterman General Hospital and flew to Denver and signed in at Fitzsimmons Army Hospital for outpatient treatment.

He never heard from Cheryl or Courtney again.

Palmer's good luck had always been both rare and strange, so rare that it could not be relied upon, and so strange, like becoming briefly the battalion commander's blue-eyed boy, that a part of him was always intrigued by what his next good luck might be, while understanding that most of his luck would always be not so much bad as mediocre. Being an MP in Vietnam was better than being an Infantryman in Vietnam, but not as good as staying home.

On his fourth evening at Oakland, one day before he was certain his name would be called for the next flight to Vietnam, Palmer was picked from the ranks along with thirteen other men for KP. He had avoided KP all during the time he had been here, and had come to think that this might be his Oakland good luck. But after the names of the men going overseas had been called, and the smaller shit-detail rosters had been filled with warm bodies, the NCO in the tower pointed directly at his rank and told the first fourteen men to fall out to the left side of the formation. It was like an ambush. There was no time to sneak into another rank, something that Palmer had never done before because of its obvious and amateurish futility.

After they had formed a new rank at the side of the formation, Palmer maneuvered himself into the last place in line. It wasn't like basic training anymore. He would never again volunteer to be first for anything as he had done at Fort Campbell, at the obstacle course and the grenade range and all the other ranges where he had wanted to show the Drill Sergeants that he was motivated and determined to receive a promotion at graduation. All he could think about now, as the NCO in charge of the detail walked down the line collecting

ID cards, was the fact that he was not going to be able to drink beer at the EM club on his last night in America. He would have to get up at three in the morning and spend the next eighteen hours sweating in a kitchen under the hard eye of some belly robber, and for all he knew his name would be called for his flight to Vietnam and he would not be there to answer up, and he would subsequently descend into the desperate limbo of men with lost orders living in transient barracks until some Spec Four sorted everything out. That was all he could think about.

The buck sergeant in charge of the kitchen detail was another GI on his way to Vietnam, and Palmer could tell he wasn't any happier with this assignment than they were. Palmer pulled out his billfold and took out the green ID card with his basic training face on it, which he looked more like now than he had at any time at the Presidio. When the sergeant took the card from his hand, Palmer felt as if his soul had been stolen.

He watched as the E5 squared the ID cards like a poker deck and slipped them into the pocket of his fatigue shirt. The sergeant then handed a clipboard and pen to the first man in line.

"Everybody sign your name, rank, and serial number on this roster."

When the clipboard got down to Palmer, he took the pen and held it to the paper but could not bring himself to sign it. He stood as if paralyzed, which he was in a way, barely touching the ink tip to the empty space below the bottom name on the list. The E5 walked up to him and said, "Are you finished?"

Palmer nodded and handed the clipboard back to the sergeant, then waited to see if the man would notice that his name was missing, feeling as he had on the day at the rifle range when Sgt. Weigand had snatched Courtney's scorecard out of his hand

But the E5 just walked away, harried by the minor bullshit of this detail, and told everyone to go to the barracks and get their duffel bags and meet back outside in ten minutes. "You're going to stow all of your gear at the KP shack, and then I'll let you go, but you have to be back at the shack by 2200 hours. And make goddamn sure you show up or they'll send the fucking MPs after you."

Palmer began to feel lightheaded, began to feel adrenaline leaking into his heart making it beat faster, as it always did when his ass was hanging over the edge. The rest of the men in the squad, those who had signed their lives away, began drifting toward the barracks, lighting cigarettes and scowling, but keeping their wretched KP thoughts to themselves. Then a complainer spoke up, the type of man who would always be threatening to go to the Inspector General with some pissant squawk, the sort of soldier that Palmer had never wanted to become but no longer cared whether he did or not.

"How are we supposed to get into the enlisted men's club tonight, sergeant?" he said. He was just a kid, skinny and red-haired. His soft southern-accent had a nasal knife-edge to it. "We can't get in without our ID cards."

The other the men stopped walking and turned to look at the E5, who returned their looks with sympathy, fully understanding the severity of the dilemma. He knew that no one was allowed into the EM club without an ID card. "I'm sorry," he said, and he did sound sorry. "I have to keep all of your ID cards until tomorrow night."

The men looked at each other, and a man at the back of the crowd muttered, "Bullshit." Another man quietly said, "Fuck the army." But the E5 just shook his head. He knew what a shitty deal they were getting, but there was nothing he could do about it.

"But sergeant," the whiner said, the complainer, the kind of dud Palmer had never liked and had always tried to avoid, "you've got our names on the roster. Why do you need our ID cards?"

The other men took up the argument, though not loudly, but with military courtesy. "You've got our names and serial numbers, sergeant. Why do you need our IDs?"

The E5 looked down at the clipboard gripped in his hand. An odd glazed expression crossed on his face, as if he was not merely thinking hard, but grappling with a situation not covered anywhere in the regulations. The logic of the kid's argument apparently suited him. He reached into his shirt pocket and pulled out the stack of cards and began dealing them out.

"Just make damn sure you show up at the KP shack by ten," he said.

When Palmer received his card, he felt as if his soul had been returned to him. He felt as if the minute-hand of a clock had rotated back to the moment he had been culled from the formation. His name was not on the clipboard and his ID card was in his pocket. He was free but for the abstract link of physical distance between himself and the sergeant who had released him from KP.

Palmer snapped that invisible link by turning and strolling slowly away from the immediate vicinity of the sullen men who were gazing down at the illusory furloughs in their hands, the ID cards that would allow them to spend a few hours in the EM club before surrendering to the kitchen authorities at 2200.

When Palmer judged that he had made enough distance, he began double-timing, but was unable to maintain this pace for long. He broke into a wind-sprint, though not in the direction of the enlisted men's club, not just yet. His breath came fast and the beat of his heart matched the velocity of his boots. His legs had not endured such strain since the day he had been clocked for the record at the end of basic, the day he had demonstrated his ability to run a mile at top speed, the day he had completed the eight weeks of training that would enable him to disappear into a dark and camouflaging labyrinth of warehouse buildings during his last night in America.